PRAISE FOR ALAF

Never Tell

"One of the finest young crime writers working today."
—Dennis Lehane

"Burke has a good eye for the many faces of New York. . . . Burke's story is complex, but her pace is fast, her prose is crisp, and her duplicitous characters ring true in the Darwinian world she creates."
—*Washington Post*

"Burke, author of last year's amazing *Long Gone,* has delivered another winner. . . . Two seemingly different storylines converge in a shocking way, demonstrating Burke's remarkable abilities as a writer. . . . Hatcher is a complex character, and her journey both personally and professionally will have even the most jaded suspense aficionado rapidly turning the pages. . . . Burke has a knack for making New York City come vibrantly alive on the page."
—Associated Press

"Alafair Burke is one of those rare writers whose books are both scary and cerebral. . . . A terrific storyteller."   —Sandra Brown

"The chilly realm of an elite Manhattan school holds a few clues to the question of why a famous music producer's daughter might have committed suicide in her family's West Village townhouse in Alafair Burke's *Never Tell*, a kind of dark-side *Gossip Girl*, complete with a dubious best friend named Ramona."
—Vogue.com, "Beach Reads You Can't Put Down:
The Summer's Best New Literary Thrillers"

"The plot of an Alafair Burke thriller doesn't just rip from the headlines. She's one step ahead of them." —Harlan Coben

"Burke's last book was a stand-alone, but in *Never Tell* she's returned to the character her readers know best, the fierce and gutsy NYPD detective Ellie Hatcher—now investigating the apparent suicide of a privileged Manhattan teen." —*Entertainment Weekly*

"The meticulous plotting, coupled with Ellie's complicated evolution as a heroine, make this Burke's strongest work to date."
  —*Publishers Weekly* (starred review)

"Once in a while, a book comes along and makes you sit up and notice. A supremely intelligent novel, masterfully created with a telling hand and unique voice, *Never Tell* is one of those books. Crime writing doesn't get much better than this."
  —*New York Journal of Books*

"*Never Tell* is a great read. Alafair Burke writes a riveting story with a strong female protagonist." —*Suspense* magazine

"Alafair Burke is a wonderful writer, with the kind of skill and confidence I most admire! I'm a big fan." —Sue Grafton

"A terrific web spinner. She knows when and how to drop clues to keep readers at her mercy." —*Entertainment Weekly*

"One of Burke's trademarks is connecting disparate plotlines, which she does here in spades. . . . Skillfully structured." —*Booklist*

"Burke's prose is clear and fast, and every move by investigators and officers of the court is the real deal. She explores genuine contemporary questions in a revealing and thoughtful way. . . . Her plot is always dynamic and intelligent." —*Portland Oregonian*

never
tell

ALSO BY ALAFAIR BURKE

Long Gone

THE ELLIE HATCHER SERIES

Dead Connection
Angel's Tip
212

THE SAMANTHA KINCAID SERIES

Judgment Calls
Missing Justice
Close Case

A NOVEL OF SUSPENSE

never
tell

ALAFAIR
BURKE

HARPER

NEW YORK · LONDON · TORONTO · SYDNEY

HARPER

A hardcover edition of this book was published in 2012
by HarperCollins Publishers.

Excerpt from *If You Were Here* © 2013 by Alafair Burke.

HarperCollins books may be purchased for educational, business, or sales
promotional use. For information please e-mail the Special Markets Department at
SPsales@harpercollins.com.

First Harper paperback published 2013.

Designed by Michael P. Correy

Library of Congress Cataloging-in-Publication Data has been applied for.

ISBN 978-0-06-199917-8 (pbk.)

13 14 15 16 17   OV/RRD   10 9 8 7 6 5 4 3 2 1

For my mother-in-law,
Ellie Hatcher Simpson.

Thank you for your name and
your son (not in that order).

PART I

JULIA

CHAPTER ONE

Second Acts: Confessions of a Former Victim
and Current Survivor

"3:14 IN THE MORNING"

It has been twenty years, but at three-fourteen this morning I screamed in my sleep. I probably would not have known I had screamed were it not for the nudge from my husband—my patient, sleep-starved husband, who suspects but can never really know the reasons for his wife's night terrors, because his wife has never truly explained them.

I could see the uncertainty coloring his face this morning as he sipped his coffee, already going cold, while I poured a fresh cup for myself at the counter, carrying the carafe to the breakfast table to top off his cup. Not uncertainty about my reasons for screaming—that was ever-present—but uncertainty about whether even to raise the subject. *Should I ask her? Are some subjects better left in the subconscious?*

I loved him so much in that moment—for loving me enough to care, for caring enough about me to let the unspoken remain so. And so, even though I would have preferred we peruse the newspaper together, sharing headlines with each other before he had to dash to work, I told him.

I screamed at three-fourteen in my sleep this morning because twenty years ago—more than half my lifetime ago—a man walked into my bedroom and changed my childhood forever. I did not hear him open the door but somehow I knew he was there. Maybe it was the sliver of light that penetrated the room from the hallway along with his footsteps. Or maybe it was simply because I had known for months that this moment—at some point, on some night—would eventually come to pass. When I opened my eyes, he was there, closing the door behind him. Unwelcome, but not unanticipated.

I remember expecting him to say something, to offer some flimsy excuse for entering my room, or maybe even to try floating some corny, flirtatious line, pretending like we were some kind of illicit couple. But he didn't say anything. He took the four steps from the door to the foot of my bed in silence. I apparently wasn't worth the expenditure of words.

I remember wanting to scream. Wanting to beat the shit out of him until he was dead. But it was as if some other part of my brain had already made the decision for me—no, at the time, it felt more like the decision had been made for us: the me in that room and the real me watching from afar. Neither of us would be screaming. We would not be defending ourselves. We would simply watch the bedside clock and wait for this night to be over.

I remember looking at the readout of the display, thinking about the squareness of those red numbers, how each digit could be formed by illuminating various combinations of seven straight lines forming two stacked squares. And the numbers on the readout at that one moment read 3:14—three-fourteen in the morning.

I saw those same numbers taunting me from my nightstand last night after my husband nudged me in our bed. They made me wish he had left me to scream in my sleep, unaware that my body and thoughts still, to some degree, belong to that man, and to that night, all these years later.

It has been twenty years since I stared at that old clock. Ten years since I married a man who was willing to look past my occasional tendency to burst out in tears during lovemaking. Seven months since I believed I was recovered enough to start this blog. One hundred and forty-three posts about my experiences as a survivor. Seventy-two thousand, eight hundred, and ninety words, not that I'm counting.

And with one scream at three-fourteen this morning, I felt once again like a victim.

But to my dear, sweet husband who was finishing his coffee before work, all I could say was, "I had a bad dream, babe. I think it was about those things that happened when I was young."

And then after I kiss him goodbye and watch him make his way down the steps of our townhouse, briefcase in hand, I walk upstairs to sit at this desk and write down the truth that I still cannot speak aloud to the people who love me, even twenty years later.

Just like the woman said, it had been seven months since she'd first started the blog. "Second Acts: Confessions of a Former Victim and Current Survivor." Even the title reeked of self-indulgence.

It wasn't surprising that she'd gone to the trouble of counting the individual posts and even the number of words. She was exactly that type. She was that prideful. High and mighty.

The blog had started out as an anonymous project, but this particular reader knew precisely who had authored the past seven months and, apparently, 72,890 words of this self-involved, self-help-through-writing garbage. The reader scrolled down to the comments section at the bottom of the screen, bypassing the predictable remarks from the undoubtedly overweight, housebound trolls who followed this woman's crap: "Hang in there, girl." "One day at a time." "Thank you for your honesty."

Those were the comments that were most disgusting—the posts that *thanked* this woman for deluding herself into thinking she had any kind of insight into her current existence and for enticing even more pitiful souls to read and admire her.

The reader contemplated the blank text box on the computer screen, then began typing:

"If you thought that night twenty years ago was bad, wait until you see what I have planned. You won't remember a single time on the clock. Maybe a day on the calendar if you're lucky. Maybe a week. Or maybe I'll keep you busy for a month. One thing I know for certain: You will not live to write about it."

The tapping sounds against the keyboard were so quick and intense that the typist did not hear the approaching footsteps until a second face appeared, reflected in the laptop screen.

It was too late.

CHAPTER TWO

Ellie Hatcher had arrived in New York City with certain expectations. Influenced by iconic images of Times Square, the Plaza Hotel, and the Empire State Building, she anticipated bright lights, rows of towering skyscrapers, wide sidewalks filled to capacity with suit-clad businessmen and their briefcases, and a perpetual soundtrack of car horns, sirens, and construction equipment.

But now that she'd lived here for more than a decade, Ellie knew that those iconic images painted a tourist's picture of New York City. Outside the movie version of this city, most New Yorkers lived quiet lives on peaceful streets, venturing into the madness only as necessary.

This morning found her on Barrow Street, among the narrow, tree-lined diagonals that formed the West Village. Nestled between Washington Square Park and the Hudson River, this was Ellie's dream neighborhood, removed from the commercial worlds of the Financial District and midtown, protected from the fumes and sounds of frustrated commuters lined up at the bridges and tunnels.

But today a different kind of chaos had found its way into that charming neighborhood. It was a form of chaos to which Ellie had also become accustomed over the years: marked cars, fleet cars, uniforms barking into shoulder-mounted radios, plainclothes and techs gathering physical evidence, even a fire truck and an ambulance. It was the chaos and energy of a crime scene, complete with the yellow tape that separated the normal from the aberrant.

She overheard the murmurs among curious pedestrians as she and her partner, J. J. Rogan, made their way toward the taped perimeter.

"What's going on? They're filming?"

"*Law and Order*, I think. Not the regular one. That got canceled. But *SVU* still films here. Or maybe it's that new show—that one with the blonde in the hat. Or was that one canceled too?"

Another bystander noticed them flash their badges to cross the perimeter. "You see that? It's for real."

"I thought that was Gwyneth Paltrow's house."

"No, she was on Fourth Street. And she sold it a few years ago."

Ellie could understand the source of the real estate gossip once she had a chance to take in the townhouse to which they'd been summoned. Four floors that she could count above ground, plus what looked like a basement. Twice as wide as the other single-family houses on the block.

Through the etched glass of the front door, she was struck by the spaciousness of the entryway. Larger than her entire living room, the area was empty but for a round table topped with a vase of what appeared to be five dozen fresh tulips and, in the back corner, a sculpture that looked like it belonged in the Metropolitan Museum. A fireplace and Prius-sized chandelier completed the look.

"Damn," Rogan said.

In short, the place was nice enough to earn a "damn" out of Rogan, who wasn't as easily impressed as his partner.

The woman who made her way down the curved staircase seemed born and bred to live in this kind of home. Black slacks and an asymmetric tan jacket, for a look that was simultaneously casual and sophisticated. Salt-and-pepper bob, fresh from a salon blowout. But when she opened the door, the redness of her eyes reminded Ellie that they weren't here to admire her lifestyle.

The woman's gaze seemed to fix on their clothing. "Who are you?"

"Detectives from NYPD, ma'am. Ellie Hatcher." She offered her hand, but the woman surprised Ellie by grabbing her forearm.

"Thank God." Ellie assumed she was being pulled to the staircase, but the woman guided them instead into an elevator. It was decorated with photographs of defining moments of New York City from the seventies and eighties. A bar owner writing on a storefront sign during the blackout of 1977: *No Lights, No Food, but Plenty of Booze.* The Ramones playing at CBGB. Transients lined up outside the Bowery Mission. John Lennon in a crowd in Central Park. The final Simon and Garfunkel concert. Forty-second Street back when it was fleabag hotels and porno theaters. A graffiti-covered 6 train. It was a New York Ellie had never known.

The woman pushed the button for the fourth floor and the elevator began to creak its way up.

"You have to do something. It's my daughter. I found her. In the bathtub. The blood. The water was so red. Her face was—so white."

"I'm very sorry, ma'am, but why are you still here?" Ellie realized her response sounded cold. "I mean, we usually separate the family from this kind of chaos."

"They're up there already, but they're not doing anything. I heard what they said. They didn't think I could hear them talking, but I'm not deaf. They don't believe me. They're saying she did this. To herself."

When the elevator doors opened, two uniformed officers were waiting—one short and fat, the other tall and lanky, very Laurel and Hardy. They looked alarmed, and then resigned, when they spotted the badges clipped to the waistbands of the latest arrivals in the hallway.

"Crap." The skinny one spoke first, trying to explain their presence upstairs while a civilian roamed freely through a crime scene. "We were heading down. Waiting for the elevator. Guess she beat us to it."

Rogan clicked his tongue as the two officers stepped onto the elevator. Ellie could tell he wanted to clunk their heads together. "Get

the hell outside and help protect your scene," he said. "Hatcher and
Rogan. Arrived at eleven-twenty-seven. Write it down." He jabbed
his index finger against the fat cop's breast pocket for emphasis.

The elevator began its creaky descent. "That's what I was trying
to tell you," their hostess said. "They're not taking this seriously.
Please listen to me. My daughter did not kill herself."

CHAPTER THREE

The top floor of the townhouse served as a separate residence, complete with its own dining room, living room, kitchen, and long hallway leading to the back of the building. The decor was white-on-white-on-white. Gleaming white high-gloss floors. White sheepskin rugs. White Lucite furniture. White throw pillows on the white furniture. Swank digs for servants' quarters.

"Julia's room is back here."

From the rear of the apartment, Ellie heard footsteps. Voices. The clicks and squawks of radios.

"And you are?"

"Oh, I'm sorry, Detectives. My name is Katherine Whitmire. Julia's mother."

"And no one has told you that you can't be here?"

"This is my home, Detective. My daughter. I said I wouldn't leave until homicide detectives arrived. I heard what they were saying about Julia, but I'm telling you: My daughter was murdered."

The callout had come to them as a suspected suicide. When they had pressed for an explanation as to why the case required two homicide detectives, none was forthcoming. Ellie had a feeling she was looking at the numero-uno reason.

"We're here now, Mrs. Whitmire. And I know you're hurting.

But you can't be in this house right now, especially if you're right about someone doing harm to your daughter." Ellie caught sight of a uniformed officer on the spiral staircase and waved him up. "This gentleman's going to take you outside. You can wait in one of the cars if you'd like, or he can take you to the precinct if you'd be more comfortable there. We just need to take a quick look around, and then we'll need to talk with you in more detail."

She could tell the woman wanted to argue but then seemed to think better of it and nodded. "I'll let you go back and see for yourselves. I can't look at her again. I can't. I just—can't." She led the way down the stairs, the uniform following her awkwardly.

The noises Ellie had heard were coming from behind a closed door at the end of the hallway. She opened it.

"Why is this door closed with a civilian running around the crime scene?"

"Because it's not a crime scene, and that crazy bitch slammed the door before she ordered us not to touch her daughter's body."

The two EMTs were young, one with a crew cut, the other with too much gel worked through his spiked hair. They stood passively by the bedroom windows, placing themselves as far as possible from the white marble floor of the en suite interior bathroom they both eyed unconsciously. It was the spiky-haired one who was doing the talking. From his colleague's shrug, Ellie could tell that he was also the one who'd gotten into some kind of confrontation with Katherine Whitmire.

"So some rich lady in a designer jacket gets a little irate about her daughter being dead, and the two of you decide to just stand in here, scratching each other's balls? What the fuck is going on here?"

"You got the same callout we got. Sixteen-year-old girl, slit wrists in the bathtub. We came up. Probably only beat your two guys by a minute or so. And it was obvious what we were looking at." He lowered his voice. "It's a clear suicide, all right? The blade's in the tub on the right side of her body. A couple hesitation marks on the left wrist, then a clean cut through the radial artery. The girl even left a note, right there on the bed."

Ellie saw a lined sheet of yellow notepaper propped neatly against the throw pillows on the low platform bed.

"So tell me again why you're calling this girl's grieving mother a crazy bitch?"

"Because I guess she heard us talking and wigged out on us. I was about to go downstairs for the gurney. We were all in the bathroom, making that initial assessment, you know—the hesitation cuts, the clear slice, the note—and the next thing I know, she's screaming at me to take my hands off her daughter's body. Yelling at us not to touch anything at all if we weren't going to investigate what happened. You've seen this place. These people obviously have some grease. So, yeah, we decided to stand in here and—what'd you say? scratch our balls?—until someone higher on the pay grade showed up. When we heard that doorbell, your guys went running out to cover their asses, but here we are, still scratching. I'll stand here and scratch all day until the ME makes the call. I'm not taking on some rich, crazy bitch. How about you, Andy? You need any help over there, or are you all squared away?"

Another shrug from the quiet one.

Rogan was already making his way to the bathroom. It was spacious enough for the two of them, plus the two EMTs and a few linebackers, but she was the only one who followed. She heard Spike call out behind her. "If you need me to explain how I know the girl's bulimic, let me know. We aren't as magically astute as you cops, but eating disorders go with depression. Suicide notes go with suicides. There's nothing for us to do here."

She hitched a thumb over her shoulder. "Go save lives, guys. We'll wait for the ME."

Rogan looked back at her from the bathroom, hands on hips. "Real sensitive for a guy who spends his days helping people."

"Some people would say that about you, Rogan."

"You didn't want to take him up on that bulimia thing? To me, she looks as skinny as every other white girl these days."

When people imagine a woman soaking in a tub, they picture those cheesy commercials with a bath full of frothy bubbles, the woman's hair tucked into a loose bun as she runs a loofah across her pampered skin, pausing to take a sip of wine in the candle-light.

There was nothing pampered about Julia Whitmire's death scene. There was wine, but it was an empty bottle toppled on the floor next to the toilet. She was nude, but there were no bubbles or loofahs or candles. Just clear pink water, a few smears of dark red on the edge of the white ceramic tub, blood that had streamed from her left wrist. The straight razor had fallen into the tub on the right side of her body.

Ellie leaned forward and saw two superficial lacerations next to the source of the leaking blood. Slitting a wrist takes fortitude. Some people try for years before they can bring themselves to go through with it. This girl only took two practice strokes.

Rogan was seeing the same scene, drawing the same conclusions. "Looks like she held the razor in her right hand and pulled her left wrist across it. Right arm falls into the water with the razor. Left arm doesn't quite make it back to the side." Julia's left hand was draped across her pubic area, as if trying to protect her privacy in death.

Ellie didn't need an EMT to explain the signs of this girl's eating disorder. "Her skin's loose. That's one of the things the EMT was probably seeing."

"She's dead. Skin gets loose."

She peered between the girl's parted lips. "No, it's more than that. See how her face is bloated even though she's gaunt around the eyes? And her teeth are gray. This girl was definitely making herself sick." She walked out of the bathroom and over to the bed, bending down to read the hand-scrawled note, filled with scratch marks and second attempts, propped against the pillows.

She took in every scribbled word, but a few lines summed it up.

I know I should love my life, but sometimes I hate it . . . I'm con-stantly being told how lucky I am, but the truth is, my so-called privileged life hurts . . . It hurts to believe that I can never amount to the person I'm supposed to be. It hurts to feel so alone every second of the day, even when I'm surrounded by other people.

Poor little rich girl.
The final sentence said it all:

And that is why I have decided to kill myself.

She left Rogan to read on his own as she did a quick walk-through of the upper-floor residence. Medicine cabinet filled with high-end hair and skin supplies, but no prescription drugs other than a birth-control packet made out to Julia Whitmire. Hairclips and magazines in the nightstand. Top dresser drawer filled with expensive La Perla lingerie, more suitable for a soft-core porn shoot than a high school girl's bedroom. No food in the refrigerator except two bags of baby carrots and a bottle of nonfat ranch dressing. Cabinets filled with liquor. Wine rack stocked with bottles.

Rogan trailed into the kitchen behind her. "So what do you think?" he asked.

"Looks like making herself throw up wasn't quite enough self-inflicted damage for her anymore."

"What were you saying about sensitivity?"

"Hate to say those tools were on to something, but this looks pretty clear-cut to me."

"The note even had tearstains on it," he said.

"And yet I noticed you didn't touch the letter. Neither did I."

"Don't need to. Got that LASIK shit. These eyes shine like diamonds and focus like laser beams."

She rolled her own, un-LASIKed, eyes. "You know what I'm getting at. Those idiots had a point about people who've got—what did he call it—grease? I don't know who that woman outside is, but she's clearly rich enough to have a setup like this, and she's apparently powerful enough to set her own terms about where she'll stand and what type of detective will be sent to her home."

They were interrupted by a towering bald man in medical scrubs.

Rogan squinted at Ellie, a sign that he recognized the new arrival's cue ball but had forgotten his name.

"Ginger," she called out with a smile. Cue ball had called her "Blondie" during a tense moment when they'd first met. Instead of making an obvious bald comment in response, she'd called him Ginger. Since then, he always returned her calls in record time.

"It's Blondie and her stoic partner."

Apparently Rogan wasn't the only one in the room who struggled with names. "Bob King, you probably remember J. J. Rogan."

"I'm told there's a tearstained note," King said.

"Our guys or the EMTs?" she asked.

"Your guys. Two of them cowering on the front porch like bitch babies. I take it they're a-scared of the mama grizzly out in the living room. Or the parlor. Whatever you call that big useless room down there."

So much for telling Katherine Whitmire to wait outside.

"Yeah, there's a note," she verified. "Body's in the tub."

She noticed that he stooped slightly beneath the doorway as he crossed the bathroom threshold, a habit of the tall, she supposed.

While he was inspecting the body, Ellie rifled through the bright-orange Hermès handbag on the kitchen counter until she found an unlabeled vial of pills. She unscrewed the cap and held an orange-and-white capsule up to the light. "Bingo."

When King stepped from the bathroom, she threw the capsule in his direction. "Correct me if I'm wrong, but Adderall's prescribed for depression?"

"Nah, more for ADHD—attention deficit hyperactivity disorder—but, yeah, it's a stimulant. Your extra-special law-enforcing eyes seeing anything that my awesome medical training is missing?"

They shook their heads.

"Haven't seen slit wrists in a while," he noted.

Despite the well-worn paradigm, Ellie knew that a cut wrist was a surprisingly ineffective method of death. The vessels in a wrist just aren't that big. And bodies fight to survive. The vessels usually close before death occurs. That's why cut wrists are often followed by cut chests or necks. But, in this case, Julia had the bathwater to help keep the blood flowing. The empty bottle of Barolo on the marble floor indicated some alcohol-related assistance as well.

Ginger placed his hands on his hips. "Well, I don't know about you two, but I get paid the same whether I'm here or back at Twenty-sixth Street. If this were a subsidized studio at the Patterson Projects, I'd be heading back to the office. But for Mama Grizzly out there? I plan on doing everything I'd do if you told me this was fishy. Better the taxpayers' dollars than my ass."

"Then it's unanimous," Rogan declared. "Let's do it."

"Yoo-hoo." Ellie waved a hand. "Not unanimous yet."

"What's the big deal? We'll get CSU to work the place up. Talk to a few of the girl's friends. Canvass the neighborhood. Make sure we're not missing anything."

"Or we could get the hell out of here and eat lunch."

"Again: Sensitivity and what not?"

"I don't know. A hamburger sounds pretty good right now. Or does your girlfriend still have you watching your cholesterol, old man?"

Rogan shook his head. "I never should have mentioned that shit to you. Like riding with my moms. A whiter, blonder, more freakily intuitive version of my mother. It's not like you to walk away from something so quickly, Hatcher."

"I walk away when I know my time's being wasted. You two stay up here if you want, but I've got a court appearance to make. I'm going to talk with the mother, then I'm out of here."

CHAPTER FOUR

Ellie found Katherine Whitmire perched on an upholstered banquette at the bottom of the stairs, a cordless phone to one ear. The officer who was supposed to have accompanied her outside stood by. "I've been with her the whole time," he offered as a consolation.

Ellie was beginning to wish she possessed whatever power this woman seemed to exert over others.

Katherine used her free hand to wipe away smears of black mascara when she noticed Ellie approaching.

"I have to go, Bill," she said into her phone. "One of the detectives just finished up in the bedroom. She might have some news. But you're heading back into the city, right? Immediately?" She muttered a soft thank-you before clicking off the line.

"My husband," she explained. "He's getting a helicopter back from East Hampton. He was talking about a meeting out there. I think he's in a bit of shock."

"It's not unusual."

"Right. I guess you're used to dealing with these sorts of things, aren't you?"

"You never get used to it. Tell me about your daughter."

"She would never do something like this to herself."

Everyone thought they could spot suicidal tendencies. Ellie knew better. Some people advertised their misery with unshowered days spent self-medicated in bed, but just as many kept up appearances as workers, students, neighbors—fathers. It had taken Ellie nearly twenty years, but she'd come to the truth the hard way.

"So tell me about her."

"I don't understand, Detective. What is it that you want to know?"

She wanted to know how this woman saw her daughter. Mostly she wanted this woman to feel like she had been given the opportunity to speak before Ellie left her to deal with the long and messy aftermath of a suicide. "I know you overheard a couple of the police officers talking to the EMTs. Obviously you believe they jumped to the wrong conclusions. So tell me what you want us to know about Julia, so we can have the whole picture."

Ellie followed the woman to the living room, where she removed a framed photograph from the mantel. "This was two Christmases ago." Katherine Whitmire had not changed since the family portrait, but her daughter looked much younger with no makeup, plump cheeks, and pink lips struggling to cover her metal braces through a smile.

"Is that your son?" Ellie pointed to the preppy-looking boy seated next to Julia.

"Billy. Bill Jr., yes. He's a freshman at Colby now. And that's my husband, Bill. I haven't called Billy yet. I—I don't know how to. He doesn't handle change well. He's very regimented, very planned—like his father. Not like Julia at all." She smiled sadly. "Julia's more like me. Or was. Independent. Free-spirited. Stubborn as all hell, but so tolerant and accepting and loving of every person she ever met. She had the kind of heart that wanted to save us all."

"Did you need saving?"

Her wistful expression was replaced by an intense stare. "I didn't mean myself personally, Detective. I meant—you know—society, the world. She wanted to save the world. I warned her. I told her that some people just couldn't be saved. They might have been decent people under other circumstances, but that kind of poverty, living on the streets—it makes people desperate. It makes them dangerous. *That's* what happened here. One of those—animals—killed her. They probably stole a few bucks from her purse. *That's* what this is about."

The words were tumbling out too quickly to follow.

"You sound like you have someone in mind."

"They're kids from the street. I found them here with her—maybe two months ago."

"And who were these kids?" In the world of the Whitmires, kids from public school might be considered bad influences.

"I don't know if they're orphans or in foster care, or maybe they're just homeless. I don't know their names. There were maybe three of them here—two boys and a girl, I think. Ramona would know. Ramona Langston. She's Julia's best friend. I told Julia not to have those people over again, but, God knows, my daughter never did listen to me. Bill said she'd only hold on to them closer if I tried to push them away. What can you do, though? She was all grown up."

"I was told she was sixteen?"

The woman blinked as if Ellie's response was a non sequitur.

"So these kids were here two months ago?" Ellie asked. "You didn't see Julia with them since then?"

"I've only been back once since then."

"I'm sorry. You told us when we arrived that this was your house?"

"It is, but Bill and I only come in about once a month or so. We've been going back and forth between here and East Hampton for years, but we've tapered off our city presence. When Billy went to college, Julia moved upstairs."

"And before Billy was at school?"

"Then the two of them would be here. Oh, they were inseparable. I don't even know how to tell him what's happened. Julia followed Billy everywhere. She has never liked being alone. That was probably why she befriended such desperate people. You know, I was here more often before Billy went to school. She had me. She had him. Now—"

"So, I'm sorry—Julia was basically living here alone?"

"Most of the time. That's right. She preferred the city. Her school. Her friends. Everything is here."

And this woman had called the street kids the orphans.

What else would a good, thorough, concerned detective ask? "Did she have a boyfriend?"

"A boyfriend?" Like the word was foreign.

"A guy in her life?"

"Well, my daughter certainly dated, I'm sure. But no one special I know about."

"I found birth control pills in your daughter's medicine cabinet. I thought that might indicate she was seeing someone regularly?"

"Oh, those? She's been on the pill since she was fourteen. Bill's idea, actually. Better safe than sorry."

There was something about Julia's father's name that felt familiar to Ellie. Whitmire. Bill Whitmire. She couldn't quite place it.

"What about other prescriptions? We found Adderall in her purse."

"Adderall? I've never heard of it. I mean, she would get head-aches. Maybe—"

"It's a prescription stimulant used for ADHD."

Katherine shook her head. "She didn't have anything like that."

"Did she see a psychiatrist?"

"No. Lord knows I do, as do a lot of her friends. But Bill thinks therapy and antidepressants and all of that are overused by over-indulgent rich people. I suppose to you we might seem to fit that description."

"Your husband's name sounds familiar to me. Do you mind if —"

"CBGB."

"Excuse me?"

"Don't tell me you're so young you don't know about CBGB?"

Ellie and her brother, Jess, had probably logged a couple thousand hours at the celebrated music venue before it succumbed to escalat-ing rent prices. "Of course I know it." Then the light clicked. Bill Whitmire was the famed producer behind bands that had played with the Ramones and Blondie.

"It's a John Varvatos boutique now," the woman said sadly. "Can you believe that?"

Ellie stayed with the woman in the living room while CSU officers came and went. She heard about the school Christmas play Julia wrote in the fifth grade, where Santa Claus went to a doctor named Cal Q. Later to lose weight so the reindeer could still fly with him in the sleigh. She learned that Julia had been the one to write her older brother's college admission essays. She found out that Julia had organized the first chapter of Amnesty International at Casden, her Upper East Side prep school. That she loved dogs but was allergic. That she once met Bono through her father and got his autograph—not for herself, but to donate to a charitable auction for an animal shelter.

Ellie interrupted on occasion to voice aloud the questions raging in her head.

Didn't you notice your daughter had an eating disorder? *Why would you ask that? She's naturally thin.* Right, despite that chubby adolescent picture on the mantel.

Did it dawn on you your daughter might have reasons to feel lost? *Have you heard anything I've been saying to you, Detective?* Have you been listening to yourself?

I assume this note is in your daughter's handwriting? *Handwriting can be imitated.* You must have learned that on *CSI.*

And though she pontificated about her daughter and their family for well more than an hour, Katherine Whitmire never once mentioned the fact that her sixteen-year-old bulimic daughter died in her bathtub from a slit wrist, leaving behind a suicide note propped against her overstuffed down pillows.

Sometimes it was easier to deny undeniable facts than to acknowledge a painful truth. Ellie knew that better than anyone.

She took a deep breath of fresh air once they left the townhouse, as if freshly oxygenated blood could wash away her unwanted thoughts, imagining what it had been like to grow up with Bill and Katherine Whitmire for parents.

"Some house, huh?" Rogan had been spared all but a few sentences of the conversation with Katherine and was still looking up with envy at the four-story abode.

"Her dad's Bill Whitmire. The music producer." She rattled off a handful of the projects he'd backed.

"You and that loud white-boy music. Give me Prince any day. *I wanna be your . . . lovah!*"

"Hurry it up, will you?" She looked at her watch as she continued her march to the car. "I've got that hearing scheduled. Told you I'd make it in time, but only if you drop me by the courthouse straight from here."

"I thought you said when we got the callout your testimony wasn't that important. You said the DA could get by without you if necessary."

"Well, I don't see anything here that counts as necessity. You said yourself no one reported anything out of the ordinary here over the weekend."

"We've still got uniforms canvassing the neighborhood," Rogan said.

"They haven't found any witnesses, and they're not going to."

"You know what's going to happen if we blow this off, right?"

"Katherine Whitmire will huff and puff and blow our house down?"

"Seriously, Hatcher, what is up with you? We've worked cases before that we knew weren't going anywhere. We don't usually walk away."

He was right, of course. How many hours did they waste a year on gang shootings where there was no such thing as a witness? But those cases were different.

"It's just pathetic, Rogan. Some people have kids just to satisfy their own fucking egos. That girl was sixteen years old and was expected to be all grown up because her parents were too cool and too impatient to have children in their lives. On the pill for two years already. Obviously bulimic, and her mom doesn't even notice. Apparently hanging out with street kids just to get some attention from her parents."

"Shit, you're confusing me. Now you're saying we're missing something?"

"No, Rogan, none of that's suspicious. It's totally, completely, one hundred percent predictable, and it all adds up to a reason why she'd kill herself. This girl slit her wrist as a final cry for help, and her mother refuses to see it. You do what you want, but I'm going to the courthouse."

They'd wait for the medical examiner's report. An autopsy. Forensic findings. Science. It would all sound more official and indisputable than the experienced instincts of cops and EMTs. But there was no doubt in Ellie's mind that by the end of the week, Katherine Whitmire would be informed with all finality: her daughter killed herself. Maybe then she'd look in the goddamn mirror and start facing the truth.

CHAPTER FIVE

Second Acts: Confessions of a Former Victim and Current
Survivor

"FORGIVENESS"

Forgiveness. Such a simple word, but one of the hardest
things to find within oneself and give to others.

I have heard people say that it is impossible to heal without
forgiving those who have hurt you. But it is not my place to
forgive the man who raped me. Shouldn't he be the one who
is expected to look into himself to understand why he did what
he did? Shouldn't he be the one who has to ask himself how he
could take from me everything he stole—not just the physical
act, but the trust, my power, my agency, my sense of self?

Maybe he should be the one who has to try to forgive himself. That is not for me to do.

One of the things he stole from me was my mother. I remained silent for so long—allowing that man to come to my
room night after night—because of my fears for her. My loyalty
to her. My utter dedication.

She had always been my only parent. Dad left before he
could make any kind of impression that stayed with me. My
mother was alone for long and frequent periods. Not complete-

ly alone. She had me. But alone as a woman. Now a man she
had learned to love—whom she had brought into our home—
was coming to me at night and threatening to kill us both if I
said anything.

But I never blamed her for his presence in my life. She
couldn't know, I told myself. He put on such a kind face for others. How could she possibly suspect he carried a monster inside
of him?

No, it wasn't the abuse that took away my mother. Ironically, it
was my absolute, unquestioned faith in her that eventually trumped
the fear he had instilled in me. I waited until he was working late
at night. It was just the two girls at home together, like the old
days. We ate those silly finger sandwiches we used to make when
I was younger. They were chicken salad on cut Wonder Bread, but
for some reason the dainty size and funny name brought me so
much joy. (Who would eat a finger sandwich? I used to squeal.)

As the hours passed, I started to feel the darkness of his im-
minent return. Girls' night would soon end. He'd hug my mother
and say how happy he was to be home. As she fell into sleep,
he'd say he was still restless. *I'm going to read downstairs. I
don't want the light to bug you, honey.*

It had happened often enough that I could picture him entering my room. I was even beginning to note certain patterns.
If he was drunk, he was clumsier. It usually hurt less, but took
longer. If he was tired, he'd be in a rush to make it happen.
Choking me with his belt seemed to help him go faster. I'd also
learned by now that my period wouldn't stop him. He would
leave me there on a bloodied sheet, admonishing me to clean
up the mess before morning.

So I told her.

I still remember the expression on her face as she raised that
stupid Wonder Bread stick to her mouth. She halted midway
and returned it to the fancy platter we'd taken out for the occa-

sion, a gift I'd received from the neighbors for my confirmation.

"Maybe you had a dream."

"Mom, I think I know the difference between reality and a nightmare. And it's not just one time."

"What are we going to do?"

"I can tell the police. Maybe they can protect us."

"That's not what I meant. What are we going to do with *you*?"

"Mom" I'm not sure what punctuation to include after that single word but I can still hear my own voice in my head. Part observation. Part scream. Part question. Period, exclamation point, question mark?

And then she'd picked up the platter and dumped the remaining sandwiches in the trash. "I had no idea you hated me so much. Making up these kinds of lies. I forgive you, but don't ever tell these stories again."

She forgave *me*.

You might think I hate my mother. I don't. I never did. I simply lost her along with everything else I lost because of that man. And without making excuses for her failures as a mother, I choose now to blame him, not her. I choose to believe that, just as he broke me, he broke her. We were both his victims.

I also choose to believe that, even though it is too late to tell her, my mother knows I have forgiven her.

Forgiveness. Such a simple word.

The reader looked around to make sure no one was watching. After the last time, more caution was necessary now. Today's screen was the public computer at a crowded luxury gym on Broadway. The distracted employees at the front desk hadn't stopped the few people who had breezed by on cell phones with a quick wave of acknowledgment, a gesture that was easy enough to mimic. In a worst-case scenario, a cover story about forgotten running shoes would provide a nonmemorable escape.

Time to type a comment to reward the most recent posting.

"Did it ever dawn on you that your mom hated you for driving
away your father and making her a single mother? Did it ever
dawn on you that your desperation to have a father figure is
what drew that man to your bed? He should have choked you
harder. He should have made you bleed more. Keep writing.
I'm reading. And I'm coming for you."

Five minutes after the comment appeared online, a phone call
would be made to Buffalo, New York. "I'm calling about a prisoner
named Jimmy Grisco. James Martin Grisco."

That phone call would change everything.

CHAPTER SIX

K atherine Whitmire bolted the door after the last of the strangers finally left.

The house was quiet. It felt strange to be surrounded by silence in this house.

The Whitmires were a family that liked living with noise. Bill—on those rare occasions when he was there—was always listening to newly recorded tracks or blasting through demos in search of undiscovered talent. The kids had inherited his constant need for sound.

With Julia, it was usually music, but lately she'd developed a penchant for old-fashioned suspense movies. Billy, on the other hand, was a 24/7 news junkie, flipping incessantly between CNN, MSNBC, and Fox, the latter bringing him to frequent bouts of shouting at the television. Then, of course, there was the yelling between the townhouse floors. Despite Katherine's efforts to persuade her family members to use the room-to-room intercom system, the rest of the Whitmires insisted on communicating with one another through screams: *Did you erase my shows off the TiVo again? . . . Is anyone else hungry? I'm calling in for sushi! . . . Julia, get down here. Tell me what you think of this tape. . . . How many times do I have to tell you not to call it "tape" anymore, Dad?*

Now the house was silent in a way she could not remember since those first months, back when she was overseeing the renovation. It was quiet like this during that short period when the construction was finally done and the painters had removed their ladders and tarps but the movers had not yet arrived.

Julia was just a baby then, not even babbling yet. Billy had just celebrated his third birthday at a party only his father could have planned—twenty toddlers and their parents for a private afternoon concert at Joe's Tavern featuring a live performance from Hootie and the Blowfish. She remembered standing in this same foyer, admiring the feel of the clean, smooth marble against her bare feet, foreseeing the life her happy family would enjoy in this spectacular home.

She'd felt so lucky back then. Bill Whitmire had lived an amazing life filled with talent, celebrity, travel, music, and beautiful women. Katherine was not his usual fare. Neither a model nor a singer in-genue, she was already in her early thirties when she met Bill. An architect with a modest career, she'd landed her biggest contract yet with the remodel of a Tribeca loft for the lead singer of the Smashing Pumpkins.

She'd been on her way out, blueprints in hand, when Bill showed up for a coffee. Coffee turned into cocktails. Cocktails evolved into dinner. And, much to her surprise, she'd woken up in his bed the next morning.

She expected it to be a one-night stand, her first—and probably only—in a lifetime. But Bill called her three days later, and three days after that. Within two months, she started to wonder if they were actually in a relationship.

And then one day, to put her mind at ease because she was nearly two weeks late for her period, she peed on a stick. And then another, and another. With the trilogy of pink plus signs lined up on the top of her toilet tank, she saw the quick end of her exciting new romance. Bill was fifty years old and had never been married. This story could not have a happy ending.

She gave him the news, fully expecting him to ask when she'd be getting it taken care of. But then, once again, Bill Whitmire surprised her. He smiled and hugged her, and then he cried and said, "Thank you for this." He held her hair when the morning sickness started. He rubbed vitamin E lotion on her belly every night, promising to love her even if her entire abdomen ended up striped with stretch marks.

Six months into the pregnancy, he asked her to marry him, so they "could be a real family." They exchanged vows on the beach at Montauk. Elvis Costello officiated with a minister's certificate from the Internet. Their wedding announcement was placed prominently in the *New York Times* Sunday Styles section. She changed her name.

When she became pregnant a second time, with Julia, it was Bill who proposed buying a townhouse with ample space for the children to play. The top floor could be an apartment for a live-in nanny to help Katherine juggle the additional chaos that would accompany another child.

Bill Whitmire had settled down. He was a good father. And he'd chosen *her* to do it with. She remembered actually spinning around with glee on this marble floor that quiet day, staring up at the bright white molded ceiling so far above her, feeling like she'd won the love-and-marriage lottery. She was living a fairy tale, and Bill was her Prince Charming.

Two months later, the house was no longer empty. Billy with his *Toy Story* bedspread. Julia with her moss-green, elephant-themed nursery. Katherine's custom closet was bigger than the apartment she'd last rented as a single woman.

Mira, the full-time nanny, had her own living space upstairs.

To this day, Katherine still wondered how long it had been going on—right beneath, or above, her nose—before she realized. She'd come home one afternoon to find the familiar sound of Bill's music emanating from his study, but no Bill. The elevator parked on the top floor. No sign of Mira, either.

She'd taken the stairs so they wouldn't hear the elevator. If she was wrong, she could always tell Mira she was just slipping in some extra exercise.

But her suspicions had been right. Bill was the one slipping something in.

Now, more than sixteen years later, she had watched her daughter's body being wheeled out of that same top-floor apartment. The detectives she had insisted upon were gone. Everyone was gone.

She walked to the bar cart in the sitting area and poured a crystal highball glass full of Bill's vodka. She hated herself for thinking about his first (known) infidelity when she should be thinking about Julia.

But in many ways, that moment was inextricably entwined with this one. When she saw Bill—panting and sweaty behind the bent-over nanny, his unzipped, age-inappropriate designer jeans clumsily dangling—everything had changed. She should have left him then. She should have taken what the prenup had to offer and made a normal life with her two, still happy children.

But by then, being Mrs. Bill Whitmire had become the very core of her identity. For their marriage to fail would mean that she was nothing but a cliché, the glamorous carriage having turned back into a pumpkin at the stroke of midnight. It would mean that Bill had never really chosen her. She would be just one in a long string of women—the one who'd gotten knocked up.

And so watching and monitoring and controlling her husband became her full-time job. If Bill said he was meeting a reporter at Babbo, she would walk him there—and step inside to say a brief hello, supposedly "on her way" to some errand or another. If he had to fly to California for the Grammys, she accompanied him—even if the ceremonies coincided with Julia's first piano recital. When he announced that he was more productive at the in-home studio out in Long Island, she chose to believe that Julia and Billy were mature enough to stay at the townhouse on their own.

She felt the vodka burn its way down her throat. She held in the sting, wanting it to burn, wanting to feel *something*. She'd seen the way those detectives looked at her. Judging her. Casting her squarely inside whatever stereotypes they held about superficial women who valued their looks, handbags, and silverware above the things that actually mattered.

She knew she deserved every last bit of their scorn. She should have been here with her baby girl. She should have been here to protect her. The least she could do now was to find out who did this to her daughter. The police might be gone, but no way was this over.

The silence was disrupted by the sound of keys in the front door. She knew who would be walking in, but part of her wished it would be her son instead. She'd called Billy at school with the awful news, but even if he made it onto the last flight to New York, he wouldn't make it to the city before nine tonight.

"Kitty?"

Bill's eyes were red and damp. He rushed to her and wrapped his arms around her.

"My God. Our Julia. Our baby—" His voice broke.

How many times had she wanted him to run to her like this? To need her. To hunger for her love and loyalty like an addict jonesing for the next hit. She felt tiny and fragile against his smothering embrace.

"It's going to be okay, Kitty. We're going to get through this. Together."

He grabbed her even tighter, palming the back of her head and pressing her face against his cashmere overcoat. She smelled the sweet floral scent of Cartier perfume on his collar and, for the first time in nineteen years, found that she did not care what became of this marriage.

CHAPTER
SEVEN

Usually, Ellie enjoyed her time in the Criminal Court Building. She'd heard it described as "hurry-up-and-wait time." She understood the term all too well.

Other people—usually the lawyers—ran up and down the hallways, struggling to herd witnesses like cattle. They negotiated last-minute deals, always in shorthand. *ROR—release on recognizance. JOA—judgment of acquittal. SOR—sex offender registration. Stip-facts bench trial—stipulate that the facts offered in a bench (no jury) trial establish the material elements of the offense.* Meanwhile, she sat and chilled on a courthouse bench, usually with some lawyer's discarded newspaper in hand, collecting her pay—overtime if she wasn't on shift.

But on this particular day, waiting in the hallway outside Judge Frederick Knight's courtroom, her thoughts kept jumping back to Rogan's look of helplessness as she'd shut the car door on him mid-sentence. She could tell her partner was pissed. The last words he said to her before she walked away were: "Should we place an over-under on how long it is before Tucker gets a phone call?"

He was probably right. The Whitmires would call their lieutenant. Or have the commissioner call their lieutenant's captain to call their lieutenant. Or have the mayor call the commissioner—

however those kinds of people managed to pull the strings that were beyond reach of the rest of the population.

But Ellie was the last person on earth who was going to make it easy for them. Nothing about their celebrity or money could change the fact that they'd raised a sad, screwed-up kid who ended it all, drunk and naked and bloody in a bathtub.

"Hey, you. I thought you said you had a callout."

She had texted Max Donovan, the assistant district attorney handling today's motion, on their way to the scene on Barrow Street. She wasn't on a texting basis with most prosecutors, but this particular ADA was her boyfriend.

"Turned out to be a quickie."

"Wasn't aware we had quickie murder investigations these days. Oh, there was that case on Wooster last year where a guy thought his neighbor was murdering a woman, but the woman turned out to be a girlfriend doll."

"This one had a real body, but it was a clear-cut suicide. Well, clear-cut to everyone but the family."

The amusement fell from his face. "And you're okay with that?"

"Any reason I shouldn't be?"

"All right. Forget I said anything. I'm glad you could make it. Maybe time for a quick lunch when we're done here?"

"That'd be good."

Owing to their work schedules, they hadn't seen each other for four days. Given the consistent routine they'd developed over the last year, four nights apart was practically a long-distance relationship.

The bailiff stuck her head out of the courtroom door. "The judge is ready."

Ellie's testimony took all of sixteen minutes. She was there to defend against a murderer's postconviction motion for release. The defendant alleged that his attorney had offered ineffective assistance of counsel by allowing Ellie to interrogate him about the death of his girlfriend. The necessary information was straightforward. The defendant had been the one to call the police, claiming he'd come home and found her bludgeoned on the kitchen floor of their shared Chinatown apartment. He wasn't in custody. He wasn't even a suspect. His alleged "counsel" was a real estate lawyer who lived in the apartment next door and came over to offer friendly support.

It wasn't the lawyer's fault that Ellie noticed the tiny lacerations marking each blow on the victim's body, or the sharp, raised edge of the defendant's pinkie ring, or the red marks on the defendant's knuckles. Just a single, plainly phrased question about a possible explanation for those three circumstances had been enough for the defendant to break down.

It would have been a straightforward hearing if it weren't for the fact that Judge Frederick Knight was known throughout the New York criminal justice system as the Big Pig.

Maybe the term was unfair, a reference to his considerable weight of at least three bills. But Ellie suspected the nickname would never have come into play if the man did not strive at every second to out-misogynize Andrew Dice Clay.

The nonsense began as she rose from the witness chair after testifying.

"I know you."

If Ellie had been at a nursing home in Queens, she would have expected the line from a patient—the really, really old one, who didn't know anyone anymore.

"Ellie Hatcher, Your Honor. This is my fifth time here." She rattled off the defendants' names. She always remembered them. She could tell you the dates of the arrests, too. Probably their dates of births as well. Ellie's brain was weird that way.

It was all a blur to Judge Knight, who shook his head with her mention of each case. "Only five times here, and I remember you? Take that as a compliment, Officer."

Detective.

"You keep yourself in shape. That's good. Pretty girl there, right, Donovan?"

Max didn't miss a beat. "No one's as fit as you, Your Honor."

Corny, Ellie thought, but what was the right response to that question, under the circumstances?

"And what do you, Mr. Donovan, think about your witness's attire today?"

"Your Honor?" Donovan asked.

"Off the record for a moment," he said to the court reporter. "Only five visits to the courthouse and yet I remembered this witness. And let's be clear here. We all know what it is about her that would have stood out in my recollection. And now here she is in these butch pants—trousers, let's say."

Part of Ellie wanted to tell this man that beneath her simple gray flat-front pants she wore a black thong bikini, but she dressed for court this way for a reason. She dressed this way because most judges and jurors had expectations. And they weren't the same as Knight's expectations.

Knight wasn't interested in her inner monologue. He was on his own roll.

"When I first joined the bench, I heralded the first wave of lady litigators. They always wore skirts. High heels. Silk blouses. And then came the menswear trend, and these women started showing up in trousers and oxford shirts. Now the gals have it back to the way it was. Dresses. Skirts. Legs. Heels. Except for you, Officer. Hatcher, you said? You've got your best assets covered up. You look like a boy. Not to mention, my clerk tells me that you and Donovan here are quite the item. I mean, what if Donovan showed up here tomorrow in a dress? How would you feel about that?"

She saw Max looking at her. Willing her. Begging her. *Don't. Do. It.*

"I would like to see that, Your Honor. But ADA Donovan was just telling me he wore out his best red silk number modeling it for you."

•   •   •

Max was doing his best in the hallway to appear annoyed, but he couldn't help breaking a smile.

"Red silk? Really? Seems a little hoochie-momma."

"Oh, you'd be much classier as a lady fella, I'm sure. Brooks Brothers. Burberry. All those blue-blood labels. Sorry, I sort of lost it with the Big Pig."

"Whatever. The motion's a slam dunk. Even the defendant's own allegations make clear he was playing the grieving boyfriend at the start. Besides, there's no way for the state *not* to be all right with Knight. He sides with the prosecution like he's on autopilot. I could tell him the court should enter an official finding of alien invasion, and he'd do exactly as I said."

"I'm praying I'll still get home at some reasonable hour tonight. You?"

He let one hand wander to her waist. "As soon as I'm done here, I have to go out to Rikers. Gang shooting. Guess a few weeks in a cell has someone second-guessing his loyalty to a coconspirator. I've got to hammer out the cooperation details."

"Could the good citizens of New York please stop fucking killing each other for a night?"

"Do you at least have time for that lunch? I've got a few minutes."

"Depends. You still got that red silk dress?"

"Those pants *are* a little butch."

"Not underneath," she said. He returned her smile. When her cell phone buzzed at her waist, she tensed up at the sight of Rogan's name on the screen. He had predicted a shitstorm to follow their walking away from the Whitmires' townhouse. Apparently it had taken little more than an hour for Julia's parents to work their way through their network back to her cell phone.

She held up a finger while she took the call. "Yeah?"

"We shouldn't have left. You told me yourself Donovan didn't really need your testimony."

"I take it Tucker tore you a new one?"

"It's not just the Lou. We should have at least gone through the motions.

Like I said: Protect the crime scene, talk to the friends, do what we do."

"Like *I* said, it's a waste of time."

"That's why I let you convince me to leave. But we screwed up."

"And how exactly did we do that?"

"I'll tell you when I get there. Meet me out on Centre Street. I'm three minutes away."

Neither one of them said goodbye.

Three hundred and seventy-five miles northwest of the city, in Buffalo, New York, Assistant District Attorney Jennifer Sugarman took a call from the front desk. "There's a James Grisco here to see you."

"Okay. Send him back."

She had heard all the terms used to describe the other stars in the office. Dan Clark was a *natural born trial lawyer*. Joe Garrett was a *genius in front of a jury*. Mark Munson was a *courtroom machine*.

Munson? Really? She'd popped in on him in trial one day to see what the fuss was all about, only to hear him argue that the defendant's story was all an "elaborate rouge." He even touched his fingertips to the apple of his cheek, just in case she was wondering if she'd misheard the word that was supposed to be "ruse." An elaborate rouge. What an idiot.

Jennifer Sugarman? Ask around the office, and they'd say she was a *hard worker. Diligent. Detail oriented. Conscientious. Burns the midnight oil.* When men were good, they were born that way. If she was just as good—better, even—it must have come by way of tremendous effort.

She didn't mind those descriptions, though. She'd made it out of misdemeanors into felonies faster than any ADA on record and was now first-chairing murder cases after only five years in the office. Rumor was she'd be named a unit chief in the next round of promotions. And when the big boss finally retired, her reputation for working hard would come in handy. Voters liked to know they were getting their money's worth with public employees. She planned to be Erie County's first female district attorney.

And she was, in fact, harder-working than most. Take the call she got from the jail this morning about Grisco, for instance. Most of the ADAs would have blown it off. At most, they would have passed the information on to the parole officer and forgotten about it.

But she had been the one to negotiate Grisco's release from prison, and she knew ex-cons feared the official power of a prosecutor much more than they feared the often-empty threats of parole officers. If there was some reason for a person to call the prison inquiring about Grisco's whereabouts, she wanted Grisco to know she hadn't forgotten about him. She wouldn't hesitate to pull his ticket if it came to that.

He removed his baseball cap when he entered her office. It was a good sign he knew who was in charge. She told him about the call that had been made to the prison that morning. She reminded him of his release conditions, going so far as to read them aloud from his file.

"You don't need to remind me, ma'am. I got no plans of messing this up."

"Good to hear, Jimmy. I stuck my neck out for you."

"Yes, ma'am. I appreciate it."

She shook his hand and walked him to the hallway. As she watched him make his way toward the exit, she found herself hoping he might actually find a decent life for himself. He wasn't even forty yet.

It wasn't until she returned to her office that she realized she should have covered up the note pad on her desk, the one on which she had scribbled the information she'd received from the prison. It was a stupid mistake, but Grisco hadn't seemed to notice. His eyes had remained on his shoes the whole time, anyway.

She flipped the pad to the next page. It was nothing. She was certain of it.

CHAPTER EIGHT

As Casey Heinz jogged up from the 6 train at Bleecker, he was thinking that, all in all, it had been a good day.

Ramona's school had some kind of teacher in-service Monday, so she'd been able to spend the day with him, starting with a snack at AJ's. On a day without Ramona, he might have had only a chocolate-chip muffin, forcing himself to chew slowly, careful not to show his hunger. The fact that he was getting sick of that particular food option would have helped to slow the pace of his eating. He was tiring of nearly all the choices at AJ's, one of the only places left on the Lower East Side that allowed them to hang out without buying too much. A cup of coffee first. A couple hours later, a muffin. Sometimes Brandon or Vonda would drop in with enough collected change for another cup of java.

AJ's was starting to feel like home.

But, today, time wasn't a problem, because Ramona was there. Girls who carried themselves like Ramona were never asked to leave, no matter who they consorted with.

Cost wasn't an issue, either, when Ramona was around. He appreciated how Ramona paid. Not just the fact *that* she paid. Of course she would, given their different circumstances. But it was cool *how* she did it. Always ordering something for herself, too, even when Casey knew she wasn't hungry enough to finish it. And she always seemed to order the things that Casey liked. Today it was chicken breast, mozzarella, and basil on a baguette. She'd picked off a bite or two, then, when Casey had finished his muffin, she'd pushed the sandwich toward him, insisting, "I'm so full. Here, can you finish this?"

As they had walked through SoHo after lunch, he had studied her profile. He'd never known a girl as pretty as Ramona. She wasn't classic pretty. Or even cute pretty, the way most straitlaced high school girls were, with their misplaced confidence and upturned noses. Ramona was actually sort of funny-looking. Her nose was a little too long and flat, and he knew from memory that one of those big eyes of hers fell a little lower than the other. And her lips were on the thinnish side, her smile a bit crooked. But all of those features together? Ramona was, by any definition of the word, a stunner.

Even cooler was the fact that she didn't try to be pretty. No highlights in that short jet-black hair of hers, the ends chunky as if cut with a razor. Plus, she wore way more vintage clothing and black eyeliner than acceptable among Upper East Siders. Plus, she hung with the likes of Casey.

Usually, they goofed around the neighborhood, making fun of the pretentious, surreal art galleries and the wannabe punk kids. And usually one of them had someone in tow—he with Brandon, or her with Julia. But today it had been just the two of them.

And they hadn't just goofed around. Today, Ramona had really *talked* to him.

"I'm worried about my mom. I think she's depressed or something."

Casey couldn't imagine what Ramona's mother could possibly be depressed about. From what he could gather, her full-time job was to shop and work out, but he held his tongue.

"I called Julia last night. She thinks I should talk to my dad. Tell him that she's spending so much time holed away in her room all day."

"See this?" Casey had pointed to his own face. "This is a look of pain and humiliation that you talked to Julia about this before me."

"Sorry." She had leaned over and grabbed his shoulders from behind in a quick half-hug. "She's just constantly in contact, you know, with text and IM and everything."

Texting and instant-messaging. Two other conveniences of a normal life that Casey did not enjoy. At Promises, there was a fifteen-minute limit on computer use unless it was related to a job search, and residents didn't have their own phones. Anyone who wanted to contact him had to leave a message at the front desk. Or with Joy, who worked the register at AJ's from noon to five on weekdays. She was a sweetheart that way.

The pain and humiliation were feigned, in any event. Ramona and Julia Whitmire had known each other since the single-digit years. Casey'd met Ramona only last December, when they were both hanging out in Washington Square Park. Casey would probably never be Ramona's best friend, but that didn't mean she wasn't his.

Julia was supposed to meet them today at AJ's but had once again been a no-show. In her absence, he made a few comments at her expense.

"Julia thinks you should tell your dad because as much as she bitches about those parents of hers, she's a daddy's girl. She'd love nothing more than a chance to tattle on her own mommy to get a few brownie points from her dear, distant dad."

"Harsh."

"Not harsh. Just true. You know I love that girl. Almost as much as you." Then he'd felt awkward, but Ramona didn't seem to mind the comment.

After the stroll through SoHo, they headed west and hung out on the High Line, then they walked store to store in the Village. Maybe if Julia had ever shown up, she would have forced them to buy something. Not Casey, of course, but Ramona.

When Ramona announced at two o'clock that she needed to go home, he wondered whether she would have stayed longer if Julia had been there. Then he wondered whether he'd ever stop having those kinds of thoughts. He hated realizing how insecure he was at heart.

But then he'd bumped into Brandon on Eighth Street, holding his latest cardboard sign. "Trying to get home to Louisiana. Need $55 for a bus ticket." If Casey had a hundred dollars, he'd bet it all that Brandon had never been south of D.C. Brandon was cockier than Casey. Bolder. Undoubtedly a little shady. Casey had been careful to keep his distance those few times while Brandon did hand-to-hand sales in the park. Casey made a point never to challenge Brandon, though, or to show that he was worried. Brandon was the only guy Casey had met on the streets who was willing to accept him.

It had been a good day.

By the time Casey made it back to AJ's, it was just shy of five o'clock, so Joy was still there. As usual, she snuck him some food with his coffee. Sometimes it was pumpkin or zucchini bread—whatever they had the most of and would likely have to throw out at closing—but today he scored with a piece of lemon cake.

"Got a message for you, too, hot stuff." Joy was only twenty years old and had a bleached white pageboy haircut and a sleeve tattoo on her right arm, but she liked to talk like a 1960s waitress slinging hash in a Waco diner. "Your favorite little lady called."

"Natalie Portman's finally seen the light, huh?"

"You know which one I mean. Little Missy Ramona's sweet self. She said to call her faster than green grass through a goose."

Casey was pretty sure that was Joy's choice of words, not Ramona's. He made a show of taking his time leaving AJ's, then hightailed it to one of the neighborhood's last remaining pay phones, at the corner of Lafayette and Bleecker. After four rings, he heard Ramona's familiar outgoing message: "Hey, there. It's Ramo—" Typical. Ramona had a habit of leaving her cell phone silenced, in her purse, and otherwise ignored. Any other person his age could leave a message and expect a call back on his cell within an hour, but Casey didn't have that luxury. He fished through his wallet for his list of contacts, dropped fifty more cents, and dialed another number.

Ramona's father answered. Damn it. "Hello, Mr. Langston. This is Casey Heinz. May I please speak with Ramona?"

Casey had met Ramona's parents only once, that night when they walked out during intermission—some play they called a "cheap Albee rip-off"—and came home early to find Casey and Ramona watching a marathon of *Arrested Development*. They didn't know the details of Casey's living situation, but it hadn't taken them long to infer from his appearance and vague responses to their questions that he was not from Ramona's usual social circle. He made a point of using his best manners on the rare occasions he called her house.

"Ramona is—well, she's very upset right now. She's in her room. I think her mother's trying to talk to her."

"Did something happen? I got a message from her and it sounded urgent."

"She wanted to speak to you, huh? Well, I guess I should let her know you're returning her call, then. Just a moment, Casey."

He heard murmuring in the background, and then Ramona was on the line. "Casey, oh my God, Casey. Please come over. Please. I need you here."

I need you. How many times had he fantasized about Ramona saying those words? But in his imagination, her voice had been soft and vulnerable. Now she barely sounded human, the syllables coughed from her throat between rasped sobs.

"It's Julia. It's Julia. She's gone, Casey. Julia's dead. She killed herself."

CHAPTER NINE

Ellie was sitting on the front steps of the Criminal Court Building when she spotted Rogan pulling a U-turn to meet her at the curb. He greeted her with a frustrated shake of his head before tearing up Centre Street.

"So where have we been summoned to now?" she asked as she snapped her seat belt in place.

He remained silent for another six blocks before he finally spoke.

"Don't try to pretend that what we did today was good work, Ellie." He rarely used her first name. "We were in and out of there faster than a straight-to-cable movie, and we spent the whole time looking to prove the conclusion we came to within a minute of entering that house. We're no different than those lazy uniforms and smart-ass EMTs. We assumed the spoiled little rich girl slit her own wrists, and we made sure not to notice anything that might pull us in another direction."

"You seemed fine when we left."

"And that's on me. I deferred to you, but I should have realized you're the last person who should've made the call on this."

"What's that supposed to mean? I made the same call as everyone else there—except that girl's mother, who's not exactly objective."

"We both know it's not our job to make calls that fast. You mean to tell me nothing else is going on here?"

Ellie looked out the window, as if that could buy her some space.

There were days when she was grateful that she and Rogan could navigate their way through an interrogation with only exchanged glances. She had even learned to accept the fact that Rogan could tell she was PMS-ing before she could. But if there was some way to lobotomize the part of his brain that knew about her father, she'd saw open his head personally.

Ellie had never talked about her father to anyone at the NYPD, not even Rogan. But she couldn't help that other people knew her background. After police in Wichita had finally arrested William Summer and named him as the College Hill Strangler, she had decided to go public. She thought the pressure would convince the WPD to reverse its decision and finally award her father's pension to her mother. Turned out to be a shit idea, but she had to try.

Now, because her face had been on *Dateline* and in *People* magazine, everyone knew that—despite what she appeared to be now—she had once been the little girl who could never accept the fact that her cop-daddy blew his brains out. She wondered if that was all people saw sometimes.

As Rogan pulled next to a fire hydrant in front of the Whitmire townhouse, she knew that even her partner suspected that, maybe—just maybe—a cold night at the side of a rural road in Wichita was the real reason why Ellie had been so quick to chalk up Julia Whitmire's death to suicide.

But Ellie knew her true motivations. She was being rational. She was acting on evidence, not emotion; on reality, not old memories. Julia had killed herself, and her parents needed to come to terms with that fact.

She noticed the engine was still idling. "So are you going to tell me why we're here? Who'd the Whitmires call?"

"Everyone, from what I can tell. I did, in fact, get an earful from the Lou. So I asked myself whether we might have missed something."

"I know, you told me that on the phone. So what is it? What did we miss?"

He turned off the engine, only to turn it right back on. "You know what kills me? This is exactly the kind of thing that *you* would notice. Think, Hatcher. Think about what we saw today."

"Are we playing twenty questions? Is it bigger than a bread box? Animal, mineral, vegetable? Oh, wait, I know: it's a screwed-up kid in a bathtub. Will you hurry up and tell me before we knock on that door again? Because we better have a damn good reason if we're going to disturb that woman just as she probably finished downing her third Valium to try to get some sleep after watching her daughter's body hauled away."

Rogan turned off the engine again, and this time took the keys out of the ignition. "You were the one who spent the most time in her room," he said. "The girl was a junior in high school—a member of her generation in every way, with every gadget in the world at her fingertips."

"Yep, every luxury money could buy, and what did it do for her?"

He shook his head once again. "You still don't see it? Ellie, you really got to get yourself right on this one." He didn't wait for her to get out of the car before making his way to the front door.

Katherine Whitmire started talking as soon as she opened the door. "It's about time. The EMTs. The medical examiner. The two of you. Your lieutenant. I lost count of the number of times I heard the word *suicide* today and the number of people who used it. All of you were lining up to tell me and my husband that our daughter did this to herself. And every single time, I believed it even less. I tried. I *begged*."

A man came up behind her and placed a protective arm around her shoulder. "I'm Julia's father, Bill Whitmire. Please, come in."

As she took the seat offered in the parlor room adjacent to the foyer, Ellie found herself distracted by the man's appearance. He was more than twice her age, but still handsome with longish salt-and-pepper hair, a strong jaw, and the kind of wear and tear considered distinguished on a man.

But Ellie kept seeing the man he'd once been—the man photographed so many times with famous musicians from her childhood, at spots like Studio 54, with then-starlets like Ali MacGraw and Carrie Fisher. He still carried himself with a rock-and-roll edge that looked out of place in this sterile townhouse. Ellie suspected the man spent little time here and had nothing to do with a decorating plan whose only reflection of his personality was relegated to photographs in the elevator.

"I'm sorry about that outburst at the door," Katherine said, "but we're just . . . we're . . . our daughter—she's gone. And I've had to spend the entire day on the phone arguing and fighting and twisting arms. But you're back now, right? You'll be listening to what I've been trying to say? You'll be treating Julia's death as a murder?"

This was exactly what Ellie had been afraid of. They were getting these people's hopes up for no apparent reason. She was going to let Rogan handle this one on his own.

"We can't imagine what you've been through today," he offered. "We want to be absolutely sure that we didn't miss anything before—"

"Before you shut the folder on my daughter and move on to your next statistic." Bill Whitmire wiped away a drop of saliva that stuck to his lip as he'd hissed the words. "You write case names on a whiteboard, don't you, Detective? Like on television? Have you crossed her name off the board yet?"

"Mr. Whitmire—"

"You say you want to be sure you didn't miss anything, but we all know the first twenty-four hours of an investigation are absolutely critical." Apparently the record producer spent a lot of time watching crime TV. "You should be talking to our neighbors and her friends, checking sexual offenders released nearby, doing whatever it is you people *do* to find whatever monster came into our home and did this."

Uniformed officers had already knocked on the doors of the other townhouses on the street, but no one reported seeing anything out of the ordinary.

She wished Rogan would cut to the chase, but he was still trying to manage the parents' expectations. "The initial evidence, as we explained earlier today, indicated that your daughter was alone in the bathroom and was the author of the note we found on her bed."

"Well, at least this time you avoided the *S*-word, but I think my wife and I heard the same message enough times today."

Katherine placed a hand on her husband's knee. "Please, let the detectives *speak*. They're here for a reason."

Rogan paused before continuing. "When we were in your daughter's room earlier, I noticed that her homework all seemed to be printed out. Did she usually do her schoolwork on a computer?"

Ellie noticed the blankness in Bill's face as he looked to his wife for the answer. Katherine nodded. "That's all kids do now. They take laptops to school for note taking. Seems recently she was even getting by just with her iPad. Kids can't even spell or print correctly anymore without a computer there to help them."

"So if she had to write a letter of some kind—"

"She doesn't write letters. No one her age does."

Ellie now saw what Rogan had been trying to get her to realize on her own in the car. Julia's suicide note had been handwritten, on paper. And not just written on paper, but drafted on paper, with false starts and crossed-out words.

Julia's mother saw the point as well. "Julia wouldn't have written that ridiculous note on her bed. Even if you could convince me that my daughter authored that note, I simply can't imagine her putting a pen to paper in order to do it. She would go to her computer. Even if she wanted us to have a handwritten version, she'd draft it first on the screen, then write it out afterward."

"That's why we're here. The note had scratched-out words and other scribbles on it, like Julia had started fresh, with a blank page, when she sat down to write."

"No, not Julia."

"What about the paper? The letter was on yellow lined paper, with holes punched on the side. I don't recall seeing a notebook like that when we went through her room. Do you keep yellow legal pads around the house?"

This time it was the wife who looked to her husband. "No, not to my knowledge," he said.

"So that means she didn't write the note." Katherine sounded hopeful for the first time since they'd encountered her. "That proves she didn't kill herself."

Ellie finally had to cut in. "It's always possible she got the paper somewhere else. We're here because we didn't want to jump to conclusions."

But like his wife, Bill Whitmire had already reached his own verdict. "Based on your experience, Detective, do you really believe this scenario makes any sense?"

"We'd like to take another look around if you don't mind." Rogan was already on his feet, heading for the stairs.

They searched through every drawer, cupboard, box, and bag of the four-story townhouse, but nowhere did they find a yellow legal pad matching Julia's supposed suicide note.

"You mentioned your daughter's friends, Mrs. Whitmire. Who knew Julia best?"

It was a simple question, but Ellie recognized the look of determination on Rogan's face. They were going to rework this case from the beginning, whether she liked it or not, and he blamed her for the crucial hours they had already wasted.

CHAPTER TEN

When asked who knew her daughter best, Katherine Whitmire hadn't hesitated. Answer: Ramona Langston. And they wasted no time, heading straight to Third Avenue for the drive to the Upper East Side.

If the day had been about developing an opinion of wealthy Manhattan mothers, Ramona's mother helped clear Ellie's palate. Where Katherine Whitmire was cold, aggressive, and uptight, the woman who answered the door at the Langston household came across more like an organic earth-mother type. She introduced herself as Adrienne—first name only. Given the woman's long, loose natural waves, Columbia Sportswear pullover, and blue jeans, Ellie could not imagine her fitting in with the other Upper East Side mothers at Casden, the ultra-elite private school where Julia Whitmire and her best friend, Ramona, were juniors.

Even the apartment felt warmer—more lived-in—than the townhouse where Julia's body had been found earlier that morning. Whereas the Whitmire house was adorned with Edwardian-era settees that were more impressive than comfortable, this place was filled with oversize sofas, plush rugs, and throw pillows that looked like you could actually use them. By the Whitmires' standards, the apartment might even be considered modest.

The man who walked into the living room after Adrienne excused herself to get Ramona seemed startled to see them. Rogan raised his eyebrows in Ellie's direction, a signal that he, too, had noticed the man's literal flinch at the sight of a black man in his house.

"Hello."

They repeated the introductions they had already made with Adrienne at the front door.

"Ah, I see. I'm Ramona's father, George Langston. Is it really necessary to pull our daughter into this? She's having a very hard time understanding what's happened. We finally called in one of her friends to help calm her down. I don't want to get her upset again."

Ellie already had this guy's number. *Just because your daughter appears calm does not mean she is calm.* She knew it was a bad habit, but she couldn't help it: Ellie formed impressions of people immediately upon meeting them. George Langston struck her as a well-meaning but rigid man, both physically and psychologically. He was very small in stature—not much taller than Ellie—but maximized every centimeter of it with perfect posture. It's not that he was unattractive. She could imagine how some women might be drawn to his clear, blue eyes and smooth skin. But to Ellie he looked like he literally had a stick running up his ass, all the way to the base of his skull.

"George?" Adrienne had returned from the rear of the apartment. "Sorry, I thought you'd gone to bed. These are—"

"We already met. I was explaining that Ramona is as shocked by all of this as anyone. I'm not sure she knows anything sufficiently useful to warrant the disruption that will come with having police officers talking to her tonight. Maybe tomorrow—"

"Not everything boils down to cost-benefit analysis, George."

Mr. Langston forced the polite smile of a man who was used to quarreling in public. And his wife offered what was probably a common apology for the display of conflict. "Sorry, Detectives. It's been a rough day—obviously for the poor Whitmires, but for our family, too. There were years when Julia literally spent more nights here than at her own home. I think Ramona would very much like to speak with you."

"Adrienne—"

He was cut off again by his wife. "She needs to feel like she's helping. I was a teenage girl once. Trust me, George. *Please*."

When George drifted from the room—no more relevant than he'd been before entering—Ellie knew which parent was calling the shots.

So did Rogan, who was already out of his chair. "So, where can we find your daughter, Mrs. Langston?"

They found Ramona Langston lying on her bed listening to her iPod, a mangled ball of tissues covering her eyes.

Despite the earbuds and Kleenex, she sensed their presence and sat up abruptly. She wasn't what Ellie expected. Black makeup smeared both of the girl's round cheeks. Her thick, spiky hair was flattened against her head on one side from lying on the bed. Ellie was starting to wonder whether two families had mixed the pieces of their family puzzles together. Uptight George Langston belonged with Katherine Whitmire in the townhouse full of antiques, while this girl and her mother, Adrienne, would be happier with a rock producer like Bill Whitmire.

"My mom said you're with the police. Was Katherine right? Julia didn't do this to herself?"

Ellie had wondered whether the girl's bedroom would be suitable for an interview, but she'd been picturing a room like her own, with barely enough space for a queen-size bed and a dresser. Ramona Langston's room was more like a studio apartment. She and Rogan settled next to each other on a sofa next to a full-length mirror and dressing table.

Rogan spoke first. "It sounds like your friend's mother has already shared her concerns with you. Do you have any thoughts about that?" They'd been partners for more than a year, but Ellie was still surprised every time he transformed his voice for certain witnesses, setting aside his usual gruff bark in favor of a sweet, warm, vocal maple syrup.

Ramona shrugged. "Thoughts? I mean, yeah, I've been *thinking* about it ever since I heard, but I didn't realize the police were actually investigating or anything. I just assumed Katherine was believing what she wanted to believe."

Ellie was liking this girl more and more by the second. "Why did you assume that?"

"If Julia did this, that means she was in horrible, terrible pain, and felt so alone and so isolated that she would rather end it all than reach out to someone, even her mom. It means Julia was willing to hurt her mother this way."

And her best friend, Ellie wanted to add. In her father's case, it was a wife and two young children who had been left behind. Ellie had spent her entire life wondering which was worse: If her father had been murdered by the serial killer he spent his entire career hunting, or if he hated himself so much for failing to find the man, that he was willing to end his life before seeing his own children grow up? And then, two years ago, the Wichita Police had finally identified William Summer as the College Hill Strangler. Summer had had an ironclad alibi for the night Detective Jerry Hatcher was found at the wheel of his car, killed by his own service weapon. The truth about his death had come twenty years too late for his family.

"Do you think Julia might just do something like that?" Ellie asked.

"Honestly? I could see her doing something dramatic like swallowing half a bottle of aspirin to get her parents to pay her some fu—to pay attention to her. But Katherine said she, you know—" She made a slicing gesture across her left wrist.

"She cut her wrist," Rogan said. "That's correct."

"It's hard to imagine. I talked to her Friday night and she seemed fine. We were supposed to hang out with Casey today, but she never showed up. Now we know why."

"Who's Casey?" Rogan asked. "A boyfriend?"

"No, just a friend. More my friend, I guess, but Julia's, too. He just left a few minutes ago."

"Where'd you see Julia Friday night?"

"It was just a phone call. Well, texting at first, but then the phone."

"How did she seem?"

"Normal. Jesus, looking back on it, I did all the talking. Me, me, me. I was such a head case, maybe she didn't want to burden me? Maybe if I'd stopped and asked how she was?"

Rogan was still using his sweet voice. "Don't get ahead of yourself, Ramona. We still don't know she did this to herself. In fact, let's assume she didn't. That leaves one other explanation—someone else did it. And there's two different ways that possibility might play out—it could be someone Julia knew, or a stranger. Let me be blunt. The Whitmires must have a million dollars' worth of jewelry and art in that townhouse, and yet nothing was missing. Detective Hatcher and I work a lot of cases, and, over time, you develop a feel for these things."

"You think she knew whoever killed her?"

Rogan was only ten years older than Ellie, but sometimes the years mattered. Had he forgotten how quickly high school students could, as he'd put it, *get ahead of themselves*? An hour from now, the Casden rumor mill would have Julia Whitmire the victim of an ax-wielding serial killer hunting down the prep school crowd.

"All I'm saying is that if she *didn't* do it, it's unlikely this was a random crime. Strangers don't get inside townhouses without forcing entry, they don't fake suicides, and they don't leave behind that kind of treasure. So what we need from you right now, Ramona, is total honesty. Your instinct right now is to remember the very best traits in your friend. You're going to want to talk about her in a way that highlights what a wonderful girl she was. But those aren't the kinds of details that might help us know the truth."

"What do you need to know?"

"Everything."

"I don't know—"

"Don't tell us what you want us to hear about Julia," Ellie said. "Tell us what you think we really need to know. Can you do that for us? For Julia?"

Ramona had tears in her eyes when she nodded.

"So what did you and Julia talk about on Friday?"

"It's dumb, looking back on it. I was freaking out about my mom and called Julia for advice. And none of it has anything to do with what happened to Julia, obviously, but I keep thinking that I should have talked less about me. I mean, it's stupid, but I was wondering whether my mother would be acting differently if she were really my biological mother. Because technically she's my stepmother. My mom died when I was a baby, but, whatever—yeah, she's basically my mom. And Julia got all serious, saying that it didn't matter whether my mom and I were related by blood or not. That she was the best mom in the world. That she'd been more of a mother even to Julia than her own mom. That kind of thing. Maybe she was depressed. What if I had called her to talk about boys and crushes and stupid stuff instead of complaining about my relationship with my mother? What if I set her off or something?"

The more Ramona wallowed, the less useful she was becoming. Ellie changed the subject. "Speaking of crushes, did Julia have a boyfriend?"

"No. Not any single boyfriend, at least."

Ding ding ding.

"Look, you said you need to know everything about Julia, so I'll tell it like it was. You've got to understand. Julia was adventurous. Fun. Crazy as hell, sometimes, but fun." She smiled sadly at some memory only she knew. "But part of the adventurousness and craziness was her—openness, let's say, with guys."

"Like who?"

"Honestly? It was a lot of people. Marcus Graze was her first kiss and probably took her V-card. He goes to Casden too. They were never really together, but constantly hooking up, if that makes any sense. And there was a trainer at her gym. I don't even know his name. And one time she"—her cheeks blushed—"she blew some guy in the parking lot of Lily Pond to get a ride back from East Hampton last summer, even though we can always call a car service. I know it sounds awful, but it's like she wanted the bragging rights."

"No one's judging your friend," Ellie said.

"But that kind of lifestyle can be dangerous," Rogan added. "Did any of these men ever want more from her than she was willing to give?"

She shook her head. "No. If anything, Julia appeared to have calmed down the last few months. She was spending a lot more time at home. For once, I was the one begging her to go out, and she'd be the one who wanted to stay in. That's why I didn't talk to her since Friday. I went to the Hamptons with my parents, and all she could talk about was how much she was looking forward to a weekend alone in the city."

Rogan moved a creepy doll with ringleted hair and a red velvet dress farther down the sofa to give himself a little more room. "Julia's mother said something about some street kids who were over at the townhouse at least once before?"

Ramona rolled her eyes. "Of course she'd have to bring them up. That's Casey. He went to Julia's, like, once with a couple of friends, but like I said, he's really more my friend. If Katherine's trying to blame him—"

Rogan cut her off. "No one's blaming anyone at this point. That's why we investigate. On that note, would you mind giving us a quick DNA sample? Just a cheek swab so the lab can eliminate any stray hairs you may have left behind at Julia's house."

Now that they were working this case as a homicide, the lab would be busy eliminating known samples to focus in on any unidentified DNA found in the house.

After Rogan took the swab, they had Ramona run through her final conversation with Julia one more time, but the girl had no new revelations to offer, only more regrets about the unspoken feelings, which led to more crying. As they reached the bedroom door, Ramona said she was sorry she hadn't been more helpful.

But as far as Ellie was concerned, Ramona had helped plenty.

Witnesses never seemed to realize that what seemed to them like an idle observation could make a case look entirely different to the police—or, in this particular case, could be construed entirely differently by two different police detectives.

Rogan started in on his interpretation as soon as they hit the car. "I don't buy for a second that Julia Whitmire had calmed down recently. A weekend home alone?"

"Exactly what a depressed girl might prefer," Ellie said.

"No way. The type of girl who bangs personal trainers and hands out blow jobs at the beach in exchange for transportation doesn't suddenly calm down because she's depressed. Julia's mom said she hated being alone. If Julia had leveled out, I bet you anything she had a new man on the side—someone she was being hush-hush about, even with her best friend."

"Either way, we're still looking at a depressed bulimic whose parents had abandoned her. No forced entry. Nothing missing. Don't forget the slit wrist and suicide note. On the other side of the ledger, we've got a missing notepad. Plus that stuff about Julia saying that Ramona's mom had been a better mother to her than her own? One more indication that Katherine Whitmire was a cold, crappy mother, and that her daughter, Julia, wasn't quite as tough about it as she let on. Who could blame her for drinking herself numb and checking out?"

"We still owe it to that girl and to those parents to be a hundred percent positive before we take her name from the board."

The car fell silent once again. Ellie finally reached for the radio but Rogan blocked her hand.

"None of your new wave Devo Flock of Seagulls shit when I'm driving." As far as Ellie could tell, Rogan thought any music by white people between 1983 and 1997 was either Devo or Flock of Seagulls.

But then the silence must have gotten to him, as well. He turned on the stereo and stopped the dial on a rap song she actually recognized. She muttered the lyrics as she looked out the window. *"Ain't nothin' but a g-thang, baby."*

It was enough to get a laugh out of her partner. "You kidding me with that?"

"What? I grew up in Kansas, not on a commune." She put a little more swagger into her performance, swaying in her seat. *"And now all you hookas and hos know how I feel."*

"Damn, woman. You got to ruin everything for me, don't you? I won't be able to listen to that again without picturing your bony butt bouncing around."

She placed a hand on her hip. "Ain't nothing bony about this. You just want *a small piece of some of that funky stuff.*"

He shook his head, but he was smiling. "This mean we're all right?"

"We're always all right. You should know that by now."

"But you still think you're right and I'm wrong."

"Yep."

"Want to go talk to this homeless kid, Casey?"

"Nope. But I will. Last time I checked, that's what we do."

CHAPTER ELEVEN

Second Acts: Confessions of a Former Victim and Current Survivor

"MAKE IT STOP"

I'm continually surprised at the way ordinary events trigger revelations about abuse and survivorship. This morning, my daughter awoke to the sounds of jack hammers thanks to a construction project on the street below her bedroom window. She wandered from her bedroom bleary-eyed and bed-headed, her palms pressed against her ears. "Make it stop. That's all I want right now: Just make it stop."

Make it stop. It's a perfectly rational reaction, isn't it? To want to put an end to whatever unpleasant stimuli one is experiencing? To crave the exact opposite?

Ear-shattering noise? Give me total silence instead. Blisteringly hot food? Hand me cold water. Blinding light? I shut my eyes to enjoy the darkness.

Rape? Make it stop.

But what does it mean to crave the *opposite* of rape? No sex? No physical contact? No men?

But rape, we must always remind ourselves, isn't about sex.

It's about power. Our abusers want to exercise dominion over us. They want to steal our agency.

And so what do we do? We take our agency back, however we can.

I couldn't force that man out of my house, but I could choose not to go to school. I couldn't bar him from my bedroom at night, but I could get a fake ID and a six-pack at three in the afternoon. I couldn't stop him from eyeing me every time my mother averted her gaze, but I could start hanging around the people my mother had always called "bad influences." I needed to know I could make choices that belonged to me.

We have all read about some rape case that goes un-charged or unpunished because of evidence that the victim en-gaged in consensual sexual activity with another man (or men) immediately after the rape. Why in the world, prosecutors and jurors ask, would a woman who had just been raped go out and have sex with someone else? They assume that a desire to "make it stop" necessarily translates into a lack of interest in sex.

But, once again, I thought we all knew by now that rape is not about sex. If "make it stop" means a craving for the oppo-site, then isn't it perfectly predictable that some of us respond to rape by exercising agency over our own sexual intimacy?

In my case, I couldn't protect my body from him, but I could choose to start sharing it with someone else. And of course I chose an unacceptable "someone else"—at once too old and too immature. That decision in turn led to its own forms of dam-age, self-inflicted in some sense and yet, it seems to me, still wholly attributable to my abuser.

Part of survival is getting to a place where we are able to exercise true free will, not just a reaction or rebellion against the abuse. Yesterday I wrote about forgiveness, not of our abus-ers, but of the people who enabled them. We must also forgive ourselves for reacting to the abuse in destructive ways, harming

ourselves and others in response to our loss of power. We have
to learn how to accept our pasts and determine our own futures.
It's the only way to really "make it stop."

This evening the blog was being read on a display laptop at the
Apple Store in the Meatpacking District. The reader made a point
to stand close to the computer, blocking the screen from view of the
crowds of shoppers who provided further anonymity.

It did not take long to type a reply to the post:

"I will show you damage. I will show you loss of free will. I will
show you harm. And you will never make it stop."

The typist did not know that on a different computer, at a public
library in the suburbs of Buffalo, an ex-convict named Jimmy Grisco
was doing some online reading of his own.

CHAPTER TWELVE

Ellie loved the arch at Washington Square Park. Serving as a frame for the view up Fifth Avenue to the Empire State Building, the arch had an impressive historical pedigree, with origins dating back to George Washington, but Ellie would always think of it as the spot where Harry dropped off Sally after their road trip home from Chicago.

She also thought of it as the usual location of Marty, the city's best hot dog vendor. They were in luck. Tonight was one of the first warm evenings of spring, and he had set up shop just west of the fountain.

After they parked on Waverly, she led the way to the snack cart. "Let's stop here for a dog."

"How is it that wherever we go you have a food stop within a one-block radius? It's like you've got a culinary map of this city implanted in your brain."

Actually, she did, but on this particular night, she was more interested in Marty himself than the fact that he used Hebrew Nationals, stocked Fresca in the can, and always had fresh buns. Marty had been her eyes and ears in this park back when she was on patrol.

She loaded her bun with yellow mustard and relish, while Rogan opted for ketchup only. "So, Marty, do you know a street kid around

here named Casey? Male, about twenty years old? Hangs out here
with some of the other homeless kids?"

"Not sure you have the right info, but I know who you mean."

"Why do you say we don't have the right information?"

"You'll see for yourself. The one you're looking for is over there."

He pointed to a kid practicing handstands in the grass just north
of the dog park. Ellie thanked Marty and she and Rogan started
making their way toward Casey. Halfway there, she realized what
Marty had been alluding to.

"You mind if I take the lead with this one?" Ellie asked.

"You still think you've got it going on for teenage boys, huh?"

"Like you don't turn on the charm for the cougar crowd when
opportunity calls. Just promise me you won't say anything that's
going to scare this kid off. In fact, just don't say anything."

"Casey Heinz?"

Casey wiped his palms on his khakis and looked around as if
someone else might step forward to have this conversation.

"That's pretty good," Ellie said. "It'd kill my wrists if I tried something like that. Probably a sign I spend too much time typing up reports at a computer. Your friend Ramona told us we might find you
here." She introduced herself and Rogan with a flash of her badge.

At the sight of Ellie scribbling his name in her notebook, he
added, "Heinz like the ketchup, not like hind legs."

"Casey short for anything?"

The pause was barely perceptible, but it was there. "Nope. Just
Casey."

"Got it," Ellie said with a smile. "You knew Julia Whitmire?"

"I knew her. I mean, only through Ramona, and not like the two
of them, but, yeah, sure, um, I'd say we all knew each other."

"Julia's mother mentioned meeting you one time at the townhouse. Did you go there often?"

Casey raised his eyebrows in surprise. "I can't believe I even registered on that woman's radar. Oh, wait, let me guess? She didn't remember me at all. Just some homeless kid?"

"I think 'from the streets' may have been her phrase of choice. She said there were a few kids over that day." She had mentioned two boys and a girl, to be exact.

"Yeah, I think it was Brandon, and this girl we see at the park sometimes named Vonda."

"Did you go to Julia's regularly?"

"Oh, huh-uh. I'd been there maybe four or five times, and usually it was just to swing by to meet her on a day out with Ramona. That was bad luck the one night her mom came in. Vonda was always fawning all over Julia's clothes the couple of times we'd hung out by the fountain together."

"Here at the park, you mean?"

"Yeah. So then Julia told me the next time I saw Vonda, I should try bringing her around because Julia had all these clothes she wanted to give away. We were just about to leave when her mom came home. She acted like we were going to walk out with the china or something."

"That was awfully generous of Julia. Was that typical?"

He shrugged. "Yeah, I guess. But she also wanted everyone to know when she did a good deed. Sorry, that sounds mean, under the circumstances."

"Were you and Julia ever alone?"

The kid looked panicked. "You think I had something to do—"

"No, no," Ellie said, taking a step backward to give him more space. "Nothing like that, Casey. I only asked to get a better sense of how well you knew Julia. It might help put your impressions in context."

"Yeah, okay. Um, we never arranged anything with just the two of us or anything. But, yeah, a few times, we'd all be hanging out and Julia and I would end up walking in the same direction afterwards. One time, everyone else had to bail early, so we walked over to see the new part of the High Line when it first opened. You know, that kind of thing. Mostly, though, I'd say we knew each other through Ramona."

"And I take it you know what happened to Julia last night?"

"That she died? Yeah, Ramona called me and I went up to her place. She said Julia's mom doesn't believe it's suicide. Is that why you're here?"

There was no reason for this kid to know that Ellie and her partner had a split of opinion on that issue. "You seem like a pretty straight shooter, Casey."

He squinted. "I try to be."

"So give it to me straight. What can you tell us about Julia that her best friend might not be willing to say?"

"There's not a lot to tell. I mean, she's super rich. Pretty. Probably had some baggage with her parents—always fighting with her mom, talking about her dad, trying to get more time with him, feeling kind of ignored. You know. But otherwise pretty normal."

"Did she have a boyfriend?"

"No, it was more like she'd just hook up. She told me she was into some guy a few weeks ago, but I never asked what happened to that."

"Who was the guy?"

"No clue. She only mentioned it once. Like I said, we were both friends with Ramona, but not as much with each other. This was during one of those few times we were actually alone. We'd gone to this place called Black and White." Ellie suppressed a smile. The bar was a little lounge in the East Village where her brother, Jess, and his band, Dog Park, sometimes played open-mic nights on Sundays. She'd always teased Jess that the place was overrun by kids with fake IDs, but Jess wanted to believe it was the next CBGB. "Ramona hopped in a cab uptown, and I walked Julia home. She was pretty tipsy and was saying she was tempted to drunk-dial the guy. I was having a little fun with her, trying to get her to call him. Then she said she didn't even have his cell phone number—that she wasn't supposed to call or something. It was a little weird."

"Does Ramona know?"

"I'm not sure. Julia said Ramona wouldn't approve."

"Why wouldn't Ramona approve?"

"You know that daddy baggage I mentioned? Let's just say it manifested itself in Julia's dating preferences. Ramona was always trying to get her to see a therapist about it. I just assumed when she made that comment about Ramona not approving that it was some old guy."

"How old are we talking about here?"

"Not, like, you know, Hugh Hefner old. But I think one guy last summer was, like, thirty! Ramona kind of lectured her about it, and since then I got the impression Julia decided the less Ramona knew about those things, the better."

In any other situation, Ellie would bristle at the thought of thirty being "old." But to have a relationship with a junior in high school? Thirty was ancient.

"What made you think she was keeping Ramona out of the loop?"

"Ramona seemed to buy Julia's act that she wanted more down time to read and study and stuff. Maybe I'm too suspicious but it seemed to me she was lying. One time she said she'd gone to the rooftop at the Standard with this guy, Marcus, but then later Ramona found out Marcus was at a birthday party for some girl at school the same night. Ramona blew it off, but other times Julia would tell Ramona she fell asleep watching TV, and I could just tell she was lying. When she didn't show up today, I assumed it was another one of her secret disappearances. I feel awful now."

"How about her friends? Would you say she was well liked?"

"Seemed like it. They're both a little more on the wild side, compared to all the matching mean girls at their school, but I think Ramona actually got hassled more than Julia for it. Julia's dad kind of gave her the cred to be a little off. Compared to the kids at that school, Ramona's family's, like, poor or something."

"And how exactly was Julia *off*, or I think you said a little wild? A lot of drinking? Drugs?"

"No, nothing more than the usual drinking. Maybe a little weed.

It's hard to explain. Just, you know, more curious about the rest of the world than rich kids usually are."

"That's funny. Growing up in Kansas, I always thought wealthy kids in New York were incredibly worldly."

"I don't mean living in Paris on your summer vacation. I mean hanging out downtown. Taking the subway." He lowered his voice. "Being friends with people of a different status. Trying *not* to be the spoiled brats they've been bred to be."

"And where do you fall on this status spectrum?" Ellie made sure not to look at the light stains near Casey's shirt collar or the spot on the sleeve where the fabric was wearing thin.

"Pretty damn low." He looked down at his canvas sneakers. "I'm currently residing—if you can call it that—at Promises. It's what they call transitional housing for at-risk young adults. It's what everyone else in the world calls a homeless shelter."

"Is that where the other kids who went to Julia's townhouse with you live, too? Brandon and Vonda?"

"Brandon does, but not Vonda. I haven't seen her in, like, a week."

"Do you have last names for them?"

According to Casey, Brandon was Brandon Sykes, sixteen years old. Casey had seen him just that day, and he was probably heading back to the shelter that night. Vonda was supposedly nineteen, but he suspected she was younger. He did not know her last name, nor did he know how to contact her.

"And the shelter's the best address for you?" she asked.

"Until I win the lottery, that's where I'm at. I guess you need stuff like ages and last names and addresses for police reports."

She rotated her wrists in front of her. "Like I said, I do an awful lot of typing in this job. And this *transitional housing for at-risk young adults* is really a better place for you than with your family?" Ellie was no social worker, but she didn't feel right about leaving this kid in a shelter without at least inquiring.

"My family's in Iowa, and let's just say they're not real interested in being my family these days."

"Speaking of that report I'll need to file, I should probably make sure to check your identification."

"I thought you said I'm not in trouble."

"You're not, but I've got to make sure we're not putting false information on a government document."

Her eyes locked on his was enough to induce an actual tremble.

"I'm sorry, Casey. I've got to document every witness. It's okay. We already know."

"But—"

"It wasn't your appearance. I noticed that pause earlier when I asked whether Casey was a nickname."

There was a full five seconds of silence before Casey sighed and pulled a beaten brown leather wallet from his back pocket.

Iowa driver's license. Same face. Same stoic expression, masking the softness Ellie had spotted when Casey had first come out of his handstand. All the basic information was there. Five feet, eight inches. DOB March 16, 1992. Green eyes. Full name: Cassandra Jane Heinz.

"Does Ramona know?"

He was looking at his shoes again but nodded. "Yeah. We don't talk about it, but, yeah."

She patted him on the shoulder, as she would to reassure any other man. "Thanks. We'll let you know if we need anything else."

Casey watched the police detectives talking as they walked back toward Waverly. Even from behind, he could recognize the dynamic. The male cop may have remained silent through the entire exchange, but Casey had seen the guy's expression at the sight of the driver's license. She was cool with everything. He wasn't.

That always seemed to be how things went.

As he watched them drive away in their nondescript blue sedan, he wondered whether he had done the right thing. He had told them what they needed to know about Julia, but he hadn't told them everything. Not really.

One little lie—not even a lie, just a secret—couldn't possibly make a difference. And the one little secret, if disclosed, would only hurt Ramona even further. He hadn't done it to protect himself, he told himself. It had been for Ramona.

He returned to his handstands, trying to set aside the terrible feeling that somehow he had made a mistake.

CHAPTER
THIRTEEN

Bill Whitmire watched his wife, who sat cross-legged on their bed, using the palm of her hand to smooth out the surface of their down duvet. He could hear her voice from the last time they'd spent more than a single night there, reminding herself aloud that it was finally getting warm enough to pack that layer into storage and replace it with the cotton coverlet she loved so much.

Since then, their visits to the city hadn't been long enough to justify even that minor change.

She was surrounded on the bed by brochures and pamphlets fanned out in front of her like tarot cards. Her therapist had dropped them off earlier tonight. He'd heard their conversation in the foyer. Grief counseling. Group therapy. Bill—never a fan of psychotherapy—might feel more comfortable in solo sessions, with a separate therapist.

The therapist had also warned that they might require couples counseling. *The sooner the better*, he had said. He'd told Katherine that the majority of parents who lost a child ended up divorced within three years.

Bill had been tempted to storm downstairs and throw the man out. Using the death of their child to instill fears in Katherine about their marriage? But for some reason, he couldn't stop eavesdropping, watching them in the front hall from his spot on the second-floor landing. He wanted to hear his wife defend herself. To defend their marriage and the family they had created. To tell him they would be just fine—together.

Instead, she'd allowed the therapist to drone on. "That's not to say that you and Bill won't weather the storm," he'd said. "Some couples become closer than ever. They find a permanent and impenetrable connection in the memories of the child who was lost." He had interlaced his fingers together to demonstrate the bond that she might suddenly form with her husband.

When Katherine had finally spoken, it was to say words he never would have expected to hear. "You've sat through enough sessions with me to know that Bill doesn't form permanent and impenetrable bonds with *anyone*, let alone me."

Julia—his Baby J—had been dead less than a day, and he could already feel the mother of his children slipping away from him.

It had started earlier this evening, after the police detectives left and before the therapist had arrived. She had been lying on the bed, and he had tried crawling next to her. Usually she was the one who sought physical proximity during sleep. She was the one who would back up into his body, nudging him to wrap his arms around her. Usually he would roll away to avoid the extra heat.

But today, he'd reached out for her. He'd pressed his chest against her back, wrapping his arms tightly around her. It had been Katherine who had pulled away, pretending to roll over in a sleep she had not yet actually found.

Unlike his wife, though—in fact, unlike most people—he was not the type to wallow among a stack of mumbo-jumbo pamphlets or numb himself with happy pills, all in the hope that life would somehow magically improve.

He recognized his wife's strengths and weaknesses, and dealing with a problem was not her strength. Making decisions was not her strength. These jobs always fell to him. Even with the studio on Long Island, he had to be the one finally to pull the trigger.

He told her he worked better out there. He told her he was getting sick of the city. But he also was very clear that he would stay in the townhouse if that was what she and the kids wanted. He knew how much she loved the house. He knew the kids still had their high school years ahead of them.

But she had refused to decide. She made endless lists of pros and cons. She talked about her love of the beach. The ease of life out in the Hamptons. Her friends who were spending more time there. She would wonder aloud whether the kids were mature enough to be unchaperoned during the week, but never ventured an answer.

And so he had made the decision. After talking to Julia and Billy—two of the strongest-willed, loudest-voiced children ever created—he had made the call to give up the lease on the recording space in the city and build the studio in Long Island. Two years later, he was still hearing Katherine's passive-aggressive comments about how much she missed the city.

Now it would fall to Bill once again to fix this problem. She was pushing him away now, but he knew she would never leave. He also knew she would eventually begin to heal, not with those fucking pamphlets and her therapist's psychobabble, but once they had answers.

He had thought at first they were on the same page. Those police officers had been so dismissive when they'd initially found Julia's body. He'd never seen Kitty so angry and full of determination.

But when those two detectives had come back later tonight to take another look around, the fire he'd seen in her had dissipated, replaced by anemic hope: *They really did seem motivated to find out what happened to Julia, didn't they? They know what they're doing, right?*

More than fifty percent of couples split within three years, the therapist had warned.

Well, not them. Not after all these years.

Bill knew how to fix this. He walked downstairs to his office and made the phone call.

CHAPTER FOURTEEN

E ven from the hallway outside her apartment, Ellie could hear the television blasting.

"Holy hell," she said, pushing the door closed hard behind her with her hip, the extra effort needed due to the many layers of old paint around the frame. "Mrs. Hennessy always said that rock-and-roll music of yours would make you deaf. Do I need to schedule you an appointment for a hearing aid already?"

Jess was barely visible on the sofa, his face peering out from beneath the comforter that she'd last seen on her bed. She heard a moan of some kind, followed by the sight of the remote control at the blanket's edge. The volume decreased.

"That crazy biddy also said my music would lead me to Satan's altar."

"And I'm sure if she were still alive, she'd say New York City was close enough. You're still home?"

"I think I'm sick."

"Great. Remind me to wipe down that remote with rubbing alcohol."

"You're back early."

"Technically I get off work at four o'clock, remember?"

"Yeah, right. You mean the way technically this apartment is occupied by the granddaughter of Mrs. Delores Macintosh?"

Ellie's rent-stabilized sublet wasn't entirely aboveboard. The fact that Jess had been the one to hook her up with the deal probably explained his comfort with long-term tenancies on her sofa.

"Don't knock my overtime. How do you think I can afford your IQ-destroying basic cable? I thought *The Hills* was your drug of choice," she said, glancing at the television screen.

"You are so 2009. I had a brief addiction to *Toddlers and Tiaras*, but it was actually too depressing, even for me, the way they tart those girls up. No offense, sis."

"Please don't compare me to a five-year-old with waxed eyebrows." Ellie had briefly made the rounds in Kansas beauty pageants—a phrase that Jess often called an oxymoron—but strictly for the scholarship money. Even with a couple of runner-up prizes, she could only swing part-time classes at Wichita State. She had less than three semesters of credit by the time she left.

"I've since moved on to those impeccable arbiters of domestic modesty and taste, the housewives. They're *real*, you know. One hundred percent authentic, real housewives. Because fake housewives just won't do. Any city will suffice, but I am currently imbibing those lovable divas of our very own two-one-two."

"From college girls to New York City cougars. I'll choose to take the development as a sign of maturity. No work tonight?"

"I called in sick."

"I would think your germs would blend in just fine at the Booby Barn." With his current job at a strip bar, her brother had beaten his longest record of employment four-fold. The so-called gentlemen's club on the West Side Highway was named Vibrations, but she and Jess preferred to conjure up their own pseudonyms.

"You planning to see Captain America?" he asked. "I can scram if you need me out of here."

Jess had been referring to ADA Max Donovan as Captain America since she and Max had first met. She was convinced that they could marry and celebrate their fiftieth anniversary and Jess would still be calling him Captain America.

"He got called out to Rikers."

"Want something to eat?"

The invitation usually led to Jess choosing the take-out place, Ellie paying, and Jess eating most of what arrived.

"I'm not hungry yet. You want me to get you something? Chicken soup?"

"No, I'll call the deli when I'm ready."

"I had a callout today to Bill Whitmire's house."

"Are you kidding me? *The* Bill Whitmire?"

"His house has an elevator."

"He's Bill Whitmire. His house should have an elevator, a water slide, and strippers in every room. Please tell me you slipped him a demo of Dog Park." No matter where—or whether—he earned a paycheck, Jess's true calling was as lead singer and guitarist for his band, Dog Park. Ten years ago, Ellie had moved to the city when she sensed that Jess's phone calls home to Wichita—filled with allusions to always-imminent but never-actual "big breaks"—were a cover for serious trouble. What she found instead was that Jess had managed to carve out something of a life for himself, albeit not the one he described to their mother. Since then, she'd done the same.

"Right. Because I carry your demos around with me. Not to mention that his daughter killed herself last night." She gave him a brief run-down of her day. "The girl's mother couldn't handle it. Says the girl would never do something like that. She kept begging me to believe her."

"You all right?"

She was losing track of the number of people who'd asked her that today. "Yeah. Fine. You didn't come home last night." Yesterday seemed like such a long time ago. "You stayed over at that bartender's place?"

"Rebecca. Bartender slash actress slash singer slash superfine hottie."

Just like Jess was a titty-bar bouncer slash rock god, the people he knew usually had multiple professions. Most recently, he had been spending multiple overnights per week with a victim on one of Ellie's cases from last fall. That particular woman was an artist slash prostitute, but she'd vowed to get out of the life after it almost got her killed. Ellie had only just gotten past her worries about the relationship when it finally ran its course, as relationships with Jess always seemed to do.

She tried joining him in front of the television, but watching the real housewives fight over who drank more pinot grigio made her want to arrest somebody.

"I love you, Jess, but I can't do it. It's like I feel brain cells seeping away with each passing minute. I'm heading to the gym."

"Keep it gangster."

Ellie remembered everything about the first time she got punched in the head. She screamed, not from the pain, but from the complete surprise of the impact itself. It was only as she screamed from the shock that the actual, physical pain registered. The piercing stab right behind her temple that seemed like it had to have cracked her open from ear to ear. The throbbing that radiated across her skull, down her jawbone into her neck. The blurring of her vision. The sincere belief that her brain was rattling behind her sockets like candy in a thumped piñata.

The punch had been delivered by a sixteen-year-old kid she caught tagging a phone booth in Hell's Kitchen. Stuck on graveyard with ten minutes to go before shift change, she had planned on confiscating the spray can and letting him off with a warning. The skinny kid with long bangs and the moniker 2SHY didn't know that, though, and caught her off guard with a right hook. What she remembered most about that first punch was her anger—not about the punch, but about the tears. She had blinked over and over again, trying to focus her vision, trying to stop the pain, but mostly trying to stop those stupid fucking tears from falling down her face in front of the shitty little kid who'd gotten a jump on her.

She was so humiliated about getting knocked by a hundred-pound teenager that she processed the criminal mischief charge but let him slide on the assault of a police officer. It was only her third month on the job. She was still getting past the beauty-queen jokes. She didn't need the house to know she'd cried from a sucker punch.

It was the first time Ellie had been punched, but she'd known it wouldn't be the last. She also knew she'd need to get better at it.

Now she was a kickboxer at the total-contact level, allowed to apply full power, force, and strength against an opponent in a ring. Instead of tears, she felt beads of sweat pour down her face as she threw jab after jab against the heavy black practice bag.

The intensity of her one-sided fight was telling her something about her own energy. She was grinding it out the way she could usually muster only inside the ring against a live opponent. Something was eating at her.

As she chopped her lower shin against the side of the bag, she found herself thinking about Julia. And not the appearance of her thin, naked body in the pink bathwater, but her words on the lined yellow pages. Every word. Every sentence. The hesitation marks and cross-outs. Without realizing she'd done so, Ellie had committed the entire note to memory.

She could picture the girl in life, sitting cross-legged on her low platform bed, staring at the legal pad, three-quarters of a page already filled with blotchy black ink, crossing out yet another word. Unsatisfied with that single deletion, she would have stabbed the pen across the last four lines of text, running the ballpoint tip across the page so many times she actually managed to poke a hole in the paper.

I know I should love my life, but sometimes I hate it. My parents tell me all the time how lucky I am. Lucky to have good schools, a nice house. Money. Them. Yes, they actually said that. I was lucky to have them.

Julia had crossed out everything after the word *money*. Maybe she didn't feel like writing about her parents. Maybe she realized they were the kind of people who never should have had children, but that the observation was better kept to herself.

Ellie followed the jab series with alternating hooks and upper-cuts, then started to throw in front and roundhouse kicks, the appearance of Julia's words still fresh in her visual cortex.

> *I understand why other kids would assume my life is easy. No one wants to hear a spoiled rich girl complain. I know some kids who would kill (maybe in some cases literally)*

She had scratched out the parenthetical. It had probably been an attempt at humor, but she'd concluded correctly that it just didn't belong there. She had tried to block the words out completely, but Ellie had been able to piece them together beneath the scratches.

> *I know some kids who would kill to have the "privileges" I know I have. But sometimes I wonder if maybe their lives aren't actually better. Or at least more free. No one expects anything from a kid who has nothing.*
>
> *I'm constantly being told how lucky I am, but the truth is, my so-called privileged life*

Ellie felt her heart pound in her chest.

She could almost hear Julia's thoughts as the girl held the tip of the pen above the page, trying to choose the right words to complete the sentence. That this life is harder than it seems. That this life can be challenging. That this life sucks. That this life—*hurts.*

Yes, Julia had settled upon that word. Maybe she had even recognized it was a little melodramatic. She hadn't suffered from actual, physical pain or paralyzing depression. But she would have felt injured from the pressures of her life that no one wanted to hear about. And so what if she was melodramatic? She was sixteen years old, after all. Shouldn't she be allowed to be a drama queen? Shouldn't she be allowed to be a lot of the things other teenagers were permitted to be? And wasn't that the purpose of the letter?

She pictured Julia writing the word she finally selected on the page:

my so-called privileged life hurts.

    It hurts to be told that I'm not allowed to waste my potential. It hurts to hear that more is expected of me because more has been given to me. It hurts to believe that I can never amount to the person I'm supposed to be. It hurts to feel so alone every second of every day, even when I'm surrounded by other people. And it hurts to know that I have all of these feelings but am not supposed to voice them.

Ellie could hear blood racing through her veins. Her damp hair was plastered against her scalp. Her arms and legs began to ache, but she kept working the leather of the bag.

Julia's thoughts moved in errant directions a few more times as she wrote, requiring more scratch marks on the page, but the words were flowing more easily now. She would have felt her emotions pouring from her like the ink from the pen, like Ellie's sweat from her pores.

And then the tear had fallen to the notepad, hitting the letter *f* in *feelings*, blurring the shape into an amorphous blob. And then words began to fail her. It was time to wrap things up.

And that is why I have decided to kill myself.

Ellie continued to kick the bag. No forced entry. No signs of a struggle. Cuts consistent with self-infliction—the bathwater and a 0.16 blood-alcohol content helping the blood flow. One bump on the back of her head, but Ginger at the medical examiner's office thought it consistent with collapsing against the tub after Julia slit her wrists.

And then Ellie started hearing snippets of voices from throughout the day.

Katherine Whitmire pleading, "You have to do something. It's my daughter."

The EMT saying, "There's nothing for us to do here."

Max, wanting to say more, but leaving it at, "You're okay with that?"

Rogan, saying they screwed up. "You really got to get yourself right on this one." Even Jess, asking if she was all right.

And then she heard voices from her past. *You just have to learn to let it go, Ellie.* How many times had she heard that damn phrase over the years? As if she could just open her hands and release the fact that her father's brains had been blasted out the back of his head by his own gun. As if she could simply set aside her own past like a discarded shopping bag.

Ellie threw a flying punch as she worked through her own thoughts.

When Ellie's mother tried to explain that Jerry Hatcher would never kill himself, no one listened to her—not the Wichita Police Department, not the city attorney's office that made the call on whether to release his pension, not the neighbors, no one—no one except Ellie. And look where that had gotten them.

So today, when Katherine Whitmire had implored her, "Please listen to me," of course she hadn't. Ellie had wanted to scream at her: "Take a lesson or two from the tale of Jerry Hatcher."

But Ellie didn't want to be that kind of cop. She didn't want to be the person who joked around about the girl's crappy mother, like those EMTs. She didn't want to passively check off the boxes like the medical examiner she called Ginger. She didn't want to be the cop who didn't at least pause to ask why Julia Whitmire's suicide note had been handwritten, not typed, and on a notepad that was nowhere to be found in her home.

Ellie didn't want to be like everyone else.

Then, like she'd been sucker-punched in the head, Ellie realized what had really been nagging at her about that scene at the Whitmires'. She suddenly stopped pummeling the bag. She held her gloves to her chest and bent over while she caught her breath, favoring one side to forestall an oncoming cramp.

Rogan had a good point. She had to get herself right on this one.

PART II
RAMONA

CHAPTER FIFTEEN

As an investigator, Ellie firmly believed she was best at her job when she could live inside the heads of her victims. That kind of empathy hadn't been as important to her when she was working property cases and vice busts. But coming up on two years of cases in the homicide squad, she knew that some little part of her would always be able to imagine what the final moments of each of those lost lives had been like for the victim.

Ellie liked to think she had a natural ability to imagine the life of another person. She'd grown up watching people. She noticed patterns. She read facial expressions. She had a good sense for what made people tick.

But, other than imagining what it must have been like to write that suicide note, Ellie was having a hard time inhabiting the world of Julia Whitmire.

She surely did remember the emotions that came with being a teenage girl. She also remembered the pressure to mold one's body into perfection. *You don't become Miss Teen Kansas with all that baby fat.*

And she knew what it was like to pine for the attention of a parent. She had idolized her father. He protected people. He was like a superhero in the battle between good and evil. She remem-

bered playing on the basement floor in the makeshift office he had
created, the walls decorated with photographs of the victims of the
College Hill Strangler and a map filled with pins—red for known
kills, yellows for suspected. Ellie would bounce her psychedelic-
colored rubber ball and pick up jacks, offering questions and theories for her father as she played. Usually he shushed her, but the
days when he'd actually talk through the case with her, despite her
mother's scolding that it "wasn't right"? Those were Ellie's most
cherished memories of her father.

But, in too many ways, a life like Julia Whitmire's was so completely unlike anything in her prior experience. From a three-
bedroom wood-frame ranch house in Wichita, Kansas, Ellie could
never have dreamed of having the independence that Julia Whitmire enjoyed. Once her dad was gone, to describe their family
as middle class was overly generous. Ellie had never been east of
Kansas City or west of Dallas until she followed her brother up to
New York City.

She'd told herself at the time that the move was to allow the one
responsible Hatcher child to keep an eye on the other, but in retrospect she knew she had hungered for a different life. As much as was
missing in her life, though, she'd never been unhappy. And she'd
definitely never been ungrateful.

She had no idea how to get into the mind of a girl like Julia. With
the Whitmires' money and the streets of New York waiting just
outside her townhouse door, Julia already had a more sophisticated
life than most people could ever imagine. And yet she was miser-
able.

Ellie and Rogan sat side by side at her squad desk, scrolling
through Julia Whitmire's Facebook profile, hoping to find some
clues about her last days.

"The girl's final status update was Friday night," Rogan ob-
served. "*Just noticed the name of this toe polish color: Ogre the Top Blue.
Groan!*' Those are some lame-ass last words. Don't you think a girl
who killed herself Sunday night would post some kind of goodbye
message?"

"She did," Ellie said. "With a suicide note."

By now, that last comment typed by Julia on Facebook was buried deep at the bottom of the page, replaced by more than two hundred comments posted since news of the girl's death had leaked out. Most of them appeared to be from strangers sending condolences to Julia's father. *"I didn't know you, Julia, but I'm sorry you weren't able to find joy in this life. May music follow you to the next." "Your father changed the face of rock and roll. RIP to his little angel."*

"I swear," Rogan said. "I just don't get people."

They continued to scroll through the comments, compiling a list of the Facebook friends who appeared to be closest to Julia in life. They had already spoken to Julia's brother, Billy, that morning. Despite being distraught and still in a state of shock, he tried his best to be helpful. Like most college freshmen, however, his recent attention had been focused on classes, parties, and hooking up, not on his little sister back home.

Rogan clicked on the Facebook tab marked "Photos."

Most of the pictures were the typical ones that teenage girls posted online these days: close-up self-portraits with a cell phone, lips pursed as if saying the word *prune*. There were a couple of bikini shots on a beach with Ramona. Snapshots of ridiculously over-priced dresses she admired. Pictures from recent trips to Rome, Paris, Madrid, and Belize. A face mask from last summer's Alexander McQueen exhibit at the Metropolitan Museum of Art. Most recently, a picture of her appearing relaxed and makeup-free on open country land.

"That's the fattest goat I've ever seen," Rogan said of the animal whose long neck Julia Whitmire had draped an arm around. In the background stood a red post-frame barn with a sloped green metal roof. It was a perfect rural shot.

Ellie spooned out a bite of Nutella from the jar she kept in her desk. "I think it's an alpaca. It's like a small, hairy llama. They've become sort of a status symbol for country homes because they're super expensive—something about their fur or whatever."

"How the *hell* do you know that?"

"When are you going to learn there are no boundaries to your partner's knowledge?" Her ex-boyfriend, the finance guy, had been close to buying two alpacas a few years ago when she'd moved out. "They also spit and make this creepy humming sound like injured cows."

"The poor thing's so ugly he's almost cute."

"You're such a softy," she said. "Any word from Julia's doctor?"

With the parents' permission, they had contacted Julia's physician about the Adderall capsules they found in her purse. "The nurse just called. The only prescription drug her doc had for her was the birth control. And no referrals to a psychiatrist, either. The bottle wasn't labeled. Maybe she didn't have a prescription for them."

Ellie opened a new window on her computer and searched for "Adderall."

She clicked first on a video titled, "Teens and ADHD Medications: Intervention or Addiction?" Four panelists sat side by side at the front of a generic lecture hall. A purple velvet curtain adorned with NYU's torch logo served as the backdrop.

According to one psychologist—her nameplate was blocked by a pitcher of water—psychotropic drugs were wildly overprescribed, especially in kids, where use was up nearly four hundred percent in a decade. About eighty percent of cases were "off label," meaning doctors were prescribing the drugs in ways the FDA never approved.

Equally convincing was the psychiatrist who saw the drugs as the best prospect to save children from needless heartache. He spoke with passion about children who worked as hard as they could, only to throw their books against walls, feeling stupid and hopeless.

Rogan reached over and clicked the mouse, pausing the video.

"Hey!" she complained.

"Clock's ticking, woman, and that video's nearly an hour long. You're digging that shrink a little bit, aren't you?"

She looked at the face paused on the screen. According to his nameplate, the doctor espousing the pro-drug views was David Bolt and, she had to admit, he was in fact attractive.

She gave Rogan a fake sneer and took control of the mouse again. "Take a look at this." The article was called "Students Seek Competitive Edge with Adderall." She scrolled down the screen as they skimmed together, catching bits and pieces. *Perfectly healthy, undiagnosed teenagers . . . Mixture of amphetamine salts . . . Usually snorted . . . Helps you study . . . Have to get any academic advantage possible . . . Buy it from friends who have been legitimately diagnosed with ADHD . . . Effects on the brain similar to cocaine or methamphetamine . . . One in five students . . .*

"Look," Ellie said, pointing to the penultimate paragraph. " 'Can cause depression and social anxiety when abused.' Let's try to get a rush on the toxicology reports. It's one more indication she did this to herself."

"Let's also try to find out where she got it," Rogan said.

Ellie clicked back to the Facebook "wall" filled with comments. She began to click on the names of Julia's friends who had left notes on her page.

She clicked on the profile of Marcus Graze, whom Ramona had described as Julia's on-and-off-again fling.

Sorry, this Profile is currently unavailable. Please try again shortly.

As she began to click through Julia's list of friends, she got the same message for several of the profiles.

"Maybe some kind of system glitch," Rogan said.

"But I just looked at a couple of these half an hour ago," Ellie said. She typed *Jess Hatcher* into the Facebook search box, and her brother's profile appeared, third down on the list and open to full view without any problem, complete with latest ironic status update: *I think I have Bieber Fever.* "Seems weird."

"Don't worry. We'll track these kids down in person at the school, anyway."

"Ah, the very two people I was looking for." Lieutenant Robin Tucker gazed down at them from the other side of the desk. "Jesus, Hatcher, how can you constantly have a spoonful of pure sugar and fat in your mouth and still fit into your pants? Never mind. Just please tell me your eyes and that computer are focused entirely on Julia Whitmire."

Rogan gave her a casual wave. "All good, Lou."

"Not all good. I must have taken fifteen phone calls about the way you marched out of there yesterday. I just got another call from the dad trying to make sure you weren't just shining him on when you went back last night."

Tucker was staring straight at Ellie as she spoke, but Rogan was the one to respond. "We're working on it."

"How the hell did it take you so long to see that notepad issue?"

Rogan was still speaking for them both. "It's generational. Suicides are for people facing terminal cancer, divorce, financial ruin. People that age write their final letters on paper. We weren't thinking."

"So is the handwriting hers or not?"

"Hatcher took the note to one of her old profs at John Jay. The guy says the script in the suicide note appears to be consistent with Julia's, but he can't give an opinion with any confidence because we have so little to go by in terms of known samples of her writing— just a few notes in old birthday cards and from Mother's and Father's Days. Like we said, kids don't write anymore."

"So you're fully on board with this, too?" This time it was clear Tucker's question was aimed directly at Ellie.

"I'm doing the work, yes."

"Wonderful. Your enthusiasm is inspiring."

"Look, I could lie if you want me to. The only thing that matters is I agree we jumped the gun yesterday. I regret it, and I want to make it right. But, no, I don't happen to think she was murdered, and I know for damn sure that no one would be complaining about us jumping the gun if we had the same exact facts with some poor kid dead in a tub in the projects. Regardless, I promise I'm working to get at the truth just as hard as if my instincts told me something different."

"Given the personal histories involved here, maybe your instincts are off on this one."

Ellie let out a frustrated laugh. "Very subtle."

Rogan rapped his knuckles against the desktop. "Hate to cut into your heart-to-heart, but maybe it's a good idea for us to get back to business."

Ellie was grateful for the segue. "We need to go to the Casden School and see these kids in person," she said, rising from her chair.

The announcement served to appease Tucker, who walked back to her office without further comment.

"You're on your own," Rogan said once Tucker was gone. "Testimony in the Washington case today, remember?" He snuck a glance at his TAG Heuer watch. "Shit. I got to move. Thirty minutes."

She remembered the Washington case. First name: Thelma. The defendant was the grandson she'd raised from the second grade. Just like his mother, thirty years earlier, he'd been ransacking the house for drug money when Thelma walked in and confronted him. Unlike his mother—who had simply walked away, leaving her seven-year-old son behind—he had strangled Thelma Washington to death and then sat on the porch until the police came, after, of course, getting in one last high.

Today was the day for a pretrial motion to suppress the defendant's confession. It was a slam dunk for the state, but in a murder case, a good defense attorney dotted all the *i*'s and crossed all the *t*'s. Either she or Rogan could give the necessary testimony for the prosecution, but there had never been any question that the Washington case—although assigned to both of them—was really Rogan's. She suspected it had something to do with Rogan's close relationships with his mother, grandmother, great aunt, and lord knows how many other Rogan women when they'd still been living.

Sometimes a case got into your blood and between your synapses and ignited a passion. Some cases brought out the warrior.

"You want to wait for me?" Rogan asked. "Or you want to go solo for a couple of hours?"

"I'll go up to the school while you're in court. Call me when you clear up."

Julia may not have been murdered, but she was still a person whose screwed-up life had ended unnecessarily, and that ending had brought her to Ellie. The least Ellie could do was to find out what had been the girl's last straw. She needed to start caring.

CHAPTER SIXTEEN

Ellie grew up being told by her mother that she and Jess were lucky to be in one of the city's "good schools." The term had little to do with academic standards or curricular content. In segregated Wichita, "good schools" was code, conveying the same message as "good neighborhoods" or "good people."

The Casden School was an entirely different story. Casden was a "day school." Until she'd moved to New York, Ellie would have thought the term redundant since she'd never heard of a night school for kids. But now she understood that day schools were in contrast to boarding schools. This particular day school was arguably the most elite coed program in the city. Its Wikipedia entry boasted that for ten years straight the small school had representation in every single Ivy League university's entering freshman class.

As she followed the directions she had received to the offices of the headmistress, Ellie took in the photographs of alumni that lined the school's ornately carved stone hallways. She'd already passed the headshots of three senators, two Supreme Court justices, and a vice president. A surgeon who conducted the first heart transplant. The first female CEO of a Fortune 500 company. The editor in chief of *Time* magazine.

It was a "good school" indeed.

Ellie arrived at the headmistress's office with certain expectations. She had expected absolute silence in the waiting area, a woman with a tight black bun who talked like Mary Poppins, and an extended song and dance about student privacy and the importance of parental consent for any encounters with outsiders.

As it turned out, Ellie didn't know much about headmistresses.

She entered the administrative suite to find several adults clustered in the doorway between the secretary's desk and the headmistress's office. She heard a voice from inside the door. *We have a grief counselor in the student lounge, though this really isn't a school matter.*

Ellie peered around the impressively coiffed hair of one of the concerned parents to get a glimpse at Headmistress Margaret Carter. No Mary Poppins accent. No hair bun in sight. A bit of a song and dance about privacy. *Our understanding is that even the police do not have a full understanding of what occurred, but whatever did happen took place off campus and is a private matter for the student's family. Please, I recognize your children are upset, but this has nothing to do with Casden.*

Ellie listened to the exchanges of complaints as the parents shuffled out of the suite. "If the girl went to Casden, then it's the school's business, which means it's our business." "I hear Julia Whitmire left a note. Does anyone know what it said?" "If that woman thinks we're just going to ignore this, she'll be out of a job by finals." "This is the second time this semester. How can she expect us to simply ignore something like that?"

After the crowd of parents had cleared out, Ellie ventured into the headmistress's office and identified herself.

"I apologize for the disarray. I'm Margaret Carter, the headmistress here. I'm afraid the rumor mill has a life of its own. My phone has been ringing off the hook with worried parents."

"What was the gist of the rumors?"

"I know the official cause of death has not been revealed, but all the kids are saying there was a suicide note. They're saying she popped a bottle of pills and slit her wrists in the bathtub."

The pills were a dramatic embellishment, but someone had obviously heard at least some of the critical facts.

"I'm hoping to speak to some of Julia's friends. They'd be in the best position to know her state of mind in recent weeks."

"I'm afraid I can't help you, Detective. Our students are minors. If you want to contact them off school premises, you can do so during nonschool hours, at their homes, and presumably with the consent of their parents. As of now, they are minor children on private premises. And I'd prefer you obtain a warrant if you want to go beyond any routine conversation with yours truly."

"How about Julia's friend, Ramona Langston? Her mother—or stepmother—Adrienne, said it would be all right. You can call her if necessary." Ellie had no need to speak to Ramona again, but she wanted to test the headmistress's commitment to stonewalling.

"You must be mistaken, Detective. Ramona's at home today." Carter reached a manicured fingernail to a button on her phone. A woman's voice came through the speaker. *"Yes?"* "Heidi, can you please check the attendance records to see who contacted us this morning about Ramona Langston's absence today?"

"No need, ma'am. I took the call myself. That's how I heard about what happened to Julia. Ramona's mother called and said Ramona was too upset to come to school today."

"Thank you, Heidi." Another tap of the speaker phone cut off the call.

"My impression is that Julia had many other friends besides Ramona," Ellie said. "I'll need to speak to them."

"And, again, I'm saying you'll need to speak to them outside of school property, and with the consent of their parents." Carter did not even bother waiting for her response before shuffling documents scattered across her desk, obvious busywork.

"Do you know anything about Adderall abuse at Casden?"

Carter stopped fiddling with her papers and shot Ellie a look as if she'd just spit on the floor. "I don't know what kind of children you're used to, but the Casden School prides itself on the creation of future leaders. We have alumni in every branch of government, including the Supreme Court, and on the boards of forty-eight Fortune 500 companies. We produce more Rhodes Scholars per capita than any other day school in the country. All of our faculty have graduate degrees in their respective fields."

"Perhaps that's exactly why you might have kids selling each other Adderall. I just heard one of the other parents say something about this being 'the second time this semester'? Was there another suicide?"

"I'm sure you can get whatever information you need elsewhere, Detective. I have an institution to run here. We all regret what happened to Julia, but I have other young people whose educations require my attention. If we are finished?"

Ellie didn't budge, so the woman led the way to the office door for Ellie's anticipated exit. "The mayor is an alumnus of this school, and he fully understands the situation here today. I suggest you call him, if necessary. You're on private property, Detective, which means you need a warrant to be here."

This was definitely not what Ellie expected of a school that had just lost one of its own.

CHAPTER SEVENTEEN

Heinz. H-E-I-N-Z. Like the ketchup."

Casey had been saying "like the ketchup" since before he'd even learned how to write the actual letters. It was the same phrase his mother had used every time she introduced herself or gave her name over the phone—at least, back when her last name had still been Heinz. For a whisper of a moment in grade school he had abandoned the family line, as a symbol of protest against the oozy red condiment that every other child seemed to consider culinary heaven. Instead, he invoked a new twist, telling people to spell the name like Teresa Heinz Kerry. He was only eleven years old at the time, but quickly learned that he already knew more about current political events than most adults.

The woman behind the counter gave him a polite smile and promised to be back "in a jiff."

More than a jiff passed—at least by Casey's definition—so he took a seat in one of the fancy modern chairs in the lobby area. He remembered Ramona spinning around in one of these at the Design Within Reach studio one day. It was the kind of store that Casey would get rushed out of if he ever walked in alone, but Ramona and her friends looked like they belonged. Ramona loved walking into that store the way some people love to roam museums. She was into the whole mid-century modern vibe. More than once she said she felt like she was meant to be born earlier, back when pregnant women smoked and men drank three martinis at lunch.

What had she called this chair? A butterfly? Camel? No, it was a swan. Casey hadn't seen the resemblance, but Ramona showed him how the lines at the edge of the seat arched backward like the angle of a swan's neck. He reached behind him and ran both hands across the slope of the cushion, remembering Ramona spinning like a child, staring up at the ceiling to make herself dizzy.

Casey liked to pretend that he was comfortable in his own skin, able to waltz into this doctor's office and give his name at the reception desk like he belonged, but he was relieved when he heard the door to the lobby open, followed by the entrance of his friend Brandon.

"Hey, man. You said you'd be here by eleven." Casey had intentionally arrived five minutes late so Brandon would already be there first.

"Sorry," Brandon said. "Subways were fucked."

"Which line did you take?"

"The A."

Casey had sailed to the Upper West Side without problems, but he'd taken the 1.

Brandon was offended by the cross-examination. "Damn, were you checking to see if I was lying to you?"

"No. Just, you know, wondering." Casey had indeed been testing Brandon, but immediately let it drop. He needed to be careful not to scare Brandon away. He liked having at least one male friend on the street.

"Whatever, dude. We're both here now. She get you hooked up yet or what?"

This office was unlike any of Casey's previous, limited exposures to doctors. At the clinics he was used to, the lobbies were standing-room-only, for pregnant teenagers, colicky babies, and old bums two quarts shy of liver failure, all battling for a second's attention from the gum-chewing fat ladies juggling phones behind the desk.

This place felt more like a living room, with its designer chairs, fireplace, and piped-in classical music.

Casey would live here if given the chance.

"All right, Casey. The doctor's ready for you now."

Casey looked at Brandon, who had already settled into the next chair with a copy of *Sports Illustrated* like a waiting father. This was their sixth visit to this office, but Casey still wasn't comfortable with the entire setup. "You sure you can't come with me? Maybe it's, like, more efficient or something for him to meet with us together."

"No way, dude. The doctor will just kick me out if we try that. Just do like I said. Like you've been doing every time, man." Brandon lowered his voice and held the magazine up to hide his lips from the receptionist's view. "Answer all his questions with half the truth, but really exaggerated—like you're totally bummed out or majorly psyched. And maybe remember to add the thing about touching the phone booths. Every single one. And if you try to pass one, you wind up circling back. Try to get that in there somehow. But, with each visit, tone it down a little. Not as much today as last time."

As Casey followed the receptionist to the heavy oak door at the end of the hallway, he felt a little guilty that he allowed Brandon to believe he was still playing games with the doctor. Brandon had his own agenda and was the one to first bring Casey here, nearly two months ago, but Casey hadn't been able to go along with it. Maybe they'd wind up messing up this doctor by pretending to be something they weren't. Or maybe there were side effects or something that could screw his brain up.

But Casey hadn't been able to bring himself to leave, either. Even now, he was still excited to be here. Sure, he'd been sent to "counselors" before, but that had been in Iowa. And they'd all been hell-bent on fixing his supposed delusions. There was usually a lot of prayer involved. They weren't real doctors like this guy, let alone successful city psychiatrists. As much as Casey liked to tell himself he was fine—it was other people in the world who had a problem—he had to wonder if maybe a nineteen-year-old living on the streets for the last two years might be in legitimate need of some fine-tuning in the head department.

He glimpsed back one more time at Brandon, who mouthed an urgent command to "go on."

As he let the doctor's office door close behind him, Casey reminded himself of the vow he'd taken on that first visit, a promise not to waste this opportunity. The chance to have a real, honest one-on-one with a legit top-notch shrink was more important than the plan that had originally brought him here. When the doctor had begun asking him the usual questions, Casey had answered them— not as Brandon had coached, but in his own way. He answered truthfully. He told the doctor everything.

Forty-five minutes later, he exited the office. Brandon was still in the lobby but now had the sleeves of his sweater hitched up to his biceps, a cotton swab taped over a vein near the crook of his left arm. He cradled a Ziploc baggie filled with pills in his lap and looked at Casey with anticipation.

"Dude, what took so fucking long? It's usually takes me, like, ten minutes."

Casey flashed him a quick thumbs-up, and Brandon broke out into a broad grin. Two minutes later, after a quick blood draw, Casey had an identical Ziploc bag and a hundred bucks in his back pocket. But he was even happier about having someone he could talk to.

CHAPTER EIGHTEEN

Second Acts: Confessions of a Former Victim
and Current Survivor

"NEVER TELL"

I almost called this post "Speaking Truth to Power."

The title was intended to be ironic, the phrase itself vacuous.
It came to use in the mid-1950s, courtesy of Quakers who were
trying to resist international violence. These days, the phrase is
invoked constantly by those who want to be seen as standing up
to oppression: the Tea Party against what they see as the "elite,"
the left against whoever dares to disagree, Anita Hill as a title to
her memoir.

But what is power on the Internet?

Many of you will have noticed that in the past few days, our
little discussion group here has drawn the efforts of someone
who craves attention from others. From what I can tell, he—or I
suppose, less probably, she—checks the site one or two times a
day for new posts from me, and then tries to respond with some
sort of intimidating comment.

If you haven't had the privilege of reading the artistic contributions of this particular writer, here's a sample of the work in question:

Wait until you see what I have planned.
He should have made you bleed more.
I will show you damage.

I want to thank you all for the moral support you have shown me here. You give me courage and strength to continue to share my experience with you, and I hope it helps you in turn.

But whoever has been making these destructive comments deserves no attention. Some of you have tried to scold him or shout him down, but please just ignore him. I have been tempted to erase the comments, which of course I have the ability to do, but even that gives this person a form of attention—the knowledge that I digested his words sufficiently to decide to erase them, the accomplishment of being the one member of the message board to have his comments moderated.

And so I have left the words there on the screen—capable of being read by you or me—but hopefully ignored upon first glance. These are the words of a person who has his (or her) own shortcomings. His (or her) own secrets. His (or her) own insecurities. Whoever that person is, he does not have anything "planned." He will not make me "bleed" or "show me damage."

Because some of you loyal readers may have called the police in response to the activity of my website, I suppose law enforcement might become involved. But I will not delete the words. Nor will I stop writing my own.

I choose not to delete those heinous comments because they are a badge of honor. Those words constitute evidence that I am speaking truth—not to power, but to those who crave it, no matter what the cost.

I will not delete the words because I recognize they are an attempt to silence me, no different from that man's words so many years ago, threatening to kill my mother and me if I spoke the truth.

The title of this post is "Never Tell" because that is the lesson I was taught by my abuser all those years ago. In my particular case, he made the threat explicit, but he didn't need to. Never Tell is the universal, underlying rule that all survivors intuit and then internalize.

The phrase is beautiful in its efficiency, isn't it? Two little words, but they convey so much more. *Never tell. Or else.*

But here's the thing. When does it happen? When do we actually read in the news about women who are killed for daring to speak of the harms committed against them? It doesn't happen, at least not here, where we are privileged to live in a modern society. Words have been used by these abusers to silence us for too long, but the cowards never follow through on their threats. They are the ones who are weak. We are the ones with strength.

They choose to threaten. I choose to call their bluff. I will not be silenced.

Back at the downtown gym with complacent staff and a public computer, those words were inducing their own kind of threat. This endeavor was proving more difficult than previously envisioned. She had not only continued to blog, she had defiantly kept the threats visible in the comments section. Now she was raising the possibility of a police investigation.

Although it was tempting to reconsider strategy, there seemed to be no other option but to leave another response.

"I look forward to proving you wrong. I know your name. I've seen your family. And I know where you live."

• • •

In his rented room at the Tonawanda Motor Inn, Jimmy Grisco finished reading the last of the letters. He hadn't thought about these things for fifteen years, but seeing the yellowed pages now had him remembering how he'd felt back then.

It was ironic. He'd been out for two months. He'd searched as well as he could—asking around, checking the phone book, that sort of thing—but had gotten nowhere. Then, yesterday, the prosecutor had hauled him into her office. *Why is this person calling the prison?* she wanted to know. *Keep your nose clean. You got a second chance, James. Don't be causing yourself any trouble.*

And then he'd seen that note next to the lawyer's computer. The name and phone number just sitting there for him, better than if he had planned it himself. He pretended not to see, but, man, how he'd started repeating those numbers in his head over and over and over again. Picturing the layout on a phone's touch pad. Imagining the shape. Anything to keep that number locked up in his mind.

Finally he'd ended up in the courthouse elevator with that guy scribbling file notes with his left hand. He asked to borrow the pen, using his own forearm as a scratchpad. Fifteen years ago, when he'd gone in, a phone number could only do so much. These days? On the Internet a phone number could get you everything.

He packed the letters away into the same Adidas shoe box he'd stored them in all those years ago. He still couldn't believe the police hadn't paid more attention to them when they searched his apartment back then. Goes to show they didn't really care about the whole story.

He'd found the shoe box in his uncle's basement last month, when he'd finally gone through all the crap that had been stored there since his arrest. He had almost thrown it out. Now he was glad he hadn't.

CHAPTER NINETEEN

As Ellie was walking to her car, she spotted a kid in a Casden uniform on the corner of Seventy-fourth Street. He was smoking a cigarette. She recognized him from Julia's Facebook page as her on-and-off boyfriend, Marcus Graze.

"You didn't get the news flash? The mayor doesn't want people smoking near schools."

If the kid was fazed by Julia's death or a police detective's harangue, he didn't show it.

Marcus Graze was only sixteen years old but carried himself like the thirty-eight-year-old investment banker Ellie had briefly lived with a few years back. Chest out. Shoulders down. Chin forward. The collar of the crested navy-blue blazer was turned up, just grazing his shaggy blond hair. If posture reflected self-confidence, this kid had it in spades.

He took a deep drag on his filtered Camel. "Don't give me that Officer Healthy routine. I noticed you breathing it in. Go ahead. I won't tell anyone."

He leaned his body toward Ellie's as he extended the cigarette toward her. She suddenly understood all those songs by men about teenage girls as temptresses.

"You're sweet but half my age."

"Older women know what they're doing."

"And Julia Whitmire didn't?"

"Julia was cool."

"All the money your parents are dropping on Casden and the best you can do is *cool*?"

"I can get fancy if you want. She was sophisticated. Tolerant. Inquisitive. Adventurous. Nonconformist. How about that? Sometimes simple's better, though. If you knew her, you'd know what I mean. She was . . . cool."

"Were you dating?"

He smiled, but with his downcast gaze and the accompanying sigh, the overall effect was more sad than cocky. "I don't *date*. Julia didn't *date*. We were fuck buddies. Oops, there I go again with the simple words."

"It's a strange way to talk about a girl you were intimate with, just a day after her death."

"Julia would have said the same about me. We weren't boyfriend and girlfriend, if that's what you were hoping to find."

"Too *conformist* for you?"

"Yeah, if you must know."

"Regardless of the terminology, don't most teenagers still couple up?"

"Our crowd isn't most teenagers. We're not from that segment of society that becomes police officers or bookkeepers or teachers."

"I'm afraid I'm missing your point."

Marcus spoke with the kind of practiced assuredness that revealed he'd delivered this lecture to others without challenge. He was used to pontificating to a deferential audience, most likely other kids eager to soak in even an ounce of what they perceived as profound wisdom. "We are told from day one that we are special. That we're not like the other, little, people. That we have to excel. That we have to be the best of the best of the best. What was your summer job in high school, Detective?"

"I sold clothes at the mall." She lied. He didn't need to know that she'd flipped burgers at Orange Julius when she wasn't trying to score scholarship money on the Kansas beauty pageant circuit.

"See? The girls I know? If they're interested in fashion, they're supposed to have internships with Marc Jacobs or, better yet, Anna Wintour. Me? I like nightlife. Entertainment. The creation of a lifestyle. I lined up an internship with the Thomas Keller Restaurant Group."

She recognized the name of a high-end restaurateur.

"Impressive."

He stomped out his cigarette butt, then immediately lit another smoke. "Not if you're Simon Graze."

"I take it that's your father?"

"He says the restaurant business is for gays and immigrants, whatever the hell that means. He finally compromised by getting me an internship with a hotel group his friend runs instead. Even that he sees as slumming. People like Julia Whitmire and I don't *date* or *go steady* or whatever you want to call it, because we've got enough pressure on us as it is. It's more like we work hard, so we party hard."

"And does a drug like Adderall help with that?"

He shrugged. "Sometimes. I've pulled a couple of all-nighters with a little bump. Ritalin makes a good combo. I've got to be careful, though, because that plus the Xanax throws me off a little."

She started to laugh but realized he was serious. She was starting to understand why that psychologist in the video debate had been so weary of these prescriptions for children.

"Where do kids get the Adderall?"

He stifled a laugh. "Sorry. *Kids*. It sounds funny, is all. Some *kids* get prescriptions for ADHD, and most of those *kids* take some for themselves and dole out the rest. It's easier to buy prescription drugs than alcohol, really. Adderall, Ritalin, Oxi, Valium. No problemo. Xanax is my fifth antidepressant since I was thirteen. I've got friends on Paxil, Prozac, Lexapro—you name it. What's any of it got to do with Julia slitting her wrists?"

"I never said she slit her wrists."

"Come on. Every *kid* north of Fifty-eighth Street knows about it by now. And I'm trying to save you some time by telling you how it is. Julia was truly a fantastic girl. But if you want to understand her, you can't look at it through the eyes of your inner sixteen-year-old Jersey City mall girl. A girl like Julia's been giving head since she was twelve. She started calling her mother Katherine when she was thirteen, around the time she tried her first blow. I'm sad she's gone, but shit happens. A couple months ago, a guy in my class shot himself up with enough heroin to kill a herd of elephants. It was on Valentine's Day. Very romantic, right?"

That would account for the "second time in a semester" comment she'd overheard at the headmistress's office.

"So you're saying some people just can't handle the pressure?"

"Apparently not."

"According to some of her other friends, Julia had been distracted lately. Busy, like she had a pretty serious relationship going with someone."

"Well, it wasn't me."

"But did you also notice a change in Julia's schedule? Was she around less recently?"

He took a drag from his cigarette. When he shrugged as he exhaled, it was as if a part of the chip on his shoulder slipped off. "Yeah, now that you mention it. Usually she was the one who'd call me to hook up—almost always when she was feeling kind of shitty about herself or her family or whatever."

"So you helped her out by sleeping with her when she was low?"

"We're both fucked up. What do you want? But I hadn't heard from her for at least a couple of months. And the last few times I buzzed her, she basically blew me off."

"Did you ask her why?"

"To what end? Not like we were great loves or anything. I figured she wasn't interested anymore. No big deal."

"If she was seeing someone seriously, do you have any thoughts about who it would have been?"

"No one on the prep scene, that's for sure."

"Why do you say that?"

"I would have heard about it. And Julia wasn't the type to get all googly-eyed for some high school kid."

"I hear she had a thing for older guys."

"Anyone she couldn't have. Ooh, you know who you should talk to?" He sounded excited by the prospect. "Mr. Wallace."

"Who's that?"

"The forty-year-old physics teacher all the girls pine for. Julia was totally hot for him, and she's not one to take no for an answer. Maybe dreamy Kenneth Wallace is your mystery man. Now, wouldn't that be scandalous? Margaret Carter will stroke out on the front steps."

"The headmistress?"

"She's in full-on bunker mode. If she could shut down the school without losing her job, she would have done it hours ago. She visited all the morning classes personally to make sure we all knew that talking to the press would be strictly frowned upon—meaning one less gold star for our college admission letters."

Ellie pictured all those online profiles for Casden students that had suddenly been "unavailable."

"Is that why I couldn't see some of the students' Facebook pages this morning?"

Suddenly he didn't want to answer. "Bill Whitmire's kid offs herself? The second Casden student this semester? The media will be all over this. We're hunkered in the bunker."

As if on cue, a *NewsOne* truck pulled in front of the school. "Told you so."

Ellie was heading back to her car when she heard the boy's voice again behind her.

"You should tell her parents a hundred grand's not enough. At least not in Julia's circle."

"What are you talking about?"

"Oh, you didn't even know? That is classic. Mommy and Daddy dearest announced a hundred-thousand-dollar reward for info. Might make a difference if she'd been killed by some gangbanger in the Bronx. But the people who knew Julia best know there's nothing to tell: Life sucks and then you die. Besides, that kind of money's only—what? Like a few months' splurge for a kid who's already got a trust fund? They're wasting their time."

Her cell phone rang as she unlocked the car door. It was Rogan.

"Hey. I just talked to one of Julia's friends and want to scrub my brain out. You can't possibly be done already." Judges insisted on promptness from everyone but themselves. By Ellie's estimation, Rogan's testimony on the pretrial motions in the Washington case should have started only minutes earlier.

"The defense withdrew the motion. They reached a plea agreement before I even hit the stand. Guess I scared them that much." Despite the bravado behind his words, he sounded disappointed.

"I'm afraid to ask." She knew how much Rogan cared about that case. She had watched him adjust Thelma Washington's threadbare housedress before they'd zipped the body bag around her corpse.

"Life with possibility of parole at twenty. I can live with it. Better than some jury feeling sorry for the crackhead and coming back with a Man One verdict. What's up on your end?"

"Have you heard anything from the Whitmires? A kid at the Casden School says they announced a reward."

"Hold on a second." She heard Rogan asking someone in the background to pull up the *New York Post*'s website. "Yep, got it right here. A hundred grand."

Just as Marcus Graze had said. "I figure we only have a couple of hours before we get hammered by all the money-sniffing whack-jobs coming out of the woodwork. Very helpful of them to mention it to us, huh?"

"Great. The phone number listed here's not even a city number. If they'd coordinated with us, we could have at least used the tip line and staffed it with our own people. Now we have no idea what kind of airhead will be manning the incoming calls. Rich people got their own way of doing stuff."

"You don't know the half of it," she said, recalling the bizarre atmosphere at Casden.

"I'm heading your way. Where you at?"

She gave him the location of her parked car. She wasn't planning on heading out yet. She sat in the driver's seat, but did not turn on the engine, watching the entrance to the Casden School. "Do me a favor before you leave? See if you can find a picture online of a Casden teacher named Kenneth Wallace. Supposedly teaches physics."

Margaret Carter might be in bunker mode, but for the first time, Ellie was starting to think that Julia's story might be more complicated than she'd first thought—and that somehow the answers would be found inside that building.

CHAPTER TWENTY

Ramona sat on the bench next to the playground south of the Metropolitan Museum of Art. Though a sign labeled it the Pat Hoffman Friedman Playground, everyone in the neighborhood called this the Three Bears Playground because of the bronze statue of three bears—one sitting, one standing, one walking. She watched two little boys climbing on top of the sitting and walking bears, just as she had as a toddler. One of Ramona's favorite childhood pictures showed her standing on the back of the walking bear, her hands held in front of her like paws to emulate the standing bear beside her, her mother hovering behind, waiting to catch her in case of a fall.

Today, she chose this bench more for its view of her own apartment building than for the bears. She stole another glance across Fifth Avenue. Nothing. She took a lick of the whipped cream on top of her Frappuccino.

She hadn't planned to cut school. Her parents had offered to let her stay home, but honestly, the thought of staying in the apartment all day with her mom was unbearable. Her mother kept trying to convince her to talk about her feelings.

How are you feeling? How are you feeling? Tell me all about your feelings.

If she heard that word one more time, she was going to throw something. So she had put on her uniform with every intention of making it to classes. Then, on her way to Casden, she realized everyone would be talking smack about Julia—either pretending they were better friends with her than they were, or knew more about it than they possibly could, or saying she was the fucked-up head case who killed herself.

Before she knew it, she was calling the school from her cell phone, telling the headmistress's secretary she was Adrienne Langston and that Ramona wouldn't be coming to school today. No school. No home. Just walking through Central Park, thinking about that last phone call to Julia on Friday night.

Julia had picked up after half a ring: "Hey."

"It happened again."

"Your little visitor? How many times have I told you there's a book about that you should read. *Are You There, God? It's Me, Margaret.* And then one day, when you meet a man you love and are ready to be married and have a baby—"

"Very cute. It's my mom again. She's acting weird."

"Your mom's not weird. Mine, on the other hand? Mindblow."

"Seriously, she hasn't been herself. If I ask her about it, she snaps at me."

"You realize that no one else in the world would find this unusual, don't you? Leave it alone, and consider yourself lucky."

Ramona absorbed what Julia was trying to say, but she and her mom had always been more like best friends than mother and daughter—or stepmother and stepdaughter. That was exactly why the recent distance between them had been bothering her. She should have listened to Julia right then and there. She should have let it drop. But instead she'd gone on and on about how she and her mom were different from other relationships. What if the entire conversation had only served to remind Julia of how screwed up her own parents were?

"It's not just the way she acts around me. She and my dad don't seem—*right* lately. Maybe whatever's bugging her, she doesn't want my dad to know about it, either."

"Oh, Jesus. George and Adrienne are like Ward and June fucking Cleaver. What do you mean, they're not *right*?"

"My mom spends a lot of time on her own, holed up in her study. They seem sort of quiet with each other. Uncomfortable or something."

"Seriously, your parents are, like, so perfect compared to mine. If you're really worried about whatever Adrienne's doing, go check it out yourself."

"What do you mean?"

"Snoop. Go on her computer, look at her search history, read her e-mails—whatever."

"No way."

"Fine, I'll come over and do it." Julia had no qualms about reading diaries, opening medicine cabinets, and otherwise violating people's privacy. As they were leaving Cynthia Lyons's holiday party last December, she'd boasted proudly about searching the entire house. Not a speck of cocaine in sight. Apparently Mr. Lyons's well-known stint in rehab had worked. "Or, better yet. Tell your dad. George will TCB."

Ramona had never really thought of her father as a taking-care-of-business type. He was, after all, one of the partners who got squeezed out of his law firm during the downsizing.

"No, *your* dad would definitely TCB," she said.

"Yeah, if you mean Take Care of Brittany, or whatever slut he's banging lately."

"You're a sick, sick girl, Julia."

"Just calling it like I see it. I learned a long time ago who my parents really were. Maybe it's time you did the same."

It was an uncharacteristically serious tone for Julia. It seemed as though lately all of their interactions were short, ironic quips. It was as if Julia had become such a strong personality that she could never be sincere. As if a moment of earnest compassion would literally melt the cool off of her.

Ramona had found herself wishing they were talking in person.

She wanted to tell her that it wasn't only her parents who hadn't seemed *right* lately. She felt like something had been blocking the two of them. She missed her best friend. She wanted them to be the way they used to be, when nothing was secret and they really, truly *knew* each other, better than they knew themselves. She wanted to know why Julia wouldn't come with her out to the Hamptons the next morning, insisting on staying in the city alone.

Instead, all Ramona had said was, "See you Monday?"

"Yep. Eleven o'clock at AJ's. Maybe in the meantime George and Adrienne will get that extra boost they need in the boudoir. *Oooh, George.*"

"I hate you so much right now."

Ramona had no idea those would be the last words she spoke to her best friend.

As she took another sip of her coffee drink, she finally spotted her mother rushing out the front door of their building. According to the clock on Ramona's phone, her mom was running a few minutes late to her Pilates session.

Once her mother was out of sight, Ramona made her way across Fifth Avenue. She had rejected Julia's advice on Friday, but it wasn't too late to heed it now.

Inside her mother's study, she jiggled the mouse on the computer. A password was required.

She thought about walking away. Her mother would never violate her trust this way.

She asked herself what Julia would do, then rested her fingertips on the keyboard to type.

R-A-M-O-N-A

Enter.

She was in.

CHAPTER TWENTY-ONE

How can you drink this? It tastes like burnt motor oil." Rogan scrutinized the name of the coffee shop printed on the side of the cup in his hand. "*Coffee Monster?* More like monstrous coffee."

In the hour since Rogan had joined her in the car at Seventy-fourth and Madison, another three news vans had arrived outside the school. Ellie was on her second helping of java from the coffee shop across the street. "It's right here. It's caffeine. Whatever. Hey, there's our guy."

In the sideview mirror of their parked Crown Vic, Kenneth Wallace looked pretty much the same as he had in the photograph Rogan had found online, posing for a team shot at a run-for-cancer-research 5K. Same dark-blond tousled hair, thin face, slightly crooked nose as if from a break. Ellie could certainly understand why this guy was the campus dreamboat.

She started to open the car door as Wallace turned to walk in their direction, but Rogan reached across her and held the door shut. "Hold up."

They watched as reporters swarmed the physics teacher. Even through the closed window, she could hear their questions. "Are you a parent? Do you teach at Casden? Did you know Julia Whitmire? We've heard that the school is refusing to make a statement, even to parents. Why are students being told not to speak with us? What is Casden trying to hide?"

The teacher held up his palms to block his face. His brisk walk turned into a jog, and the reporters finally gave up once he hit Madison Avenue.

"*Now* we go," Rogan said. They hopped out of the car and caught up with him just as he crossed Madison at a diagonal, ducking into a café around the corner on Seventy-third.

Once he'd placed his order—something called a Panini Americano—they identified themselves. She saw him eyeing the door and wondered if he was considering bolting.

"I guess I don't need to worry about being seen. The rest of the teachers were too afraid of the reporters outside to leave campus for lunch, and our headmistress is infamous for bringing in her own portion-controlled meals."

"And you?" Ellie asked.

"A guy's got to eat. I told the vultures I had nothing to say, and now, voilà—" The man behind the counter handed him a white bag and a paper cup. "I can eat this sandwich and pretend I'm in Paris. Plus the coffee's a hell of a lot better than *that* crap."

Rogan gave his Monster Coffee cup another look of disapproval before tossing it in the trash. "You mind eating here?" he asked. "We'd like a few words with you. Probably better to do it away from the vultures."

Ellie ordered two coffees from the counter before scoping out a small corner table.

"We've been surprised at the school's reluctance to cooperate," Ellie said. "On the one hand, we've got Julia's parents so eager for answers they've announced a cash reward. Meanwhile, Julia's own school has—well, it sounds like you know."

"Our headmistress, Margaret Carter—have you met her yet?"

Ellie nodded.

"She rounded all the teachers up this morning to break the news about Julia. She expressed the appropriate amount of sadness, et-cetera, but the message was clear. She'd be the point person for all communications, even with students—and it was pretty obvious she was going to remain as tight-lipped as possible."

"And yet," Rogan said, "you leave the building for lunch. You're sitting here with us."

He finished swallowing a huge bite of his sandwich before speaking. "I graduated first in my class in college with a degree in physics. Then I got a master's at UC Berkeley. I'm about two years away from finishing my Ph.D. thesis. I wanted to be an astronaut."

"Past tense?" Ellie asked.

"Turns out you may as well want to be a rock star. And until I get a Ph.D., there's no tenure-track jobs to be had. Then you've got the private sector, where it's pretty much impossible to do interesting work without somehow being part of the military-industrial complex." He smiled. "I know, I should have been born earlier. I'm, like, the youngest hippie in America. And so, at least for now, I'm Mr. Wallace, mild-mannered physics teacher to the future leaders of the Free World. But I'll tell you what: there's no way I let some bureaucrat like Margaret Carter dictate what I can and cannot say when one of my students is dead."

An antiauthoritarian free-spirit might be just the type to cross boundaries with an underage student. Ellie decided to let the topic rip. "We've been told you and Julia had a particularly close student-teacher relationship."

He smiled and looked up at the ceiling. "Ah, classic. These kids are totally predictable. Let me guess: the always-provocative Marcus Graze?"

Her silence resolved any doubt.

"That would be the same Mr. Graze who just got a D for refusing to show any of his work on most of his assignments this semester. Pretty sure he's cribbed some answers here and there from his peers."

"So you don't mind telling us where you were Sunday night?" she asked.

"Depending on the time, either with my wife's family in Boston, or next to my wife on a plane headed back to New York. You can check with her if you'd like. Her family, too. The airlines, whatever you need."

She nodded.

"Don't get me wrong. God knows, Julia tried. So have others, but trust me, I'm quite unavailable." Wallace pulled out a wallet from his back pocket and flipped it open to a photograph of a knock-out gorgeous brunette and a tiny baby. "This amazing woman is my wife. In addition to being breathtakingly beautiful, she's a wonderful mother and a brilliant physician to boot. I've been off the market since I met her my freshman year in college. When these girls at the school start sniffing around, I wonder if it's because I put out this air of complete unattainability. It's like they all want the designer handbag that's back-ordered for five months. It's probably for the best that the attention seems to fall to me, because, honestly? I know some pretty decent guys who might not have been able to resist. Julia was—precocious. And more persistent than most. Pretty aggressive for such a young girl. She may have even told Marcus Graze something happened with me, just to have a story to tell."

"You make her sound pretty troubled. Did anyone ever try to help?"

"There are too many of them to help, quite frankly. I saw my share of indulged kids at Occidental and Berkeley, but the crew here? Part of it's the wealth, but a lot of it's generational. They're pressured to be absolutely perfect, and yet simultaneously told they can do no wrong. No one ever says no to them. If something isn't right, it's someone else's fault. They blame someone like me for their D, or they call a doctor for a diagnosis."

Ellie was glad he raised the topic. "We're under the impression that the students take prescription drugs like they're multivitamins."

"That's not just here. I mentioned that my wife's a doctor? She might be even more idealistic than I am. She refuses to take handouts from the pharmaceutical industry or to write prescriptions people don't need—especially for children who have nothing wrong with them. Between the two of us, we've managed to make ourselves broke, but at least we can look ourselves in the mirror. Get this." He had abandoned his sandwich on the table, now animated by the current conversation. Ellie could imagine him as a college lecturer. "I talked to Maria—that's my wife—about this last year when I found out a bunch of students had taken Ritalin and Adderall to help study for finals. It turns out the number of kids on psychotropic drugs is staggering. There have been cases of two-year-olds on Prozac. They now permit diagnosis of ADHD in children as young as four. And Maria thinks almost all of the diagnoses are bogus. Then, about ten percent of kids who *haven't* been diagnosed take their friends' drugs, just to get high. Was Julia messing with that kind of stuff?"

"You'll understand we can't tell you her medical history," Ellie said.

"Well, the rumor is she killed herself but that her parents think otherwise. I'm not sure which is worse."

Ellie did. She knew which was worse. And she knew why Bill and Katherine Whitmire so desperately needed another answer.

"At any other school, we'd expect to get access to every single student to find out what she may have been going through, who she was seeing, whether she was having problems. But here, kids are even shutting down their Facebook pages. Is it possible Julia was being bullied?" She wouldn't be the first teenager to kill herself after a relentless campaign of torment that kids were capable of launching these days, typical schoolyard teasing now amplified by a thousand with a turbo boost from technology.

"I hate to say this, but Julia would have been more likely to be the bullier than the bullied in that kind of scenario. They're pulling down their profiles because the school put the fear of God in them—no, worse, the fear of tackiness. Some kids might trade a lung for the infamy of some lame song on YouTube, but Casden's all about propriety. The headmistress made it very clear: even if they set their pages to 'private,' all it takes is for one friend to cooperate with the media."

"Next thing the kid knows," Rogan said, "his party pictures are on the front page of a tabloid, the poster child for prep school dysfunction."

"Exactly. So to make sure nothing is taken out of context, no Facebook, Twitter, Google Plus, all that nonsense. One of the administrators told me that the school even hired a public relations firm to search the Internet for stories about the school and have the negative ones *scrubbed*. It's like *1984*."

"But we saw parents lobbying the headmistress. They were angry, and they wanted information. Won't a private school need to listen to that kind of pressure?"

Wallace was back to his sandwich, pausing to swallow before responding. "It'll be interesting to watch the fallout. The kind of people who send their children to this school are used to having their way. But it's ultimately about supply and demand. You wouldn't believe some of the family names we've turned down. Even the head of the Fed needed a friend to pull strings to get his kid in. Parents can complain, but at the end of the day, what are they going to do? Yank their kids? There are a hundred other families lined up who are willing to tell themselves that two dead teenagers is just a coincidence."

"Is it?" Rogan asked. "Just a coincidence?"

Wallace crushed the empty wrapper of his sandwich into a tight ball. "I think even I have said enough at this point, Detectives."

As they were heading back to the car, Rogan's cell phone buzzed. "Rogan. . . . Yeah. . . . Can't you just tell me? . . . All right. We'll be right down."

"Now what?"

"That was the CIS detective. He found something on Julia's laptop."

CHAPTER
TWENTY-TWO

Most law enforcement jobs came with cool-sounding titles, as with the forensic scientists who worked as *criminalists*, or the dispatchers, who were *communications technicians*. Even the clerical staff at least got nifty acronyms—*PAAs*, short for police administrative aides.

And so, unsurprisingly, the cops who did the increasingly important work of analyzing computers for the NYPD weren't merely detectives: they were CIS detectives.

Typically, a victim's computer would have been inspected at the precinct by one of the department's "computer associates"— civilians who tended toward the long-haired, lanky, Dungeons & Dragons techno-nerd variety, more comic-con than *Columbo*. But when the daughter of Bill Whitmire was involved, Rogan had sent the laptop directly to headquarters to be examined by a CIS detective.

Because Julia was dead, they did not need a court's permission to search every byte of the computer's data. They could read her documents, follow her Internet surfing trail, and pore over her e-mail history. With her death, Julia had lost any right to privacy.

Today's CIS detective introduced himself as Peter Pettinato. From the first glance, Ellie could see he was not the usual only-left-the-basement-to-answer-the-door-for-carry-out type. He was an actual grown-up with short black hair and an equally tidy mustache. There were, however, signs of a creative personality. His cubicle was decorated with photographs of his pets and a few appearances he'd made in local theater productions. In place of a typical office chair, he sat on a bright blue yoga ball.

As Pettinato reached for the closed laptop on his desk, Ellie noticed a sticker of a yellow bird with a white belly on the back of the computer, right above a sticker that read: "Mean People Suck."

The bird image was familiar. Where had she seen it before? *The Brady Bunch*? Something about it reminded her of the oldies repeat-channel she used to watch when she was little. That was it. *The Partridge Family*! It wasn't an identical cartoon, but the bird reminded her of *The Partridge Family*.

"Yo. Earth to Hatcher. You there, girl?"

Rogan waved a hand in front of her eyes, as if to check her sight. "It's like that parakeet hypnotized you for a sec."

"Sorry." The bird sticker made her sad. Sadder than Julia's water-pruned and lifeless body in the bathtub. With all the emphasis on the Whitmires' wealth and Julia's life of privilege and precocious-ness, Ellie had neglected to remember that she was still only a sixteen-year-old girl. A part of her had still been childlike. It was yet another fact Ellie had overlooked during that initial callout to the townhouse.

Pettinato motioned for them to look over his shoulder. "All right, so here's what seems relevant based on what you told me yesterday—suspected suicide, slit wrist, found in the tub. You asked me specifically to search for first drafts of the goodbye note, or for any Internet research about depression or suicide. I got zilch on both fronts. The only documents I found on the hard drive all appeared to be school papers—Shakespeare, Civil War, that kind of stuff. I didn't find any Googling for methods of death, for mental heath issues, for anything like that."

"So what *did* she look at online?" Rogan asked.

"Typical teenage fare. Facebook. Twitter—though that was more one-way communication."

"What does that mean?"

Ellie braced herself for the usual loud sigh that followed questions that struck CIS detectives as stupid, but Pettinato showed no signs of attitude. "It's how a lot of quote-unquote *real people* use Twitter. They don't actually post—or tweet, in the lexicon. But they have accounts so they can follow their favorite celebrities. She followed twits like those big-butt sisters and smack-talking rap stars. That kind of nonsense. So, anyway, Facebook. Twitter. Lots of online shopping. Fashion sites. Yelp for reviews of restaurants and clubs and stuff. Celebrity gossip like *TMZ*, *Us Weekly*, and Perez Hilton. Really, not all that much activity as far as surfing goes. But I did find one hit over the weekend to a blog about childhood sex abuse. I thought maybe that could be related, you know?"

If Julia had been abused, it would put her eating disorder and promiscuity into context. It would also make her a prime candidate for suicide.

"And explain to us exactly how you can be sure Julia accessed the blog?" Rogan asked. "And, to be sure, we're not total Luddites—we get history windows, time stamps, etcetera. It just helps when you break it down."

Pettinato was waving away the explanations. "I may be CIS, but I'm also a detective. I get it. So, like you said, there's a history window involved. If we open Safari here . . . that's the Internet browser"—he smiled at the exaggeratedly elementary level of the tutorial—"and hit Show All History, and then look at this column called Visit Date? Now we have a list of every site she went to, and the date and time when the visit occurred. And here, on Saturday night, you'll see three entries for this blog."

He clicked on the link and the website opened. "Second Acts: Confessions of a Former Victim and Current Survivor."

Pettinato scrolled down the screen slowly so they could get a sense of the subject matter.

"Can you tell if she'd been following the blog for long?" Rogan asked. "Or going to other websites related to sex abuse?"

"No, this is the only one."

"It could be a complete fluke," Ellie offered. She herself had wound up at countless unintended online sites thanks to random hyperlinks, pop-up ads, mistaken mouse clicks, and search-engine snafus.

"That's what I thought at first," Pettinato said, "but I swear there's a reason I thought you'd want to see this."

He pulled up the history page again, and this time Ellie noticed that the "Second Acts" blog was listed three consecutive times. "Wait a second. Why are there three entries in a row if she only went to the website once?"

"Ah. Because the fact of three different entries in the history window doesn't mean three separate visits to the blog. Otherwise we'd see the names of other websites in between if she was doing other surfing. Those three entries are for navigation within the blog itself. See: if we click on this first entry here"—he moved the cursor and clicked accordingly—"we pull up the home page for the blog. This is the main page, what you get whenever you enter the main website address. Got that?"

He looked to both Rogan and Ellie for confirmation they were following his step-by-step tour.

"Okay. Then we go back to the history to see what happened next. We click on this second entry, and now we see the comments that came in response to the blog post for that day."

Rogan nodded. "So Julia would have first seen the post of the day on the home page, but then she clicked to see the comments."

"Correct. Now here's what's interesting. If you click on this third entry in her history, it takes you to the 'Create Journal Entry' box in the comments section."

"Meaning that she posted a comment?" Rogan asked.

"Well, I can't tell you that with a hundred percent certainty just from the laptop. The only way to do that would be if she had a keystroke recorder on her computer. But, yeah, I'm pretty confident that's what happened."

"Explain to me how you know that?" Ellie said. Pettinato was a detective—and perhaps a talented one at that—but she didn't want his inferences. She needed to conclude for herself that two and two added up to four.

"Okay, but if I'm right, am I allowed to claim the hundred-thou reward? Just saw it online."

"I'm quite sure the three of us aren't eligible."

"What I know for certain is that the three listings in her history correlate to these three actions. One, she pulled up the home page Saturday at 10:02 p.m. Two, she pulled up the comments, also at 10:02 p.m. And, three, she pulled up the page for entering comments at 10:03 p.m. Now, if you look here on the blog post that went up on Saturday, there's only one comment posted within ninety minutes of that time, and it was finalized at 10:04 p.m."

She understood now why Pettinato had concluded that Julia was the author of the comment posted at 10:04.

"And here's the kicker." He pushed back from the laptop to make sure they could get a clear look. "This is the comment that was posted that night."

"If you thought that night twenty years ago was bad, wait until you see what I have planned. You won't remember a single time on the clock. Maybe a day on the calendar if you're lucky. Maybe a week. Or maybe I'll keep you busy for a month. One thing I know for certain: You will not live to write about it."

Ellie remembered the physics teacher saying that Julia was more likely to have been bullying someone else than being bullied herself. Julia may have only been sixteen years old, but these were not the words of a normal teenager.

"I assume you have no idea why your victim would say such a thing?" Pettinato asked.

They both muttered their no's, still taking in the new information.

"Now, here's where things get really perplexing. Your victim died Sunday night? Well, that's all and well if we're right about her posting the one comment on Saturday night. But guess what? There have been five other threats since Monday. Unless Julia Whitmire is surfing the Web from the afterlife, someone else out there is continuing whatever she started."

CHAPTER TWENTY-THREE

Ramona was not usually an angry girl. She had been told over the years that she had plenty of reason to be an angry person. The word *bitter* had been used at times, too.

Usually the words came from people who thought their job was to tell Ramona how she should feel.

The first person she recalled telling her she was "allowed to be angry" was a school counselor in the—what?—the third grade? Yes, she was in Mr. Masterson's class at the time, so it was the third grade. She didn't get long division, so Dad got her a tutor. And when she still had trouble with long division, despite the private tutor, she saw the school counselor.

Why wasn't she paying attention in school? Why did she seem so distant? Was she angry about her mother? *You're allowed to be angry,* she was told. She was barely nine years old. What was there to be angry about?

Sometimes Ramona wondered how much she even remembered about her mother. Her dad was good about keeping photographs of her around, like that one of her and her mom by the bears statue. He also talked to Ramona about her—not so much anymore, but while she was growing up. She knew that memory could play tricks on a person. You could convince yourself from pictures and stories that you remembered a person, when really all you knew were two-dimensional images and rehashed anecdotes.

But Ramona was confident she had at least some true, authentic memories of her mother. Her name was Gabriella. Her girlfriends had called her Gabby, but at home, Ramona's father always called her Gabriella. She wore this lotion that smelled like ginger and honey. When she was done applying it, she'd run her still-slick hands along Ramona's forearms and say, "Now you and Mommy smell just the same." That wasn't a story Ramona's father had ever told her, and someone can't make you remember a fragrance that distinctively. That's how Ramona was certain she really did remember her mother, Gabriella Langston.

Oddly, though, she could not remember learning she had died. She knew, because she certainly had been told, that her mother died shortly after Ramona's fifth birthday. She knew because she had been told much later that a car on Egypt Lane had struck her mother during her ritual walk home from the Hamptons Equestrian Stables. She knew that the state police department's accident-reconstruction experts believed that the car involved was a red Pontiac of some kind. Something about the tire tracks and paint transfer. A hit-and-run, they said. Probably a drunk, though there was no way to know since they never caught the guy. Ramona also knew that her mother's ashes had been scattered in the ocean at Montauk, because she had loved the taste of the salty wind hitting her face as she stood on the rocky beach's edge.

And she knew that, not eighteen months after her mother's ashes had been scattered, her father had married Adrienne. She had been working as a nanny for another family in the building, back when she was still Adrienne Mitchell. The transition from neighbor's nanny to supportive presence to new wife and stepmother was quick.

Then Ramona was in Mr. Masterson's third-grade class and couldn't do long division and got asked a lot of questions about being angry.

Then, in the fifth grade, she started complaining about being tired in the mornings. Her father sent her to her first therapist, who also asked Ramona if she was angry. In fact, she may have been the first to throw in the *bitter* word, not Mr. Masterson. The therapy sessions got down to once a month until a couple of years ago, when her father found pot in her purse. Somehow pot meant she needed to talk to a doctor once a week, like so many of the kids Ramona knew. And somehow all these trained experts seemed to think that Ramona should be angry.

The truth was that Ramona just wasn't the angry type. She only remembered getting really angry about her mother's death once. It was the first time Adrienne had tried to discipline her. Ramona must have been eleven. She pierced her ears without permission, and Adrienne had dared to express her disappointment. Ramona screamed at her—"You're not my mother, *Adrienne*!" emphasizing the use of her first name—then ran to her bedroom. She could hear Adrienne crying in the living room but couldn't bring herself to apologize.

When her father finally came home from work, she heard their voices in the kitchen. Maybe Adrienne wouldn't mention the episode to him?

But then her father had come into her room and sat on the foot of her bed. She'd never seen him like that before. He was usually so flat in his affect. He didn't show emotions. But that night, after putting in thirteen hours at the law firm, he had cried in front of his daughter. He said how much he missed her mother. He talked about the day he first met her, at a jazz concert in the Museum of Modern Art's sculpture garden.

She would never forget how matter-of-factly he had said that Adrienne was not Gabriella. *Love at my age isn't the same as meeting someone when you're in your twenties,* he had said. She hadn't even questioned it at the time, because children instinctively think of their parents as old. But in retrospect, he was all of forty-six at the time but reminiscing as if his best days were already past. Adrienne wasn't Gabriella, he had said, but Adrienne was a good person. She was young. She brought a different energy into the house. She was fun. She made him feel happy again. They had been married four years by then, and she was still helping him learn how to be happy without Gabriella. "And," he said, "she loves you and really wants to be a mother to you."

But Ramona wasn't done pouting. "She's *not* my mother."

And so her father told her that her mother hadn't really been her mother either, not according to the DNA. They had tried. They kept a calendar. She took all the expensive drugs that were available. They tried one round of in vitro, but still nothing. Some of their friends resorted to surrogates and egg transplants, but Gabriella cared more about being a mother than about the biology. They called a lawyer. They arranged a private adoption. Gabriella had been the one to choose the name Ramona.

Adrienne wasn't her mother, but neither was Gabriella.

And so just as the baby version of herself must have come to accept Gabriella as her first mother, she resolved to accept Adrienne as her new one. Now, five years after that episode with the earrings, she didn't think of her as a stepmother. Or an adoptive mother. Adrienne was her mother. She had never again questioned the truth of that relationship, not only because she'd made a promise to her father, but because Adrienne had earned it.

Ramona returned her gaze to her mother's computer screen, the browser open to the page that had appeared when she had typed in the password.

The website was called Second Acts: Confessions of a Former Victim and Current Survivor. And the page wasn't the blog as it would appear to any casual reader. No, Ramona was looking at the administrative "dashboard" on a blog-hosting service called Social Circle. This was the place where the author of the blog could draft new posts, delete comments, and modify content.

Ramona was always so proud of the fact that, unlike her friends, she had a "real" relationship with her mother. But here she was— alone in her mother's study, snooping around on her mother's computer when she should have been in school, finally discovering why her mother had seemed so secretive lately.

Her mother was a sex abuse survivor. Her mother was the author of this blog.

And now, after all these years of being told that she had every reason to be angry, Ramona Langston was actually angry.

Someone was threatening her mother.

Five miles south, at NYPD headquarters, Ellie and Rogan were also reading the "Second Act" blog, paying special attention to the threats that had been posted since Julia's death.

"Can you tell if Julia accessed the blog anytime after that comment on Saturday night?" Rogan asked. They had evidence suggesting that Julia had been the one to post the first threatening comment on Saturday. Clearly she had not authored the threats written since Monday, but she was still alive on Sunday and may have checked in on the blog then.

"Nope," Pettinato said, pivoting back and forth on his fitness ball. "Just the one hit the night before she died. But if I'm right and she was the one who posted the comment, she must have known the website well because she navigated through it so quickly. However, I have found no indication that she ever used *this* laptop to visit the website previously."

They had more questions than answers.

"So how do we find out whose blog this is?" Ellie asked. "And what computer was used to post the more recent threats?"

"The blog was created with a hosting service called Social Circle. They should be able to give you the IP addresses. That stands for—"

"Internet protocol address," Ellie said. She and Rogan had come up against these Internet situations before, where the bad guys cloaked themselves in anonymity. The IP address was like a computer's numeric address on the Internet.

"Good luck getting it, though," Pettinato warned. "Unless you're working with some corporate behemoth, the dudes who run these webites usually won't cooperate without a subpoena."

She and Rogan were familiar with that world as well. Fortunately, she knew an assistant district attorney who liked her.

Her cell phone buzzed at her waist. She didn't recognize the number.

"Hatcher."

"Detective Hatcher? This is Ramona Langston. You came to my apartment last night to talk to me about my friend, Julia Whitmire? You gave me your card?"

"Sure, Ramona. What can I do for you?"

"It's not about Julia. But, um—I'm not sure who I should call. It's about a website?"

"What website?" Rogan and Pettinato both perked up on hearing her side of the conversation.

"Um, it's at secondacts-dot-com. I'm pretty sure it's my mom's? And, it's about stuff that happened to her when she was young. But, um, I think—well, someone's basically threatening to kill her. Can the police find out who it is?"

CHAPTER TWENTY-FOUR

The city of New York is home to nearly nine million people. Within it sits the island of Manhattan, only twenty-three square miles of land, but with nearly two million residents, the most densely populated area in the United States. Two million people buzzing around on just twenty-three square miles of land bred a certain culture: efficiency in moving from point A to point B; no eye contact or small talk; no connection to the people one passed on the way. And along with that culture came a distinct feeling of anonymity.

But the sense of anonymity was not the same thing as actual privacy. Among the hundreds of people a busy Manhattanite buzzed past on a daily basis was the guy at the deli counter who poured the same large cup of coffee each morning, two sugars with nonfat milk; the pedicurist who feigned obliviousness to prolonged cell phone calls while she scraped away dead skin from her clients' cracked feet; the clerk at Duane Reade who pretended not to notice when a husband purchased condoms six hours after his wife picked up her birth control pills.

The Manhattan economy was propped up by people whose very jobs depended on feeding the feeling of anonymity, even as they were entrusted with the most private secrets. And no one knew more about the lives of the seemingly anonymous than a New York City doorman.

The doorman stationed at the entry of the Langstons' Upper East Side apartment building was the epitome of professionalism, with a neatly pressed navy blazer, perfect posture, and a prompt greeting. "Good afternoon. How may I help you?"

While she and Rogan displayed their shields, Ellie squinted at the name embroidered on the doorman's jacket. "How are you doing today, Nelson?" The personal touch never hurt. "We're here to see Mrs. Langston. We were here last night as well. It's about a friend of Ramona: Julia Whitmire?"

If the name meant anything to Nelson, he certainly wasn't showing it.

"Of course. Let me call up." His expression was blank as he placed the call. "Good afternoon, ma'am. There are two detectives here to see you. . . . Detectives Hatcher and Rogan. . . . Yes, they are right here in the lobby now. . . . Very good." He hung up the phone and extended a white-gloved hand toward the elevator. "To the twenty-first floor."

"They seem like a nice family," Ellie offered.

"Very," he said with a nod. He might have meant exactly what he said. Or he might have meant the Langstons were devil-worshiping cat torturers. His face revealed nothing.

"Do you remember Ramona's friend, Julia?"

"We have many visitors in a large building like this."

"My understanding is Julia spent a lot of nights here. I'd think you'd get to know the kids' friends pretty well."

"Sometimes, yes. We have very nice families here."

"Was Julia Whitmire 'very nice'? Did she seem to still be on good terms with Ramona and her parents?"

"She visited regularly, I believe. Please, Mrs. Langston is expecting you."

Once they were in the elevator, Rogan gave her an "atta girl" punch in the arm. "Good job interrogating the domestic help there, partner."

Not all doormen were like Nelson. Some of them were refrigerator-size versions of Joan Rivers, happy to dish endlessly about the residents. It wasn't her fault that, compared to those guys, Nelson was Fort Knox.

Adrienne Langston was standing just beyond the elevator doors when they opened.

She was dressed in yoga pants and a hoodie from the Pilates session that had given Ramona a chance to hack into her mother's computer. Ramona had chosen to leave the apartment after speaking to Ellie on the phone, asking Ellie to be the one to tell Adrienne that her daughter had discovered the blog.

"I'm sorry you came all the way up here, Detectives. I'm afraid Ramona is still at school. I tried to convince her to stay home today, but she insisted she wanted to keep her normal routine. She should be home soon, but if it's important, you can of course pull her from class if necessary. She's at the Casden School."

"I appreciate that, Mrs. Langston," Ellie said. "We're actually here to speak with you. It's about a blog."

No response.

"A blog called 'Second Acts'? I think the full name is 'Second Acts: Confessions of a Former Victim and Current Survivor.'"

Ellie considered herself a pretty decent poker player. She was good enough that, some months, she brought home more money from Atlantic City than from the NYPD. She did not, however, want to play cards with Adrienne Langston, who was up there in Nelson the doorman's league of unreadable mugs.

"Do you know of a website by that name?" Rogan nudged.

"What is this relating to, Detectives?"

"It's just a simple question, Mrs. Langston." Rogan had used his sweet voice when they were here the previous night, but now he'd upped the ante to what Ellie called his military tone.

"And I asked you one in turn."

Most people shared a natural tendency to acquiesce to authority.

They accompanied police to the station without an official arrest. They answered questions from detectives despite Miranda warnings advising them of their right to remain silent. They consented to searches without warrants. In Ellie's experience, only two categories of Americans departed from this trend. The first were the hardcore recidivists who could look a cop in the eye and say, "Fuck you, bacon. I want my lawyer." The second were rich people. And while Adrienne Langston might not be Whitmire wealthy, she was rich enough to think she was owed an explanation.

"We assure you," Ellie said, "that our questions about the blog are related to the death of Julia Whitmire. I think *your* question is intended to protect your privacy."

"I value privacy a great deal." Adrienne was adjusting the floral arrangement on the foyer's center table, even though every last stem was meticulously placed.

"Is that why the blog was supposed to be anonymous?" Ellie asked.

"It's sort of a contradiction, isn't it?" Adrienne said. "A person claiming to want privacy, while placing every last personal detail on the Internet for every prying eye to see?"

"My father died under horrible circumstances when I was little. All my life I wanted the details of his death to remain private. But two years ago, I found myself in the media spotlight, sharing all of these stories I never wanted to talk about. I did it to help my mother get access to my dad's pension—it's a long story—but I have to admit that the process of unloading all of that onto a curious public was strangely healing. If I could have done it anonymously, as with a blog—well, I can see the appeal of that."

Ellie truly did value privacy. She hated every second of those ridiculous interviews. But, despite what she said to Adrienne, she did not understand people who blogged, Facebooked, and Tweet-ered (or whatever) their every irrelevant moment. She did not enjoy hauling out her own drama, even for the sake of getting a witness to trust her. Luckily, the trumped-up common ground did the trick.

Adrienne invited them into the living room, gesturing toward an oversize floral-print sofa. Ellie felt herself sink into the plush down cushions.

"I suppose there's no point in denying the blog is mine," Adrienne said, claiming a spot on the rocking chair next to them, then tucking one foot beneath her. "You are the police, after all. All these years, I thought I'd put my childhood behind me."

"So why did you decide to write about this now?" Ellie asked.

She wrinkled her face in confusion as she considered the question, obviously not for the first time. "Who really knows why we do *any* of the things we do. But my best guess? I look at Ramona. She's the same age now as I was when I finally told my mother I was being raped." She used the word without any hesitation or discomfort. "I remember, at the time, forcing myself to understand why my mother didn't want to believe me when I went to her. She didn't want to be alone again. My dad left before I was born. She was poor. She was forty years old but looked sixty. Men weren't exactly pounding on her door."

"But you were her daughter." Ellie felt strange talking to this woman about something so personal, when she'd already read the details on her blog.

"Exactly. And when I was a teenager, I really did try not to hate her. I made all kinds of excuses. And it wasn't hard, you know, because boys were my first consideration, too, at the time. And I wanted to love my mother. But now?"

"You're not a teenager anymore," Rogan said.

"Exactly. When you're a kid, it's like you don't have enough experience to gauge how wrong your situation is. It's not until you grow up that you can truly and honestly evaluate just how *off* something was when you were a child. I knew enough to understand that my mother's boyfriend should not have come to me at night the way he did. But I would have also known it was wrong for him to borrow a CD without my permission. It was like I somehow convinced myself they were close to the same level of offense, so I was able to forgive my mother for not reacting more strongly. And, ultimately, I still forgive her, because I know that in some way, it was that same man who made her weak. But, wow, I see my Ramona. If any man ever touched her like that, I'd kill him."

"And you never spoke to Ramona about the abuse?" Ellie asked.

Adrienne shook her head quietly. "That part of my life is over. I write about it as a way to rid myself of those events, but I don't want my family to see me as that person. I need it to be separate. Wait, if this has something to do with Julia—does Ramona know about my writing?"

Ellie broke the news that the woman had started to piece together on her own. "She found your blog. She saw the threats, too. She called us because she's afraid for you."

"I guess I'll need to talk to her about it now. And, of course, George."

"You never told your husband?" Ellie had met George Langston and had filed him away mentally as Mister-Stick-Up-His-Ass, but she still couldn't imagine marrying someone without telling him something so important. "Not that it's my business."

"You're right. It's not your business. What does any of this have to do with Julia?"

"Would you say that you knew Julia well?" Rogan asked, still with the military voice.

"Very. She and Ramona were practically joined at the hip since they were in the fifth grade. Slumber parties. Late-night cookie baking. They got their ears pierced together, way too early if you ask me, but that's another story. Future maids of honor for each other would have been my guess. Ramona—well, I don't know what she's going to do without Julia."

"And everything was okay between them?" Ellie asked.

"Two peas in a pod."

"And what about Julia's feelings toward you?"

Adrienne was clearly perplexed by the question. "Me? Oh, I don't know. I liked Julia. Very much, actually. I felt bad for her. Her parents—well, you met them. You probably gathered that parenting was not their top priority. Sometimes I wished she would just stay with us instead of being downtown in that museum, all by herself. But her feelings about me? I'd like to think that she liked me. And respected me. And recognized that I cared about her. But my guess is that, like all children, she just saw me as the woman who happened to be around Ramona's house every now and then." She smiled sadly.

"When we were talking about your blog, you didn't mention that someone had been posting threatening remarks in the comments."

"Oh, those drive me crazy." Adrienne waved a hand as if the remarks were nothing to worry about, but Ellie noticed she was rocking in her chair more aggressively. "I thought about deleting them, but then I figured, if some crazy person wants to attack me, I'll let my readers see it for what it is. Speaking the ugly truth is a sacrifice. There are people who think survivors should all shut up and keep it to themselves. And that's why it's all the more important for survivors to have their voices be heard."

"Don't you wonder who's posting the comments?"

"Of course I do. But I've read enough in the newspaper to know I really can't do anything about it. Words are only words, right?"

Her impression of the law was accurate. If Adrienne had called the police about the threats on her blog, her call would have been transferred to ten different departments until someone finally explained to her that problems of jurisdiction, anonymity, freedom of speech, and antiquated penal laws all conspired to leave only one option: suck it up.

It was time to drop the other shoe. "We have uncovered evidence that Julia Whitmire posted one of those comments."

Adrienne's face was initially unchanged, but then the truth must have registered. She looked like she'd been slapped.

"I don't understand. How can you know that? Julia's dead."

Ellie gave her the truncated, nontechnical version of the information they'd pulled from Julia's laptop. She left out the part where they wouldn't be a hundred percent certain until Max subpoenaed the Internet protocol addresses from the blog's hosting site. She had called Max before leaving for the Upper East Side, and he was working on it at that very minute. But Ellie knew what she knew, even without the records. The timing revealed by Julia's Internet history was good enough evidence for now.

"That doesn't mean Julia wrote it," Adrienne protested. "Anyone could have used her laptop."

"True, the author wasn't necessarily Julia, but not just *anyone* would have access to her computer. It stands to reason that Julia had something to do with that original post, and someone else has continued making similar threats since she died. Maybe a friend of hers?"

"I know where you're going with this. Absolutely not. Ramona would never. We're very close. You just said she was the one to call you, for goodness' sake."

Once they obtained the IP addresses linked to the other posts, they'd know for certain whether Ramona could have been involved, but Ellie shared Adrienne's assumption that the girl wouldn't have called them if she'd been the one responsible.

"You said yourself that Julia and Ramona were extremely close. We've seen cases where teenagers lash out at their friends' parents, without the victims' own kids even knowing about it. You're Ramona's stepmother, if I'm not mistaken?" Ellie was on a roll now, so Rogan was letting her lead the questioning uninterrupted.

Adrienne's eyes drifted upward and she shook her head in frustration. "Unbelievable. I've raised that girl since she was seven years old. She calls me Mom."

"So you've legally adopted her?"

"No. It was never—it wasn't necessary. It isn't necessary. She's my daughter. We have a good relationship. She wouldn't do something like that. We are very open with each other."

"And yet you had a secret in your past. And you had a blog. And she even learned about that blog and that secret. But neither of you spoke to the other about what you knew."

"That doesn't mean—"

"And yet you don't want to believe that Julia would have posted those comments, either, but we're telling you—she did."

She took a deep breath before answering. "Julia was a wonderful and generous girl, but she was also reckless. She had a darkness within her."

"Dark enough to post such horrible threats on your website?"

"I don't know what to think. In a way, it would be nice to know that whoever is writing those comments isn't actually dangerous. But I have a really hard time believing Julia would do this."

"You don't seem all that troubled by either prospect. We've seen the comments posted on your site." *He should have choked you harder.* That was from Monday morning. Then Monday afternoon: *You were a good lay. Wonder what you're like now. Is that ass still tight? I might have to find out.* Monday evening: *I will show you damage.* This morning: *I'm still here. I touch myself when I read your words. I'm thinking about you.* Ellie had worked her share of stalker cases but couldn't imagine what it must have been like for a rape survivor to find those words waiting for her when she turned on her computer.

"I've spent a long time getting past the things that happened to me when I was younger. Writing about it has been the best form of healing, after all of these years. I put it all out on the table—maybe not with Ramona, because, however misguided this may seem, I want to preserve her innocence. But on a page, in words, I'm laying it all out there. And I've resolved not to let some idiot with a keyboard and the shelter of the Internet get to me. All I can tell you is that I would bet my life that my daughter had nothing to do with those vile comments. And I'm nearly as sure that empty threats on my silly website have absolutely no relation to whatever happened to Julia Whitmire. You can't seriously think *I* did something to her? I was at a fundraising dinner for breast cancer research out in Sag Harbor that night, if you need to check on my whereabouts."

"I wasn't accusing you of anything, Mrs. Langston. And I'm sorry if it sounded like I was questioning your relationship with Ramona. But for now, we're treating Julia's death as a homicide. And when we find out that a homicide victim was holding on to a secret, that secret often sends us down the road to a killer."

"It makes me very sad to say this, Detective, but my guess is that you'll find that Julia was carrying around more than one secret."

CHAPTER
TWENTY-FIVE

Nelson the doorman had just finished putting an elderly woman
and her pocketbook-size dachshund into a cab.

"You were right, Nelson. The Langstons seem like a very nice
family."

He smiled politely. "Have a nice day, ma'am."

"Ramona seems to get along with Mrs. Langston?" Unless Julia
Whitmire had a reason of her own to threaten Adrienne, the most obvious explanation was that she was doing it on Ramona's behalf, and that
someone else was now continuing the pattern. "I'm sure at that age it
must be typical for a teenaged girl to fight with her parents."

"I just watch the door."

Outside on Park Avenue, Rogan shook his head. "Seriously? You
thought he was suddenly going to tell you all he knows? Like, some
magic doorman interrogation code, where all you have to do is ask
three times?"

She was too busy reading a text on her phone to bother with a
comeback. "It's from Max. He's working on the subpoena for Social
Circle."

"Good. Maybe the IP addresses will tell us something."

"In the meantime, was it just me, or is that woman in serious
denial about those threats? She's trying to convince herself they're

only words, but I could tell that part of her was terrified. She's working so hard not to be scared that she refused to focus on whether
Julia might have had some motive for posting a comment like that
on her blog."

"You're not thinking of her for the perp, are you?"

"No, I don't get that vibe. Plus, she said she was at a party in the
Hamptons Sunday night. Easy enough to check that out. Add it to
the to-do list."

"Maybe she honestly doesn't know," Rogan said. "If she and Julia
had some kind of beef, presumably she'd just tell us, especially if
she's got a rock-solid alibi."

"Unless the beef somehow involved Ramona. She seems pretty
protective over that girl. If Julia was lashing out at Adrienne on
behalf of her friend, Adrienne might not want to admit there's a rift
in her perfect stepmother-stepdaughter relationship."

"So let's go talk to Little Miss Truant again."

Ramona was waiting, as she had promised, on a park bench next to
the playground by the Metropolitan Museum of Art. She was fiddling with her iPod but stood up and pulled out her earbuds when
she spotted them walking toward her.

The words started tumbling from her mouth before they had a
chance to speak. "Did you talk to her? Does she know who's threatening her? Are you going to be able to find out who's doing this?"

Ellie pointed to the bench, and Ramona returned to her seat.
"Slow down for a second, okay? So, we talked last night about the
importance of your being extremely honest with us about Julia."

"Of course."

"We need to know: Did Julia have a grudge against your stepmother?"

The girl's mouth moved but nothing came out. She looked like a
beautiful goth puppet. "My mom?"

"Yes."

"Why would you even ask that?"

Ellie was starting to wonder herself. First-year cops learned the maxim of Occam's razor: the simplest explanation was also the most likely. When you're in Kentucky and hear hooves, think horses, not zebras. Here they had a dead high school girl in the bathtub and an Upper East Side housewife receiving online threats. Because Julia had posted the first threat, they'd automatically concluded the two events were related. Made sense. But maybe the threats were just one more indication that Julia Whitmire was, as Ramona had put it, the fucked-up head case who killed herself, while some mean-girl friend of hers was continuing to wreak havoc against Adrienne now that Julia was gone.

Rogan was the one who broke the news. "When you called us about your mother's blog, we were completing a search of Julia's computer to see if we could get a better idea of the circumstances that might have led to her death. Those offensive comments on your stepmom's blog? Well, it turns out that Julia's laptop was used to post one of them the night before she died."

"That's impossible. She didn't even know about my mother's blog. I just found it today."

"You may not have been aware of it, but Julia apparently was. We searched her computer."

"You can't know that she's the one who posted it, though, right? It just means it came from her laptop. So whoever's still posting those threats against my mom somehow knew Julia?"

"That's right," Ellie said. "We're trying to figure out who that might be."

"I have no idea. It doesn't even seem possible."

"This might be hard to talk about, but if there's a simple explanation for this, we need to know about it. Ramona, is there *any* chance that maybe you were having some kind of tension with your stepmother? If Julia was aware of a fight between the two of you and stumbled upon the website—"

"No. No way. I mean, I know you keep saying she's my step-mother, but I call her Mom. I always have. And, I love my dad and everything, but you met him. He's—well, he's, like, you know, lucky to have found her. And so was I. That's why I was so freaked out when I saw those comments. We're, like, really *close*. I couldn't believe she didn't tell me. No way would Julia do something like that to her."

Ellie still didn't know what to think about the possible connection between Julia's death and the comments on Adrienne Langston's blog, but she was convinced that, if there was a connection, Ramona certainly didn't know about it.

CHAPTER
TWENTY-SIX

Katherine Whitmire threw yet another dress on Julia's bed. The pile of clothing was now three garments wide and at least ten deep, its own weight threatening to pull it from the comforter to the floor, a heap of imported fabric, designer labels, and cedar hangers. Never mind, she would stand here all day building a wardrobe tower if she had to. You only dressed your daughter for her coffin once.

She reached for another dress at the back of the closet. This one wasn't a candidate for the burial outfit, but Katherine remembered buying it three years earlier.

Bill had promised to take Julia and Ramona backstage to a Justin Timberlake concert. Not the dime-a-dozen backstage passes, he had boasted. The *real* passes, for insiders. The ones that put you right next to the artist—not just for a quickie photograph and a shuffle to the nearest exit, but for however long the after party lasted.

It had been a big deal for the girls. Sure, Julia and Billy were both used to being carted around to industry events with Bill. There were some months when that was their only time with their father.

But the Justin Night, as they'd called it, wasn't about Julia being in tow just so Bill could multitask parenthood with work. Justin

Night was Bill going somewhere he'd never otherwise choose to go, just because it meant something to his daughter. On Justin Night, Bill's professional identity—instead of taking him away from his family—would actually work to Julia's advantage for once.

The day had started well enough. It was summer. Katherine had gone back to the city in the car with the kids in the morning. Bill was scheduled to meet one of the long-term artists on his label for a casual lunch at Cyril's, then planned to take a helicopter in time for the concert.

She started worrying when she hadn't heard from him by five o'clock but tried to hide her concern from the girls as they practiced their dance moves to "SexyBack" in the foyer. She started calling Bill's cell phone at six. By seven, the girls were worried they wouldn't have time to buy T-shirts from the stadium vendors before the opening act started. And by nine, Julia had locked herself in the bathroom to cry. They all knew he wasn't coming.

Bill had all his excuses prepared when he finally showed up at eleven, wearing a fresh shirt and still smelling of soap. That drama-king of a singer-songwriter had shown up drunk at lunch and continued to get drunker as they dined. He had to drive him out to Montauk to make sure he made it home in one piece. Then the man's latest wife had bent his ear about the crappy sales of his last album. Then he missed the last helicopter.

None of it explained why he hadn't answered his phone. None of it explained why he'd broken his daughter's heart.

But as angry as the Whitmire girls had been that night, Bill had somehow managed to get himself back in their good graces the following day. He woke them both at eight a.m., declaring it Julia Day—"Trust me," he'd said, "Julia Day kicks Justin Night's skinny white ass."

The driver was already at the curb, waiting to take them to breakfast at Norma's, where the kitchen had Julia's favorite banana-macadamia flapjacks all ready to go. Bill even let thirteen-year-old Julia have a mimosa, though when Katherine balked, he assured her the drink was heavily orange-juiced.

From there it was on to Bliss Spa, where even Bill participated in the mani-pedi-facial-mudbath combo. When Julia laughed at the sight of her father sticking out his pink tongue from a mask of green clay, it was a childlike belly giggle like Katherine had not heard from her daughter since grade school.

And then the crowning moment of Julia Day had come with this dress. This crazy, beaded, one-shoulder-strapped, hot-pink monstrosity.

Bill had led Julia through the Nina Ricci department at Barneys, covering her eyes with his palms.

"Bill, what did you do?" Katherine had asked. "Where are we going?"

As futile as it was, Katherine did try not to spoil the children. When it came to clothing, it's not like Julia was shopping at the Gap, but Katherine had so far managed to keep her *Vogue*-obsessed little girl away from the adults-only couture that she so desperately craved.

Katherine remembered the squinty-eyed stares of her annoyed fellow shoppers when Bill had finally uncovered Julia's eyes. The girl screamed. Literally screamed, that high-pitch squeal that only young girls and certain large birds are capable of making.

"Daddy! How did you know?"

How, indeed, had he known? The previous night—while Julia had been completing another round of bawling in the bathroom, and Katherine had been slamming cabinets in the kitchen—multi-Grammy-winning producer Bill Whitmire had pored through the stacks of fashion magazines on his daughter's nightstand, noting the dogeared pages, searching for the most extravagant, expensive, completely over-the-top magnet of his daughter's attention. His wife had no idea Bill even knew that Julia liked those magazines. Or where she kept them. Or had a habit of folding corners on the pages that best captured the look she so longed to have, and which her mother would not allow.

Julia had emerged from that dressing room like a future princess, ready for the offical engagement announcement.

"You look beautiful, Baby J."

"Amazing, Julia. But, Bill." Oh, how Julia's face had fallen with just those two words from Katherine. But, Bill. "Where is she going to wear something like that?"

"I was thinking she'd fit right in at the VMAs next month. I think Justin might even like it."

Julia's eyes opened to the size of saucers. To a thirteen-year-old girl, the MTV Video Music Awards were like the Super Bowl.

"I made some calls this morning. We'll be sitting right next to him. What do the Whitmire ladies think of that? It'll be all three of us together." He pushed Katherine's hair aside and planted a soft kiss on the side of her neck.

"Do I get a five-thousand-dollar dress, too?"

"Whatever you want, my love."

Katherine had stopped telling those stories to her friends a long time ago, because she knew how they sounded. But at the time, days like that with Bill made her so incredibly happy, that all of the wrongs he was trying to make up for somehow fell away.

Even now, she found herself smiling as she held that dress out in front of her. She was surprised Julia had hung on to it. The dress had worn out its fashionability long ago, and Katherine was pretty sure it wouldn't have even fit Julia after that summer, when her chest had suddenly sprouted another cup size.

Julia must have remembered that day at Barneys, too. She must have kept this ridiculous dress because of that memory. Now it was just another item of clothing to go in the charity stack. Onto the pile it went.

Money. It had taken Katherine years to adjust to having *this* much money. But eventually she'd come around to Bill's view that money might not buy you happiness, but it sure could solve your problems. Busy? Hire an assistant. Too much traffic to the Hamptons? Get the helicopter. Sick of the city? Build your own recording studio. Stand up your daughter? Buy her a dress.

It wasn't surprising, then, that the idea of hiring a private in-vestigator had come to Bill last night. And given that her husband gnawed at an idea like a dog with a bone, it wasn't surprising that he had already made the necessary calls about the big reward before she'd managed to drag herself from bed that morning.

As she understood it, they had a designated number for the tip line. Bill's PI firm would handle the incoming calls. The head guy— Earl Gundley—was a retired cop, with contacts in the NYPD, but who worked solely for them. Bill had his publicity people put out the press release.

She pulled another dress from the closet. This one was a bone-colored, cotton-lace sheath by Stella McCartney. This would be a nice choice. Simple. Timeless.

She hung the dress on a hook inside the closet door. She'd ask Billy to take it to the funeral home in the morning. He was looking for ways to be helpful, and Katherine had seen more than enough of that place when she'd chosen the casket this morning.

She barely heard the sound of the doorbell above the music blaring from Bill's office. She heard the stereo volume drop, followed by muted voices three floors below. Then she heard Bill's voice in the intercom he never used. "Katherine, I think you need to come down."

"What is it, Bill? I'm busy up here."

"I know, but I think you'll want to hear this too. The press release worked. There are two people here who say they know what happened to J."

CHAPTER TWENTY-SEVEN

But my neighbor is taking me to Small Claims Court. He claims that Peanut scratched up his front door, but Peanut is innocent. Who is going to represent me? Who is going to represent *Peanut?*"

"I'm sorry, sir, but the district attorney's office does not defend either individuals or dogs in private, civil matters. Wait. What's that in your bag? Is that Peanut? You can't be having a dog in here, sir."

The receptionist on the fifteenth floor of the courthouse clearly had her hands full. She waved Ellie and Rogan back to Max's office.

"Hey, you." He stood to give her a kiss, but she turned her cheek. Even if only in front of Rogan, it seemed inappropriate to share PDA with an assistant district attorney in his office.

Rogan apparently noticed the exchange. "Damn, Hatcher. You're cold."

Max offered Rogan a handshake. "About time someone took my side. Turns out it's your lucky day, guys. Social Circle was pretty cooperative, as far as these Web companies go. We weren't gonna get the IP addresses for every comment posted without a fight, but we settled on the ones that were obviously threatening."

All Rogan had to hear was the word *fight*, followed by *settled*, to protest. "That's some bullshit—"

So much for the male bonding. "Rogan, do you currently know *anything* about the origin of the other threats on the website? And do you actually *need* information about the other comments? Because, you know, if tracking down the identity of the Illinois housewife who posted '*You go, girl*' three weeks ago is essential to the investigation, then by all means, I'll drag Social Circle into court."

Rogan brushed a nonexistent piece of lint from his suit lapel and looked directly at Ellie. "I do believe someone has picked up on your tone."

Ellie flashed a proud smile. "I think that means we'll take what we can get for now."

"That's what I figured. Here's the deal: the blog's been up for about seven months. Pretty typical traffic initially for an amateur blog—meaning, zilch. But she kept at it, and apparently people started to find her and to comment. Other bloggers started to cross-link to her site. That all leads more people to the blog. Anyway, she was up to more than ten thousand hits after five months. Twenty thousand as of last week."

Ellie couldn't imagine anyone wanting to read someone else's self-analysis. "Seriously? Reading all that therapy-lite garbage made my head hurt."

"But get this: since that first threat was posted Saturday night, traffic has skyrocketed. Yesterday, she had seventy thousand hits. The commenters talk more about the threats than her actual posts."

"Adrienne gave us some mumbo jumbo about wanting her readers to see how people try to silence survivors. She never mentioned it had also been good for business."

"Very good, in fact. But now let's get down to brass tacks. *Where* did these posts come from? We already suspected that the post on Saturday night came from Julia's laptop. Sure enough, the IP info for that comment comes back to her computer, just as we expected."

"And the rest?" Ellie asked.

"That's where things get pretty interesting. The other comments all originated from Manhattan, but not from Julia's computer. We've got a couple that came from Equinox gym by Union Square. Another gym on the Upper West Side. Apple Store in the Meatpacking District. Whoever's doing this hides their tracks pretty well."

Rogan sighed. "We can take the times of the posts at each place and see if we get lucky with video."

"But to what end?" Ellie asked. "We still don't even know that Julia Whitmire was murdered, and we certainly don't know there's any connection between her death and these comments. After getting a feel for the kinds of kids who go to Casden, I wouldn't be surprised if one of those brats somehow found out about Adrienne's website and decided to screw with their friend's mom. Julia might not have even known that someone used her computer."

Rogan's phone buzzed at his waist. He held up a finger and excused himself to the hallway.

Ellie plopped down in Max's chair and stretched her legs out. "Seriously, Max, you should've seen this Casden School." Like her, Max was strictly a public school kid. "Creepy headmaster more concerned with secrecy than education. Spoiled sociopaths drugged up by parents too busy to notice their kids are little monsters."

"Tell me how you really feel."

"Trust me, it's worse than I can even make it sound. After a day on the Upper East Side, even Bill Whitmire doesn't look so bad. Thank God I'll never have to deal with any of that stuff."

"Public schools for the next generation, too, huh?"

"More like the miracle of birth control."

"Ah, for now, but what about when that biological clock starts ticking?"

"For now and forever. Or I guess until menopause. Then it's hot flashes, a hairy upper lip, and—oh yeah—still no kids."

"That's not funny, Ellie."

"I'm not trying to be funny. Okay, maybe a little, with the hair thing, but—"

"But someday—"

"No. No someday. No clock. Clock never ticked, never will tick." She heard Rogan's voice in the hallway, and then lowered her own. "I mean, you *have* met me, right?"

Max let out a huff. "Are you kidding me with this?"

"Of course not. You knew that."

"Um, I think that's the kind of thing I would have noticed. We've been dating for a year."

"Plus two and a half weeks," she corrected. She remembered the timing of their first date, because one night later she killed a man. She and Max had celebrated their one-year anniversary by going back to the same restaurant of that first meal.

"And this is how you tell me you're not interested in children? When you're venting about yet another run-in you've had with people you've deemed not quite as morally good as you? Really nice, Ellie."

"Now who's the one not being so nice?"

"Isn't this the kind of thing normal people work out together? Don't normal people talk about these things and negotiate?"

She swiveled in his chair, fiddling with the documents from Social Circle. "Fine, then, I'm not normal, because, as far as I'm concerned, there's nothing to negotiate. It's not like there's a split of opinion about one kid or three, like we'd meet in the middle at two or something. I can't have half a baby. It's a totally different life, and one I'm not at all interested in."

"You could have told me that."

"And you could have told me you were all into the idea of babies and diapers and playdates and the exhaustion of having a whole other human being need every ounce of your energy every single day. I just assumed we were on the same page on this."

"Well, we're not."

She heard Rogan saying goodbye to whoever was on the phone. "Can we please talk about this later?" she said.

Max nodded, but in that moment it was clear something had shifted. Since their very first conversation, she had wanted to see only what they shared: commitment to the job, dark humor, and a certain matter-of-factness about life. She had been so proud of herself that, for once, she was in a relationship in which she emphasized only those attributes she should cherish.

But now, with this one grudging nod, an agreement to postpone this conversation, Max was focusing on what separated them—him, so close to his devoted and adorable parents; her, with the dead dad and screwed-up mom. He was looking at her and feeling the yawning absence of the next Donovan generation.

She reached for his hand, but then Rogan walked in, slamming the door shut behind him. "Tracking down our cyber-stalker is going to have to wait."

"What's up?" she asked.

"So we knew a fat reward offer from Julia's parents would bring out the crazies?"

She looked at her watch. "Don't tell me we're already being inundated."

"I wouldn't say inundated. Not yet, at least. But I just got a call from Tucker." Their lieutenant didn't make a habit of tracking them down when they were out in the field. "Bill Whitmire called the commissioner himself. He's got a witness at their house."

"Who?"

"No clue, but he told the commissioner she's already getting squirrely. The Lou said we better get there before she bails, unless we want the wrath of the Whitmires crashing down on us."

"So the witness is there right now?"

"Yes, *now*. Damn," he said, looking at Max. "I swear, sometimes she intentionally doesn't listen to anything she doesn't want to hear."

Max didn't meet Ellie's eye as she walked out the door.

CHAPTER TWENTY-EIGHT

Bill Whitmire was smoking a cigarette on the front steps of his townhouse. "Detectives, thank you for coming."

"I didn't get the impression we had much choice in the matter." It was the kind of comment she had learned by now not to make, but her mind was still back in Max's office, and she'd had about enough of these people. She'd grown up collecting albums by bands this man had made. But every piece of evidence showed that Whitmire was a crappy father, and now he was trying to make up for it by using his influence to control their investigation. "Where is this alleged witness?"

"There are two, actually. Right inside." He used the handrail to help him stand. "My wife tried to tell you from the very beginning this wasn't self-inflicted—"

"And we *are* treating this case as a homicide, Mr. Whitmire." *Against my best instincts*, she wanted to add. "We've been following all relevant leads. In fact, we've found some information on your daughter's computer that we'd like to talk to you about."

"Okay, that's fine. But talk to these two people first. My wife told you she thought it had something to do with those strange kids she found here with Julia. And now it turns out she's right."

"You already *interviewed* these witnesses?" she asked. "We assumed you were simply collecting information from the tip line to pass on to us. Even *that* goes far beyond the typical involvement of private parties in a criminal investigation."

"My intention was to do this the right way." The front door cracked open and Katherine Whitmire stuck her head out, but her husband didn't bother to pause. "We hired Earl Gundley's firm. He served his full twenty-two years of service. The plan was for him to handle it all just like he would have as a cop, but with full-time attention to only one case. But then these two showed up, right at our doorstep, ready to talk."

"Then you should have sent them directly to the precinct," Rogan said.

"I told you it was a bad idea, Bill." The flat, quiet voice did not belong to the same bossy woman who had met them at the door yesterday morning. The spark was gone. Ellie suspected a pharmaceutical influence.

Bill Whitmire had enough energy for both of them. "Did you really expect us to wait? We didn't want to lose them. We had to act fast. Even after they talked to us, it was hard enough to convince them to cooperate with the police. We had to promise to give them ten thousand dollars of the reward money now, just to get them to stay until your arrival."

Terrific. Now it looked like straight-out bribery.

Rogan jumped in before she raised the confrontation level even further. "Look, what's done is done. Let's hear what they have to say, and we'll take it from there."

"I can live with that." Whitmire held the front door open, then followed them into the foyer. "They say they know who killed our daughter. They say it was some girl who tells everyone she's a boy. She goes by the name of Casey. Casey Heinz."

Jimmy Grisco took another look at the schedule he'd picked up at the Buffalo Greyhound station.

Packing was easy enough. His uncle'd thrown him out two weeks earlier. Grisco didn't mind. He'd already stayed two weeks longer than the month he'd initially been promised.

Jimmy lugged the same duffel bag out of this shithole that he'd carried into it, holding all the same familiar clothes, plus the Adidas shoe box containing all the old letters.

He took one last look around the motel room before shutting the door behind him. There was an 11 p.m. bus leaving that night. He'd be at the Port Authority Bus Terminal by 6:30 the next morning.

PART III

CASEY

CHAPTER
TWENTY-NINE

The boy and girl waiting for them in the Whitmire living room looked like forgotten children.

The girl's long, sandy, blond hair had matted into unkempt dreadlocks. Her already ruddy skin was further marred by acne. Ellie couldn't even tell what the male sitting next to the girl actually looked like beneath all the self-imposed ugliness. All she saw above his long, pointy beard were the nickel-size discs stretching his earlobes like plates, a silver bar piercing the cartilage of his nose, and a tattoo of a green bar code on his left cheek. Maybe she was just too old, or midwestern, but she'd never understand how these kids who couldn't afford food or a roof over their heads always seemed to have enough dough for another tat.

Bill Whitmire was about to join his wife on a narrow upholstered banquette in the corner of the living room, but Ellie stopped him.

"I think under the circumstances we'll stick to the convention of speaking to these two alone, if it's all the same to you, sir." It was bad enough that the couple had gotten to the kids before the police. They didn't need to exacerbate the appearance of special treatment by allowing Julia's parents to sit in on a witness interview.

The Whitmires vanished up the townhouse's winding staircase.

If they could have politely taken their pristine furniture with them, they surely would have done so. The kids smelled as if they hadn't bathed in days, maybe weeks.

Ellie chose the farthest seat from them, the same corner bench the Whitmires had just vacated. Rogan remained standing at the edge of the foyer, but wasted no time getting down to business.

"How about we start with names."

The two kids just looked at each other.

"All right," Rogan said, pretending to head for the stairs. "I'm sure we can have the DA persuade the Whitmires not to give one penny to you guys."

The boy spoke up first. "Brandon. And Vonda."

"For ten grand, I think we'll need last names, guys."

"Sykes. Brandon Sykes." Brandon made sure to add enough sullenness to his tone to register his resentment.

"And how about you, Vonda?"

She sat there with crossed arms. These two were real cheerleader types.

"It's Vonda Smith. Scout's honor." She held up three fingers, which struck Ellie as somehow different from whatever she'd done as a childhood pledge, but she wasn't about to start an argument.

Vonda and Brandon. The two kids Casey mentioned when Ellie asked him about that day Katherine Whitmire came home to find them at the townhouse with Julia.

"The Whitmires say you have information about their daughter's death," Rogan said. "The medical examiner's preliminary findings indicate suicide."

"That's not what we hear," Vonda said.

"That's the funny thing about gossip," Rogan said. "It's not always reliable, especially when it's swirling around the homeless kid community with the promise of a hundred grand coming down the pike."

"It's not gossip." Brandon's voice jumped an octave and echoed in the high-ceilinged room. The shift from withdrawn to angry was immediate. "Casey told us what happened."

"That's Casey Heinz?" Rogan clarified.

"Yeah. You know he's not a boy, right? She just pretends she is. Total fucking freak."

This, from Tattoo Face. Ellie shook her head. "Casey said you guys were his friends. In fact, he stuck up for you when I told him that Julia's mom was sure you guys had something to do with her death."

"He probably didn't want to be on our bad side. He knows we know he did it. He told us all about it."

"Told you what?" Ellie asked.

"That he killed Julia."

"And when did he supposedly say this?"

"Last night," the boy said, "at the park. We saw him at the park."

"Casey said they got into a fight about Ramona and he just snapped," Vonda said. "Then he started crying like the girl he is, saying he wished he hadn't done it."

"If someone killed Julia, they went to great lengths to make it look like a suicide. I don't think it *just happened*." Ellie was careful not to reveal any details about the way Julia died or the appearance at the scene, but she wanted them to know that she and Rogan—unlike the Whitmires—weren't going to swallow down every word they said. "How exactly did Casey say the killing happened?"

"Casey. Didn't. Say." Brandon mimicked sign language with his words. They'd obviously expected this to be easier. "It's like he regretted saying anything to us, and so he stopped talking about it. We asked him more about what happened, but he just kept bawling like a little bitch baby."

"And why would he and Julia have a fight about Ramona?"

"Because Casey's totally obsessed with Ramona," Vonda said. "He thinks Ramona's eventually going to love him back, like he's a real dude or something. It's pathetic, but that's the truth. You should see the way he looks at her. Then you'd know what we mean."

Ellie recalled the way Casey had talked about Ramona Langston, like she was an angel.

"If you ask me," Brandon said, "that fight probably had something to do with him hooking up with Julia."

"You just said Casey's obsessed with Ramona," Rogan said. "Now you're claiming he was with Julia?"

"Yeah, man. He's totally into Ramona, but she's, like, platonic or whatever, like Casey's a girlfriend or something. But Julia, she'd try anything once, you know? Maybe she was gonna tell Ramona about it. Blow Casey's chances forever."

If Casey did have a physical relationship with Julia, then he had lied to her and Rogan. She didn't want to believe Casey had actually confessed to these kids, but they also couldn't ignore that kind of lie.

She continued to press. "And so after Casey told you he killed a girl, you did nothing until you heard about this reward?"

"Casey's our friend, okay?" he said.

"A friend that you just referred to as a, quote, total fucking freak."

The kid looked down at his hands and scraped some dirt from beneath his nails. "I feel bad. But, yeah, we could use the money."

"It doesn't mean we're lying," Vonda added.

"Then you won't mind if we talk to you separately." Ellie noticed the two exchange glances as Vonda followed Rogan into an office adjoining the sitting room.

Once she and Brandon were alone, she switched gears. Every instinct told her these kids were only here for the money, but unless one of them admitted they were lying, Julia's parents were going to believe what they wanted to believe. Maybe if she could connect with this kid, she'd have a better shot at getting him to come clean.

"Where are you from?"

"Roseburg, Oregon. I started out in Portland. Some girl told me it was better here, so I took a bus eight months ago."

"How'd you get the money?"

"I told some church I was heading to New York to go live with my parents. They handed me a ticket, and now, here I am."

"Is it better?"

"Nope. Guess it would be if I was living in a place like this. But, nope. The panhandling's better, but, you know, the cops mess with us more. And winter was colder than shit."

Ellie resisted the temptation to explain that shit wasn't especially cold.

"What was so bad about Roseburg?"

"Nothing, until my stepdad went medieval on me for cutting class."

"Just how medieval?"

"Broke my left arm pretty good."

"Seems like an overreaction."

"Yeah, well, when a school social worker did a little unannounced pop-in on a Wednesday morning while he was cooking meth in the garage—my stepdad didn't seem to think it was an overreaction."

"And your mom?"

"Doesn't matter. She got sick of dealing with me a long time ago. I'm now what you call *emancipated*. That means I'm legally responsible for myself."

"That must have been hard."

"Whatever. They don't require a license for parents. Did Casey tell you about his family? They sent him to some brainwashing camp where a supposed counselor tried to rape him back into being a girl."

"You say Casey's a freak but I notice you refer to him as *him*, not *her*." Ellie had heard enough about gender identity to correct Rogan's initial use of feminine pronouns, but she had to admit, the preferred terminology did require conscious effort. "I know what you're doing. You actually accept Casey at heart, but you want to make him sound troubled enough to do something like kill Julia."

"And I know what *you're* doing. I don't need your friendship."

"And I don't need two selfish kids who would lie to churches for bus money taking advantage of these grieving parents. This isn't a joke, Brandon. You may not have given a shit about a rich girl like Julia, but she's dead. You may want us to believe that Casey killed her, but I could just as easily tell her parents up there that you and Vonda are making up this story to cover your own asses."

"Cover our asses for what?"

"For killing their daughter."

Beneath the tattoos and piercings, the color dropped from his face. "But—that—no, no way, lady. I *knew* we should've bailed. I *knew* the cops wouldn't listen to us."

"Tell me the truth and I'll listen plenty."

His moment of panic passed. The next time he spoke, the stammer was gone. "Point the finger at us all you want, but we're not the ones who were messing around with Julia. Or have a key to this place."

"What are you talking about?"

"Casey may not have given us a play-by-play of what he did to Julia, but we are telling you the truth. You're right. He is my friend. And, yeah, me and Vonda are only here because of the money. But Casey said he killed Julia. And he—not us—could have gotten in here to do it. Julia gave him a key to this place when they hooked up. Why don't you ask him about that?"

Ellie was starting to worry about the growing contradictions between Brandon's statements and the impression Casey had created. First the hookup with Julia. Now a key. If Casey had access to the townhouse, he had access to Julia. And her computer. He could also be the one posting the threats on Adrienne's blog.

"What did Casey think about Ramona's family?"

Brandon chuckled. "You mean his future in-laws?"

"Casey loves Ramona that much, huh?"

"Totally. He'd fucking *die* for that girl, you know? But her parents? He thought they were spoiled pricks."

"Why was that?"

"Because they are."

"You know them?"

"The type. Sure." He looked around his current, opulent surroundings as if the decor explained his point.

"Did he ever say anything specific about her parents?"

"Not really. Just that he'd gone over there once and could tell they were eyeballing him. You know, like something wasn't right."

She still didn't believe Casey confessed a murder to these two kids, but parts of Brandon's story had the ring of truth to them. She realized now that her compassion for Casey's personal situation had caused her to give him too quick a pass. She should have done a more thorough interview while she'd had him at the park.

Brandon stared at his crossed feet. When he looked up, Ellie saw a surprising softness in his expression. "Like I said, Casey's my friend." Ellie forced herself to remember he was only sixteen years old and had lived a young life so horrible that his current existence—alone on the streets of New York City—was an improvement.

"So when do we get our money?"

And, just like that, the moment of sympathy passed.

CHAPTER THIRTY

Ellie and Rogan found Katherine Whitmire in the den on the second floor. Like the sitting room downstairs, this space was filled with stuffy, hard-edged furniture and ornate rugs. It had neither a television nor a bed, making it useless as far as Ellie was concerned.

Katherine immediately rose from her chair as Ellie and Rogan approached. Down the hall, they spotted her husband, Bill, on his BlackBerry in the kitchen. It struck Ellie as a strange moment for the two of them to be apart. If the appearance in their home of two teenagers claiming to know the identity of their daughter's killer was not enough to bring the pair together, Ellie wondered whether the two were ever in the same room.

They all convened in the kitchen. "Have you put out a warrant for this Casey Heinz girl?"

She did not have the time to explain to a record producer the process that was required for obtaining an arrest warrant.

"We're going to check out Heinz right now," Rogan said. She noticed that her partner omitted the fact that they'd already spoken to Casey the previous night. "I'd suggest that you hold off on giving those two scroungers down there any money for now."

"But Bill told them—"

Rogan shook his head. "Trust me. You give those kids ten grand, and they'll be in Seattle by tomorrow night. Slip them a couple hundred bucks and tell them it'll take time to pull the rest together? They're not going anywhere."

Bill Whitmire was pacing back and forth in the aisle between his kitchen island and cabinets. "Can't you arrest them to make certain we don't lose them?"

Ellie shook her head. "They haven't done anything illegal."

"They waited until a reward was announced to tell anyone they knew about a murderer!"

"I'm afraid the law doesn't require people to come forward with knowledge about illegal activity, Mr. Whitmire."

"But that's ridicu—"

"Otherwise, you'd be required to call the police every time someone lit a joint in your recording studio. You see?"

"It's not the same—"

"I'm just explaining why we can't take these two into custody."

"Aren't they runaways?"

"Vonda is of age, and Brandon claims to be legally emancipated, in which case he's also considered an adult."

"But what about, what's it called? Material witnesses, or something?"

"That's only if they're uncooperative. Like my partner, I'm quite sure they'll stay exactly where we need to find them unless you suddenly give them enough money to leave." She was getting sick of fielding Bill Whitmire's legal questions. This wasn't a citizen training academy. "We've had some other leads in the case as well. We need to ask you about your daughter's relationship with Adrienne Langston."

Bill Whitmire's expression was completely blank. It was his wife who spoke up. "You know who she is, Bill. Ramona's stepmother. You mention how *youthful* and *natural* she is every time you see her." Her voice became slightly less bitter when she returned her attention to Ellie. "Julia was very fond of Adrienne. Always saying what a wonderful mother she was. The underlying message wasn't lost on me," she added sadly.

Now that Bill understood the question, he was not about to wait for answers. "This is ridiculous. You should be looking for Casey Heinz."

"And we will, soon enough," Ellie said. "But we'll be better prepared to question any suspect if we fully explore all the other information available to us." She had just gotten to a description of Adrienne's blog when Katherine interrupted.

"So Adrienne's big writing deal is just a blog?"

"I'm not sure what you mean."

"A couple of weeks ago, Lanie Marks told me Adrienne had some big book deal. Lanie works at *New York* magazine. She heard that Adrienne had sold a memoir to the editor in chief at Waterton Press. Everyone assumed it would be one of these Upper East Side tell-alls. The only question was whether Adrienne would be naming names. Shows what gossip will get you. By the time some pathetic blog hits the whispers of Madison Avenue, it's become a healthy six-figure book deal."

Ellie wondered whether there was any hope for the woman. Whoever she was two days ago, Katherine was now a person who took pleasure in the fact that a woman she'd known for the better part of a decade—a woman who had come from humble means and had loved a stepchild as her own, a woman who had treated *Katherine's* daughter as her own—had written as a mere blogger, not as a soon-to-be-published author. This woman was being eaten away, not just by grief, but by jealousy now as well.

She quickly summarized the evidence they had to show that Julia's laptop was used to post one of several threats on the blog. "Did Julia have any reason to dislike her friend's mother?"

Bill was sighing impatiently, but his wife simply shook her head. "That just doesn't make any sense. I've never heard her say anything bad about Adrienne."

"What about keys to this townhouse? To your knowledge, did Julia have extra keys she gave to friends?"

Another blank stare from Bill Whitmire. He obviously had no idea what his daughter's day-to-day life had entailed.

Katherine, however, walked to a narrow drawer next to the refrigerator, pulled out a red leather keychain, and continued to rum-
mage through the drawer's contents. "A copy is missing. We keep
two here. The other's got a—um—what is it called? A unicorn. It's
on a silver unicorn keychain. I know it was here last Thanksgiving
because I gave it to Billy's girlfriend for the weekend, but now it's
gone. Why?" Katherine's tone was panicked. "Did someone take
keys to our home? Do I need to change the locks?"

Ellie used her best stay-calm voice. "We don't know that for
certain, but, yes, according to these two sources, your daughter
may have shared a key to your townhouse with a friend of hers and
Ramona's."

"One of the homeless kids?" Bill yelled. "Jesus Christ. That is
just like Julia."

Katherine's moxie briefly reemerged as she shot her husband a
sharp look that immediately quieted his outburst. "Like I told you,"
she said calmly, "our daughter was overly generous. I will call a
locksmith, to be safe. And I assure you that my husband and I will
continue to provide any information you require, but now will you
please go find this Casey Heinz person?"

In the car, Ellie and Rogan compared notes about their separate
interviews with Brandon and Vonda.

Their stories lined up perfectly. The location. The time. What
Casey was wearing. The words he'd used. His explanation spilling
out so quickly they could barely follow. An argument with Julia,
somehow related to Ramona. *I snapped*, he'd said. *It just happened*.
More tears. *I wish I could take it back.*

"They're definitely singing the same tune," Rogan said.

"It's a little *too* in sync for me. They both happened to remember
exactly what Casey was wearing? And that he was doing handstands
near the dog run?"

"Sounds like that's what Casey wears and does every day, based
on what we saw. Not really surprising they'd remember it."

"And the same exact phrases?" she said. "Verbatim?"

"Hate to say this, Hatcher, but isn't that what defense attorneys argue all the time after the two of us testify to identical details?"

"We're not two homeless kids trying to get reward money from a famous record producer."

"We've had worse witnesses. Remember Otis Jones?"

Of course Ellie remembered. They'd built an entire murder case around the word of a convicted drug dealer who boasted on the stand about spending the first part of the day in question smoking a blunt while "being bathed" by three crackheads who served as his "harem." Cops didn't get to pick their witnesses.

"Yeah, but we believed Otis Jones because his testimony matched what we knew about the murder. Brandon and Vonda? The only thing their statements match are each other's statements. There's no insider detail."

"Maybe that's because Casey stopped talking before any of the insider detail got out. Isn't that possible?"

"I guess."

"Damn, Hatcher. Those two are lowlifes, but if Casey slept with that girl, had a key to her place, and didn't tell us? We've got to be looking at the kid, right?"

"Obviously."

"So, I'll say it once again: you best open your damn mind."

CHAPTER
THIRTY-ONE

Ellie had seen more than a few homeless shelters. During her years on patrol, she tried to avoid the dispatch calls to shelters the way most cops tried to avoid the domestic beefs. They were dirty, desperate places filled with broken, desperate people. It was as if the physical buildings had somehow absorbed their occupants' collective regrets and hopelessness.

But the Promises Center for Young Adults was not that kind of place. With a new, clean brick façade and a glassed-in atrium at the entrance, the structure felt more like a community center than a homeless shelter—except the receptionist at the front desk had a bright-pink mohawk and a silver chain draping from her right nostril to her ear.

There had been no sign of Casey Heinz at Washington Square Park. Ramona's cell phone had gone directly to voice mail. That made Promises the next step in the search for their only person of interest in the death of Julia Whitmire. The pink mohawk woman hadn't seen Casey that day but assured them she'd locate the center's director for them right away.

Two minutes later, a woman with jet-black, blade-straight hair and flawless alabaster skin greeted them. There was an old-fashioned formality to her tailored suit and black stockings, but she opened her arms and flashed a warm smile, as if she'd known them for years. "Detectives, my name is Chung Mei Ri. Welcome to Promises. I understand you are looking for Casey?"

Rogan took the lead on introductions, and then gave the woman an edited explanation for their visit. "We believe Casey has some information relevant to a case we're investigating."

Her smile grew even wider. "Casey is a wonderful person. If he has any information that would assist you, I have no doubt that he will be more than forthcoming. He is smart, too. He'll be one of our success stories. Of that I have no doubt."

"I've seen a lot of shelters, Ms. Ri," Ellie said. "I didn't know there were many successes."

"That's how Promises is different. There are shelters for mothers and their very young children. And there are the adult shelters, which are filled with grown men—usually who are addicted to one thing or another, or mentally ill, or who have given up on life, or vice versa. Promises is for young adults who are still getting started in life, but with rougher beginnings than others. We like to think of ourselves as a kind of belated Head Start. We're leveling the playing field a little bit so these kids can find their legs and make a decent life for themselves."

"And what was Casey's rough beginning?" Ellie asked.

The woman's eyes dropped, but the smile never faltered. "I think it's for Casey to choose whom to share confidences with."

"We know he's transgender, if that's what you mean."

"The preferred terminology is transgender *person*, but very close, Detective. And do you not believe that's reason enough for needing a new beginning?"

"What about Brandon Sykes and Vonda Smith? Are they also finding the new beginnings they need?"

A worried look crossed Ms. Ri's open face.

"I don't hear you predicting further success stories for your center, Ms. Ri."

"Please. Come with me."

They followed her through the shelter, passing a workout room and then a series of small rooms with bunk beds. They ended their journey in a tiny office with just enough space for a desk and two chairs.

"I apologize for the pinch. When we built this center, I thought it best to devote the maximum amount of square footage to the residents."

"You've been here since the beginning?" Rogan asked.

"Yes. We've been open for three years. I was previously the director of Operation Nightwatch." Ellie recognized the name of one of the transient shelters in midtown where people checked in night by night with no promise of a long-term bed. "I saw what happened to our younger clients. They were weaker. More naïve. They had the greatest likelihood of making another kind of life, but they just fell through the cracks. Did you know that half of all runaways have been physically abused at home? That a third will attempt suicide? These are kids who still have a chance in life—without the chronic mental illness and addiction you see in older populations. That's why at Promises we only accept clients aged sixteen to twenty-four."

Ellie shook her head. "There shouldn't be a large enough homeless population in that age group to keep you in business."

"Here's another statistic for you: a third of America's homeless are children. At any given time we have a waiting list with more than fifty names."

Ellie thought about all the medicated kids up at Casden. They had no idea how lucky they were. "You brought us back here when we asked about Brandon Sykes and Vonda Smith."

"I do not like to say negative things about the young people we are trying to help."

"But?"

She placed a hand over her heart. "I have a special place here for Casey. If those two have anything to do with the reasons you are contacting him—well, I worry."

"We got the impression they were all friends."

"Casey tries to be a friend to everyone he meets. Not everyone is as accepting of him as he sometimes so desperately wants to believe. Now, Brandon—I do believe that Brandon has been good to Casey at times. Mostly Casey gets along with the girls here. But the boys? It's a problem. I have to give him his own room because of the gender issues. Brandon, however, has been different. He sticks up for Casey with the males."

"And yet?"

"This is Brandon's third and final chance here. We've had to ask him to leave twice previously for evidence of drug usage."

"What drug?"

"Heroin. We don't call the police on our clients, but we do have zero tolerance. We found a small quantity the first time, which we flushed down the toilet. Two months ago, it was a needle. We let him back in about a month ago, but let's just say, I have reason to worry."

"What about Vonda?" Ellie asked.

"Vonda I can't take back again, I'm afraid." She shook her head. "I'm sure it's not the girl's fault. But her presence here was completely counterproductive to our mission."

"How so?"

"She is—there's no other way to put it—she is toxic. She is like a poison that taints everything around her. One of the girls—Lisa—she had completed her applications to CUNY. We had loan and grant forms filled out. She was really going to do it. She was going to start college. The first in her family ever to do it. And then Vonda comes along and—like they say—she pissed all over it." The word sounded odd coming from this woman's dignified voice. "She tells Lisa she's *too pretty* to go to college. That she'd be wasting her most valuable years in a classroom when she could be meeting men. That's what it's always about with Vonda."

"Forgive me for saying this, Ms. Ri, but Vonda didn't look like a girl who gave much thought to whether men would find her attractive."

"You mean she is ugly."

Ellie shrugged.

"And that's precisely why she would try to destroy Lisa's ambitions. Because Lisa is a beautiful girl. And Vonda is not, but would like to be. And if someone else is healthy, she will try to get them to eat junk. And if someone else is about to start a new job, she will keep them out so late the night before that they oversleep and get fired. Rather than try to pull herself up, she tries to drag everyone else down. When I meet two detectives looking for Casey, and telling me it has something to do with Vonda—well, it makes me very worried. Is Casey in trouble?"

"We didn't mean to alarm you," Rogan said. "Just a few quick follow-up questions for the kid. Give us a call when he gets in?"

When Rogan and Ellie returned to the squad room, Detective John Shannon looked up from his desk with the smile of a fat kid who'd just snuck a cookie without getting caught.

"What's up, Shannon?" Ellie asked. "Krispy Kreme having a two-for-one sale?" Her words would be harsh if said to anyone else, but with Shannon, full-on hate speech was friendly banter.

"More like two for one in the dog house. As in, the two of you."

"What the hell?"

"Go ask the Lou. She came out about ten minutes ago, totally *en fuego*. Either the two of you fucked up good or she ran out of tampons."

Robin Tucker called out from her office. "Did I hear Hatcher?"

She started talking before they'd even crossed the threshold of her office.

"Where were you two?"

Rogan pointed a thumb over his shoulder. "Working Whitmire." He checked the screen of his cell phone. "We didn't get any calls from the house."

"Shit. I was giving it five more minutes. I was hoping you were pulling a major break in the case out of your asses."

Ellie wanted to make a joke about giving new meaning to "crack"-ing the case, but figured the comedic timing was off.

"Tell me you at least know who some homeless kid named Casey Heinz is and how he-she fits into this investigation?"

"He prefers *he*," Ellie said. "We talked to him last night. Now we've got two kids pointing fingers at him. Questionable reliability, but still, we'll track him down."

"And do you happen to know who Earl Gundley is?"

"He's the private dick Bill Whitmire hired."

"Based on what Mr. Whitmire tells me," Tucker said, "this Gundley guy worked the job for twenty-two years, solved a gazillion murder cases, and, while we're at it, he might've been the one to pull the trigger on bin Laden, the way I heard it."

"The family also offered a huge reward without talking to us first," Rogan said. "We're pretty sure that's why these homeless kids are yapping some story about Casey."

"Yapping a story, huh? Well, maybe this Earl Gundley is Mister Super Detective of the Century after all. Because supposedly he has Casey Heinz in his custody and is currently searching his room at a homeless shelter. I suggest the two of you catch up."

CHAPTER
THIRTY-TWO

Casey looked a lot happier when he was doing handstands in Union Square Park. Now he was hunched over in a plastic chair in the lobby of Promises, his head burrowed in his crossed forearms, flanked on each side by large men dressed in matching black suits. Ellie could tell from his trembling shoulders that he was crying.

He jerked up at the sound of the door opening.

"What is going on here?" Ellie asked.

One of the men in black rose to his feet. He had to be at least six-four.

"Miss Heinz came with us of her own accord. She consented to a search of her property."

Ms. Ri was storming down the hallway toward them. "Thank goodness. Real police. I was just about to call you. These people arrested Casey. I told them to get out, but Casey told me to let them in his room. I still tried to stop them, but back they went."

"Is that true, Casey? Did you tell Ms. Ri that you wanted these people to go into your room?"

He nodded but still hadn't spoken a word.

"Look at these people," Ms. Ri said, waving an angry hand in no particular direction. "They obviously forced him."

From the grass stains on Casey's clothing and marks on his face, Ellie already had her suspicions.

"If these men have done something—"

The standing security officer cut her off. "Which side are you on, lady? Nobody forced anybody to do anything."

Rogan was already making his way past the lobby toward the hallway adjoining the tenant rooms. When they got to the third room on the right they found two more men in suits, one young and enormous—an identical triplet to the two towers in the lobby— the other equally handsome, but with light-gray hair and a regular human-sized body.

The older man beat them to the punch with introductions. "Earl Gundley, Detectives." The firm, confident handshake matched the man.

"We would have appreciated a call," Rogan said.

He gave them a smooth smile. She could imagine why he would be successful as hired corporate security. "I would have said the same thing when I was on the job."

"Casey Heinz looks terrified," Ellie said. "What did your guys do to him to get him to let you in here?"

"*Him?*" He shared an amused look with his younger colleague. "Times, they sure do change, but I can be progressive, too. We didn't do anything to *him* I didn't do on the job. And even if the kinder, gentler NYPD has a new *pretty please with a cherry on top* consent policy I don't know about, here's the beauty of being strictly private. No government action means no constitutional violation, which means no motion to suppress. Whole lot faster than a search warrant."

"Except now we're here," Ellie said. "So there's your government action. We need you and your monochromatic giants to leave. We'll be retaining custody of Casey Heinz, and we'll determine whether to search further and with the proper legal authority."

"Nothing more to search." Gundley pointed to a cardboard box filled with evidence bags identical to the NYPD's. "You'll see they're all properly marked. Chain of custody begins now. You'll be particularly interested in this one here, I suspect."

She noticed he plucked two bags from the box. He handed her one, holding the other against his suit jacket.

Inside the bag was a single key attached to a dangling silver unicorn. Gundley looked very pleased with himself as he extended the second bag. "Not entirely certain about these, but I'm pretty darn sure they don't belong to *him*."

The second bag contained a pair of black lace bikini panties, the tiny La Perla tag visible at the waistband. Ellie had seen a neatly folded stack of identical pairs inside Julia Whitmire's dresser.

Ellie followed Gundley to the lobby. She wanted to make sure he and his hired help were out of here before she and Rogan decided what to do next.

Casey's eyes moved directly to the evidence bags in her right hand. A glimpse of recognition crossed his face.

"Am I under arrest? Because I want to talk to a lawyer."

CHAPTER
THIRTY-THREE

As they unhooked Casey Heinz's handcuffs to place him in the holding cell, Ellie heard a voice call out to them. "Detectives? Hello? Rogan? Hatcher?"

Ellie recognized the PAA who worked part-time at the reception desk. He had strawberry-blond hair and a gap in his teeth. The guys in the squad called him Doogie, and she had forgotten the kid's real name too many months ago to ask now. For tonight, he was the lucky guy who got to deliver the news: "Your lieutenant said to see her ASAP."

As if they needed another reminder of the mounting political and media pressure, they arrived at Tucker's office to find that she'd already called in the riding ADA. Max rose when they entered, choosing to lean against Tucker's office window as they took the two guest chairs. Max at least made eye contact with her, but the usual crooked smile was still absent.

Rogan brought them up to speed on the last few hours. As it turned out, Promises had a signed agreement with each client making clear that individual residents had no expectations of privacy. After convincing Ms. Ri to allow them to "double-check" what the private investigators had already done, Ellie got her to agree to a search. CSU was looking for physical evidence, but they had left with nothing other than the items Gundley's team had inventoried. Casey had invoked, so an interrogation was a no-go. He was in a holding cell downstairs. Of most obvious relevance were the missing key to the Whitmire townhouse and a pair of Julia's underwear.

"Casey could always say Gundley planted it," Ellie said. "One look at that guy and I can tell he makes Mark Fuhrman look like the ACLU's dream cop."

"We've got no proof of that," Tucker said. "I made a few calls. Gundley had a good reputation."

"Are you seriously telling me that every detective who retires with a good reputation is beyond placing a thumb on the scale, especially if his access to Bill Whitmire's wallet is at stake?"

"Except you saw that look on Casey's face," Rogan said. "He knew exactly what you were holding."

"Unfortunately, we've got to make a decision, campers." Ellie felt a moment of melancholy, knowing that Max had picked up the term from her. "If we cut Casey loose, he'll disappear. If we charge him, we can't mess around."

They all knew this wasn't how things were supposed to unfold. Sometimes they hit that sweet spot in an investigation—that moment when they knew it would happen. A piece of evidence falls into place that makes you sure there will be a prosecution and that you'll be able to give the district attorney what he needs to make the case.

There was still so much they didn't know about Julia Whitmire. Why had the wild child recently calmed down? Had she started seeing someone? If so, who, and why hadn't she told Ramona? Because it was Casey? And why had she been threatening her best friend's mother?

Gathering the answers to all those questions would take time. And time was something they no longer had. They could only hold Casey for twenty-four hours without a probable-cause hearing.

"There's no way we can build this thing up to PC for murder in a day," Rogan said.

Max drummed his fingertips on the wall behind him. "Here's

what we do. We've got the key to the Whitmire house, the panties, and the previous statement from Casey, making it sound like he barely knew Julia. We put all that together, and I can get a burglary charge past a judge: unauthorized use of the key, the taking of the underwear—we'll be fine."

Rogan was nodding in agreement. "That might at least keep the press off our backs." Unlike murder, a burglary charge wouldn't trigger a closer read of the blotter by reporters.

"But the kid's got no ties," Tucker said. "He makes bail in a couple of hours, and then he's on the next bus to God-knows-where."

Max was already prepared with a response. "In a closed courtroom, I'll make sure the arraignment judge knows about the connection between the burglary charge and the Julia Whitmire investigation. If we're lucky, we'll get our no-bail hold and also keep news of the arrest quiet."

"Not sure that's so lucky," Ellie said. "You get a no-bail hold, and we only have a few days to convene a grand jury for an indictment, right?"

"Six days or the defendant gets released."

They would have six days to return a murder indictment. Once the case was indicted—*if* it was indicted—it would be scheduled for trial. They wouldn't be able to backpedal. The DA's office wasn't in the habit of dismissing murder indictments.

They'd lost all control over the timing of the investigation.

CHAPTER THIRTY-FOUR

She climbed into the backseat of Rogan's two-door BMW, yielding the front to Max. Rogan's offers of a ride home were part of their daily routine. So were her *no thank you*'s. Her apartment was only a fifteen-minute walk from the precinct.

But today she had taken him up on the suggestion. She had also accepted Max's offer to come over. They hadn't been alone since the drama at the courthouse. The short car ride with Rogan would delay the conversation she knew was waiting for them.

It started the second they stepped into her elevator. "I've been thinking about that conversation we had today," he said.

"Not right now, okay? Let's see if Jess is home." Max had wanted her to spend the night at his place, but she honestly had run out of clean laundry in the dresser drawer she kept there.

Part of her had hoped to find Jess in his favored position on the sofa, concocting dinner from open boxes of Special K, Apple Jacks, and peanut butter Cap'n Crunch, but she unlocked the door to find an empty, quiet apartment. She knew they couldn't continue ignoring the land mine they had stumbled upon in their relationship. This time, she was the one who broached the subject as she kicked off her shoes and tossed them in the corner.

"I'm sorry if what I said today caught you off guard. I really did think you and I were on the same page when it came to children."

"Why would you think that, Ellie? We've never talked about it."

"But you know me, probably better than anyone ever has. You know my life and my work and, well, just the way I am. How in the world would I ever fit a kid in?"

"These are the things couples work out. People make it work."

"That's only if they want to. I don't *want* that. I've never wanted it."

"This is crazy, Ellie. You're barely thirty years old. There's plenty of time—"

"It's not a matter of time. It's a chip in my brain that's missing, okay? I don't melt when I smell a newborn. I don't suddenly have a higher voice and a lisp when I talk to babies. I don't hate them, but I also don't need them. I know exactly who I am, and I'm not a mommy-person."

"You know exactly who you are right now, and that's one of the million things I love about you. But who you are changes over time. And if we're together, maybe life would be different enough for kids to be in the picture."

"No. Life isn't going to be different. Not *my* life, at least."

"I can't believe you never thought to mention any of this."

"It's not like you ever asked. What was I supposed to do? Declare on our first date that my womb was strictly off limits?"

"That is so *you*, Ellie. Instead of having an honest discussion, you throw out some sarcastic one-liner."

Things went downhill from there.

During her second round of crying in the bedroom, she caught sight of the digital readout of the alarm clock. They'd been at it for over an hour. They were no longer talking about the prospect of children. They weren't even talking about who was to blame for never having revealed their preference on the subject. They were fighting about the fight they'd been having about the original fight.

They were both fading. She knew where this was going. This was turning into one of those horrible nights where they would keep talking at each other until their voices gave out. Nothing would be better. Nothing would get resolved. And they'd both be spent in the morning, stumbling to make it through the day without sleep.

They needed to stop. At least for tonight.

"Max, I can't do this anymore."

"That's not fair, Ellie. You can't just walk away because it gets rough."

"I'm not walking away."

"You just said you can't do it anymore. You've done this before. You push me away. You say you're not cut out for relationships. You try to sabotage your own happiness."

She reached for his hand and held it in both of hers. "No, not like that. I just can't fight anymore. Not tonight. I'm exhausted. I just want to go to sleep. And I want to go to sleep with you, okay?"

His eyes softened, but he wasn't done talking yet. "I love you, Ellie, but I don't know how to help you when you do this. You do it to me, but mostly you do it to yourself. You cling to this caricature of your own identity. You're so tough. You've seen it all. Everything's so cut-and-dry. And that attitude gets you into trouble. Not everything's black-and-white."

She loved Max. She trusted him. And she knew he had a point about her rush to judgment. But, inside, a part of her was screaming that he was wrong. That it was condescending to suggest she didn't know something so basic about herself as whether or not she wanted to be a parent. And damn it if a part of her didn't want to end it right then and there. But she didn't want to lose him over a child neither one of them was ready to have right now. Maybe someday it would come to that, but not tonight.

She moved to kneel at the foot of the bed between his knees.

"I hate it when we fight," she said, looking up at him. "I really am sorry this came up the way it did. I've missed having you with me."

He bent down to kiss her, gently at first, but she returned the kiss more deeply. They had been apart for the last five nights. They both knew how to find temporary peace.

When they were finished, she lay naked on her back, the air cooling her damp skin. He turned on his side next to her and brushed her hair away from her face with his fingertips.

"It's almost back to where it was," he said, kissing her shoulder.

The night after their first date, a madman had chopped her hair off and nearly killed her after she had gone by herself into a serial killer's house, willing to trade her own life for another's. The episode had earned her a Police Combat Cross, but she knew why Max was mentioning it now. *That attitude gets you into trouble. Not everything's black-and-white.*

She rolled over to face him. "I really do love you, Max."

He gave her a soft kiss on the lips. "We're going to figure it out. As long as we don't give up on each other, we'll be okay."

She smiled and kissed him again, then closed her eyes, needing to find sleep. But when she heard that first click in the back of his throat—a sign he was out for the night—she felt a tear slide down her cheek into the pillow.

She was so sure Max was different. He was supposed to be the one. But now he had become yet another man who had convinced himself that in exchange for his patience she would eventually change.

A grinding sound pulled her upright. Had she even been asleep? Her hand automatically slapped at her nightstand, searching for the cell phone buzzing its way across the wood top.

She didn't recognize the number.

"Hatcher."

"Detective Hatcher, it's Ramona Langston."

She had to stop giving her cell phone number to witnesses. Beside her in bed, Max rolled toward her, draping one arm across her thighs.

"Hi, Ramona."

The teenager sounded out of breath. "You're wrong about Casey."

Ellie looked at the nightstand. It was just past seven in the morning. Ellie was sick and tired of the Whitmires, but they did lose a daughter. The last thing she wanted to deal with now was the

Langston family. Daddy George, the anal-retentive lawyer who had no idea how to handle the chaos that had just been thrown into their lives. Evasive Adrienne, who was obviously in denial about Julia's connection to those vile comments on her blog. Now Baby Langston had robbed her of her last opportunity to get a few minutes' sleep before she had to return to the real world.

She took a deep breath and kept her voice strong and steady. "The district attorney's office will be the one to make the charging decisions—" She neglected to mention that the ADA who'd be making that decision was in bed beside her at the moment.

"You've been wrong about everything. You said Julia was the one who was posting that crap on my mom's blog? Well, pull up the website. Look at the blog right now. Read the comments."

Ellie wanted to hang up on the girl but instead walked into the living room, finding her laptop on the floor next to the sofa. She typed the website's URL into the address bar of her Internet browser, then scrolled down to the most recent comments.

Ramona's words were still spilling out through the phone. "I don't think my mom's seen it yet. She went running and left her stupid cell phone at home again. Whoever's been doing this crap is still at it. That means Julia couldn't have been the one. And neither could Casey. My mom is still being threatened. And whoever's doing it knows who she is."

Ellie stared at her computer screen.

"Blog by 'Anonymous'? Yeah, right. I know who you are, Adrienne. Stop writing your drivel or die."

According to the time stamp next to the post, the threat was typed that morning, only twenty minutes earlier.

"Are you there, Detective? You were wrong. And you're wrong about Casey. I think whoever's threatening my mom was the one who killed Julia. You have to do something. You have to help my mom."

"I'll be right there."

Max was standing above her, also reading the screen. "Great. Even if we do decide Casey's our killer, that post gives the defense attorney a convenient red herring. Any way you cut it, we're going to have to figure out who's been posting this stuff. It obviously isn't Casey or Julia."

She still felt in her gut that Julia Whitmire's death was a suicide, but even she had to admit there was no easy explanation for the connection between Julia's laptop and the threats on Adrienne's website.

And then just like that, Ellie saw it.

CHAPTER
THIRTY-FIVE

Ramona had phoned the detective because it was what you were supposed to do. Police were supposed to help people. Plus, these were the police who had interviewed her about Julia's death. They knew her. They would be better than the random cops dispatched by 911.

The female detective—Hatcher was her name—had gotten to the apartment quickly enough. She even had documents showing the locations of the computers that had been used to post the threats on her mother's website. It was almost overkill when she unfolded the Manhattan map on their living room coffee table.

"The threats prior to today came from different locations. The first was made from Julia's computer, connected to the network at her home. Since then, the posts have come from various public locations in Manhattan—primarily downtown, like the Union Square Equinox, an Apple Store—but also a couple on the Upper West Side . . . here at Seventy-second Street and Broadway." She circled the locations on the map with a highlighter.

"Okay," she said. It was a dumb response, but Ramona had no idea how she was supposed to confirm that she understood.

"Now, here's the interesting thing about this morning's post," the detective said. "We were able to get hold of the company that hosts

your stepmother's website. The comment that was made this morning came from a public computer in the lobby of a hotel at Madison
and Seventy-second."

She made yet another mark on the Upper East Side of the map.

"That hotel's only about eight blocks from here. You said your
stepmother's out on a run?"

"Stop saying 'stepmother.' She's my *mother*. And you can't possibly
think she has something to do with this."

"You told us before there was no way Julia would do anything
to hurt your step—your mother. But what if she thought she was
helping her? You said the two of them were close. If your mother
had asked Julia to write that post while your family was out in East
Hampton—"

"My mom would not do something like that. I told you before
that Julia had been distracted. She was busy all the time. And she
wasn't telling me where she was or who she was with. Maybe it was
whatever guy she was hooking up with. He could have used her
computer." Ramona couldn't tell if the detective was even paying
attention anymore, but she couldn't make the words stop pouring
from her mouth. "And he's still posting those ugly words now. You
have to find whoever's doing this. You have to help my mom. And
let Casey go. I'm telling you—these threats *have* to be the key to
Julia's murder. What if they come after my mom, too?"

Ramona had been so busy yelling that she hadn't heard the front
door of the apartment open. All she knew was that Adrienne—her
stepmother, her mother, the woman who had taken on the respon-
sibility of raising Ramona when she was only five years old—was
standing in the foyer, still out of breath from her early-morning run
in the park. Ramona could tell from her expression she was scared.

"What is going on here? What are you saying to my daughter?"
Ramona must have looked afraid too, because she understood now
that her mother's fear was on Ramona's behalf, not her own.

Ramona rushed to her and wrapped her arms around her waist. "I
tried to call you. You always leave without your cell phone. What's
the point of having it if you don't carry it with you?"

"Are you okay, sweetie?"

Ramona grabbed her tighter. "I'm worried about you, Mom. It's your website. There's a new threat today. And this time the guy used your name. Whoever's doing this to you knows who you are, Mom."

Ramona saw a different kind of fear in her mother's face. Then her mother bent down and kissed her on the top of the head before patting her on the back. "Go on to your room. I want to talk to Detective Hatcher alone."

"What the hell is going on here?" Adrienne demanded. "I walk into my own home and find my kid terrified in her living room with a cop standing over her?"

"If your kid looked scared, it was because she's terrified about those comments you're pretending to ignore on your website. A new one was posted this morning. And this time, the person used your name. I apologize if you thought I was the one scaring her, but she *is* scared. She's scared for you. And she called me to help."

The previous two times Ellie had seen Adrienne Langston, she had been unflappably composed. Now she seemed genuinely worried.

Ellie pointed to the map that was open on the coffee table and explained the tracking information they had gathered from Social Circle.

"As you can see, today's post was made from a different location than the previous comments."

"I don't understand, Detective. Aren't you looking into Julia's death? Why are you even bothering with this?"

"We have one of Ramona's friends—Casey Heinz—in custody as a person of interest. But because Julia was connected to at least one of these prior posts, a defense attorney for anyone we might eventually charge in her death will make an issue of them."

"I told you before that there's no way Julia would have done something like that."

"You don't seem very worried about the fact that someone is threatening you, Mrs. Langston. You haven't even asked for details about this new post." Ellie had always found it odd that Adrienne hadn't simply erased the grotesque comments that had been posted on her blog. She'd given her all that mumbo jumbo about wearing the signs of her victimhood proudly, but she never mentioned that traffic to her blog shot through the roof after the threats started. There was also the rumor Katherine Whitmire had passed along, that Adrienne had apparently scored herself a significant book deal. And from the very beginning, Adrienne seemed entirely too certain that Julia could not have been the person writing the anonymous comments, suggesting she might have known the author's identity all along.

"I told you before that if some crackpot wants to live it up with meaningless comments, I'm not going to let it get to me. I walk in and see my kid getting bullied by a cop, and I'm worried about her." She wiped away a tear that was beginning to form at the inside corner of her right eye. "I'm sorry. I'm sorry I'm yelling. I'm scared, but not for myself. I'm scared for Ramona. Her best friend is dead, and we don't even know if someone killed her. What if they come after my daughter?"

"There's no reason to believe Ramona's in any jeopardy. You're the one who's being threatened."

"It's just a bunch of stupid words."

"Except your daughter's right. It's more than meaningless words now. Whoever did this seems to know your identity. They used your name." Ellie read the comment verbatim from her phone screen. *"Blog by 'Anonymous'? Yeah, right. I know who you are, Adrienne. Stop writing your drivel or die.* Not just words. That's an explicit threat. We've been told, Mrs. Langston, that your blog has earned you a contract to write a memoir? Is that true?"

"What does that have to do with *any* of this?"

"I asked you a question."

"You've asked an awful lot of questions, Detective. Did it ever dawn on you that you don't necessarily have a right to know every single thing about my family?"

"If it's true you have a book deal, these threats on your website could make for excellent publicity. Is that why you don't erase them?"

Adrienne shook her head. "If you must know, Detective, I do have a book deal. And I earned it. And I signed it before these threats even started. Check with my editor if you'd like. Janet Martin at Waterton Press. You know, first you show up here not sure whether Julia's death was a suicide or murder. Now you say you have some friend of Ramona who is a 'person of interest,' whatever that means. And you're asking questions about stupid threats that were supposedly made by Julia but continued even past her death. You're ruining everything. My website was anonymous for a reason. Even the book is to be published under a pseudonym. I wanted to help people by writing about what happened to me, but I never wanted Ramona to know." She blew air up toward her eyes, obviously frustrated by the onset of tears. "I don't want her to know things that might scare her. Ramona's just a little girl in so many ways. This is scaring her. Julia being gone scares her. Your being here scares her."

As they were leaving the apartment, Ellie spotted Ramona watching her from the apartment's back hallway. Her lips were moving silently, first subtly and then with more urgency. It took Ellie a few attempts to make out the words she was mouthing: *You have to do something. Help her. Help Casey.*

Outside the Langstons' building, Ellie was still replaying the episode mentally. She kept coming back to Adrienne's confident assurance: I earned it. Ellie had thought she'd finally figured out who was responsible for the threats on Adrienne's website, but her theory fell apart if Adrienne had signed the contract for her book prior to the first threat. She was just about to call the publisher to confirm the timing of the book deal when her phone rang.

"This is Hatcher."

"Detective, this is Janet Martin at Waterton Press. Can you please explain to me why the NYPD is trying to silence an abuse victim?"

As Ellie drove away in the Crown Vic, she did not notice the man standing on the corner at Park Avenue, staring up toward the twenty-first floor. He had arrived at the Port Authority Bus Terminal at 6:30 that morning on a Greyhound Bus from Buffalo with nothing but his gym bag.

CHAPTER THIRTY-SIX

Waterton Press was located in the Flatiron Building, a triangular structure marking the juncture of Broadway and Fifth Avenue. Considered a skyscraper when erected in 1902, the historic building was now dwarfed by nearby condo towers. Size wasn't everything, however. Waterton's offices were only midway up the building's modest height, but Ellie still felt herself marveling at the unencumbered views of Madison Square Park from the editor in chief's windows, right at the northern tip of the triangle.

"Janet Martin," the editor said, standing behind her desk to offer a surprisingly firm handshake. "Thank you for heading right over. Well, aren't you the best-looking police detective I've ever laid eyes on?"

Ellie didn't enjoy pretty-for-a-cop comments, seeing them as insults to other female police officers rather than compliments to her. But she needed Janet Martin to like her. "Actually, I'll let you in on a little secret. We get an extra stipend for appearance-related expenditures. A few highlights, a wee bit of Botox . . . It's all part of the mayor's new plan to revamp the department."

"Oh, and funny, too. Gorgeous and funny."

"That's very nice of you. And I'm sorry again that we got off on the wrong foot. I know Adrienne has concerns about maintaining her anonymity, but I certainly didn't do anything to dissuade her from writing about her experiences." Ellie had already primed this pump when Martin had called her in a huff, but she figured a little extra obsequiousness couldn't hurt.

With a single hand wave, Martin let her know it was all bygones. "I should've known it was Adrienne being Adrienne—blowing things out of proportion. I've never met an author so afraid of success. Hey, I bet you have fabulous stories about catching the bad guys, saving the good guys, and doing it all in your Jimmy Choos. Ever thought of writing a book?"

"One pair of Jimmy Choos would eclipse my entire shoe budget, and the only writing I have time for is police reports," Ellie said, taking a seat in one of the guest chairs.

"You adorable girl. You wouldn't actually have to write it. That's how we do it these days, haven't you heard? Snooki's a *New York Times* best seller. A witty girl like you? I could sell TV rights tomorrow."

"Thank you very much, Miss Martin, but the only book I'm interested in right now is Adrienne's."

"Now *she's* a real writer, doing it all herself. Such a doll. And she's got a fantastic story. And now defending herself against this crazy stalker?"

"That's actually what I wanted to talk to you about. Did you sign a book contract with Adrienne before or after these threats started?"

"Before. My niece—she's also a survivor—was following the blog and forwarded it to me as a possible book project. I signed the deal with Adrienne three weeks ago. Paid more than I wanted to, frankly, but, like I said, she's that rare reluctant author. Not like she needs the dough, either."

"But I'm right that the threats will only help in terms of book publicity?"

"I'm upping the print run to a quarter million copies. The only problem now is that this little shit has Adrienne terrified. She called me today trying to return her advance. She wants to pull out of the deal. I even offered her more money, but, like I said, she doesn't need it."

"I don't suppose you have any theories about who the little shit might be."

"Who knows why these kinds of crackpots do what they do? And just in case you're thinking it's me, take a look through our catalog. Even a quarter million print run won't make this a lead title for me. I bought Adrienne's book because I think it will help a lot of women."

"To be honest, one of my colleagues suggested Adrienne might be doing this herself." Always better to let a nonexistent *colleague* be the bad guy.

"I'd bet every dollar I have against it. I've been in publishing thirty-two years, and I've worked with authors concerned about privacy. We've published under pseudonyms. Forgone the tours and the interviews."

"Doesn't that hurt the book?" Ellie asked.

"Are you kidding? It makes the writer's story all that more interesting. The mystery becomes the marketing hook. Who *is* she? Who are the people she's writing about? So, you know, we'll tell the reader we've got to change some names and dates and cities and details, and then the author gets to remain anonymous. But I've never seen anyone quite like Adrienne. So skittish. I've lost count of the number of times she's threatened to pull the plug. When I told her about the fact-checking, I thought her head was going to explode."

"Fact-checking?"

"Haven't you heard? That 'Million Little Pieces of Bullshit' has us all investigating our own writers. We can always tell readers that we've changed details to protect anonymity, but we have to know the heart of the story is true. When Adrienne found out we'd be verifying the underlying narrative, she even insisted on a nondisclosure clause in the contract. The only reason I'm talking to you is she told me you already know about the book. The woman's gonna drive me nuts by the time this thing comes out."

"She told me she doesn't want the past to bleed into the present."

"Whatever. I've read enough of her work to get a feel for that husband of hers. Don't get me wrong: it's part of what makes her journey so sellable. Upper East Side wife and mother, all prep schools and high society. People eat that WASPy shit up. But if I had to guess, I'd say her husband finds this whole thing a bit too messy for his taste."

Ellie had to hand it to the woman: she had good instincts. But if Janet Martin's instincts about Adrienne were right, then Ellie's were necessarily wrong. Whoever was stalking Adrienne was still out there.

CHAPTER THIRTY-SEVEN

It was Thursday—three full days since Julia Whitmire's body had been found, nearly two since they'd arrested Casey Heinz—and Ellie was the last to arrive at the conference room of the district attorney's office.

"You see the cover story on this week's *New York*?" She tossed her copy of the magazine, fresh from the newsstand, onto the faux veneer of the table for Rogan and Max to see.

"Prep School's Deadly Pressures?" was the cover story, complete with side-by-side headshots of Julia Whitmire and a boy named Jason Moffit, smiles beaming, full of life.

Max flipped to the article. "Says here the NYPD continues to investigate Whitmire's death but that inside sources say it's almost surely a suicide."

"Don't look at me," she said. "I don't leak to the press. There was no shortage of people at the callout who were thinking the same thing, though. The article's not really about Julia, even. They're using her death plus this other student's heroin overdose to shine a light on the pressures those Casden kids are under. That headmistress is probably tearing up the pages into little pieces as we speak."

Donovan looked at his watch. "Folger sent me an e-mail saying he was running a few minutes late. Traffic on the FDR."

They were waiting for Casey Heinz's defense attorney, Chad Folger. A sit-down between the investigating detectives and the defense attorney wasn't typical, but from the start nothing about this case had been normal. The initial label of suicide. The involvement of a hired investigative firm. The reward money.

"Folger's a heavy hitter," Rogan said. "How'd a kid from a homeless shelter swing his retainer?"

"He didn't. Folger's doing it pro bono. The lady at the shelter—"

"Chung Mei Ri," Ellie offered.

Rogan pointed at her. "Rainman, right here."

"Ms. Ri called one of the big, national LGBT advocacy groups. Folger's on their list—a gay brother or something. Now Folger says he has important information and wanted a meet as early as possible. This case is such a quick-moving target that I insisted you two participate."

They heard a rap on the door before it opened. A well-suited man in his early forties walked in. Ellie recognized him most recently from daily trial coverage of one of the country's biggest corporate fraud prosecutions. The defense had won.

"Hey, sorry for the wait. You must be Ellie Hatcher and J. J. Rogan. Casey told me you guys have been pretty decent to him, under the circumstances."

Rogan raised a skeptical brow. "Can't say we're used to defendants calling us the good guys."

Chad Folger smiled broadly. "Maybe 'good guys' is pushing it a little. But decent. He definitely said you were decent. High praise, though, compared to what I usually hear." He offered a quick handshake to Max. "Donovan."

Once they were seated at the table, Folger immediately leapt to his feet again, taking over the small room with his pacing. "So, let me start by thanking you for hearing me out today. I want to make clear at the outset that Casey isn't raising any allegations of wrongdoing or abuse against you guys, or anyone at the NYPD for that matter."

"Because we're decent," Rogan said with a smirk.

"Precisely. But Earl Gundley's another matter. And the Neanderthals he hires as quote-unquote security associates are even worse." He reached into his briefcase, pulled out a Redweld folder bulging at the seams, and dropped it to the table. It landed with a loud thud. "Those are complaints filed against Gundley when he was still with the department."

"We were told he was never disciplined," Max said.

"True, the complaints were eventually dismissed, but I think we all know that smoke sometimes means fire."

"Only sometimes," Max emphasized.

"And *that* is why I also have three file boxes in my office, each filled with civil complaints against Gundley's security company. Excessive force. Breaking and entering. One lady whose husband hired Gundley to document her infidelity alleged that these guys snuck into her bathroom to photograph her and the personal trainer going at it in the shower. They call themselves security, but they're glorified thugs."

Ellie could only imagine what a lawyer with Folger's talents would do with the fact that someone had threatened Adrienne Langston—a continuation of activity that began with Julia—yesterday morning while his client was in custody.

"With all due respect, Mr. Folger, I was unhappy about Gundley's involvement, too," Ellie said. "But it doesn't change the fact that Casey had a key to Julia Whitmire's house and a pair of her panties."

"She gave him the key two months ago, just in case he ever needed a place to stay in an emergency. It was an act of kindness on her part, but not one he intended to take her up on. He honestly forgot he had it."

"Big thing to forget," Max said.

"It's not like you guys asked if he had a key. You asked how many times he'd been alone with her, and he told you the truth. As it turns out, during the last of those times, they were intimate together. She tucked the panties in his jacket pocket as a little surprise for later or something."

Ellie couldn't recall a defense attorney ever confirming such an incriminating fact.

Apparently neither had Max. "Chad, you sure you're not working for us on this one?"

"I spent six hours with this kid yesterday, and I think I get it now. He is seriously in love with one of Julia's friends."

"Ramona Langston," Ellie offered.

"Exactly. Even the way the kid says her name, you think his eyes are going to roll out of his head. But not every girl's ginning up to date someone in Casey's . . . situation. And then here's this adventurous, beautiful girl, Julia, laying it on pretty heavy. It happened one time, and that was it. Casey didn't want Ramona ever to find out."

"Not even when his arrest was at stake?" Ellie said. "He didn't say a word when he realized what we'd discovered."

"The kid was absolutely terrified. Gundley's guys were completely out of control. They yanked Casey off the street. They threatened him. They hurt him. And that was only the beginning. What they did to him amounted to psychological torture."

"Oh, come on," Ellie said. "Torture?"

"I don't use that word lightly, Detective. These men should have been the ones placed under arrest. Initially, they grabbed at Casey's chest from the outside of his shirt. When they realized he had flattened his breasts with an Ace bandage, two of them reached beneath his shirt and pulled the bandage down. Then they moved on to placing their hands against his crotch, mocking him for the obvious absence of male genitalia. One of them even said, and I quote, 'You're obviously confused, sweetie. You just need me to straighten you out.' Casey would have confessed if they'd told him to, but they probably knew anything he said would've been completely inconsistent with the crime scene. So instead they coerced his consent to search his room at the shelter."

Ellie thought about the grass stains on Casey's pants. They could have come simply from the attempt to get hold of him at the park. Or they could've been from exactly the conduct Folger described.

Max tapped his knuckles against the conference table. "Anything else?"

"I know that lobbying for a client preindictment is old hat, but not from me. I'm telling you: Casey did *not* kill Julia Whitmire. In your gut, do you really believe you would have hooked him up if he had explained to you about the key and the underwear at the shelter Tuesday night? I'll also have psychiatric experts testify that Casey is particularly susceptible to coercion. The trauma he has suffered in the past as a result of being female-to-male makes him especially fearful of the type of abuse that these men were threatening. He is also under psychiatric treatment for bipolar disorder, which can reduce a person's ability to resist pressure."

"Casey was doing handstands in the park a couple of days ago," Max noted. "And these detectives talked to him at length. He didn't seem either depressed or manic."

"Manic-depressives aren't constantly at one pole or another. Many can maintain periods of a normal mood for large segments of time. They can also suffer from mixed states in which signs of mania and depression occur simultaneously. You'll see on the jail intake form that my client was carrying two powerful antipsychotic drugs prescribed to him by a Dr. David Bolt."

As Ellie jotted down the name in her notebook, she realized it looked familiar. When she'd watched the online video of that debate at NYU, Bolt had been the expert defending the use of psychotropic medications in children.

"My understanding is that it's an experimental use of the drugs. Ironically, it was your star witness, Brandon Sykes, who told Casey about the clinical trial. I'm still gathering information about Casey's diagnosis, but I'm confident it might also help you understand why Casey seemed so resigned when he was arrested. As for Brandon Sykes and Vonda Smith, I'm just beginning to scratch the surface with those two, but I can already tell you, Max, you don't want them in front of a jury. Vonda's an addict who routinely flirts with old men and then steals their wallets once grandpa takes her home."

Ellie shot Max a concerned look. The lawyer's characterization was consistent with what they'd learned from Chung Ri.

"And that drug trial Brandon got Casey into? Turns out Brandon faked his diagnosis. Think about that: he's taking an experimental antipsychotic for a mental condition he doesn't even have, all for the hundred bucks a week being paid by the researchers. You don't think he'd lie about Casey with a hundred grand on the line?"

Folger finally took a seat and placed both palms firmly on the table. "Look, I'd usually just wait for trial, but I really think if you take a close look, you'll see that dismissing this mess before it goes any further is the right thing to do. Otherwise, I *will* advise Casey to exercise his right to testify in front of the grand jury. You might think you can control what happens in a grand jury room, but I guarantee you that someone on that panel *will* want to hear the full story. The grand jurors can then call their own witnesses. They will ask Gundley the hard questions, whether you want them to or not. They'll want to meet Vonda and Sykes. They'll want to know more about Julia, which means hauling in her parents and those zombies from Casden. We've got a *New York* magazine article saying it was suicide. And even if the grand jury indicts, we still have trial. Right now, neither the DA's office nor the NYPD is implicated in what has happened to my client. But if you side with Gundley's team on this, I won't have a choice. You will become responsible by association."

She could see why clients paid a pretty penny for this guy's services. It didn't always come down to skills in the courtroom. Folger had read the politics of the situation perfectly. He knew that the Whitmires and Casden were already pulling the district attorney's office in two different directions. Now there was the prospect of front-page stories pitting the city's wealthy and powerful against an abused homeless kid.

If Max was feeling the pressure, he didn't show it. "I need some time to look at this."

"Let me know what you decide. You've got until Monday to go to the grand jury before Casey gets sprung."

CHAPTER THIRTY-EIGHT

The only psychiatrists Ellie had ever known were ones who worked for the state. The experts who evaluated defendants who claimed insanity. The ones who'd shown up for civil-commitment hearings back when she was on patrol and concluded someone had crossed the line from merely off their rocker to an official danger to themselves or others. The ones she'd been forced to meet with for her own supposed benefit at various times in her career—after the Wichita Police finally caught the serial killer her father had spent his entire adult life hunting, after she had killed a man at Gerard's Point, after she had witnessed her lieutenant put two bullets in the neck and stomach of a former friend.

Based on the appearance of his Upper West Side digs, Dr. David Bolt wasn't like any of those state-employed shrinks. Rather than utilitarian faux-mahogany office furniture, Bolt had opted for sleek, minimalist decor. Small footprint, they called it. White irises adorned the corners of the waiting room. A faint scent of ginger lingered in the air. The terrace in his office offered expansive Central Park views.

It didn't seem like a place for crazy people. The space reminded her of the day spas her ex-boyfriend the investment banker used to try to send her to. According to him, those hours were supposed to teach her the values of "rest and relaxation." He was trying to persuade her to "spoil herself." But Ellie's idea of rest and relaxation was a bottle of Johnnie Walker Black and an entire season of *30 Rock* in one sitting. Trapped in a dark room, being rubbed down like a piece of Kobe beef to the recorded sound of chirping birds, was her version of being drawn and quartered.

As for the man himself, she placed him at about fifty. She would have expected him to look slicker, based only on the office decor, but she'd already had a brief preview of his appearance online. Today he wore a gray wool sweater over a button-down shirt and black trousers. He had floppy, longish brown hair and a genuine smile.

As they explained the reason for their visit, he scribbled some notes on a Post-it and then crossed his arms like an umpire watching an instant replay.

"Ah, damn it. I've been out of med school twenty-six years, and, you know, this is only the third time I've been in this jam."

"And what jam is that?" Rogan asked. Ellie noticed that Rogan had crossed his arms, too. Sometimes she wondered whether men had learned to mimic each other's body language back in cave times.

"See? I am just not good at this. You come here asking me about someone named Casey Heinz. I'm not allowed to tell you whether I even know a person by that name. I guess you can probably draw some inferences from the fact I think this is a jam. My sister's husband's a cop. He's in Detroit, though. My point is, I want to help you out."

"So . . . sounds like we're all on the same page," Ellie said.

"Except I cannot reveal any individual person's relationship to me as either a private client or a participant in a clinical trial. Were I to do so, I could have my ticket pulled by the American Medical Association and the American Psychiatric Association, not to mention problems with the FDA for my research approval."

"Casey Heinz told us that he was under your treatment," Ellie said. "That waives privilege."

"Except it doesn't," Bolt said. "A patient can reveal the fact of a doctor-client relationship without intending to disclose all of the details of said relationship. Or, at least, that's what I've been told during my required continuing education classes. Not to mention, police officers sometimes bluff about what they already know about a person's identity as a patient—not you, I'm sure, but I have colleagues who have fallen for those sorts of stunts."

"So I guess we'll meet with the district attorney and get a subpoena."

"I really would like to help," he said.

"Obviously."

Usually that kind of sarcasm directed by Ellie at someone in Bolt's socioeconomic status triggered phone calls to the lieutenant or lectures about respectful treatment of the public, but Bolt laughed. "Wow, I've become that dick my brother-in-law's always complaining about. Tell you what, Detectives. I can't reveal anything about individual patients, but I can tell you a little bit about my work in general."

He extended his arm in the direction of two chairs on the opposite side of his desk.

"Equivan is a new pharmaceutical treatment for bipolar disorder, also known as manic-depressive disorder, or simply manic depression. Both the diagnosis and treatment of bipolar disorder in young people are controversial. Critics argue that kids will be kids. They say, for example, that while impulsive life changes might be clinically abnormal in an adult, young people aren't yet able to gauge the seriousness of these decisions. Similarly, they say feelings of hopelessness and despair might be red flags in adults, but are simply a normal part of adolescence."

"We just talked to a teacher this week who believes his students are all overmedicated," Rogan said.

"Easy to say until you've got a child who's slipping away." Ellie remembered the passion Bolt had displayed in the NYU debate when he spoke about the pain and frustration he saw in his underage patients. "That said, many of the drugs on the market are experimental, and their use in young people is highly contentious. That brings us to my research. The idea behind Equivan is to use the active ingredient of an antidepressant, which can be quite risky as a treatment for bipolar disorder, but in combination with a mood stabilizer that has been found to be more effective alone than an antipsychotic."

"You're losing us, Doc."

"Basically, we're trying to blend the best of all worlds here. Take the good and counteract the bad. Equivan is actually an off-label combination of two currently available drugs. Equilibrium is the mood stabilizer; Flovan is the antidepressant—hence the name Equivan. We're testing it specifically on subjects ages ten to twenty. This allows us not only to measure the effectiveness of the drug, but also to determine whether there is any interplay with age. Perhaps what works like magic in a young adult twenty years of age is detrimental to a ten-year-old. Obviously we want to know that. To participate in the trial, subjects must meet the criteria for Bipolar I disorder, the classic manic-depressive form of the illness according to the *DSM-IV*."

Bolt started to explain the acronym but Ellie waved him along. Given the prevalence of mental illness among criminal defendants, every cop had heard of the *Diagnostic and Statistical Manual of Mental Disorders*.

"Subjects cannot be under any other current medication for depression or other mental illness. They must agree to the conditions of a drug research protocol, which includes a provision that subjects are randomly assigned to receive either active treatment or a placebo."

"Not all the subjects are actually *getting* Equivan?"

"That's correct. The use of a control group is standard in any respectable drug trial. If we gave every subject Equivan, we'd have no way of knowing whether improvements in mood and stability were due to treatment or some other factor, like weather changes, better employment stats, or plain, old-fashioned coincidence. So a quarter of our subjects get Flovan, a quarter get Equilibrium, a quarter get the Equivan combo, and the rest get a placebo."

"So let's say the drug combo works," Rogan said. "That means you're knowingly depriving some of these subjects of treatment, all in the name of science. Sorry, Doc, that sounds a little cold."

"It's not easy, Detectives, but that's the scientific method. And that's why our subjects have to sign rigorous disclosure and waiver forms. If it makes any difference, we can't yet say we're really depriving them of anything. Every subject receives outpatient therapy from me, a service for which some people in this city pay healthily, if I may say so. The whole point is that we don't know yet whether the drug even offers a benefit. Equivan might do nothing. It might even make matters worse."

"Our understanding is that subjects are paid to participate," Ellie said. The Casden kids pay a fortune to be numbed, while the drug companies pay to get the rest of the population hooked as well.

"That's not unusual. It's not a tremendous amount of money, just modest compensation for time and transportation."

Maybe it wasn't a lot to an Upper West Side psychiatrist, but a hundred bucks to a sixteen-year-old homeless kid like Brandon Sykes was an entire day of panhandling plus a lot of luck. "Could someone fake a manic-depressive diagnosis?"

"In theory. It has happened before. But the *DSM* includes criteria that are specifically intended to help weed out false reports."

"Got it. Now, still sticking to general information . . . is it true that someone with manic-depressive disorder might be more prone to coercion?"

"Certainly. In a depressive state, the person might not have the will to withstand pressure. They don't really care about the downside because they're feeling hopeless anyway, plus they don't have the mental energy to counter the coercion."

"And in a manic phase?" she asked.

"That one's less intuitive. You might think that mania would cause a person to fight back. But in a manic episode, the person is not thinking about consequences at all. They start out dropping a buck in a homeless man's donation cup. It feels so good to help another person that they hand the guy a twenty instead. The next thing you know, they're at the bank, closing out their accounts to hand out cash on the street. In the situation you describe, a manic person might comply with one request, and before they know it, they've lost all control."

"What about credibility? Might a manic-depressive be more likely to lie if he thought it would somehow help him?" She was thinking now about the credibility of Brandon Sykes.

"I mean we're talking generalities, but, yes, that would be fair to say, for essentially the same reasons."

"What about murder?" she asked.

"Excuse me?"

"Might a manic-depressive suddenly become violent and kill a friend during what should have been a minor argument?"

"It has certainly happened before. Manic episodes can be completely uncontrollable."

"So if we have a homicide defendant who may be manic depressive, we'll need to know whether they were taking drugs for the condition, right?"

"Well, the whole purpose of treatment is we hope it helps people. We hope that, with continuous use, it keeps them at normal for longer periods of time. We may not be able to cure the disorder, but we try to reduce the frequency, longevity, and severity of the swings between the two poles."

Ellie smiled. She had thought Dr. Bolt's offer to speak only in generalities would be a waste of time. She jotted down his last sentence verbatim in her notebook. He had just given them what they needed to force him to turn over Casey Heinz's and Brandon Sykes's patient files.

CHAPTER THIRTY-NINE

Max leaned back in his chair and let out a small groan. "Fuck. First Social Circle's Internet traffic records, and now a doctor's files from a drug study? These document demands could mark a new circle of hell for lawyers."

Ellie gave his shoulders a quick squeeze until she felt the tension drop. "Sorry, dude. Catching bad guys is, like, soooo hard."

"Fine, I'll stop whining, but this is a little tricky." He stared at the keyboard in front of them. On his computer screen were the beginnings of a search warrant application for David Bolt's files. Max was planted at one computer, drafting the affidavit in support of the warrant, while Rogan helped pull up information as necessary on a separate laptop. "Okay, we've got everything in here about what you learned from Dr. Bolt. Tell me what you know about the expert himself—education, credentials, that kind of stuff."

Rogan pulled up a copy of Bolt's *curriculum vitae* and let out a whistle. "Academic appointments at NYU and Harvard. Hospital appointments from New York Presbyterian, Columbia Medical Center, and Sloan-Kettering. Recipient of all kinds of NIH and private grants. A trillion awards. Two books. Residency at Mount Sinai. Graduated from Harvard Med, Yale for undergrad, oh—and how sweet, the Casden School as a wee lad. That enough?"

Max was typing away. "Looking good. Just want to make it sound like we've done our homework. And what about the two drugs in Equivan?"

Rogan looked up the information for Equilibrium and Flovan. Ellie laughed as he struggled to pronounce the drug's ingredients. He finally gave up and turned the screen toward Max.

"Got it. And the companies who produce the drugs?"

Ellie recognized the names of two large pharmaceutical corporations. "Does the judge really need to know all this?"

"Hopefully not. My worry is that the judge will want us to pull in the drug companies, too, in which case we're looking at months of stalling. We only have four days to make a decision on Casey."

"Would they really care about two patient records?"

"If the drug companies are funding the research, they might have privacy interests at stake: confidential business information, proprietary research and development stuff, etcetera."

Rogan was still surfing for additional information to fatten up the warrant application. "Based on Bolt's history, I'd say the likelihood of private funding's high." He swung the laptop back toward Max and Ellie.

"The Blood Pact Between the Psychiatric and Big Pharm Industries."

It was a post from two years earlier on a website called Healthcare Is a Right. The author purported to document the incestuous relationship between pharmaceutical companies and the psychiatric industry. The American Psychiatric Association was phasing out the funding of its trade conventions by drug companies to avoid the appearance of a conflict of interest. The decision followed a multipart exposé in the *New York Times* highlighting the millions of dollars' worth of perks flowing to the very doctors responsible for writing the prescriptions that fueled the burgeoning business of psychopharmacology.

At the bottom of the post was a list of the twenty "poster children" for the "blood pact" between psychiatry and "big pharm." Number twelve was Dr. David Bolt, thanks primarily to the research money he'd received from drug makers in recent years.

"This is interesting," Rogan said, scrolling back up into the heart of the article. "It says here that in the wake of the recent controversy, the leading med schools required their faculty and attending physicians to disclose to their boards of trustees all income received from private sources. Looks like Bolt resigned his appointments at NYU and Harvard rather than comply with the new regulations. Apparently most of his research is sponsored by pharmaceutical companies."

Ellie had never had occasion to think about the sources of funding for drug research. "That's ridiculous that companies control the testing of their own drugs."

"Given these days of reduced spending, who else is going to pay?" Max said. "One blogger says David Bolt is the medical equivalent of a war criminal, but *New York* magazine lists him as one of the top child psychiatrists in the city."

"But it's not just a matter of opinion if Bolt's research is being funded by the companies that manufacture Equilibrium and Flovan. Bolt said Equivan was about combining the best of two treatments. Obviously both companies would have an interest in the tests going well. More kids medicated means more drugs sold."

Max was too busy reading his own composition on the screen to continue following her rant. "Let's just stick to Casey and Brandon's files for now, okay?"

Ellie thought there was more to the story, but she also knew that an investigation into a drug company's research practices would take far longer than the few remaining days they had to make a decision about Casey Heinz's guilt. Not to mention that the last time she checked, drug research protocols were well beyond the NYPD's jurisdiction. She'd have to settle for a phone call to the Food and Drug Administration. Hopefully they'd see the same red flags.

"The request for Casey's records is pretty tight," Max noted. "He's a suspect in Julia's murder. We've got his lawyer telling us he's in this study, and we've got the shrink telling us that manic depression could be relevant to both the murder and his disposition on the night of the arrest."

Rogan slapped his palms and then rubbed them together. "All right, then. Let's get this show on the road."

"But you're also looking for Brandon Sykes's records."

"And we've got it all spelled out here." Ellie reached around Max for the keyboard and scrolled down to the relevant paragraphs of the affidavit. "If Brandon lied to get into the study, then we need to know that before you put him on the stand. Conversely, if he *is* manic-depressive, then Bolt says it's possible he'd be more likely to lie to us. It's relevant either way. We lay that all out here."

"Except the records won't actually tell us if he lied to get into the study. We don't even know if he's *in* the study. It might be too tangential. And if the judge thinks we haven't done our work on the Sykes part of the warrant, he might ding us on the request for Casey's records, too. I don't think we can risk it."

"So what choice do we have?"

"Talk to Brandon Sykes first, just to be safe. At least see what he says, so I don't look like an idiot when the judge asks me."

Ellie looked at her watch. "It's already seven o'clock. Unless Bolt takes appointments on the graveyard shift, we won't get to Brandon and a judge *and* to Bolt's office tonight. You only have four more days before the clock runs out on Casey's hold."

"I know, but if I go to a judge now and get slammed, it'll be even worse. Go find Brandon."

CHAPTER FORTY

Chung Mei Ri was not happy to see them.

Even when Gundley's people had stormed into Promises with Casey to search his room, Ms. Ri had been exceedingly polite to Rogan and Ellie, despite her displeasure. She offered them coffee and joked that they worked even longer days than she did. She also told them they were wrong about Casey. She insisted that this was all a misunderstanding and that they would see they were mistaken. But she maintained the same calm voice and warm smile throughout the encounter.

Today, though, something had changed at the Promises Center for Young Adults. Same welcoming glass atrium. Same girl with the pink mohawk stationed out front. Same Ms. Ri charging into the lobby with her no-frills suit and black stockings. But this time there was no warm smile. And the calm voice had been replaced by a low hiss.

"I tried to tell you. I tell you that Casey is innocent. I tell you I know he could not hurt a flea." What had been a faint accent grew stronger as she seethed. "I also tell you about Brandon Sykes and Vonda Smith. I do not *like* to say bad things about the people we are helping here. It goes against everything we stand for. But I did it. I told you about them so you would know not to trust them."

"We're still looking at the case, Ms. Ri. The DA's office has a few days before convening a grand jury. That's why we're here to talk to Brandon. We're still gathering information."

"Thanks to you, there is no Brandon. There is no Vonda or Brandon or Casey."

"I'm not sure what you mean, Ms. Ri."

"What were you thinking, giving them that kind of money?"

"We didn't give them anything. Julia Whitmire's parents—"

She waved an irritated hand at them. "You, the parents. You work together. What were you thinking? I turned her away last night because she causes so many problems. Then today he comes back and takes all of his things."

Ellie was having a hard time following her from one sentence to the next. "Brandon left because Vonda couldn't stay here?"

"I don't know if that was his reason or not. But ten thousand dollars to two drug-addicted children? He says he doesn't need to be here anymore."

"Who said that? You mean Brandon?"

"Yes. Brandon. They got their reward money. They're gone, Detectives. He said they were going west. Until they shoot up all of that money or die, they're gone. I hope you're happy with yourselves."

CHAPTER
FORTY-ONE

FOUR DAYS LATER . . .

"Are you two okay with this?"

"Yes," Rogan said. "No question. Absolutely. *Sí. Oui.* We are totally down."

Max had asked them the same question three different ways already. Ellie cut in before her partner could continue with his list. "I think what Rogan's trying to say, Max, is that we can't recall having an ADA be so concerned with what we thought about a charging decision."

"And I can't recall ever having two detectives who were so peachy keen about springing a suspect loose from custody."

"This case was a no-go from the very beginning," Rogan said. "This whole mess with Casey is all that damn Bill Whitmire's fault. You best be boycotting his records from now on, woman."

"Request noted," Ellie said. Bill Whitmire had sabotaged their investigation. He had been the one to wave that exorbitant award money around. He had been the one to hire Earl Gundley, the private investigator whose team had taken Casey into custody. They still weren't entirely sure what Gundley's people had done, but Gundley had since admitted some of his tactics might have been "aggressive."

It was a mess.

The tipping point had come when Casey had volunteered for a polygraph over the weekend and passed it.

Granted, the test results were inadmissible. And knowledgeable experts could assure them that well-versed liars can beat the machine.

But then they'd met the previous night with the Whitmires to detail the status of the case. Although Max said he could probably get a murder charge against Casey through the grand jury, he explained why he would never be able to prove the case beyond a reasonable doubt at trial. Casey had a key to the apartment, but there was no evidence he had used it that night. Vonda Smith and Brandon Sykes were gone, and there was no guarantee they'd be found before trial. And on top of it all, there would be no shortage of red herrings a good defense lawyer like Chad Folger could use at trial: the possibility (probability, in Ellie's view) that Julia had in fact committed suicide; Casey's diagnosis as bipolar and his use of an experimental treatment; and evidence that Julia had been threatening her friend's mother, perhaps with a still-unidentified accomplice who continued to harass the woman. Plus, Max had added, there were the troublesome polygraph results.

At Max's mention of the poly, Ellie had known immediately that something wasn't right.

Bill looked huge on the tiny settee in the Whitmires' living room, his feet crossed at the ankles like a child. He stared at his hands, planted on his knees, and did not look up when he finally spoke. "I was only trying to help."

"Excuse me, sir?" Max had asked.

"I was trying to help."

Ellie couldn't hold her tongue. "Like you helped by paying Vonda and Brandon before trial, even though we specifically warned you against it?"

He nodded. "I'm sorry. I was—oh my God, are you telling me I may have been wrong?"

She'd wanted to scream at him. Of course what he did was *wrong*. But that is not what he meant.

"I was so sure she did it. This fucked-up girl who thinks she's a boy had a key to our house, and two of her friends told us she did it. I was so sure. Damn it, I screwed this up. I told Gundley to do what he had to do. That's what I told him, exactly: '*to do whatever you have to do.*'"

And that's when Ellie knew. "You paid him, didn't you?" Ellie had asked. "Not just for manning the tip line. Or for finding Casey. You paid him extra to seal the deal. What did you expect would happen?"

He had broken down in tears at that point. He had apologized. He reached out a hand to his wife in search of some sign of forgiveness, but instead received a view of the back of her turned head. Ellie had felt sick to her stomach as she watched him, so oblivious to the harm he had inflicted by trying to buy private justice.

"So you guys are okay with this?" Max asked one more time, pen in hand over a motion for dismissal.

Rogan let out a small scream of frustration. "Just sign the damn thing already."

It was a lighthearted moment, but Ellie took no happiness in it. As pissed as she was at Bill Whitmire, she was angrier at herself. She had known in her gut that Casey wasn't guilty but had allowed the investigation to get away from her. He had spent nearly six days in custody.

Ellie had been wrong about so much, from the very beginning of this case. She was off her game. She was still tiptoeing around Rogan, even around Max. Now they were correcting at least part of the harm by dismissing charges against an innocent, troubled kid.

She knew one thing, though. Even if Julia wasn't murdered, she had left this world shrouded in secrets she never had a chance to tell. It was another wrong that Ellie had to correct.

CHAPTER
FORTY-TWO

E llie was nestled into the space between her couch and her trunk-doubling-as-coffee-table, pen in right hand, nan bread in left. She was prepping a huge scoop of saag paneer onto her flatbread when she heard keys in the door. Before she realized it, she had dropped her pen and was checking her breath in her hand. She and Max had exchanged house keys nearly three months ago, but she still got a little rush when he popped in unexpectedly.

"Oh God, I detect the distinct odor of dirty diaper and singed hair. How can you eat that stuff?"

Not Max. Jess. Just as well. She was still trying to settle back into a comfortable rhythm with Max, but she could stink up both her breath and the apartment with the stench of curry, and her brother couldn't say boo about it.

She ignored Jess as he continued to feign holding his breath, then choking, then fainting on the sofa behind her.

"You mind?" he said, reaching for the remote.

"If I minded the sound of a television, I would most definitely *not* choose you as a roommate."

To her annoyance, she recognized the two women arguing on her television screen. Even though she'd never actually watched the reality show, she somehow knew who these D-list celebrities were, what products they were shilling, and the details of their screwed-up love lives.

"I swear I'm going to get one of those parental control chips for the cable box."

"It took you four weeks to call the super when your bathroom sink was clogged. If you can brush your teeth in the tub for a month, I don't see you lining up at Time Warner Cable just to deprive me of my housewives." She noticed that he kept the volume lower than usual. "How can you work and eat at the same time?"

"I'm just making some notes, is all."

"Again: How can you work and eat at the same time? Take a break. You've been killing yourself lately."

"Not anymore. We let Casey Heinz go today."

"Didn't you call that when it first went down last week? Why'd you even bother busting your ass?"

"Because when it comes to murder, we don't usually let people go because we have *a feeling*. I really expected we'd have some answers by now."

"You'll get them."

"Doesn't always happen that way, Jess. I think we both know that."

"I also know *you*. You'll get there."

She considered arguing with him, but chose instead just to thank him and continued brainstorming on her notepad.

She started drawing lines of connection between the principals. Julia Whitmire's threats against Adrienne. Julia's friend, Ramona. Ramona's friend, Casey, research subject to Dr. David Bolt. The Adderall—without a prescription—in Julia's handbag. The Casden School, alma mater to Bolt, where prescription drug abuse ran rampant. Missing witness Brandon Sykes, another subject to David Bolt.

That psychiatrist's name was popping up a little too frequently.

She pushed her plate to the side to make room for her laptop. She entered "David Bolt" into Google and hit enter to search. As she scrolled through hits relating to a southern lawyer, a freelance graphic artist, and a hotshot middle school hockey player, she realized her job would be a lot easier if everyone in America had a name as unique as Rumpelstiltskin.

Fortunately, a fair share of the hits concerned the man she was interested in. There was his practice's website. Various celebrations of his professional achievements. Announcements of the Phase I clinical trial of Equivan, one making special mention of Bolt's earlier decision to forgo his academic appointments rather than disclose the income he made from the pharmaceutical companies that funded his research. Consumer-focused websites protesting the funding of the research by the drug companies that manufactured the two drugs that went into Equivan.

Her surfing came to a halt. On the screen was a photograph from a twenty-five-year class reunion at Yale, a group shot of the Delta Kappa Epsilon fraternity. Second row, third man from the left was Dr. David Bolt. Next to him was Ramona Langston's father, George.

She tried to slow her impulses. She'd been reacting on emotion, not facts, ever since they'd caught this case. She told herself there could be a rational explanation. To a certain segment of the population, there were only ten acceptable high schools, and three acceptable colleges. It wasn't so coincidental that Bolt would go to college with George Langston, or have graduated from the same prep school as his kid. Casden and Yale probably went together like peanut butter and chocolate.

But these two men didn't just go to the same college. They were in the same frat. And in this photograph, Bolt had his elbow crooked around George Langston's neck, giving it a playful squeeze. These guys were tight.

She searched for their names together: "George Langston and David Bolt."

She got one hit, a *New York Post* article with the headline "Suicide Leads to Lawsuit." She clicked on the link. It was a short article from March.

*The parents of a Manhattan high school student who died of a drug
overdose last month have filed a civil lawsuit arising from the experimental combination of two leading psychiatric drugs. According to the
complaint, filed yesterday in the district court for the Southern District of
New York, Wallace and Janet Moffit claim that the drug Equivan—an
experimental combination of the anti-depressant Flovan and the mood
stabilizer Equilibrium—caused their son, Jason, to suffer severe depression and take his own life. The lawsuit seeks $20 million in damages.*

*Jason Moffit, 17, a student at the prestigious Casden School, was
found dead in Central Park on February 14 from a heroin overdose. A
representative for Dr. David Bolt, the acclaimed researcher overseeing
the drug trial, declined comment, as did the Moffits' attorney, George
Langston.*

CHAPTER FORTY-THREE

Mom, what are you going to do?"

Her mother's face was white.

"Mom. This isn't just words anymore. He knows who you are. He found you. He's stalking you. We have to *do* something."

Ramona knew that the world her friends inhabited wasn't real. It was real for them, but it wasn't the world that normal people lived in. Regular people didn't have chefs and drivers and private SAT-prep coaches. Regular mothers didn't have lines of credit at Tiffany. Regular dads didn't trade in their wives every decade or so for a newer model, like a car.

Ramona also knew that she wasn't rich the same way her friends were rich, with parents who had been raised rich, as had the parents' parents. Ramona wouldn't even be at Casden if her family didn't have a friend who'd pulled strings to get her in.

Still, Ramona had always been grateful for what they had. Ramona's mother made sure of that. She hadn't come from wealth, that was for sure. She'd been raised in Chico, California, by Ramona's grandmother, a single mother who waited tables for a living and who died before Ramona could meet her. Ramona's grandfather had never been in the picture. When her mother met her father, she was working as a nanny.

Maybe it was because Ramona was appreciative of what she had that she tried so hard to stay grounded in the actual "real" world. In retrospect, Ramona realized that a shared yearning to know another world was what bound her and Julia together.

Julia and Ramona had been different in a lot of ways. Julia was long and lean and lithe, with flowing blond hair and classic good looks. She was the kind of girl who attracted men. She also had a recklessness and darkness about her that Ramona liked to think she had managed to avoid.

But Julia was the only friend from Ramona's world who was happy to join in her hobby of talking to strangers everywhere they went. They both believed they could learn at least one interesting thing about human nature from any person they encountered. That was how they had gotten to know Casey, Brandon, and Vonda. Brandon had been the one holding the panhandling sign claiming they needed money for a bus ticket to Missouri.

"Do you really want to go back to Missouri?" Julia had asked.

Brandon had assumed Julia was messing with him and started in with the spoiled rich girl comments. But then Julia sat down cross-legged on the sidewalk next to them and said she just really wanted to know. They'd spent the next four hours sitting in that same spot. Just talking.

But nothing Ramona had learned from the world outside of hers had prepared her for what was happening now, in her real life. That privileged little bubble from which she'd been so eager to peer out was now being deflated, one slow leak at a time. Julia was dead. Brandon and Vonda had lied about a person who had been nothing but kind to them. And now she was terrified that something was going to happen to her mother.

"*Mom!*" Ramona was shouting now. "We have to call the police."

Her mother was staring at her, but her mind was clearly somewhere else. Her lips were parted, but no sound was coming out. And at her feet, on the freshly polished hardwood beams, lay the package Nelson had handed them as they'd entered the lobby, stuffed from dinner at Fishtail, one of their favorite mother-daughter spots when Dad worked late.

The top had spilled to the side when her mother had dropped the box to the floor.

Maggots. Hundreds of them, rushing to escape from their temporary housing.

PART IV

ADRIENNE

CHAPTER FORTY-FOUR

The next morning, Ellie and Rogan stood on the stoop of a nondescript brick apartment building on Anderson Avenue in High Bridge.

"Some kid from Casden Prep lived *here*?" Rogan asked.

Whereas Julia and Ramona grew up in the poshest townhouses and penthouses of Manhattan, Jason Moffit had been raised by his parents in this rent-controlled apartment in the South Bronx, just blocks from Yankee Stadium.

"According to that article in *New York*, he was a scholarship student. Casden takes them to ensure both class and racial diversity."

"Yeah, right."

"Jason supposedly had test scores off the charts. A total genius at chess. Parents who were devoted to his education. A real success story."

"And the kid winds up a heroin OD in Central Park?"

"According to the suicide note, it was all too much pressure, trying to keep up with these kids who had everything. He went from being the smartest kid at JHS 151—getting shit from his peers for carrying his books home—to being the poor kid at Casden, getting shit for not being able to afford the restaurants and stores where these kids hang."

"Damn," Rogan said as he rang the buzzer marked Moffit. "Life can suck."

Janet Moffit was waiting for them at the family's open apartment door. They entered to find the space filled with moving boxes. Discolored rectangles marked the walls where pictures had once hung.

"Watch your step around these boxes. We still have the couch to sit on for now. You said this was about Jason? Should I call my husband? He's working a shift down at Madison Square Garden—he's a security guard there—but he can come home if there's something important."

"We just have a few questions," Ellie said. "It's our understanding you have a lawsuit against David Bolt?"

"Yes. Or, well, we *did*. I never thought we'd be the kind of people to sue someone, but, that's correct, ma'am, we did indeed have a lawsuit."

"'Did,' as in past tense?" Rogan asked. According to the newspaper article, the suit had only been filed in March.

"That's right, but we reached a settlement. Wallace and I are still trying to figure out what to do with the money. We're getting out of here obviously. Too many memories of our son."

Rogan nodded sympathetically. "Where y'all heading?"

"A little further north, to Mount Vernon. It'll be my first time having a yard. Wallace grew up down in Georgia, but Jason and I never knew anything but apartment living. It'll be something to look forward to."

Certainly not the most affluent New York suburb, Mount Vernon was nevertheless a big improvement over High Bridge. A security guard wouldn't be able to swing a mortgage for a single-family house in that kind of town. The settlement must have been a good one.

"Had your son suffered from manic-depressive disorder for long?" Ellie asked.

"No, you see, that's the thing. He never had anything like that, not as far as we knew. I mean, he had hard times, like kids do. But he wasn't *crazy*. He didn't have a *mental disease*."

"So why was he in that study?"

She shook her head. Ellie assumed it was a question the woman might never be able to answer.

"And your lawyer was George Langston?"

"Yes, ma'am. He came to us right away. Said he'd worked defending drug companies his whole career and knew how they operated. He offered to represent us pro bono—without charge. His daughter, Ramona, goes to Casden. Jason always told us how nice she was to him. Even came up here once to see the park where he played chess on weekends."

"Did Mr. Langston tell you that he personally knows the doctor you filed your lawsuit against?"

"We knew he worked for drug companies at his old law firm. Is that what you mean?"

"We think it's more than a lawyer-client relationship with the drug industry generally, Mrs. Moffit. Your lawyer is very close friends with David Bolt, the doctor overseeing the research."

"I don't know anything about that. He said he knew the ins and outs of how these companies worked. That's how he was able to negotiate a quick settlement for us."

"Was that the basis of the lawsuit? That your son shouldn't have even been taking this drug if he didn't have a mental illness?"

"I'm not sure I should say anything else, Detective. Our lawsuit has a confidentiality agreement. They were very clear about that."

"It must have been a good amount of money for you to be moving, and, like you said, so fast. Did your lawyer even have enough time to conduct discovery?"

"He thought we'd do best to settle early, and we didn't want things to drag on. Like I said, ma'am, with all due respect, I think I'm done talking about what happened to my son."

Ellie had been pulled into this case against her will, but it had finally worked its way beneath her skin and would not leave while there were still more questions than answers.

As they started down the stairs, Ellie could picture Janet Moffit making a phone call to her trusted lawyer, George Langston. They had just wasted nearly a week clearing Casey Heinz, and now it felt like they were on the clock all over again.

CHAPTER FORTY-FIVE

Ramona held her mother's hand as they entered the 19th Precinct station house. She felt like a little girl, but having her mother's hand in hers also felt comforting. She was supporting her mother, her mother was allowing it, and that in itself was comforting.

So was the fact that they were filing a police report.

The two of them had shoveled the maggots back into the shoe box together. Ramona had held the box. Her mother had wrapped her hands with plastic shopping bags and swept them inside, the two of them turning their heads away as if that would stop the urge to gag.

They had secured the box with packing tape, then wrapped it in a garbage bag. Then they put it outside on the terrace. This morning Ramona's mother decided to file the police report.

It took forever to explain all this to the police officer, along with everything else that had happened. The blog. The threats. Now this crummy old Adidas shoe box filled with maggots feeding on a rotten piece of chicken.

The police officer took one look inside the box and slammed it shut. He was playing it cool, but she could tell he was pretty grossed out. "Any idea who might be doing this, ma'am?"

"No. We already talked to our doorman. He found the package just outside the building entrance yesterday afternoon. The security cameras don't reach that area. That's what he told me, at least. Can you run fingerprints or something?"

"We'll file a report and forward it to detectives. Someone will contact you."

Ramona could tell he wasn't taking them seriously.

"You need to take *our* fingerprints, don't you?"

"Excuse me?"

"Well, if they're going to search the box for prints, you'll need to eliminate us from consideration." She held up her hands. "We both touched the box."

As they walked out of the station onto Sixty-seventh Street, wiping their blackened fingertips with paper napkins, she felt that they should be doing more.

"Maybe we should call those detectives on Julia's case. They at least know the background."

"The last time they were at our apartment, Ramona, they basically accused me of doing this to myself to attract publicity."

Part of Ramona wanted to call them, just to remind them once more that they'd obviously been wrong about Julia harassing her mom. But her mother was right. They couldn't trust them. Those detectives had screwed up everything. Casey'd spent five days in jail because they wouldn't listen to anyone.

Maybe it was better to start fresh with the cops at the local precinct.

"I'm worried about you, Mom."

"I know. And as much as I haven't wanted to scare either you or myself, I'm not exactly comfortable with this, either. It's going to be okay, though. Thanks for coming with me. I'll miss you this weekend."

"Are you *sure* you won't stay home?" Her mother had planned to spend the weekend at the beach house to work on her book, though Ramona thought this latest escalation of the threats required a change in plans.

"I'll be fine, sweetie. Going away for a few days is going to help clear my head. Why don't you come, too?"

After Ramona had overheard those detectives grilling her mother about her book contract, they had finally had an honest conversation about the blog. Her mother told her all the horrible things that had happened to her when she was young. How her mother hadn't believed her. How she tried to forgive her mom after she died, but never did get past it. How she started keeping a journal two years ago. How she started the blog on a lark, then received an online comment from a book editor asking Adrienne to contact her.

And after telling her daughter the entire story, Adrienne still remained worried only about Ramona. She assured her that the book was being published under a pseudonym. That no one would need to know her mother had written it. But Ramona didn't care about any of that. She had hugged her mother and said, "If it were up to me, I'd want the whole world to know. I'm so proud of you." And since then, they were back to the way they were. No more secrets. They promised.

"You know I have debate team." She tried one more time to persuade her mother to stay in the city. "Can't you write at home?"

"I'll get more done out east. And, honestly, the further away I can get from the scene of the maggot crime, the better. We may need to replace those floorboards." She feigned a shudder. "Trust me. I'll be fine."

"You promise?"

"I promise."

They both knew that unlike their promise not to keep any more secrets, this was a promise they had no control over. But, just like the feeling of her mother's hand in hers, the words were a comfort.

CHAPTER
FORTY-SIX

The lobby of the Park Manhattan was typical for a midtown office tower. Lots of marble. Lots of glass. Expensive but nondescript art. Post-9/11 security guards manning the front desk, insisting on identification and issuing electronically monitored guest passes before granting entry.

On this particular day in this particular office tower, one of the security guards had already made the phone call they'd requested. The call was to a Margene Waters, former secretary to George Langston, former partner at the law firm of Mascal & Blank. Could she please come downstairs? She had a floral arrangement requiring a personal signature.

"How do you know she'll talk to us?" Ellie asked.

"I don't," Rogan said. "Worst thing that happens is she tells Langston we're asking about him and his farce of a lawsuit against his buddy, Bolt. Pretty sure the Moffits will have already let that cat out of the bag. The way I see it, secretaries feel one of two ways about any given boss: fiercely loyal to the ones who are good to them, and eager for karma to catch up to the rest. You met George Langston. He seem like the kind of guy to remember Secretary's Day?"

The security guard nodded in their direction when the woman they were looking for stepped out of the elevator. Margene was about forty years old, dressed professionally in a navy sheath dress. Her five-inch, bright-white heels were the only giveaway that she wasn't one of the lawyers at the blue-chip firm.

When they explained they had some questions about George Langston, she glanced back toward the closing elevator doors, already planning her retreat from the conversation.

"We can talk somewhere else if that would be better," Rogan said. He flashed the smile Ellie had seen work magic so many times before. "Bet you know a coffee shop around here that brews a way better cup than whatever insta-java stuff they have upstairs. On us. We just need some background info."

"You're real police, right?" She had a heavy Long Island accent. "Not some fringy private investigators or something?"

"Why would a private eye be asking questions about George Langston?" Ellie asked.

"Half the partners who got pushed out last year have either sued the firm or are getting sued for poaching clients. It's like *Lord of the Flies* since the downsizing. All the staff knows we'll get fired in a New York minute for helping any of the old guard."

Now Ellie had a smile to match Rogan's. Ladies and gentlemen, they had found themselves a talker. They assured her they weren't interested in the internal workings of the law firm, and then made their way to a Starbucks on Sixth Avenue.

Margene didn't even wait for them to ask a question before launching in. "So the suspense is killing me. What in the world could two police detectives want to know about *George*?" She emphasized his name as if it alone captured the very essence of his uninterestingness.

Rogan followed their game plan of easing into the subject gently. "Something bad happened to one of his daughter's friends. It would help us put some of the information in context if we had a better sense of the family dynamics."

"Ramona's okay, though, right? You don't think she did anything wrong."

"Oh no, nothing like that," Rogan assured her.

"Oh, thank God. That girl is such a little sweetheart. Hard to believe she grew up with George. I mean, not that he's a bad guy, but—well, have you met him?" They nodded. "Okay, so then you know. I mean, some of the girls upstairs thought he was adorable in this old-fashioned way, but I never quite got it. He's just . . . he's so . . . pent-up. Maybe the fact that Ramona's so laid-back is proof of the whole nature-over-nurture thing. Or maybe it's because of Adrienne. Now, boy, did George get lucky there."

Ellie was beginning to wonder whether this woman was even breathing between sentences. "So it sounds like you know Ramona was adopted, and that Adrienne came into the picture later?"

"Oh, of course. Everyone knew. I mean, I wasn't there when it all went down, but people talk. No one—not even the girls who were kind of into him—could believe George was marrying someone like Adrienne. I mean, she's gorgeous. And such a doll. So, on the one hand, it's like, how the hell did he land her? But on the other hand, you could kind of tell that George would be watching all the other partners when Adrienne was around, like she might embarrass him or something. Don't get me wrong. He absolutely loves her. But George is so class-conscious, you know?"

They didn't, but they were about to.

"Seersucker suits in the summertime. Bow ties. He wants to be taken so seriously. But"—she lowered her voice to a whisper—"you know his father was a building superintendent? That's right. He didn't come from money. You'd think he'd be proud of it, but—whatever. At least he married a great woman and raised a great daughter. That's gotta say something."

"How about friends?" Rogan asked.

"Same kind of thing. Always chasing the social ladder. Honestly? I think it's why he got pushed out. The partners here didn't respect him enough. And he was having a hard time bringing in clients, too. People issues, you know? People can tell when you're not comfortable in your own skin."

"Isn't he friends with some muckety-muck doctor?" Ellie said it like she wasn't sure of the details.

"Oh, that's David. David Bolt. Yeah, those two go all the way back to middle school. David told me once—I'm sure George didn't like it—that George's dad was the super in David's family's apartment building. That's how they got to be friends. More like brothers—you know how guys can be? Better friends to each other than us girls, I hate to say. David was actually the one to get Ramona into that fancy school. I was the one who drafted the letter to the headmistress. In fact, George might've been pushed out earlier if it weren't for David throwing him business here and there."

"What kind of work?" Rogan asked.

"You know, a drug company matter, usually litigation. Sometimes it was work for the patent department. One matter was a construction project for NYU Medical Center. But it was always one little thing or another, not enough to make George a rainmaker or anything. Not even enough to save him from the ax, as it turned out."

Margene had nearly drained her frothy whipped-cream coffee drink and was starting to look at her watch. They thanked her for the information and got her home number in case they needed to contact her again.

"I didn't mean to make him sound like a bad guy," she said. "Once I get on a roll, I'm hard to stop. And it's always so much easier for some reason to go straight to the imperfections. George is a very nice man at heart."

Her post-gossip pangs of guilt must have still been kicking, because as they walked out onto Sixth Avenue, she pulled her cell phone from her purse. "The week he asked me to draft Ramona's recommendation letter from Dr. Bolt, I wound up having to work eighty hours because of a deal that exploded. To thank me, he gave me a weekend in the country. Got me a car service both ways and everything. They had these cute little llama things. Look, isn't that sweet?"

Ellie took a look at the picture on the screen to be polite. A Long Island gal like Margene thought she had spent the weekend with llamas.

The two animals in the pictures were not llamas, but alpacas. And in the background behind them stood a distinctive red barn with a sloped green metal roof.

She could tell from Rogan's expression that he'd made the connection as well. When he'd seen the animals on Julia Whitmire's Facebook page in front of that same barn, he had thought they were goats.

"Oh, those *are* cute," Ellie said. "That was very nice of him to thank you so generously. Is that the Langstons' place?" If Ramona's family owned alpacas at a country property, that would certainly explain how Julia could have spent time there as well.

Margene nodded. "Up in Pound Ridge. Nothing fancy—seemed almost like a cabin or something—but tons of land, and definitely relaxing."

Ellie's phone buzzed. She let Rogan handle the goodbyes and stepped to the curb to answer the call.

"Hatcher."

"This is Detective Sean Doherty from the 19th Precinct. I was just handed a potential stalking report from a walk-in up here. I was about to write it off as a lost cause, but I found the victim's name in an incident report you filed in a homicide case you caught last Monday. Your vic, Julia Whitmire, posted some kind of harassment on a blog belonging to Adrienne Langston?"

"That's correct. Are you telling me Adrienne Langston finally filed a police report about those comments on her blog?"

"It's more than comments. We've got a box full of maggots courtesy of Mrs. Langston's own personal evidence collection."

"I'm sorry," she said. "You have *what*?"

"Her doorman handed her a surprise delivery: an Adidas shoe box nearly full of those nasty little fuckers. The fella in the property room had stomach enough to forage through the pile. Guess there was half a rancid chicken at the bottom. So is this for real or what?"

"If the maggots were real, then, yes, I'd say it's for real."

"No need to get feisty. I'm asking whether this should go to you as part of your homicide."

Ellie hated that word. When Ellie heard *feisty*, she thought of tiny, yippy dogs who nipped at ankles. She didn't nip at ankles. She bit. And when she bit, she went for the jugular.

But she *had* been a little bitchy. "Yeah, refer the report to us. We'll handle it out of our squad. But can you send the box full of nastiness straight to the lab for analysis?"

"Already done."

"That was quick."

"I'd tell you it's because we're here to protect and serve, but we were just glad to get those suckers out of here."

As she ended the call, Rogan clicked the Crown Vic's doors unlocked. "Do I even want to know why you were talking about maggots?"

"I need to schmooze the crime lab. And we need to talk to Adrienne Langston again."

CHAPTER FORTY-SEVEN

Thank you, Nelson. Send him up."

Ramona propped the apartment door open, the way she always did after telling the doorman to send someone upstairs. But then she thought better of it and walked out to the hallway. She wanted to see Casey as soon as possible.

When he'd finally been released from jail the previous evening, he had called her immediately. But she had to be with her mother. That awful box. Cleaning up the mess. Helping Mom pack for the trip to Long Island. By the time she finished, the curfew at Promises had passed, and Casey couldn't leave.

The least she could do was wait in the hallway.

She was surprised by her own reaction when he stepped from the elevator. This had been the worst week of her life, worse than anything she ever could have imagined. Julia was gone. Her mother was being stalked. The police had falsely accused Casey of doing something he could never do.

But the minute she saw Casey in person, she felt herself smile for the first time since she'd heard about Julia's death. It was a big smile, the kind that moved through your entire body. And before she knew it, she was hugging Casey. They had never hugged before. Sure, they'd done the hand-on-shoulder, peck on the cheek style of greeting, but now they were really holding on to each other. To her surprise, she found herself burrowing her face into the crook of his neck before quickly pulling away. She hoped he didn't sense the guilt in her movement.

"I'm so glad they finally realized they were wrong about you," she said, shepherding him into the apartment. "Are you doing okay back at Promises?"

"You know you've had a bad week when you're ecstatic to be sleeping at a homeless shelter."

"Maybe you can stay here for a while. I can talk to my dad tonight—"

He waved a hand. "I wasn't dropping hints for a place to stay. Ms. Ri is trying to get me to see the bright side in all this. My lawyer thinks I might have a lawsuit against Julia's dad and those security guards, but I don't really know whether I want to do that or not. Julia's mom feels so horrible she actually offered to let me stay at their house with her until I get my act together. Plus, the group that got me my lawyer is going to help me find a job. They even asked me about starting college classes. I feel like I might be able to turn this into something positive."

"That's great, Casey."

"Not like Columbia or anything like that. Community college, but whatever. We'll see what happens. I don't want to get my hopes up."

"Maybe you deserve to get your hopes up, after what you went through."

She saw a hunger in his eyes, and then looked away. More guilt.

They were interrupted by the telephone. It was Nelson from downstairs. Detectives Hatcher and Rogan from the NYPD were here to see her mother.

"Send them up," she said. "Speaking of last week, I think a couple of detectives owe you a serious apology."

Ellie was used to dealing with attitude. That was pretty much a typical day in the life of a cop—dealing with attitude. But sixteen-year-old girls had a certain brand of attitude that she found especially trying.

"My mother is out at the beach. She's working on her book. And hiding from some nutjob who's stalking her. But at least Casey's here—now that he's finally out of *jail*."

Apparently Rogan wasn't in the mood to sit through the tirade. "You done venting, Ramona?"

"No, not really. I told you that Julia would never threaten my mom. I told you that Casey was innocent. And I told you that I was scared for my mother. I practically begged you to listen. I *trusted* you."

Ellie wanted to write the girl off as a spoiled brat, but that last remark—that the girl had trusted them, and they had failed her—hit too close to home to ignore. "Is that why your mother filed the police report with the 19th Precinct instead of with us?"

Ramona looked at her feet. "We didn't think you'd listen. We thought someone else might take it more seriously."

"We're taking it seriously. I already cashed in some chips with the lab to get them to rush the analysis of the shoe box. But you're right. We got waylaid there for a few days. We made some mistakes."

Ramona started to argue, but Casey interrupted. "No, it's okay. They did what they thought was right under the circumstances."

"But that's because—"

"I know. Trust me—I *know* what those asshole security guards did to me. Not to mention Brandon and Vonda."

Ellie groaned at the mention of their names. "If we find those two idiots, I'll escort them to jail personally."

"I don't think they'll be back. You know, Brandon had the audacity to send me an e-mail this morning, apologizing?"

The news gave Ramona a new direction for her anger. "Right. Because an apology makes up for trying to frame you for murder. *Oops. My bad.*"

"He said it was Vonda's idea, which I absolutely believe. Plus, Vonda took off in the middle of the night with all the cash they got from the Whitmires, stranding him in Idaho. Now Brandon's in Portland. No money. No Ms. Ri."

"Any chance you can make them come back here?" Ramona asked.

Ellie shook her head. There was already a warrant out for both Brandon and Vonda for obstruction of justice and defrauding the Whitmires out of the reward money, but they'd probably never be extradited to New York.

"Stupid idiot actually thought Promises might take him back in," Casey said. "He was all, *I can't believe how bad I messed things up. We had a good thing going with Promises and people like Julia and Ramona trying to help us.* Way to show your gratitude. Send the police off on some wild goose chase when they should've been finding out what really happened to Julia."

"We do regret the way things have played out. But we're here now to try to help your mom, Ramona. That's what we all want, right?" She could tell Ramona wanted to show some more fight, but the girl eventually nodded. "Is your mother out in East Hampton alone?"

"Yeah. My dad's working."

"Is that typical—for her to go there alone?"

She shrugged. "Not typical, but, you know, my dad works pretty hard, trying to get his own firm off the ground. So she and I do our own thing sometimes. And lately she's been more on her own. I didn't know why until I found out how important this blog thing is to her. All these months, she's been sneaking off to write."

Ellie hadn't thought of it when they'd been talking to George's secretary about the alpacas, but she didn't have the Langstons pegged as wealthy enough to own so much property. "Do you guys also have a place up in the country?" Ellie asked.

Ramona shook her head. "Just the apartment and the beach. Oh, and yeah, my dad has that farm up in Pound Ridge, but it's land he bought with some friends right out of law school. It's more of an investment."

"A real working ranch, huh?"

"Yeah. Cattle and alpacas, even. They hire local guys to do all the work, but I think my dad likes the idea of being a weekend cowboy."

"How about you? Are you infected with the country bug?"

"No way. My mom says I'd hate it. There's nothing to do, and the house is barely even a house. More like a cave for my dad and his friends to play poker twice a year and pretend they're still twenty years old. She's only been there, like, twice. I've never even bothered."

"*Never?*"

She shook her head.

"I hear you." The picture of Julia in the country was taking on new meaning. Maybe a few of the secretaries at his former law firm weren't the only girls who saw an appealing side to George. "The Hamptons sound much nicer. Hopefully, your dad at least got to take some time off work to go with you and your mom last weekend?"

"Yeah. Well, the first part, at least. He went back on Saturday night."

Rogan gave Ellie a small nod. It was J. J. Rogan code for *nicely done*. They were just about done here.

"Do you mind if I use the bathroom before we head out?"

As the elevator doors closed, Ellie studied Casey and Ramona, standing side by side at the apartment entrance. Casey had that same adoring look he'd had on his face whenever he had talked about Ramona. And, contrary to what they had been told by Brandon and Vonda, Ramona no longer seemed oblivious to Casey's attention. She leaned slightly in toward him. She seemed comfortable with his hand on her back.

Ellie found herself wishing—for their sakes—that the world was less complicated.

"You took long enough in the bathroom," Rogan said. "I was running my mouth so long I wound up telling that Casey kid to sue the hell out of Bill Whitmire. Meanwhile, you were off violating the Fourth Amendment, weren't you?"

"It's not like I tore their bedroom apart or anything." Like most police, they both knew the difference between a little shortcut and the kind of screw-up that led to evidence getting thrown out of court. "I got a list of all the incoming phone numbers on their caller ID. Way faster than the phone company." She waved her notebook proudly.

"Damn. I hope you can read your own handwriting, because that looks like chicken scratch to me."

"Sorry, wrong number." She dialed while Rogan drove. "That was Duane Reade."

"Sorry, wrong number." She ended yet another call. "Hair salon."

"Sorry, wrong number. Some place called Marea?" It sounded familiar.

"Restaurant," he said. "Central Park South."

"Ah, right." One meal probably cost more than her entire month's take-out budget. "Yes, hello. I'm sorry. What business did I call? . . . Attorney at law? . . . Yes, can you tell me why someone from this number may have called George Langston last Thursday?"

Rogan shook his head. They both knew there was no way a receptionist would answer that question.

"All right. Well, I assume Mr. Wiles does some kind of drug or medical malpractice type of litigation?" It wouldn't be unusual for a lawyer to call Langston at home.

"Exclusively? Okay. Thank you very much."

Not the pharmacist or the hair salon or a fancy-pants restaurant. Not even an adversary on a pending case.

"That was the law office of Mr. Michael Wiles, Esquire, Attorney at Law." She mimicked the receptionist's professionally pleasant voice.

"Esquire, Attorney at Law? Isn't that redundant?"

"Yes, but here's the excellent part. This particular Esquire, Attorney at Law, practices nothing but family law. We suspected Julia might have an older man in her life. Now we find out George Langston has a private little alpaca ranch—and now maybe a divorce lawyer?"

"Everyone seems to agree Julia was sexually adventurous. What did that teacher say about wanting men who were off limits? Can't get much more forbidden than your best friend's sort-of-handsome but rigid and inaccessible dad. It would certainly explain why Julia didn't tell Ramona who she was dating."

"It could also explain the threats on Adrienne's website."

"Well, only the first one, right? Maybe George found out about Adrienne's blog and told Julia. In a fit of jealousy, she posts a late-night comment, just to fuck with her. But then who's messing with Adrienne now?"

"Maybe status-conscious George doesn't want her writing about her background—her trashy family, her abuse, the fact that she was a babysitter before she was Mrs. George Langston. He could have been the one to post the first threat, too, using Julia's computer. He wasn't in East Hampton that weekend, after all."

Rogan pointed a finger at her. "Aha! You're starting to think we're actually on to something."

"Maybe," she said grudgingly. Her cell phone buzzed in her hand. "Hatcher."

"Hey, Ellie Belly. It's M and M."

Michael Ma was by far the nicest analyst in the entire NYPD. He also liked nicknames. And cookies. Three Christmas Eves earlier, Ellie had passed off a dozen Bouchon Bakery nutter-butters as her own home-baked recipe to persuade Mike to stay late to compare a latent pulled from a stolen handgun to Ellie's favorite suspect. One of these days he'd figure out that he, too, could score a hand-made nutter-butter for two-twenty-five a pop at the Time Warner Center. Until then, Mike was Ellie Belly's go-to guy for a lab rush.

"I got seven latents off that shoe box. Five of them belonged to your vic and her daughter. And two come back to the same guy: James Grisco, DOB March 13, 1972."

"Any chance he's the doorman who handed them the package?"

"Park Avenue address? I don't think they hire murderers as door-men."

"Grisco has a murder conviction?"

"Served fifteen years. Got out two months ago."

"Cool. Anything else?"

"I'm just the print guy. You guys figure out what it all means. And bring the cookies."

"Will do, Double-M. This Friday at the latest. I promise." She ended the call before he could argue about the timing. "If George Langston is Adrienne's 'secret admirer,' we may have found the guy who can help us prove it."

CHAPTER FORTY-EIGHT

Their lieutenant had her head tilted back in her chair, a bottle of Visine trembling over one fluttering eye. "Fucking LASIK. You're the one who convinced me to do this, Rogan. What about you, Hatcher? Contacts?"

"Some days, but I can go without."

"Another reason to hate the both of you. Now, how many times are you going to change your minds about this one case?"

"You can't hold the Casey Heinz bump in the road against us," Hatcher said. "That was all Bill Whitmire. We said from the beginning that his guy Earl Gundley was bad news."

Ellie's remark wasn't quite a told-you-so, but the groan that came out of Tucker's throat was a sign she recalled vouching for the former cop.

"Pretty damn big bump in the road. So tell me again what you've got on George Langston."

Ellie gave Tucker a quick update on Langston's investment property up in Pound Ridge and the photograph of Julia. "We thought all along Julia was probably seeing someone she didn't want her friends to know about, even Ramona. We also knew she had a thing for men who were inaccessible. And men who were older. If the man was George Langston, that would certainly explain why Julia never told Ramona. And it would also explain why Julia might have posted threatening comments on Adrienne's blog."

"And what do you know about George Langston?"

"A family law attorney phoned the Langston house two days ago, which means George might be looking into a divorce. And he had multiple motives to kill Julia—she may have been close to telling Adrienne or Ramona about the affair, or she could have discovered that something wasn't so kosher about George and his representation of Jason Moffit's parents. It looks like he sidled into the Moffits' good graces to convince them to sell out quick in their lawsuit against his friend David Bolt. He shuts them up, and Bolt continues business as usual."

"That's a lot of mights and maybes," Tucker said. "And why would Langston take a case where he had such an obvious conflict of interest? He could lose his license."

"We've seen people do worse out of friendship. Or maybe Bolt paid him to help keep it quiet. From what we can tell, Langston isn't making nearly as much money as he used to draw from the firm, but there's been no change in the lifestyle: same school for Ramona, same luxury apartment, same vacation house in East Hampton."

"We're just asking for a couple days more to see these leads through," Rogan said. "No additional staff. Just the two of us."

"You two are always scheming, working the brass. 'No additional resources. Only a couple of days.' But here's the thing. You two have been all over the place since this case started. Now you think you've finally got a theory, but Adrienne Langston is still being threatened. Where does this James Grisco guy fit into the picture?"

"Minimal information on him as of now," Ellie said. "A DUI and a burg in the early nineties, then arrested in '95 for murder at the age of twenty-three in Buffalo. Victim was a forty-nine-year-old white male, an insurance agent named Wayne Cooper. The state alleged Grisco lay in wait before stabbing him to death. Agreed to life in prison to avoid the death penalty, but got out four months ago after testifying against a cellmate."

"Is there a parole officer?"

"I called him this morning," Rogan said. "The PO had no clue the guy was in the city. Grisco's been clean as far as he knows. He's got a New York State driver's license that puts him in Buffalo, but his fingerprints are on a hand-delivered box here in Manhattan. Until we've got something better, our best guess is that Grisco's in the local area and Langston slipped him a few bucks to dump the package in front of their apartment building."

"Be nice to get that nailed down."

They both nodded, because that's all they could do. There was still so much they didn't know.

"And if George Langston is your man, why is he sending a shoe box full of maggots to his wife?"

"The threats started after Adrienne signed her book deal," Ellie said. "She might be all about opening up and not having secrets, but maybe he doesn't share that point of view. We need to know exactly how he feels about her blog and her book. Now that Adrienne's actually scared, we're hoping that fear might motivate her to open up to us a little more."

"Right. Because she's really going to like you when you tactfully broach the subject of her husband possibly banging their kid's best friend."

"I know," Ellie said. "We've got some serious sucking up to do. I can apologize very profusely when necessary."

"Funny. I've never noticed." Tucker looked at the notes she'd been jotting down. "All right, keep working it. Talk to Adrienne first. See just how much her husband knows about this book and how he felt about it."

"Adrienne's at their house in East Hampton. You want us to wait until tomorrow?" It was already four o'clock. Driving out there today would mean serious overtime.

"You finally have a suspect that feels right to you. I know the two of you. Just go. And bring me back a lobster roll. And tomorrow you try to find that James Grisco person. If he can give you the connection between Langston and that shoe box, you might actually have something."

CHAPTER FORTY-NINE

Ellie emerged from Tucker's office to find Max sitting at her desk.

"Hey, you."

"You got a second?"

She didn't. Not really. But Rogan, overhearing, said, "I gotta get some stuff from the locker room. We can head out in ten."

They walked together onto Twenty-first Street, neither of them speaking until they were away from the crowd of cops on a smoke break outside the precinct station house.

"Sorry to just show up at work like this."

"You never have to apologize."

"I did a lot of thinking last night." She had called him to see if he was coming over. For the first time since they'd gotten together, he hadn't returned her call. "I didn't get any sleep. I'm totally exhausted. And I can't do it again tonight."

"Okay. What can I do?" He was really scaring her.

"I wanted to make sure I saw you in person. We need to talk. I was upset with you for having made a decision that affected both of us, but now I've made one, too."

She knew it would come to this. It had been a week since they'd both realized they were picturing different futures together. They'd been pretending to have moved past the issue, but of course they hadn't. How could they? "Please don't do this, Max. Not like this."

"Will you just listen?"

She knew somehow she would find a way to blow it. He was breaking up with her. On the sidewalk. At work. Before she had to get in a car with Rogan for a three-hour drive.

"I—can we just talk about it later?"

"Did you not hear me before? I left work because I couldn't get anything done. I need to say this now."

"Please—" She hated the pleading sound in her own voice.

"I love you, Ellie."

"I love you, too." Unlike his statement, hers didn't have the sound of a "but" at the end.

"We can't keep doing what we're doing. One day at a time. Never knowing where we're sleeping or when we'll see each other. We've been dating a year and you've never even met my parents. Or my friends, for that matter."

"I've met your friends," she protested.

"No, you've run into a few of my friends at work. It's not the same. We have a lot of fun, Ellie, and we talk shop really well to-gether, but this isn't a real relationship. I know we have the potential for more, but I need to know you're going to be there."

"Of course I'm here. And of course it's real." It was the most real relationship she'd ever had.

"I want us to live together."

This was not what she was expecting. She felt a lump build in her throat from relief.

"We practically live together now."

He shook his head. "No, we spend practically every night to-gether. That's not the same. I want us to share a home. To share a life. To plan around each other. To take vacations together."

"When was the last time either of us had a vacation?"

He shared the brief smile. "Fine. I want us to plan a vacation that we'll take five years from now. I want us to take each other into consideration, no matter what."

"I consider you. I always have, ever since we met."

"Will you please stop disagreeing with everything I say? Maybe I made a mistake wording it like I'm fixing a problem. My point is that I love you, I want us to be together, and I was so pumped to tell you that I bailed on a unit meeting so I could get up here and talk to you right now. Just say yes and I'll leave here satisfied."

She'd thought about living together. Of course she had. And on those previous occasions, she had run through all of the logistical questions: Where would they live? Was either of their apartments large enough to accommodate both of them? If they got a new place, how would they split the bills? Could she really bring herself to walk away from a rent-controlled apartment?

Max had obviously analyzed the same considerations. "We'll get a bigger place. If we combine our rents, we could even get a two-bedroom. And Jess can sublet your apartment in the meantime— just in case."

Jess had held his current job longer than any previous work, but he still wasn't up to carrying a lease on his own. "Then I need to talk to him to see—"

"Those are all just details, Ellie. Say you want it to happen, and I'll know it's going to happen." He pushed her hair back behind her ear and stroked her cheek. "You're looking for reasons to say no."

He had it wrong. She wanted to say yes. She wanted to unpack moving boxes with him and argue about how to arrange the furniture. She wanted to wake up with him every morning.

And it wasn't the logistics of leases and square footage and rent control that kept her from leaping at the invitation, one she'd been hoping for at some level for months. As much as she wanted to, she couldn't ignore the real reason he was asking her for this now.

"Do you really think we should move in together when you know we ultimately are going to want different things? It'll just make things that much harder on both of us down the road when you—"

"We don't need to decide that now. It's taking it to the next step. We'll make bigger decisions later—together."

She saw Rogan standing in front of the precinct, watching them, keys in hand.

"But I told you, that one big decision has already been made. You're asking me to change."

Ellie had lived with a boyfriend once. He had wanted her to change, too. He couldn't understand why she had to keep working as a cop when he was offering her the life of an investment banker's wife. When she realized she had to leave, she had nowhere to go. She was stuck under his roof, still sleeping in his bed, still sleeping with him, until one of Jess's friends decided to move to Nashville and Ellie scored her apartment.

"You've told me before about every guy you've ever dated wanting you to change. I don't want you *ever* to change, at least not for me, not for anyone but yourself. But I know you, Ellie. You may not believe me, but I know there's room for evolution in your life. That is not the same as asking you to change. I'm asking you to make room for some flexibility. To let yourself *not* make final decisions. To make room for another person in your life. To open up your mind to the possibility that life is a constant process of getting to know yourself, and that sometimes you get to know yourself better when you're not so *alone*."

She'd heard him say all this that first night, when they were fighting. Not everything was black-and-white. Maybe so, but most things were.

Rogan was staring at his shoes now, jiggling the keys.

"Damn it. Rogan's waiting. We've got to find Adrienne Langston."

"You can't say yes before you leave?"

"Not like that, Max. I want to, but I want it to be real. I want us *both* to feel right about it."

"Okay, I get it. The offer still stands."

"We'll figure it out, okay? I promise. I love you."

He nodded, but didn't respond as she turned to walk away.

CHAPTER
FIFTY

For the sixth time in a mile, Rogan hit the dashboard lights to cut through a snarl of traffic on Highway 27.

"What is it about white people and the Hamptons?"

To call 27 a highway this far east was misleading. The state should relabel it Gridlock 27. Parking Lot 27. Fancy Car Show 27. Come Memorial Day, this two-lane road that connected Southampton to Watermill to Bridgehampton to East Hampton to Amagansett to Montauk would be a knot of Porsches, Range Rovers, and Jaguars filled with beautiful people bouncing between the beach, gourmet restaurants, and designer boutiques. Cars were at least moving this time of year, but at a crawl.

"And what's up with you?" he said. "You been staring out that window the whole ride. This got something to do with that pop-in from Donovan?"

She didn't want to talk about Max to anyone else. It would feel like a betrayal. "I think you'd fit right in here with your black BMW and fancy Joseph Abboud suits."

"Hate to break it to you, but Abboud's not fancy. This here's Valentino."

"See what I mean? Wait. Turn right up here." They had decided not to call ahead. Sometimes a witness's startled face said more than her words. They wanted to see Adrienne's expression when they showed her the photograph of Julia at the country house. They wanted to watch as they asked her about a phone call to their home from a family law attorney. They needed to be there in person as they raised the possibility that her husband had been sleeping with a girl she'd treated like a daughter.

Sometimes their work was cruel.

Ellie continued to navigate. As they passed the turnoff for the Maidstone Golf Club, they saw water ahead. "This is it. The last turn. Take a right. The Langston house should be on the left."

As soon as Rogan made the turn, she saw the overhead lights of an East Hampton Town Police patrol car to her right. At first it was just the one car near the intersection, but further down, she caught sight of at least one more East Hampton marked car, a Suffolk County Police car, two unmarked fleet cars, and an ambulance.

A uniformed officer next to the first car held up a hand to stop them. She rolled down her window, and Rogan leaned over to speak.

"What's up, guy?" The question was code, the kind of easy line retired cops gave during a traffic stop. To call an officer *guy* meant you were on the job.

Ellie found that badges worked just as well as macho code words. She wiggled hers near the open window.

"Home intruder," the officer explained. "Smashed a back window out with a rock to gain entry. Good thing the resident was armed. Turns out you can be a pretty crappy shot as long as you've got six bullets."

"Was this at the Langston house, by any chance?" Ellie asked. She rattled off the address.

"How'd you know? The poor lady's terrified, but she got lucky. Suffolk County homicide detectives are here. They pulled a wallet off the intruder. I hear the guy did a dime and a half upstate. Murder. Was supposed to be life in prison but he got out early. Shoulda stayed inside, I guess. Good guys, one. Bad guys, zero."

Life sentence for murder. Served fifteen. It all sounded too familiar. "The bad guy didn't happen to be named James Grisco?"

"Yeah, that's the name I heard. Seriously, how do you know all
this?"

Rogan was on his third cup of coffee since they'd arrived at the East
Hampton police station. It was two in the morning, and everyone
was exhausted. "I'm surprised she hasn't lawyered up." He drained
the rest of his cup.

They were watching Adrienne Langston and Suffolk County
Homicide Detective Marci Howard through a one-way interrogation room window.

"She doesn't need a lawyer if it's justified," Ellie said.

"That's how poor people think. Rich folks from Manhattan call a
lawyer every time they sign their name on a piece of paper."

"So far she's doing just fine on her own."

Detective Howard was reluctant to involve them at first, insisting
that the shooting had occurred in her jurisdiction. But when she realized that they had a head start on the background, she had at least
permitted them to stick around and observe. She'd even stopped a
few times to give them updates in a voice that hinted of a southern
upbringing.

Everything they had learned indicated that James Grisco had arrived at the house with the intention of harming Adrienne. A rock
was found inside the back kitchen window, surrounded by broken
glass. Signs of the resulting struggle ran from the kitchen, through
the dining room, to the adjacent study, where Adrienne had gone
for the gun in her husband's bottom desk drawer. The legally registered .38 had been purchased nearly twelve years earlier when
George's first wife complained that she thought she saw someone
watching their house. Adrienne had fired all six rounds, managing
to clip Grisco first in the shoulder and then deliver a fatal shot to the
head. A knife was found next to his body.

Through the glass, they watched as Adrienne walked Detective
Howard through the lengthy story of her blog, the book deal, the
harassing comments, the box delivered to her apartment, and now
Grisco's arrival to her home this evening.

"And you filed a police report when?"

"After the box showed up at my apartment. Until then, I figured
words were only words and the police wouldn't be able to do anything."

"And you have no idea who this James Grisco is? Or why he'd be
wanting to hurt you?"

"No, I've never heard of him."

Howard rapped her knuckles against the tabletop. "All right. I
know you're tired. Let's see about getting you out of here pretty
soon."

When Howard emerged from the interrogation room, she seemed
surprised to see them standing there. "You guys are still around?"

"Of course," Ellie said. "We know tonight's shooting is yours,
but we think it could be related to our case in Manhattan."

"The teenaged girl."

"Correct." They had given Howard an abbreviated version of
the facts, but could tell she was having a hard time tracking all the
moving pieces.

"Well, I'm about to call the riding ADA, but I think we're about
set here."

"That's it?"

"What else do you want, Detectives? I've got an upstanding citizen with a legal gun defending herself against a convicted killer
whose fingerprints—as you told me—were found all over a box full
of maggots left at her primary residence, and who now drives all
the way out here to break into her other home while she's alone. I
mentioned the knife by his body, right? Just next to his right hand."

"We think Grisco may have been sent here by Adrienne's husband, George Langston."

"I know. You already told me that, Detective. Here's how I look
at it. You've been dealing with this crowd for, what? A week? And

all that business with the drug research and the online stalking and the girl in the bathtub all happened in Manhattan. As far as I know, James Grisco came out here one time only and got himself killed over it. I'm pretty damn sure I know exactly how and why that came to be. We'll run the prints on the knife. Have our ballistics and blood experts look over the shooting for anything fishy. But until I learn different, I am treating Mrs. Langston in there like an innocent citizen. In fact, some might say she's a hero. There may very well be more to the story, but unless you're telling me that James Grisco's death wasn't justified, I'll consider it to be your story and not mine."

"But—"

Ellie felt Rogan's arm on her bicep.

"Looks like your partner's getting my drift, Detective Hatcher. Some of my colleagues would be trying to fight you for jurisdiction. They might've asked you to leave hours ago. What I'm telling you is that you're now free to answer any remaining questions you have about what may have happened back in the city. I'm not in your way."

They were interrupted by the sounds of a panicked voice beyond the interrogation rooms.

"My wife. Where's my wife? Adrienne Langston? I need to see her. Adrienne? Adrienne? Is she okay?"

Detective Howard walked toward the sound of the voice. "Are you Mr. Langston? All right, sir. It's okay. I've got your wife right back here. I think it's about time we sent her home."

As she led him to the interrogation room and opened the door, George Langston did not appear to notice their presence. He ran to his wife, fell to his knees, and wrapped his arms around her.

Howard let out a loud sigh. "Like I said, the rest is pretty much up to you, but if you want my two cents: that's not the face of a man who sent James Grisco out here to kill his wife. He looks even more scared than his wife did fifteen minutes after she killed a man."

The couple seemed oblivious to the three of them watching their reunion through the window. George's sideways hug around his still-seated wife was awkward, but he managed to rock her like a baby anyway. It was Adrienne who finally pulled away, wiping tears from her husband's face.

The first thing Adrienne said to him was, "Where's Ramona?"

"I told her there was an emergency at work. I knew you'd want to be the one to explain this to her." He held her tightly again.

If George Langston was faking concern for his wife, he was a hell of an actor.

"Careful on the drive back," Howard said. "Nothing but drunks on the road this time of night."

Ellie looked at her watch. It was nearly three in the morning, and they still had a long drive back to the city.

"And I've got a present for you before you leave. We found a 2004 Malibu on the street outside the Langstons' house, registered to Grisco at the same address as his driver's license. Looks like it's a relative's place. Nothing of interest in the vehicle, but we did find directions to the Langstons' address. Follow those backwards, and you'll probably find out where he was staying."

"You're not going to check it out?"

Howard looked at Rogan. "Will you please explain to her I'm doing you two a favor?"

Rogan gave her an exhausted smile. "Trust me. She appreciates it."

"All right now. You let me know if you hear anything I need to care about. Otherwise, I'll tell you when our ADA clears this bad boy. As it stands, I'm willing to bet a paycheck on it."

The sun was coming up by the time Ellie made it back to her own bedroom. She had hoped to find Max waiting for her there. Instead, she fell asleep alone, telling herself she might have to get used to the solitude.

CHAPTER FIFTY-ONE

She was still yawning at eleven o'clock the next morning.

"Damn it, Rogan. I'm telling you, I'm about to burst. I don't have any choice. I'm doing it."

"That is disgusting. You are officially a disgusting person."

"God, you are such a germaphobe. I'll wash my hands when I'm done."

"Don't be counting on any soap in there. Or you know it's going to be all funked up."

Ellie hovered over James Grisco's toilet. The bathroom, like the rest of the apartment, was filthy. She tried not to think about the yellow streaks beneath her feet.

Rogan was right. The only soap was in the mildewed shower stall, and she had no interest in touching soap that had been rubbed on the body that had occupied this space. She found a bottle of dish soap in the kitchen, then rubbed her hands on her pants to dry them.

"Told you it'd be nasty," Rogan said.

"You and your Starbucks." That's the last time she'd suck down a Venti Americano before heading to an ex-con's crash pad. Regular deli coffee in a normal-size cup was just fine for her.

They'd found the apartment just as Detective Howard had suggested, working backwards from the handwritten directions to the

Hamptons that Grisco had left in his car. That had landed them on Ninety-first Avenue in Jamaica, Queens. She took the north side of the block; Rogan took the south. The fourth door she'd knocked on belonged to a sweet old man who had no idea the new tenant living above his garage was a convicted killer.

The landlord could use a lesson in property management, because he confirmed that Grisco had rented the filthy prefurnished apartment only six days earlier. He also confirmed that Grisco lived alone. Now that the sole tenant was dead, so were his expectations of privacy, which meant they didn't need a warrant.

As it turned out, there was very little to search. The single room was no bigger than four hundred square feet. No computer. No television. Just a few items of clothing in a rickety dresser, undoubtedly unpacked from the empty duffel bag in the closet. Milk, cereal, and two frozen dinners in the kitchen.

"Why can't this be easy?" Rogan asked. He was searching through Grisco's clothing more thoroughly.

"What did you expect to find? A neatly typed memo from George Langston to one Mr. James Grisco, subject line 're: Murder My Wife'?"

"A computer. A phone. The kinds of things that hold people's secrets. Wait, I got something." He reached into a balled sock and pulled out a roll of money. "About fifteen hundred dollars. How much did the old man say Grisco paid for this place?"

"Twelve hundred a month."

"You could get a palace in Buffalo for that."

"It may be a dump, but how was he paying for it, and with fifteen hundred bucks to spare?" They had no explanation for why Grisco was in New York City. Now they had learned that Grisco had paid his landlord first and last months' rent plus deposit—all in cash, despite having no apparent source of income.

Ellie crouched next to the bed, supporting her weight with her knees so she would not need to place her clean hands on the threadbare carpet.

"Grisco was a reader." She used a pen to slide the stack out from beneath the bed. "Two pornos and a paperback. Hey, look—he's got the same taste as you."

She recognized the image on the cover—the trunk of a Lincoln Town Car—as a series Rogan was always raving about.

"I'm strictly online now for all my pornography needs."

"Very funny. I meant this." She held up the paperback, and two small cards fell from the pages. She immediately recognized the first as a MetroCard for the buses and subways. The other was one of those frequent-customer cards promising a freebie after the requisite number of purchases. Ellie's own wallet was bursting with them, and she hadn't filled one yet. She was about to replace the cards in the book when she pulled the frequent-customer card out again. Grisco had been halfway to a free cup of coffee, but it wasn't the regularity of his beverage consumption that caught her attention.

The card was from Monster Coffee. "Check this out."

"Monstrous Coffee. Still have the taste of burnt oil in my mouth."

Ellie pulled up the Monster Coffee website on her BlackBerry. Eleven locations scattered throughout Brooklyn and Manhattan. Maybe it was only a coincidence, but she didn't like the fact that one of those branches was right across the street from the Casden School.

They moved on to the less obvious places to search: above the kitchen cabinets, behind the dresser, inside the toilet tank.

Rogan must have seen the disappointment in her face. "Maybe we'll find something in George's bank records." They had sent all the major banks a request for account statements for the Langstons, hoping to find proof that George Langston had paid money to James Grisco.

But Ellie's mind was elsewhere. "You know, I keep thinking about Langston showing up at the police station last night. He looked terrified."

"If we're right about him, then things didn't exactly go as he planned, did they? He might have been terrified of getting caught."

"No. He looked genuinely worried about Adrienne. Plus, I did some Googling this morning on that family law attorney whose number I got from the Langstons' caller ID. We assumed George was looking for a divorce, but it turns out Michael Wiles, Esquire, Attorney at Law, is seventy-eight years old with an office above a Chinese restaurant on the Lower East Side. Not exactly the kind of hired gun a guy like Langston would need for a high-priced divorce fight. And why would he send Grisco to the Hamptons house with a knife when he knew Adrienne would have access to a loaded gun?"

"Damn. Are you actually rethinking this?"

"We already made a mistake with Casey. I just don't want to jump to the wrong conclusion."

"But you never did jump to any conclusions with Casey. You said all along it didn't feel right. George, on the other hand, is the one person who ties it all together, remember?" He used his fingers to count off all of the relevant points. "We know one of the threats about his wife came from Julia's computer. Julia has a mystery boy-friend. Julia is Langston's daughter's best friend. And, oh yeah, don't forget about that picture we have of her at his country house."

He suddenly stopped talking and looked up at the ceiling.

"What?" She followed his gaze. "You see something?"

"No. But the country property. Ramona said her dad bought it right out of law school with a group of friends. What do you want to bet one of those friends is David Bolt?"

"We've been focusing on George because he's married to Adri-enne and obviously knew Julia. But if Adrienne knows that George helped Bolt sweep the Moffit family's lawsuit under the rug—"

"Then Bolt might have more to lose than even George."

"Shit. Remember Casey said yesterday that Brandon sent him an e-mail apologizing? According to Brandon, Julia was the one who originally hooked him up with Dr. Bolt, which means she knew about the drug testing, even though Ramona didn't. Maybe she knew Bolt."

"As a shrink, Bolt could have slipped her those Adderalls we found in her purse."

"And David Bolt seems more like Julia's type than George, anyway," Ellie said. "She went after her science teacher, so I could imagine her being drawn to someone like Bolt. They could've met through the Langstons, or at some Casden alumni event."

"So now we're back to Bolt's drug trial. Assuming Adrienne knows what those guys are up to, is it all so bad that they would not only try to scare her, but send Jimmy Grisco to kill her?"

"We need to talk to Casey."

CHAPTER
FIFTY-TWO

Chung Ri allowed them to use her office to talk to Casey privately. Ellie pasted on her best, most helpful, smile as Ms. Ri threw them one last disapproving scowl before closing the door.

"Sorry about that," Casey said. "That woman kind of loves me."

"I think you can hold the 'kind of' on that," Rogan said. "I, however, think she's *kind of* planning a voodoo spell for us."

"Can we make this quick? I just got a message from Ramona about everything that happened last night in Long Island. Her parents are back in the city now, but she's really freaking out."

"Tell you what," Ellie said. "Let us have a word with you, and we'll give you a ride up there when we're done. We need to know more about the drug-testing program you were doing with Dr. Bolt."

"Okay." She noticed he looked down at his hands as he spoke. He seemed nervous. "Like I said, Brandon was the one who knew about it. I guess he found out from Julia. We went once a week for counseling and stuff. We'd talk to the doctor and fill out these questionnaires. Mostly we got a hundred bucks."

"Do you know how Julia knew about the study?"

He shook his head. "No. I mean, I didn't even know she was the one who told Brandon until that asshole e-mailed me yesterday trying to apologize for setting me up like that. Julia was always trying to find ways of helping people out. She probably told him so he could get some easy cash. I don't think she knew I was doing it, too, because she never mentioned it. Why are you asking me about this?"

"Sorry, but we can't tell you. And you can't tell anyone that we asked you about this. Not even Ramona. Do you understand? We're taking a chance on you. We need to be able to trust you."

"Yeah, okay."

"You said Brandon faked the test to get into the experiment. Do you know how he did that?"

"He looked on some website about manic-depressives and then just tried to answer the questionnaire the way he thought a manic-depressive should. Some of the stuff he was talking about sounded more like OCD to me. I'm surprised it worked."

So was Ellie. According to Bolt, the diagnostic tests were intended to weed out the fakers.

"And how about you? Did you fake the test, too?"

He stared at the table, lips pressed together nervously.

"It's okay, Casey. We're not interested in putting you through anything else. We need to know what's going on with the study."

"I told Brandon I was faking it, but at the last minute I decided not to. I've been told my whole life that I'm not normal. That the way I think of myself is unnatural and a sign that something is wrong with me. I figured here was a chance to get a real diagnosis from a legitimate doctor. I was pretty surprised when he said I fit the qualifications for the research."

"Could you tell any difference in how you felt once you started the program?"

"Yeah, at first. But then, I don't know. I started to feel kind of . . . flat. Like, when all of that stuff went down with Gundley and the way those guys treated me—*terrified* me—it was like I didn't really care what happened. Like I was outside of my own body or something. I mean, in some ways I've lived outside of my body my whole life, but this was different. I was just so . . . yeah, *flat* is the best word to describe it. Like I just didn't feel anything."

"And that was a recent change?" Rogan clarified. "You said the drugs were helpful at the beginning?"

"I didn't really mean the drugs. It was more having a trained person to talk to. I got sent to quacks back in Iowa, and I could never really tell them what it was like—you know, to feel like I'm supposed to be different from the way I was born. Dr. Bolt didn't seem to judge me. He was actually trying to help me deal with my own self-doubt and guilt. I think he has a lot of young patients. He's all about separating yourself from your parents—being honest about who they are and how they treated you, but then letting go of it."

It was all getting a little touchy-feely for Rogan. "But what you're saying is that the drugs might have been causing you to feel depressed?"

"Yeah, I mean, I've wondered about that. I stopped taking them, even though they say you're not supposed to go cold turkey. But I miss talking to Dr. Bolt. He's pretty smart. Like, he had me do this exercise where I wrote a letter to my parents. Not that they talk to me anymore. They said I could come back once I was willing to be Cassandra again. But he had me pretend that I could open up to them. He had me write down all of the things I was never able to say to them. Even though you don't mail the letter—no one even reads it—there's something about the process of putting it on paper: the rage, the fury, the scribbling, the crossing out."

Wasn't that what Adrienne had said about her blog? That writing about the abuse she'd suffered was a way to purge herself of the past?

When Ellie had undergone department-mandated therapy after an officer-involved shooting, the counselor had asked her to do the same thing. In her case, the letter had been to a woman killed by the man Ellie eventually shot to death. If it was a common therapy tactic, writing must bring a form of enlightenment to some, but Ellie hadn't seen the point. Sure, she had experienced the rage and the fury and the scribbling and the crossing out that Casey described, but she hadn't let any of it go. She still woke up thinking about that dead girl. And she still had nightmares about her father.

And then Ellie pictured herself writing that fake letter. The pad of paper from the therapist's office. The crossed-out words.

She knew why Julia Whitmire had written that suicide note to her parents.

"You ready for that ride uptown?" she asked. It was about time she and Rogan had a heart-to-heart with George Langston.

CHAPTER FIFTY-THREE

The storage room?" Rogan pushed the top of an encrusted mop away from his face. "This was the best we could do?"

They hadn't been able to contact the photographer who leased the office next door, so this tiny janitorial storage closet was the only other space for them to camp out near Dr. David Bolt's office. Given the circumstances, they needed to be close.

"Shh." She pressed the headphones closer to her ears. It had taken George Langston only a day to strike an agreement with the district attorney's office. He would come clean about his part in the Equi-van drug-testing scheme. He would testify against Bolt. He would also set up a meeting and wear a wire. All he got in exchange was a promise of sentencing consideration. It was a lousy deal, but the man was seriously pissed. What had started as a favor to a friend had turned into an attack on his wife.

She heard George's voice through her headphones. Rogan nodded to indicate his audio was also working.

"Sue's gone?" George asked. Sue was the receptionist.

"You were the one who said you didn't want anyone to see you here. I canceled three sessions for this. What's with all the James Bond action?"

"My wife. Don't tell me you didn't get my messages yesterday. A man followed her out to East Hampton. He tried to kill her."

"And it sounds like she did a good job defending herself. Shouldn't you be with her?"

"This has gotten totally out of control."

"What is your *deal*, George?"

"It was supposed to be comments on a website. A few words to scare her—to make everything right again. That's all I agreed to."

"And I swear, that's all it's been."

It was only that morning when they'd watched George Langston sob in an interrogation room. *You have to understand,* he said through the tears, *it didn't seem so terrible at first.*

It was only one lawsuit. One screwed-up kid, Jason Moffit, had killed himself during a drug trial. A fluke. A statistical anomaly. But Jason Moffit had been taking Equivan, and the parents were telling anyone who would listen that the experimental drug combination had caused their son to inject himself with enough heroin to kill four junkies.

It was the kind of story that would send the drug companies running and accountability boards ordering the research team to start over from scratch—a larger sample size, a longer study, years of delays. Bolt swore that to interrupt the research would hurt an entire generation of kids who desperately needed better treatment options.

Less selflessly, any kind of investigation could destroy Bolt's career. To get the manufacturers of Equilibrium and Flovan to fund the research, he had practically guaranteed them a successful trial. He had forecast the likely profits once the two drugs were prescribed together. There were documents. Even a PowerPoint presentation. The drug companies would throw him under the bus. Bolt would lose everything.

And so George had agreed to help him. After Bolt assured him Moffit was a statistical anomaly, George helped make the Moffits' lawsuit go away, complete with a confidentiality clause and no report to the Food and Drug Administration.

Meanwhile, Bolt went about ensuring his study produced the promised results. He started taking a few kids who didn't meet the criteria for the clinical trial. Despite the protocol of "blind" testing, he placed these kids in the active drug group, overstating their initial clinical symptoms. Because these kids had never been bipolar to begin with, their "results" would show improvement as they continued the medication.

But then Adrienne had seen that tiny little article about the lawsuit in the *New York Post* after the parents had called a reporter without notifying him. *How can you sue David?* she'd asked. *He and Anne are two of our best friends.* As he recounted the conversation in the interrogation room, he nearly choked on his words. "I've always been a terrible liar. Ironic, isn't it? I told her what I'd done. I didn't want her to think I'd do that to our friends. I compromised everything I believe in, just to help David."

And then Adrienne started to change. Those unexplained periods at her computer became longer and more frequent. She pulled away from him in bed at night. And then he heard the same rumors as Katherine Whitmire about his wife's book deal. He snuck into her e-mail and learned the truth: a six-hundred-thousand-dollar advance that she never bothered to mention to him. He had always known on some level that she'd married him not for love but for station and security. That's why they had a prenup. That's why he had never wanted her to legally adopt Ramona. He needed to know she couldn't leave.

Now she had a measure of autonomy, and he was losing her.

Maybe if he hadn't told his best friend, nothing would have come of it. Book deals fall apart. Women learn to forgive. But then David Bolt came up with a plan. If Adrienne was too afraid to publish the book, she would have to stay with George. And if she stayed with George, there would be no messy divorce where she threatened to reveal what she knew about Equivan.

Like George said, *It was supposed to be comments on a website. A few words to scare her—to make everything right again.* Now, in Bolt's office, George was trying to get the man who took it beyond words to admit the true extent of his wrongdoing.

"Drop the act, David. I should have known you were lying when the police said one of those posts came from Julia's laptop. The girl you're screwing just happens to kill herself?"

"I told you: Julia was a very disturbed girl."

"You don't think I know that? She practically grew up in my home. What kind of man—a psychiatrist, no less—has sex with a teenage girl who's so obviously troubled? What happened?" Suddenly they heard muffled sounds through the headphones. "Jesus, David, what the fuck!"

"Are you wearing a wire? Are you fucking recording me?"

Ellie had one hand on the closet doorknob, the other on her holstered Glock. This was it.

"Don't be ridiculous." George's voice again. "What do you want? A strip search?"

"Sorry, man. This shit is—it's, I don't know what to do. It just wasn't supposed to be like this."

Ellie let her hand drop from the gun. They had caught a break. Bolt must have stopped with a cursory search, expecting one of those wires strapped to his friend's chest like in the movies. This particular audio transmitter was hidden in a fountain pen in Langston's front jacket pocket.

"Don't ask me to feel sorry for you. What I agreed to about Adrienne was wrong. But sending someone after her? Trying to hurt my child's mother? That's not acceptable. Not in any universe."

"I swear—on Nate and Charlotte's *lives*—I did not have anything to do with that."

"Oh, come on, David. That doesn't make any sense. You really expect me to believe that Julia killing herself and some murderer coming after my wife is all just a big coincidence?"

Ellie heard the sound of a sliding door, followed by the squeal of a siren and horns blasting below. Someone had opened the terrace door. Did Bolt still suspect a wire? *Don't go out there*, she willed. She could barely hear them over the sound of the wind. She could read Rogan's lips next to her. *Idiot.*

They made out only bits and pieces. *Julia . . . didn't know what to . . . could tell . . . research . . . nowhere . . . my files . . . threatened.*

It was hard to distinguish Bolt's voice from Langston's. They'd lost all track of the conversation. As minutes passed, Ellie and Rogan exchanged worried glances.

Their voices were getting louder. *Liar . . . family . . . police . . . coming out.*

And then they heard Langston's voice even louder now. "What? No!" There was more whooshing, but it wasn't the sound of wind anymore. Physical contact with the audio transmitter. A loud crash.

She was moving already, Rogan right behind her. She yelled into her radio. "Go. In the office. Now. Now!"

Eight officers poured from the stairwell at the end of the hallway, but she and Rogan had a forty-yard head start. This is why they'd stayed close.

Bolt's reception area was empty. They ran straight for his office door. Locked.

Rogan slammed his left shoulder hard and low against it like a linebacker. Nothing. They heard a yell inside.

Another low, hard hit, and the door gave way.

Bolt had backed Langston against the railing. Langston had only one foot in contact with the concrete, his weight beginning to tip over the terrace edge.

"David Bolt," she yelled. "Police."

He removed his hands from Langston's jacket and held them high. "Whoa, whoa, whoa. It was an argument. That's all. Right, George? Tell them."

Bolt looked at Langston with a look of hope. It was a hope that came from certainty that weak-willed George Langston would do anything to cover his own ass.

"It's over, David. It's over." Langston checked his blazer pocket for the pen-recorder. "You got all that, right?"

CHAPTER
FIFTY-FOUR

Four hours and seventeen minutes.

Some suspects blurt out the all-important words immediately. Usually these were repeat players, burnt too many times by their own instincts, finally following the advice they'd received previously from their court-appointed attorneys. Some suspects never did learn. They kept talking and talking and talking, hoping to eventually land on just the right version of the facts—some story that will get them sent home.

Dr. David Bolt lasted four hours and seventeen minutes. From handcuffs to transport to the 13th Precinct to his spot in a chair in the box with Ellie and Rogan, he was able to weather their questions. He feigned confusion or ignorance. He had the strength to sit in silence, his demeanor unfazed, while the minute hand ticked away. He gave them little in the way of evidence, conceding only that he had met Julia at a Casden alumni event. She had sought out his advice about bulimia, he said. He even admitted giving the girl a few samples of Adderall, but only after she assured him that her original prescription had recently lapsed and that she would follow up with her regular physician.

But through it all, he failed to take the one step that would put an end to their relentless interrogation.

Four hours and seventeen minutes passed before he finally said the magic words: I want a lawyer.

They were done, once and for all.

Max was waiting for them in the hallway outside the interrogation room.

Another ADA might have chastised them for their interrogation tactics. Prosecutors like to do that. If you turn on the charm, they believe pressure is called for. Go aggressive, and they say you get more bees with honey. But Max took one look at her exhausted face and said a single word: "Sorry."

"We tried. Funny, we've been able to get lawyers to sink themselves. But apparently all that psychology training helps in the fortitude department. Bolt's not budging."

"I know a little something about dealing with people who won't budge. It takes incredible patience."

The comment wasn't lost on her. It had been two days since he'd asked her to live with him, and she still hadn't reached a decision. There hadn't been time to talk or think about anything other than this case.

Once they were seated at their desks in the homicide squad, they ran through the strength of the evidence against Bolt. They had rock solid proof of the underlying plan to cover up the Moffits' claim that Equivan had caused their son's overdose. A search of Bolt's computer revealed a PowerPoint presentation assuring the drug companies in advance that the tests would go well. Even their initial perusal of his drug trial records suggested that he was doctoring evidence to support that claim.

An attempted murder charge also seemed strong. As much as Bolt insisted that the incident on the terrace was a shoving match between longtime friends, both Rogan and Ellie could back up George's testimony that the man was trying to throw said friend from a thirteenth-floor balcony.

But on the actual Julia Whitmire murder charge, they still had work to do.

"Maybe the sound technician can cut through some of that background noise," Max offered.

The recording of George's conversation with Bolt became choppy once they had stepped out onto the terrace. According to George, Bolt did confess to killing Julia. They'd begun an affair three months earlier. Bolt said Julia was the one to pursue him, but they'd never know the truth—not that it mattered, given her age. The weekend Julia had died, Bolt's wife had taken the children to London for a three-day weekend, leaving him free to spend time with Julia. Tipsy from two martinis, he had used Julia's laptop to post the first threat on Adrienne's website.

He hadn't heard her heading back to the bed. She asked him what he was doing. He knew from the look on her face that she'd seen him typing that comment. He tried chalking it up to professional research, but he could tell she wasn't buying it.

Listening to the recording of their conversation, George had been able to fill in the blanks. *Julia confronted me. I didn't know what to do. She could tell I was lying. She was furious. Then she started asking me about my research. It came out of nowhere. She'd obviously gone through my files. She threatened to tell. She threatened to call my wife. I didn't plan it. I just snapped.*

But then George had asked Bolt about the suicide note. *What did you do, David? Tell her you wanted her to try out a new exercise you had for your clients? That's pretty damned planned.*

That's when their voices had gotten louder. George calling Bolt a liar. Bolt saying he was trying to protect his family. George saying that the police were involved—the truth would be coming out. And then Bolt trying to push George off the terrace.

George's testimony, bolstered by a choppy recording, might not be enough for trial, but it was still early in the game. Like Max said, the recording might get cleaned up. They would pore over Bolt's office, home, and car, searching for physical evidence to shore up the affair between him and Julia. They'd offer evidence of Julia's habit of snooping to suggest she'd learned what Bolt was up to. They'd be comparing Bolt's fingerprints and DNA against samples taken from Julia's bedroom.

A week ago, she never would have believed it: Katherine Whitmire had been right. Her daughter had been murdered.

It wouldn't be a lock, but eventually they'd have a decent circumstantial case to prove Bolt was her killer.

Then there was also Grisco's attack on Adrienne Langston. If Bolt had hired Grisco, he was guilty of attempted murder. They might even be able to hold him responsible for Grisco's death since he set the fatal confrontation into motion.

But even in George Langston's enhanced version of the recorded conversation, Bolt never admitted to any connection to Grisco.

Ellie rewound the file, now uploaded on the computer, and listened for the umpteenth time.

First Langston's voice: *What I agreed to about Adrienne was wrong. But sending someone after her? Trying to hurt my child's mother? That's not acceptable. Not in any universe.*

Then Bolt: *I swear—on Nate and Charlotte's lives—I did not have anything to do with that.*

She hit stop, then listened again.

"You can play it a hundred more times and nothing's going to change," Rogan said. "Not the first time a guy who's guilty as sin swears innocence on his children's lives."

"I'd feel a lot better about this if we had something—*anything*—connecting Bolt to Grisco."

The civilian's aide known as Doogie was backing his way toward them with a stack of Redweld files looped together with rubber bands. "This just came for you two, Detectives. It's from the Buffalo Police Department's records archives?"

She had requested the reports from Grisco's homicide case when they had first identified his fingerprints on the shoe box left at the Langstons' apartment building. She snapped the thick rubber bands from the files. One was from the court system, documenting Grisco's case from arraignment forward. She handed that one to Max, then split the police records in half, between Rogan and herself.

"Damn. Buffalo was still typing in triplicate in 1995?" Rogan said. "What exactly are we looking for here?"

She continued to shuffle through the pages. "The more we know about Grisco, the better. Why did he come to the city? How would he have crossed paths with David Bolt? Maybe something indicating he was subject to post-supervision psychiatric counseling?"

"Nothing yet," Max said. "Looks like he was indicted for murder. The state filed an intent to seek the death penalty, back when New York had one. He then pled guilty to murder, mandatory life in prison. No appeal. Pretty thin file. Whatever happened in plea negotiations isn't in the record."

"So far I'm looking at property receipts and lab tests," Rogan said.

"I've got the original incident report." She gave them a quick summary as she read. "Like the parole officer told us, the vic was a forty-nine-year-old insurance agent named Wayne Cooper. Looks like Grisco waited outside Cooper's office and then stabbed him in the parking lot—twice in the stomach, then once in the chest. No witnesses to the actual stabbing, but Grisco took off in such a hurry that another driver wrote down his plate as he sped away."

"Lying in wait would make it premeditated," Rogan said.

She flipped to another report. "Search of Grisco's car, a 1988 Pontiac Firebird. No weapon found, but blood on the passenger seat."

Rogan held up a page from his file. "I got that. DNA came back to the victim. Sounds like a lock and load."

She continued rifling through the pages, looking for evidence of a psychiatric evaluation. She ran the math in her head. Nearly seventeen years since the murder. Fifteen years since the plea. David Bolt would have been a psychiatrist already. Maybe he took patients in western New York as part of his early training.

"Okay, here's the report from Grisco's interrogation: Mirandized. Waiver followed by an initial denial. Said the blood on the passenger seat was from a buddy cutting himself in a fall on some gravel at a tailgate party. They bluffed with the DNA results even though the labs weren't back yet. Yada, yada, yada. Okay, here we go. Grisco then admits to being at the office building parking lot. He said he only went there to confront Cooper after learning that Cooper had sexually assaulted Grisco's girlfriend. Cooper attacked him first.

Grisco said he was only defending himself. The detective noted no injuries on Grisco to support the claim of lethal defensive force."

"Did the girlfriend back him up?" Rogan asked.

She flipped to the next page and read verbatim from the report: "Grisco declined to name the alleged victim of Cooper's sexual attack, i.e., Grisco's own girlfriend. Grisco claimed he did not want to get her in trouble. When I pointed out that there was nothing against the law about being a rape victim, he suddenly said that she had nothing to do with his acts and would now be getting a fresh start in light of Cooper's death. I asked him then if that (i.e., giving his girlfriend a fresh start) is why he killed Cooper. He then stated, 'I told you it was self-defense.' I then pointed out that all evidence suggested that Cooper was a happily married family man, i.e., with no propensity for sexual violence. He then said, 'I want to talk to a lawyer now.' End of interview."

"I.e.," Rogan said in an exaggerated staccato, "Grisco realized his story sounded completely bogus."

She kept shuffling through the reports, but the investigation appeared to come to an abrupt halt. No indication that the police had looked for Cooper's alleged rape victim. No evidence that Grisco underwent a mental health evaluation. No explanation for why, fifteen years later, Grisco had come to New York, or how he might have crossed paths with David Bolt.

Max slid Grisco's court file across the table toward Ellie. "Pretty cut-and-dry plea deal to avoid the death penalty. Only reason he got out was he witnessed his cellmate stick a shiv in another prisoner last year. He cut a deal with the state."

"Still seems lazy," Ellie said. "If Grisco's motive for killing Cooper wasn't revenge, then why did he do it? It doesn't sound like the Buffalo police could find any reason Grisco would go after some ho-hum, middle-aged insurance agent. If it were us, we would have at least looked for a connection. At least find out who Grisco was dating. I wouldn't clear the case without finding the girl. If the girl doesn't exist, then Grisco's entire story is a lie, and he's a cold-blooded murderer. No pleas allowed."

Ellie began reorganizing the Grisco files when she noticed a stack of envelopes addressed to Rogan from various banks. She tossed them in his direction. "Bank statements at work? If Shannon and Danes get a glimpse, you'll never hear the end of it."

He starting ripping the envelopes open as she wrapped a rubber band around the file folders. "These are the requests we sent out for the Langstons' bank records."

"Guess we don't need those anymore. Too bad we don't have Bolt's yet."

He was flipping through the pages he'd removed from the envelopes. "Hold up a second. When did Grisco rent that apartment out in Queens?"

"The landlord said he looked at the place last Thursday. Agreed to rent it the same day." It had been exactly one week. Grisco could have been in the city long before that, but so far they had traced him only to the Queens apartment.

"All cash. First, last, plus deposit, a total of thirty-six hundred dollars. I got a cash withdrawal here of nine thousand, nine hundred dollars that very morning."

Any cash transaction of ten thousand dollars or more got reported to the federal government, making any transaction slightly less than ten thousand dollars a little suspicious.

"No way, Rogan. We put the fear of God into George Langston. No way did he hire Grisco. Maybe they're paying a housekeeper under the table or something."

"Except the withdrawal's not out of the Langstons' joint account. You better take a look at this."

She looked at the bank statement, then passed it to Max. They were all seeing the same thing. They were all drawing the same inference.

"Let's pull the Langstons' phone records," she said. "What else have we been missing?"

PART V

JAMES GRISCO

CHAPTER
FIFTY-FIVE

Janet Martin stared out her Flatiron office window, as if the answers to life's mysteries might be lying in Madison Square Park. "I hope you're barking up the wrong tree," Martin said. "Adrienne might just be the real deal. A true survivor giving voice to the damage of her past, strong enough to protect herself in the present. Her story will help a lot of women out there."

They had first heard about Adrienne's book contract from Katherine Whitmire. When Adrienne confirmed the deal, the only fact that concerned them at the time were the threats on her website.

But what they'd learned in the last twenty hours had changed everything. As a result, they needed to know more about the contents of the book.

Fortunately, Martin had mentioned during Ellie's first run-in with the editor that the publisher fact-checked all of its memoirs. Now Ellie and Rogan were back at Waterton Press, hoping finally to nail down how Adrienne Langston's blog connected to the events of the last two weeks.

"This would be a lot easier if you'd just tell us what you know."

Martin smiled. "If I'm mistaken about Adrienne, I'll apologize later, but for now, maybe I don't want to make your life easy. The documents are all there. You can let yourself out when you're finished."

Because Waterton Press had conducted its fact-checking through its legal department, the publisher insisted that any observations, opinions, or summaries were protected by the attorney work-product privilege. Max had finally persuaded Waterton's lawyers to turn over the raw information they had collected in the course of the fact-checking process, but Martin would not be answering any questions or otherwise cooperating with their investigation.

They knew Adrienne had been consumed with preserving her anonymity during the publishing process. But they were hoping that the publisher's actual records revealed the truth about Adrienne Langston's past.

Maybe if Adrienne hadn't landed a book deal, they would never have suspected a connection between her and James Grisco. But when they sent all the major banks a request for information on accounts held by George and Adrienne Langston, they found the account she had opened in her own name using her initial advance from Waterton Press. They saw the $9,900 cash withdrawal she made on the very same morning Grisco paid cash for his apartment in Queens. Now they needed stronger evidence of the link they suspected.

It was a single entry in the Langstons' telephone records that had gotten their attention. An outgoing call to the 716 area code, in western New York State. It was the previous Monday morning, just five minutes after David Bolt posted the second threat on Adrienne Whitmire's blog. The call was to the central administrative number for the Wende Correctional Facility, just outside Buffalo.

Martin had left them a tidy Redweld binder labeled "Adrienne Whitmire's Second Acts" on the office conference table. Ellie opened it and removed several manila file folders.

The first contained a printout of the entire "Second Acts" blog. They had read it all before. They had even known from Janet Martin that some of the personal details of Adrienne's background would be changed to protect her anonymity. What they hadn't suspected was that Adrienne may have already been changing biographical details her entire adult life.

In the story she had been telling, she was raised by a single mother who waited tables in Chico, California. When her mom died, she dropped out of high school, came to New York City, and worked as a nanny before becoming Mrs. George Langston. In the story she was telling, her path would never have crossed James Grisco's.

But wipe away the geographical details, and another narrative emerged. In the story she was telling on her blog, she was a teenage victim, abused by a man brought into her home by her mother. She was a girl who dealt with that abuse by turning, in her words, to *"an unacceptable 'someone else'—at once too old and too immature."*

And then there was James Grisco's story, that of a twenty-three-year-old man with nothing but a DUI and a small-time burglary on his record who suddenly decides to lie in wait outside an insurance agent's office and plunge a knife into him three times, later claiming that the victim had raped his girlfriend.

The phone call from Adrienne Langston's home to the Wende Correctional Facility connected the two stories.

The second folder in Waterton Press's file was labeled "Public Records." A copy of the marriage license of George Langston and Adrienne Mitchell. A birth certificate, documenting the birth in 1980 of baby Adrienne to mother Carmen Watson and Henry Mitchell, unmarried. Ellie felt a rush of adrenaline as she flipped to the next record, a marriage license for Carmen Watson and her new husband in 1988. "We've got it, Rogan. We were right."

What was it that Grisco said when the Buffalo police had asked him about his girlfriend? She was getting a "fresh start."

Ellie reached for the final file, labeled "Newspaper Articles." The headline on the first article read "Man Brutally Slain Outside Cheektowaga Office." It detailed the stabbing of Wayne Cooper. A twenty-three-year-old suspect named James Grisco was in custody. The police had not yet established a connection between the two men or a motive for the killing. The victim was survived by his wife, Carmen, and their fifteen-year-old daughter, Adrienne.

She handed the article to Rogan. "Stepdaughter, actually," she said. "There's no adoption records here. That's why she was going by Adrienne Mitchell when she married George."

"But it looks like she was using Cooper's name all through childhood." He was flipping through a file of what appeared to be photocopies of pages from school yearbooks. Ellie looked at one of the photos.

Where today's Adrienne went for a natural look, with long, caramel-colored waves, the 1995 version had choppy, jet-black hair, charcoal eyeliner set against white-powdered skin, and an extra twenty pounds.

The girl formerly known as Adrienne Cooper was almost unrecognizable.

Almost.

Janet Martin was waiting for them in the reception area. "I take it you found what you were looking for?"

Ellie nodded. "We're all set."

"You don't have to look so happy, Detectives. There's legal justice, and then there's moral justice. Not everything is black-and-white."

"I've been hearing that a lot lately," Ellie said.

"But here's the thing, Detective. When most people say that, they're asking you to see shades of gray. But some things can be black *and* white—right *and* wrong—all at the same time."

Ellie's cell buzzed. She didn't recognize the phone number, but it was from the 716 area code.

"Hatcher."

"Detective Hatcher, this is ADA Jennifer Sugarman from the Erie County district attorney's office in Buffalo, New York. I understand you're handling the shooting of James Grisco back east there."

"That's right." Ellie remembered seeing Sugarman's name on some of Grisco's court papers. She would have been the prosecutor who cut the deal for Grisco's early release in exchange for testimony against his cellmate.

"I'm sorry to be late getting this information to you, but I just saw Grisco's PO at a parole-violation hearing, and he told me about Grisco's death."

Ellie was eager to catch up with Max to let him know they'd been right about Adrienne's connection to Grisco. "What can I do for you, Miss Sugarman?"

"I got a call two Mondays ago from a corrections officer up at Welde. Seems they got a call from Cooper's daughter—Cooper was the man Grisco killed in '95. Anyway, the daughter wanted to know for some reason whether he had Internet access there at the prison. When they told her Grisco had been released, she wasn't real happy about it. Anyway, since I'm the one who signed off on letting Grisco out, I called him into my office to make sure he firmly understood his parole conditions prohibiting contact with any of his victim's family members."

Apparently that conversation had been a real Come to Jesus moment for him, but Ellie didn't have time to explain the entire story to this lawyer.

"I got the impression there was nothing to worry about at the time. I'm not sure if you know why he wound up there in the city—"

"We think we're getting a handle on it, but thanks for calling."

"No, wait, here's the thing. When Cooper's daughter called the prison, they automatically logged in the caller ID information. They, in turn, passed the phone number on to me. Seems I had it written down on my desk when I hauled Grisco in here, right there next to her name—Adrienne Cooper. It was a Manhattan number. I'm sure it's nothing, but I thought I better let you know, just in case."

Ellie listened as the assistant DA rattled off the digits that Grisco would have seen scrawled next to Adrienne Cooper's name, but she didn't need to write them down. She'd read through the Langstons' phone records thoroughly enough to recognize their number.

CHAPTER FIFTY-SIX

They looked up at the Langstons' high-rise.

"You ready to do this?" Ellie checked her watch. It was almost three o'clock. Hopefully Ramona wouldn't be coming straight home from school.

They had manufactured a reason to call George at the office, so they knew he was at work. They had just watched Adrienne enter the building alone. The gun registered to George Langston was tucked away safely in a property room in East Hampton.

"All right. Let's see what we can get."

Adrienne met them at the apartment door, still in yoga pants with a thin ring of perspiration around the V-neck of her pink T-shirt. She held a glass of water in one hand.

"Sorry for my appearance, Detectives. I just got done with a workout."

She led the way into the living room. When they had first arrived here eleven days earlier, Ellie thought she'd had a perfect read on the family. George the uptight lawyer. Adrienne the breath of fresh air who made the house a home.

Sometimes more than one truth defined a family.

"How are you holding up?" Ellie asked.

"I'm making it through. I got a call from Detective Howard this morning from Long Island. The district attorney's office there has officially closed the investigation. I'm still waking up in the middle of the night thinking about that back window crashing and him walking into our house, but—well, at least the official part of the matter is over."

Ellie searched Adrienne's face for any sign of the woman who had orchestrated that event with such calculation. She had to have broken the window herself before Grisco arrived. She'd given him the address, perhaps even directions to the house. Staged the signs of a struggle. Planted a knife in his hand.

Now they were the ones setting her up. The phone call from Howard was intended to make her feel safe. All Ellie saw in Adrienne's expression was the security of a woman who believed she'd gotten away with it. Ellie hoped that same arrogance would keep her talking.

"Unfortunately, we probably won't be able to say the same about the David Bolt case for several months. The DA's office assumes he'll opt for a trial, so we're still trying to shore up some of the loose ends."

"Well, I want to help however I can. I hope you realize that I would have told you about George's terrible role in settling that lawsuit against David if I'd had *any* idea it was related to Julia's death. I'm still having a hard time coming to terms with the fact that he knew about those threats on my website. He was so worried about our marriage, but it never once dawned on me to leave. Now, frankly, I'm not sure we're going to make it past this."

"That's actually why we're here, Adrienne—about those comments on your website. The first one, as you know, came from Julia's laptop, and we believe David Bolt typed it. Then we had several other comments posted at public computers around the Upper West Side and down near the Village. We now know that those were located near Bolt's office and residence, respectively. But the final post—the one mentioning your name—was created on a computer in the lobby of a hotel just eight blocks from here."

"With all due respect, Detective, you already asked me about that last week."

"That was before we had this." Rogan slid a printout with six photographs, including Adrienne's, onto the coffee table. "We showed this photo montage to some of the hotel employees yesterday afternoon. See those initials at the bottom of your picture? That means the concierge identified you as a woman he saw in the lobby last Wednesday."

It was a bluff, but Adrienne didn't need to know that.

"Obviously there's some mistake. I use the Internet here at home. Maybe this person just recognized me from the neighborhood."

"We thought that might be the case," Ellie said. "But then we learned more about James Grisco. We know about your past, Adrienne. You didn't grow up in Chico. You grew up in Buffalo, New York, and your boyfriend there was James Grisco. He killed your stepfather, Wayne Cooper, the man who raped you."

She held her composure for multiple seconds, but then her lower lip began to tremble. Ellie wondered whether it was out of fear that the world she had so carefully constructed was about to crumble, or if this woman was really just that good.

"I—I didn't even recognize him that night. When Detective Howard told me the name of the man who broke into our house, I just froze. Maybe I should have said something right then and there, but I panicked. Before I knew what I was doing, I said I didn't know who he was. David must have found out about my past. He must have hired Grisco just to add another layer to the madness."

"But, see, that's the thing. We haven't been able to find any connection at all between David Bolt and James Grisco, let alone evidence that Bolt hired Grisco. But we did find out about that phone call you made to the prison up in Buffalo, right after Bolt posted the second threat on your website." Ellie set a single page of the Langstons' phone records on the table. "You assumed Grisco had found you after all these years. You thought he was the one harassing you online, but, Adrienne, you were actually the one who brought him back into your life. He might never have found you if you hadn't made that phone call."

Rogan laid yet another sheet of paper on the coffee table, this one her bank statement with the transaction at issue highlighted in yellow. "A ninety-nine-hundred-dollar withdrawal from an account in your name, right before Grisco paid cash to a landlord in Queens."

"I've never had my own money before. I took out some cash to splurge."

"So you have receipts for whatever purchases you might have made?" Ellie asked.

"No, I mean—it was just an extra facial or massage here and there. It all adds up."

"That's a lot of spa time," Rogan said. "We think it was Grisco who found out how quickly the expenses add up. He went away a long time ago, and at a young age. He probably thought ten grand was a lot of money, but before he knew it, he was broke again. Did he come back for more? Blackmailers usually do."

When the shoe box full of maggots showed up at the Langstons' building, Adrienne had been the one to insist that her precinct check it for fingerprints. Their theory was that her initial ten thousand dollars bought her that Adidas shoe box, filled with whatever incriminating documents Grisco was blackmailing her with. She then used the weathered box to set him up for stalking her, setting the stage for the shooting in East Hampton.

"What Jimmy Grisco did back then was insane. Wayne said he'd kill me if I ever told anyone. It took all of my strength to tell my mother, and instead of believing me, she called me a jealous bitch. I went to Jimmy because I had nowhere else to go. I told him what my stepfather was doing to me. I had no idea he'd go after him. I'll admit it: part of me was glad, but I had nothing to do with it."

"And then Grisco showed up in New York City after his release."

"I know how it looks, and that's why I didn't say anything. But I'm telling you: David Bolt is the one who did this. What could Grisco have even blackmailed me with? My husband already knew about my past. Maybe he didn't know the details, but he knows everything that matters. I'm the high school dropout who married up, and all his friends know it. Who cares?"

"Grisco obviously thought you cared. Why would he have come to New York?"

"You know, I just can't win with you people. Fine, believe what you want, but I'm done trying to explain myself to you."

Rogan rose from his place on the sofa and waited for Ellie to do the same. They had known going in that this woman wouldn't break easily. She had been lying to them from the very beginning. A few more threads of fiction would be no trouble for her to spin.

But they had also known going in that they wouldn't be leaving empty-handed. They let her lead the way from the living room. She saw Rogan reach for his cuffs once Adrienne had entered the narrow hallway heading to the front door.

"Adrienne Langston, also known as Adrienne Mitchell and Adrienne Cooper, you are under arrest for the murder of James Grisco." As Ellie read Adrienne her rights, Rogan handcuffed her arms behind her back. It had taken some negotiating, but Max had persuaded the Suffolk County district attorney that any plan Adrienne had to kill Grisco would have originated in Manhattan, giving the New York County DA's office concurrent jurisdiction. The arrest warrant had been signed just that morning.

Ellie had reached the final sentence of the Miranda recitation when she heard keys in the front door.

She placed her hand on her Glock, then relaxed it when she saw Ramona in the doorway, Casey standing behind her. The girl's face initially brightened, until she realized the full implications of what she was seeing.

"Mom? Mom! What are you doing? Let her go."

"It's okay, Ramona. It's okay. It's okay. Just call your father."

Ramona ran to her mother, pulling at her T-shirt as Rogan and Ellie marched Adrienne past Ramona and toward the front door. Ellie held out an arm to create distance, but Ramona reached around her, grabbing again at Adrienne's T-shirt. Casey did his

best to pull Ramona away, but she punched her fists against his
forearm.

Even in her handcuffs, Adrienne tried arching toward her stepdaughter. "Please. Please just let me hug her. She's scared."

Ramona kept screaming, "Mom," and "Don't take her," over and
over again.

As they pulled Adrienne into the elevator, Ellie looked back at
the apartment door. Ramona's arms were outstretched toward her
mother, but she was letting Casey hold her back now.

She couldn't believe she hadn't noticed the resemblance earlier.
The yearbook picture from 1995 back in Buffalo looked nothing
like Adrienne Langston. It had been nearly twenty years. Appearances change. The woman next to her in handcuffs had lost all of
that teenage angst and awkwardness.

And yet the picture should have been familiar. It didn't look like
Adrienne, but it looked a hell of a lot like Ramona.

When they had found the phone number of a family law attorney
in the Langstons' caller ID, they had assumed George was considering a divorce. Now Ellie understood that the client hadn't been
George, but Adrienne. The representation wasn't new, but began
sixteen years ago. And the subject matter wasn't divorce, but adoption.

Once they had their car's latest occupant secured in the backseat,
Ellie latched her own seat belt up front and made a phone call she
was eager for Adrienne to overhear.

"Double M, it's Ellie Hatcher. You get those cookies I dropped
off?" She had delivered Michael Ma's nutter-butters as promised.
She didn't want to lose her best contact in the crime lab.

"Just polished off the last one an hour ago."

"I'll whip you up a new batch if you can do me one more favor.
Look for evidence collection on Julia Whitmire. You'll see a DNA
swab for a known acquaintance named Ramona Langston."

In the rearview mirror, Ellie could see Adrienne looking out the window, pretending not to listen as Park Avenue sailed by.

"What do you need me to compare it against?"

"I'll have a sample to you within an hour. But I'm not looking for a match. I need you to tell me if I've found the girl's biological mother."

And then Ellie saw it—a crack in Adrienne Langston's confident veneer. It was the tiniest movement, somewhere between a blink and a flinch. But it was there.

She knew why James Grisco had been buying coffee across the street from Ramona's school. And she knew why Adrienne had killed him.

PART SIX

FOUR WEEKS LATER

CHAPTER FIFTY-SEVEN

O ne killer down, one to go."

Max held up his glass of red wine and clinked it against Ellie's Johnnie Walker Black. David Bolt had just entered a plea of guilty to the murder of Julia Whitmire. He wouldn't be sentenced for another week, but the agreement called for a minimum of thirty years in prison.

In the end, it was his clever attempt to leave behind a suicide note that sealed the case against him. Julia had pressed down on the paper so hard as she was writing the letter that she'd left indentations on the next page in the pad. They found that sheet of paper, now filled with Bolt's own handwriting, in his notes about the Equivan drug trial.

They were celebrating the closure of at least part of this investigation at their usual after-work spot, the bar at Otto. It was only 5:30 on a Tuesday, so they could actually speak to each other without yelling.

"And to our apartment," Ellie said, adding in a second clink.

"You mean *sort of* our apartment." Max had signed a lease for a large one-bedroom just off Union Square Park. She wasn't ready to walk away from her rent-controlled apartment, but Jess seemed to think he could take over the rent for now. She'd be moving her things into Max's new place next week.

Their new place. She'd have to get used to calling it that.

In theory, the decision should have been one of those joyous moments in a relationship, like the wedding-proposal stories people never tire of repeating. But they both knew the dubious origins of the arrangement. His quasi-ultimatum. His insistence that there was a difference between asking her to change and asking her to *get to know herself* more. Her desire to prove to him that she was trying. His anger at her refusal to relinquish her legal right to occupy another space without him.

Their first shared address had been the result of nights of fighting, not one of those great stories they'd be sharing with friends.

They both took a sip to commemorate the second toast, but she quickly changed the subject. "Anything else we can do on Adrienne Langston's charges?"

If there was an A-level felony for lying, they'd have Adrienne dead to rights. The DNA tests confirmed that Ramona Langston was the biological daughter of Adrienne Langston and the late James Grisco. Records subpoenaed from Michael Wiles's law office confirmed that in January 1996, Adrienne Mitchell placed a newborn baby girl in a closed, private adoption. According to the adoption documents, Adrienne had claimed not to know the identity of the biological father.

Within two years, Adrienne was living in New York City, working as a nanny for a family that lived two floors down from the Langstons. Even Adrienne now admitted that the job was no coincidence. She was in no position to raise a child on her own, but she could at least watch the baby she'd given up grow with her new parents. After Gabriella's car accident, the entire building was abuzz about poor George and his little girl. It was only natural that she volunteered to step in. The way Adrienne told the story, the fact that she, George, and Ramona became a family was nothing but a happy Hollywood ending.

Until, of course, James Grisco resurfaced and threatened to ruin it all.

"I still can't believe Ramona showed up at your apartment."

It had been two days earlier. Ellie and Jess were leaving the building for a run, and there was Ramona, sitting on the front stoop.

Ellie took another sip of her whisky, recalling the ugliness of the interaction. Somehow the tale Adrienne had spun sounded better coming from a sad sixteen-year-old girl. Grisco the blackmailer. Grisco who came back for more when the ten grand ran out. Grisco who broke into the house in East Hampton to attack Adrienne after she refused to pay him any more money.

"I swear," Max said, "if Adrienne sent her kid to beg on her behalf, I should be entitled to tack another couple of years onto the sentence."

But Ellie could tell that Ramona's pleas came entirely from her own desire to believe the very best about the only mother she knew.

"You really think a jury will buy self-defense?" she asked.

"I've learned never to make predictions. Adrienne's a proven liar, time and again. And the whole thing with the maggots shows just how far she was willing to go to cast herself in the role of victim. But at the end of the day, she's a pretty, rich, white lady, and James Grisco was a convicted killer."

"I hate jurors."

"You'd rather have judges like Fred Knight make the call? I'm hoping the husband will talk some sense into her. The defense attorney told me George spent all of yesterday poring over the entire trial file. He's a husband, but he's also a lawyer. Hopefully he'll see she should take the deal." He downed the rest of his wine. "Fuck it. I'd rather try a good case and lose than budge another day with her."

The current offer was twenty years. Adrienne would barely be fifty when she got out. She could still see Ramona get married. She could be a grandmother to whatever children Ramona might eventually have.

Max's cell phone rattled against the bar top. He excused himself to take the call on the sidewalk on Eighth Street.

The bar manager, Dennis, reappeared once she was alone. "It's a dumb man who puts a phone call above his girlfriend."

"You know us. When duty calls—"

"I do indeed, and as a taxpayer I suppose I should thank you." He refilled Max's glass. She held up her half-full rocks glass to show she was still working on the first round. "Watch yourself there. That's how the power balance gets off in a relationship. You've got to match him one for one."

"Half a Johnnie Walker's good for at least one glass of his wussy red wine."

She checked her e-mail on her BlackBerry as she continued to sip. Most of it was junk, but she opened a message from Detective Marci Howard with the Suffolk Police Department.

Hatcher, Last I heard, you two were all set on what you needed from us re Langston shooting in East Hampton. Saw husband (George) coming out of records department today. Checked to make sure no interference with current investigation.

Like a lot of cops, Howard apparently saw no need to use complete sentences in e-mails.

Records clerk told me Langston asked for copies of docs re 2001 accident investigation—fatal on Egypt Lane near Hook Pond involving Gabriella Langston (which is same name on Langston gun registration; first wife etc.). Know you two are sticklers for every last detail (ha ha) so thought I'd give you a heads up. Hope the case goes on the side of justice. Still sounds like a clean shoot to me FWIW.

Great. Even a cop took one look at the rich pretty white lady versus the scumbag ex-con and gave Adrienne a pass.

Ellie hit the reply button on her e-mail system and pecked off a response:

*Thanks for keeping us in the loop. To prove that
I am in fact the most obsessive-compulsive person
you've ever met, can you please ask your records
department to fax us a copy of the reports George
Langston requested? You never know . . . Don't
forget. We owe you. Thx!*

Max looked happy when he returned to the bar. "I was about to
say 'another round to celebrate,' but I see Dennis already got here."

"What are we celebrating now?"

"That was Adrienne Langston's defense attorney. She's taking the
deal. As is."

"You're kidding? Just like that? I thought she said she wouldn't
take anything other than Man Two."

"The attorney was surprised too. She said it was all George's
doing. Plus, they're in a rush. Adrienne will enter her plea tomorrow at nine a.m., straight into sentencing. So let's drink to George."

Ellie still had her phone in her hand.

"Sorry, babe. I hate to tell you this, but I've got work to do tonight."

His disappointment was obvious. "Come on. I thought we were
finally both out early for once. I was sort of looking forward to
talking about the new place. What to keep, what to get rid of. It'll
be fun."

She knew it should sound fun. It didn't. "I really need to work.
You stay here and chill with the other regulars. I'll make it up to
you tomorrow. Take you to Bed Bath and Beyond to look at shower
curtains with all the other ladies."

He feigned a stabbing motion to the gut. "Fine, I deserved that.
I'm soft." He gave her a kiss on the lips, and she waved goodbye to
Dennis on her way out.

From the sidewalk on Eighth Street, she pulled up Marci Howard's phone number from her call log, then plugged one ear with
her fingertip to block out the sound of a passing bus. "Hey, there,
it's Ellie Hatcher. Did you happen to get the e-mail I just sent you?"

"Didn't surprise me at all. You're definitely thorough. We'll get those records to you this week."

"Don't kill me, but I actually need them tonight—as in, right now."

They were still missing something.

CHAPTER FIFTY-EIGHT

Ellie waited in the hallway outside of Judge John DeWitt Gregory's courtroom until they spotted George Langston exiting the elevator. He was flanked by Ramona on one side and his wife's defense attorney on the other.

Behind them came Casey Heinz, walking alongside Katherine Whitmire. Katherine's pending divorce against Bill was all over the tabloids, but from what Ellie heard, Katherine's higher priority had been getting Casey moved into the top floor of her townhouse and enrolled in classes at Hunter College. Apparently she had found a way to try to make up for her and her husband's previous failures.

Ellie intercepted George before he made it to the courtroom. "Mr. Langston, I'd like to have a quick word with you, alone, before your wife's case is called, if that's all right with you."

Adrienne's attorney was a straight shooter named Bernadette Connor. A gorgeous Asian woman with a French first name and an Irish last name, she had also gone on three dates with Max four years ago, a fact Ellie tried very hard to forget whenever her name came up.

"No way. You can talk to George after Adrienne's plea is entered."

"I need to talk to him now," Ellie said.

"Then you can talk to him with me present."

"You represent Adrienne, not George."

"Then we'll call George's attorney."

"Mr. Langston," Ellie repeated, "I need to talk to you. I think you'll want to have this conversation with me privately, but if you want to call counsel of your choosing, that is of course your prerogative."

"No. I'm fine. Thank you, Bernadette."

Ellie led the way into the vacant jury room she'd scored from Benny the Bailiff. (Never underestimate the value of finding time to talk Mets games with the courthouse staff.)

She waited until they were alone and the door closed to speak. "I got a call from Marci Howard yesterday from out in Suffolk County."

No reaction.

"She told me you had requested the incident reports involving Gabriella's car accident."

"You can't do a thing without all of government knowing about it these days?"

"Why would you want to see those reports after all these years?"

"It's funny how the mind works. I loved that woman like—well, the way you maybe get to love only one person your entire life. When we finally got Ramona, it was the happiest day either of us had ever experienced. And then the phone call about the accident was the worst. It's not like I ever stopped thinking about her, but I'd finally gotten to the point where I didn't *always* think about her. Now I find out that Adrienne is actually Ramona's mother, only to be losing her now to prison for trying to protect our family? I don't know—it had me thinking about losing Gabriella, too."

"It's a very touching story. I suspect it's even partially true."

"Of course it's true."

"But it's not the whole truth, is it? If you don't want to lose Adrienne to prison, why were you the one to help talk her into this plea?"

"It's better than a maximum sentence, isn't it? I saw the discovery. I know the evidence against her. Neither one of us wants to put Ramona through a trial."

"It's always been about Ramona, hasn't it?"

"What do you mean?" he asked, looking at the jury room door. Ellie knew he was thinking about the clock's minute hand working its way toward 9:00 a.m.

"Don't worry about the time, George. It always takes the deputies forever to transfer prisoners into the courtrooms. We've got a good half hour before the judge takes the bench. I mean that it's always been about Ramona, for both you and Adrienne. Ramona was the reason Adrienne found a way to get close to you and your family. Her devotion to your child was probably the reason you married again, even though you were still in love with Gabriella."

"Adrienne and I came to love each other. We're a family now."

"You're a family, but only because of the bond you share with your daughter. And that daughter is the reason you convinced Adrienne to take this deal. You don't want Ramona to know the rest of the story."

"There's nothing else to tell, Detective. Like I said, we just don't want to put her through the trauma and publicity of a trial."

"Adrienne's attorney told the ADA you spent all of Monday studying the case against your wife. The very next morning, you drove out to East Hampton to get copies of Gabriella's accident reports. That same night, you suddenly convinced Adrienne to take a deal she practically laughed at for the last two weeks."

"I don't want to have this conversation. Please. I know you think I'm a terrible person, and I have given you every reason to believe that. But I *swear*—I have been trying to do everything in my power to make it right. This plea agreement is what's right."

"I followed the same paper trail you did, George. The Suffolk County Police faxed me those same accident reports last night."

"Please don't do this. It's not right. There's no need."

"The police always suspected a drunk driver in the hit-and-run that killed Gabriella. She was walking home from the stables in East

Hampton, just like she usually did after she rode. Based on the tire treads and paint transfer to a light pole, they suspected one of four Pontiac models, red in color. You probably hadn't thought about that detail for fifteen years. You asked for the accident reports to confirm what you suspected when you saw your wife's file."

His lips were pressed together, and he was shaking his head violently, as if somehow he could will her to stop talking.

"The Buffalo Police searched James Grisco's car in 1995 after someone turned in his license plate number from the scene of Wayne Cooper's murder. Grisco drove a red 1988 Pontiac Firebird. He gave Adrienne that car when he went to prison. He wanted her to have a fresh start."

"There were a lot of Pontiacs on the road back then."

"But not that many, George. And the gun at your beach house? You told the police that you bought it after Gabriella said she saw someone watching the house. That was right before she died, wasn't it?"

"Why are you doing this?"

"This is what I do. I clear cases. I answer questions even after people stop asking them. This one's not hard to figure out, George. You can probably find the family Adrienne nannied for with one quick phone call. They might just remember her red Firebird suddenly being damaged. And if not, eventually that car got sold or totaled or sent to a junkyard, and a record got entered with the DMV. This is a question that can be answered. But you, a meticulous, cautious lawyer, said nothing. You confronted Adrienne, didn't you? That's how you convinced her to take this deal today."

"Not all questions need to be answered. Some resolutions are good enough."

"And what makes this good, George? You *know* in your heart what she did. She stalked Gabby. She followed her from the stables. She accelerated her car into the love of your life, left her to die on the side of the road, and then pretended to care about you, just so she could get another shot at the daughter she'd abandoned."

"Adrienne didn't *abandon* Ramona. Did it ever dawn on you how much she had to love that child to do what she did? She was sixteen years old. She couldn't have even known who the father was—Wayne Cooper the rapist or James Grisco the killer. She could have gotten rid of the baby, but she carried her to term. Now, what she has done since then"—his words were coming slower now—"is absolutely unforgivable. But punishing her isn't the only interest at stake here, Detective."

"You're worried about Ramona."

He looked at the door again. "Right now, my daughter believes that she had an adoptive mother who loved her as much as she possibly could before she died, and a biological mother who loved her so much that she found a way to be with her and then ultimately killed a man, just to protect her. If this thing goes to trial—"

"She might find out the truth—that the only mother she has ever known may have killed the one she can barely remember, and all because of her."

"Please don't do that to my daughter. She's the one innocent person in this picture."

"It's not right—"

"You said this wasn't a hard question to answer, and maybe you're right in one sense. We can track down my old neighbors, or dig up some ancient DMV records. But Adrienne will never, ever admit to what you suspect she did."

"Not all defendants confess."

"You're an experienced detective. You mean to tell me that's proof beyond a reasonable doubt? How many other vehicles might have left a certain kind of red paint and tire tread as the car that *may have*—in the words of the accident reconstruction report—been involved in Gabriella's death? And how many such vehicles were on New York's roads in 2001? You've got just enough to mess with my daughter's head, but you'll never get a conviction." He looked at his watch. "And maybe you're wrong. Maybe Adrienne had nothing to do with Gabriella's death. She killed James Grisco, but there was mitigation. Do you know what was in that shoe box when it originally showed up at our apartment? All of the letters she had written to him back in Buffalo when she was only fifteen years old."

"That's not mitigation. That's a bad case of puppy love. We assumed he was blackmailing her."

"No, he did worse than that. He still wanted her, or at least that version of her. She gave him money hoping he'd go away, but he didn't. He said he had been watching her family. That if he couldn't have her, maybe—I can't even say the words, they're so disgusting—*maybe he'd try out that little Ramona instead.* His own flesh and blood, not that he knew that. Adrienne wasn't sleeping at all for two weeks. Julia had just died. This guy comes out of nowhere and starts talking about Ramona that way. She snapped."

Ellie remembered Adrienne talking about her mother's failure to protect her. She could still hear Adrienne's voice: *I see my Ramona. If any man ever touched her like that, I'd kill him.* "She didn't snap. She lured him to your address in East Hampton and staged the entire scene to look like self-defense."

"Look, I'll be honest with you. I don't even know the woman I'm married to. Maybe she's the coldhearted Lady Macbeth you're describing. But maybe she's a woman who has tried at every turn—however wrongheaded—to protect this life she's created for us and for our daughter. Leave it alone, and a few minutes from now she'll be a convicted murderer. She'll be in prison for twenty years. When she gets out, she'll have nothing. I plan on filing divorce papers while she's in custody."

"She'll still have Ramona."

"Maybe. That will be up to them. Or maybe Ramona will start taking another look at the facts when she's older and come to some other conclusion for herself. Maybe she'll even bring in a strong-willed detective like you. There's no statute of limitations on murder, right?"

"You know that's not realistic—"

"With all due respect, Detective, you don't get to talk to me about being realistic. Trust me: I'm being a cold, hard pragmatist right now. My daughter's entire universe—not just her external world, but her very sense of self—will be permanently and fundamentally altered if you go on poking at this. Maybe you don't have children—I really don't know—but what kids know about their parents affects how they see themselves. Ramona may think she's all grown up, but she's too young for this."

There was a knock on the door, followed by the bailiff's round face in the open crack. "Time's up, you two. Gregory's taking the bench. You coming?"

CHAPTER FIFTY-NINE

The squeak of Judge Gregory's courtroom door earned them an annoyed scowl from the bench. George took a seat next to Ramona in the first spectator row behind the defense's counsel table. From the prosecution's table, Max gave her a pleased look of surprise before returning his attention to the plea colloquy.

"Did you sign this agreement and initial each page to show you read it?"

"Yes, Your Honor."

"Are you satisfied with your attorney's representation?"

"I am."

"Mr. Donovan, on behalf of the people, please summarize the terms of the plea agreement."

Even from her spot against the wall at the back of the courtroom, Ellie could see Ramona's shoulders shake at the mention of the twenty-year sentence. Adrienne turned and gave her a sad smile. *It will be okay*, she mouthed. Ramona took her father's hand. Casey placed a comforting arm around her shoulder.

"Ms.—okay, I see a couple of names here. Legal name is Adrienne Langston, née Adrienne Mitchell. Also an alias of Adrienne Cooper. Got all that? All right, Ms. Langston, are those the terms of the plea agreement as you understand them?"

"Yes, Your Honor."

"Do you understand that under the plea agreement you give up your right to appeal both your conviction and any sentence?"

"Yes, Your Honor."

The words of a plea colloquy are scripted and mechanical, but the phrases replaying in Ellie's head were scrambled and chaotic. *How many other vehicles? Adrienne will never, ever admit . . . You'll never get a conviction.*

"Do you understand that you have a right to be tried by a jury, and that by pleading guilty, you are giving up that right?"

"Yes, Your Honor."

"And at such a trial, you would be presumed innocent. The government would have to prove your guilt beyond a reasonable doubt. You would have the right to be represented by a lawyer at that trial, and if necessary have the court appoint a lawyer. You would have the right to confront all witnesses and to call witnesses on your behalf. You would have the right to testify on your own behalf, or to remain silent. Do you understand all of these rights?"

"Yes, Your Honor."

"And do you understand that by pleading guilty, you are giving up all those rights?"

"Yes, Your Honor."

Leave it alone, and a few minutes from now, she'll be a convicted murderer. She'll have nothing.

"Mr. Donovan, please make a representation concerning the facts that the people would be prepared to prove at trial."

Max's voice felt far away as he methodically ran through the web of evidence against the defendant. "The defendant, rather than report to police the victim James Grisco's attempt to blackmail her, took matters into her own hands. Taking advantage of a previous experience in which threatening comments had been posted to her website by another individual, she continued to post additional comments herself to create the impression that her stalker was escalating his conduct. She also sent herself a threatening package which had Mr. Grisco's fingerprints on it, furthering that impression. Finally, she instructed Mr. Grisco to meet her at an address in East Hampton, where she shot him and then staged the scene to look like self-defense."

What had George Langston said—Ellie had just enough evidence to mess with his daughter's head but could never get a conviction? The evidence in her own father's death had been just enough to suggest that Jerry Hatcher had committed suicide, but never enough to give Ellie the firm answers she so desperately needed. She had spent her entire life wondering whether her father had loved his family so little that he chose voluntarily to leave them.

Please don't do that to my daughter. She's the one innocent person.

"How do you now plead to the charge contained in Count One of the indictment, Murder in the Second Degree?"

"Guilty."

"Very well. It is the finding of this court that the defendant is fully competent and capable of entering an informed plea, is aware of the nature of the charge and consequences of the plea, and that the plea of guilty is knowingly and voluntarily entered and supported by a sufficient basis in fact. The defendant is adjudged guilty of that offense. I understand there is also an agreement to proceed straight to sentencing, with no evidence from either party to challenge the joint sentencing recommendation."

She thought about Casey, revisiting what he'd learned during his short-lived therapy with David Bolt: *He's all about separating yourself from your parents—being honest about who they are and how they treated you, but then letting go of it.*

"Ms. Langston, it is the judgment of this court that you be committed to the custody of the New York State Department of Corrections, to be imprisoned for a term of twenty years."

As the deputy took Adrienne back into custody, Ramona reached toward her from behind the courtroom railing. "I love you, Mom. Don't forget. No matter what."

And then Adrienne was gone.

When Ramona started to cry, George placed an arm around her shoulder and kissed the top of her head before guiding her from the courtroom. Casey followed behind. Only Katherine Whitmire acknowledged Ellie's presence with a polite nod.

Max was the last to make the trip down the center aisle of spectator seats. He looked behind him to make sure the coast was clear before giving her a peck on the cheek. "To what do I owe this surprise?"

"Just wanted to see it all go down."

"Taking pleas is not exactly the most exciting part of my job. You got time for a cup of coffee? I missed you last night. Did you get any sleep? How late did you work?"

The work itself hadn't taken long, but she never did manage to sleep.

She had been so certain about so much, from the very beginning of this case, but at each turn the people involved had surprised her. Julia had not taken her own life. Katherine Whitmire was leaving the husband who had defined her. Casey Heinz was finding family among people who had shunned him. Simple, rigid George Langston turned out to be remarkably complicated and empathetic.

What had that book editor said? Not everything is black-and-white, or even shades of gray. Things can be black *and* white—right *and* wrong—all at the same time. A week ago, Ellie would never have kept quiet through that plea colloquy.

"Yeah, coffee sounds good." For the first time since they'd met, she let Max hold her hand in the courthouse as they walked to the elevator.

George had said not all questions needed to be answered, but maybe some questions didn't need to be asked. Maybe she was still getting to know herself after all.

ACKNOWLEDGMENTS

I continue to be grateful to the many people who labor behind the scenes to support my work and bring it to readers. I have known my agent, Philip Spitzer, since I was twelve years old. He and his wife, Mary, and daughter, Anne-Lise, are my surrogate New York family and biggest champions. His colleagues Lukas Ortiz and Lucas Hunt round out the posse, making the Spitzer Literary Agency the Jerry Maguire of book agencies.

Thank you, also, to the incredibly supportive and professional crew at HarperCollins: Amy Baker, Erica Barmash, Jonathan Burnham, Heather Drucker, Mark Ferguson, Michael Morrison, Danielle Plafsky, Nicole Reardon, Jason Sack, Kathy Schneider, Leah Wasielewski, and Lydia Weaver. Special thanks to my editor, Jennifer Barth, who has been with me from the beginning and continues to push me at every stage to write the best book I can write. She represents the very best in publishing, and I'm forever appreciative to have her on my side.

Thanks as well to Ed Cohen, retired NYPD Sergeant Edward Devlin, Jen Forbus, Jonathan Hayes, McKenna Jordan, Ruth and Jon Jordan, NYPD Detective Lucas Miller, Erin Mitchell, and Richard Rhorer. Thank you, Duffer, for lending your name and image to the Duffer Awards. (Check Google. Trust me.)

And, finally, thank you to my husband, Sean Simpson. If I were to write down all the mushy stuff I feel for you, my readers might never forgive me.

A SPECIAL NOTE TO MY READERS

I try to block out all the doom-and-gloom forecasts for the future (or lack thereof) of books, reading, publishing, and, gosh, even literacy. But I know enough to realize how lucky I am to have my words moved to paper pages and digital screens so I can tell my stories to you. And I know enough to understand that wouldn't happen without your tremendous and often vocal support. Every writer thinks he or she has the very best readers, but I surely do.

I've gotten to know many of you through my Web site, Facebook, and Twitter. Writing is a solitary activity, but I'm not a solitary person. Where I used to pop into the hallway for quick comedic relief back at the prosecutors' office, I now pop onto the interwebs to chat with many of you when I need a little break. My thanks go to Holden Richards at Kitchen Media, Steffen Rasile at SRA Design Studios, and Catherine Cairns of Cairns Designs for their technical assistance in creating an interactive, online community.

Some readers have gone the extra mile by serving as an online kitchen cabinet, helping me think through decisions like *Never Tell*'s title, character names, and the details of Jess's reality television choices. For their helpful (and fun) comments during the writing of *Never Tell,* I thank the following readers: Adele Sylvester, Alan Williams, Alice Wright, Allison Freige, Amber Scott Guerrero,

Amy Fleer, Amy Hammer, Amy Nagdeman, Amy Turner De-Selle, Andrea Napier, Andrea Stacy Kirk, Andrew Kleeger, Andy Gilham, Andy P. Barker, Angie Burton, Angie Thomas-Davis, Ann Abel, Ann Hyman, Ann Rousseau Weiss, Ann Smith, Ann Zerega, Anne Ward, Anya Rhamnusia Gullino, April Smith, Arllys Brooks, Art Battiste, Barb Finnigan, Barb Lancaster, Barb Mullen Gasparac, Barbara Bogue, Barbara Detwiler, Barry Nisman, Becky Decker, Becky Rathke, Ben Small, Beth Rudetsky, Betsy Steele Gray, Bettie Kieffer, Beverly Bryan, Bill Amador, Bill Hopkins, Bill Horn, Bill Strider, Bob Briggs, Bob Fontneau, Bob Horton, Bonnie Spears, Brantley Watkins, Brenda K. Gunter, Brenda LeSage, Brian Corbishley, Brian Highley, Brian Rosenwald, Bruce DeSilva, Bruce Southworth, Bud Palmer, Carl Christensen, Carl Fenstermacher, Carla Coffman, Carol Clark, Carol Johnsen, Carol O'Gorman, Carole M. Sauer, Caroline Garrett, Cele Deemer, Celeste Libert Mooney, Charlene Wigington Hulker, Charlie Armstrong, Charlotte Creeley, Cheryl Boyd, Cheryl Thompson, Chevy Stevens, Chris Cooper Cahall, Chris Hamilton, Chris Knake, Chris La Porte, Chris Schuller, Christine McCann, Christopher Zell, Chuck Bracken, Chuck Palmer, Chuck Provonchee, Chuck Stone, Cindy Current Griffin, Cindy Spring, Cindy Whitson, Clair Leadbeater, Connie Meyer, Connie Ross Ciampanelli, Cyndie Lamb, Cynthia Poley Parran, Dana Lynne Johnson, Danielle Holley-Walker, Dannii Abram, Danny Nichols, Daphne Anne Humphrey, Daryl McGrath, Daryl Perch, Dave Hall, Dave Kinnamon, David Bates, David Greensmith, David McMahan, David Michael Lallatin, David Stine, Dawn M. Barclay, Deb Sturgess, Debbie Clark Trolsen, Debbie Hartley Holladay, Debbie Hoaglin, Debbie Rati, Debi Kershaw, Debi Landry, Debi Sussman, Debra Eisert, Debra Manzella, Deda Notions, Dee Hamilton-Worsham, Denise Berger, Denise Sargent, Denise Shoup Andersen, Diane Donceel McDonald, Diane Griffiths, Diane Howell-Arp, Dick Droese, Dolores Melton, Don Lee, Dru Ann L. Love, Dudley Forster, Edward Foster, Elaine Meehan, Elaine Meehan, Elena Shapiro Wayne, Elizabeth Julia, Elizabeth Salisbury Anderson, Ellen Blasi, Ellen

Montroy Doe, Ellen Sattler Harpin, Ellen Wills Bailey, Elyse Dinh, Erin Alford, Erin Mitchell, Etienne Vincent, Faye DeBlanc, Fran Burget, Francena Parthemore, Frank Guillouard, Fred Emerson, Fred Littell, Fred Pat Heacock, Garry Puffer, Gayle Carline, Gene Ruppe, Georgia Whitney, Glen Manry, Glenda Voelmeck, Glenn Eisenstein, Gretchen Gfeller, Hailey Ellen Fish, Hayden Wakeling, Heidi Moawad, Helen Carlsson, Ilene Ratcheson Ciccone, Ilene Renee Bieleski, Jackie Denney, Jackie Schmidt Welcel, Jacqueline May, James R. Bradbrook, Jan Wilberg, Jana Johnson, Janet Lindh, Janice Gable Bashman, Janie McCue Lynch, Janine Grondin Brennan, Jay Drescher, Jeanne Adcox Lockett, Jen Forbus, Jen Mullins Keae, Jenet Lynn Dechary, Jennifer Abelson Whitney, Jennifer Ellis Lindel, Jennifer Irvin, Jennifer Little Beck, Jennifer Mueller, Jennifer Murtha Kountz, Jerrica Furlong, Jerry McCoy, Jill Fletcher, Jill Porter Connell, Jim Boylan, Jim Cox, Jim Lewis, Jim Snell, Jimbob Niven, Jo Ann Nicholas, Jo Boxall, Jo Scott-Petty, Joan Long, Joan Lumb, Joan Moore Raffety, Joan Nichols Green, JoAnne Rosenfeld, Joe Carter, Joe Shine, Joey Mestrow, John Buckner, John Chester, John F. Armstrong, John Jones, John K. Peterson, John Karwacki, John P. Eperjesi, John Thomas Bychowski, Jon Schuller, Jordan Foster, Jordana Leigh, Josh Lamborn, Joyce Joyner, Joyce Wickham, Juaan Prescott Gibbs, Judith McCarrick, Judy Bailey, Judy Gehrig, Judy Jongsma Bobalik, Judy Lambert Watson, Judy Waren Bryan, Jules Davies-Conjoice, Jules White, Julie Ebinger Hilton, Julie Kosmata Elliott, Karen McNeel Meharg, Karin Carlson, Karla Davis Glessner, Kate Wood, Kathleen Andrews, Kathleen Geiger, Kathy Collings, Kathy Goodridge Poulin, Kathy Sammons, Kathy Schmidt, Kathy Vraniak Aldridge, Katie Blackmon, Kaye Wilkinson Barley, Kayla Painter, Kelly A. Gunter, Kestrel Carroll, Kim Baines, Kimberley Stephenson, Kristy Knox Taylor, Lance D. Carlton, Lance McKnight, Laura Aranda, Laura Bostick, Laura Piros McCarver, Leah Cummins Guinn, Leann Collins, Lee Walton, Leigh Sanders Neely, Liam Moloney, Lincoln Crisler, Linda Gilmer, Linda Hanno, Linda J. Myatt, Linda Jaros, Linda Maxine Williams, Linda Napikoski, Lisa Bergagna, Lisa Fowler, Lisa Wilcox,

Liz Patru, Liza Kosiadou, Lois Alter Mark, Lola Troy Fiur, Louis Brunet, Louise Maughan James, Lovada Marks Williams, Lynda Pendley Bennett, Lynelle Russell, Lynn Ashworth Peters, Lynn Comeau, Lynn Hirshman, Lynne Dalton, Lynne M. Lamb, Lynne Victorine, Marc Davey, Margaret Franson Pruter, Margie Watts Iverson, Marie Horne Jackson, Marion Coro, Marjorie Tucker, Mark Gould, Mark O. Hammontree, Marlyn Beebe, Martha McConnell Greer, Martha Paley Francescato, Martha Stephenson La Marche, Martin Cook, Martin Treanor, Martyn James Lewis, Mary Geary, Mary Hohulin, Mary Phillips, Mary Stenvall, Mary Thompson Bullock, Maryann Mercer, Matt Foley, Matthew Jeanmard, Maureen Lennon Kastner, Maureen Wiley Apfl, Mauricia Sledd Smith, Melissa Costa, Michael Bok, Michael Charles Woodham, Michael Gallant, Michael Honeybear Cotton, Michael Ma, Michele Hendricks, Michelle Goad, Michelle Pabon Pharr, Michelle Phillips, Micki Fortenberry Dumke, Mike Forehand, Mike Houston, Mike Newman, Mitch Smith, Monica Niemi, Nancy A. Nash Coleman, Nancy M Hood, Nancy McCready, Nancy Rimel, Naomi Waynee, Nils Kristian Hagen Jr., Pamela Cardone, Pamela Jarvis, Pamela Pescosolido, Pamela Picard, Pat Neveux, Pat Winfield, Patricia Hawkins, Patricia Medley, Patsy Green, Patti James Anderlohr, Patti MacDonnell, Patti O'Brien, Patty Hudson, Patty McGuire Moran Kilkenny, Paul Hansper-Cowgill, Paul W. Stackpole Jr., Paula Rossetti, Pepper Goforth, Perry Lassiter, Pete Sandberg, Peter Robertson, Peter Spowart, Phil Messina, Phillis Spike Carbone, Rand Hill, Rebecca Turman, Rebecca Woodbury, Rhonda Tate McNamer, Richard Fox, Rick Miller, Robert Carraher, Robert Hartman, Robert Ray, Roger Vaden, Ronda Smittle Aaron, Rosemary Lindsey, Russell Meadows, Ruth Mariampolski, Ruth Miller Blackford, Ryan Dorn, Sabine Pilhofer, Sal Towse, Sally Channing, Sammi-Rexanne Huskisson-Bonneau, Sandra Jean Krna, Sandra Speller, Sandy Cann, Sandy Holcombe Olson, Sandy Maines, Sandy Plummer, Sandy Schwinning Hill, Sara Baldwin, Sara Glass Phair, Sara Gremlin, Sara Weiss, Sarah Pearcy, Scott Irwin, Shanna White, Shannon Keane English, Sharon Brown,

Sharon Faith Graves, Sharon Woods Hopkins, Sherri Young Coats, Sherrie Saint, Sheryl Cooper, Sheryl Ditty Hauch, Shirley Anderson Whitely, Sita Laura, Soules Wanderer, Stacy Allen, Stella Mullis, Stephanie Angulo, Stephanie Doherty Rouleau, Stephanie M. Gleave, Stephanie Smith, Stephanie Stafford Roush, Stephen Burke, Sue Christensen, Sue Hollis, Sue Smith Stewart, Sue Stanisich, Susan Connolly, Susan Cox, Susan Dineen Kritikos, Susan Feibush Braun, Susan Ferris, Susan Jarrett Carey, Susie Cowan Hudson, Suzanne Abbott, Tammy Helms Baker Meyers, Teri James, Terry Butz, Terry Parrish, The Signal Grill, Thomas C. McCoy Jr., Tirzah Goodwin, Tommye Baxter Cashin, Tonett Mattucci Wojtasik, Tony Sannicandro, Tori Bullock, Tracey Edges, Tracy Nicol, Trena Klohe, Victoria Waller Ranallo, Viola Burg, Wallace Clark, Wayne Cunnington, Wayne Curry, Wayne Ledbetter, Wendy Brown, Wendy Burd-Kinsey, Wendy Weidman, Will Boyce, Will Swarts, William Bruner, and William Penrose.

ABOUT THE AUTHOR

ALAFAIR BURKE is the best-selling author of seven previous novels, including the stand-alone *Long Gone* and the Ellie Hatcher series: *212*, *Angel's Tip*, and *Dead Connection*. A former prosecutor, she now teaches criminal law and lives in Manhattan.

Nicky Cervantes smiled to himself as two Wall Street boys pressed past him, one reporting excitedly to the other that Apple stock was up six percent with the release of the company's new iPhone. He could tell from their tone that the good news for the market meant a hefty check for the duo.

Nicky was smiling because one might say he was sort of invested in the market himself these days. And those boys in suits and ties might be whistling over a six percent bump, but Nicky's own payback on the brand had nearly tripled in recent days. When demand for the latest gadget was this red-hot, no one seemed to care where the hardware came from. No additional work for Nicky, either. If anything, he felt a little less guilty about it. Anyone dumb enough to buy jack the day it came out deserved to lose it, was how he figured.

In truth, he never had felt much guilt over it. The first time, he expected to feel real bad, like maybe the lady would start crying or there would be pictures on there of her baby that she'd never get back. But when he finally worked up the courage to do it—to just grab that shit out of her hand while she was preparing some text message to send aboveground—the girl didn't seem to care. He still remembered her reaction. One hand protecting the thousand-dollar bag, the other covering the cleavage peering from the deep V in her wrap dress. In her eyes, he was dirt, and the phone was a small price to pay to protect the things that *really* mattered.

He knew he wasn't dirt. But he also knew he wasn't VIP, like those Wall Street dudes. Not yet, anyway.

He was just a kid whose mom needed the six hundred dollars a month he'd been able to kick in to the household since he'd been working at Mr. Robinson's hardware store on Flatbush the past year. And he was the star pitcher for the Medgar Evers High School baseball team with a .6 ERA, an 88 MPH fastball, a .450 average, and a sweeping curve and change-up that consistently racked up strikes. With numbers like that, the nine bucks an hour he was getting from Mr. Robinson had to go once the coach told him he was spread too thin. If all went according to plan, Nicky might even be drafted right out of high school. He could donate a thousand phones to charity out of his first paycheck to make up for what he was doing now.

Nicky was already fifty reach-and-grabs in, but he was still careful, compared to some of the dudes he'd met who also sold hardware. Tonight he was waiting on the N/R ramp at Times Square, six-thirty P.M. Packed trains. High ratio of Manhattanites to outerborough types. Low odds of resistance.

It really was like taking candy from a baby. But the candy was a five-hundred-dollar phone, and the baby was some hot chick whose sugar daddy would buy her a new one. The standard play was to linger on the platform, like he was waiting to get on the train. Look for someone—inattentive, weak, female—standing near the door, fiddling with a gadget.

Reach. Grab. Run. By the time the girl realized her phone was gone, Nicky was halfway up the stairs. Easy.

He heard the rattle of the approaching train. Watched the lights heading his way. Joined the other cattle gathering close at the edge of the platform in eager anticipation of scoring a New York commuter's lottery ticket—an empty seat.

Six trains had come and gone without a baby and her candy.

This time, as the train lurched to a halt, Nicky saw what he'd been looking for through the glass of the car doors. Eyes down, phone out.

Reddish blond hair pulled into a ponytail at the nape of her neck. Long-sleeved white sweater, backpack straps looped over both shoulders. Despite the train's lurch, she typed with two hands, stabilizing herself against the bounce with her core strength.

Maybe that should have been a sign.

He stepped one foot into the car, grabbed the phone, and pivoted a one-eighty, like he had fifty times before. He pushed through the clump of angry riders who had followed him into the car and stood before him, all hoping to secure a few square feet on the crowded train before the doors closed.

Had he known what would happen next, maybe he would have run faster for the staircase.

It wasn't until he hit the top of the landing that he realized he had a problem. Somehow he heard it. Not the sound of the shoes but the sound of surprised bystanders reacting.

Hey!

What the . . .

You lost your shoe, lady!

Oh my God, David. We have to leave the city.

Nicky sneaked a glance behind him to see the woman kicking off her remaining ballet flat as she took two steps at a time in pursuit. She had looked sort of average middle-aged through the subway doors, but now she had a crazy look of determination on her face. In her eyes. In the energy of her forearms as they whipped back and forth at her sides.

At the top of the stairs, he spun left and then right, up the ramp toward the electronics store positioned between the N/R tracks and the 1/2. Why were some trains labeled with letters and others with numbers? Strange how random thoughts popped into his head when he was stressed.

He could hear the thump of an old Run-DMC song that his father listened to when he was still around. Nicky was in luck. The break dancers always attracted a dense semicircle of onlookers.

He leaped over a stroller on the near side of the audience, evoking an "ooooooh" from viewers who thought his vault across the make-shift stage was part of the act. Picked up the pace once again, gaze fixed on the stairs that would take him to the 1/2 platform.

He heard more shouts behind him. The crowd hadn't stopped her. A kid cried as he fell to the ground.

Girl wasn't messing around.

He sprinted down the stairs, hoping to hear the familiar clack of an incoming train. No luck.

He thought about abandoning the phone, but the platform was too packed. The phone would fall to the ground, unnoticed by her, scooped up by someone whose good luck today rivaled his bad.

He decided to use the crowd to his advantage. He analyzed the platform that awaited him like an obstacle course, plotting out three or four weaves to maneuver his way to the next exit.

He risked another look behind. The woman had gained on him. She was just as fast, maybe faster. And she was smaller, more nimble. She was finding a more direct path than he'd navigated.

Up ahead, he spotted a busker warbling some "Kumbaya" shit behind a cardboard sign he couldn't read from his vantage point. Something about the message must have been magic, because there was a mass of people huddled around the open guitar case.

They were spread out across the platform. No gaps that he could see.

She was gaining on him.

He heard the distant clack of a train. Saw lights coming on the left. A local train north.

One pivot around the crowd and he'd be fine. He'd keep run-ning until the train stopped. Hop on board at the last second. Wave goodbye to all this once the doors closed behind him.

Almost over.

He dodged to the left, turning sideways to scoot around a pillar.

He saw long black hair swing like a shampoo ad. He heard him-self say "sorry" on impulse as he felt the heavy thud against his right hip. As he fell backward, he saw the object that had hit him—the brunette's hot-pink duffel bag—followed by the message on the busker's cardboard sign (THE PREZ AIN'T THE ONLY ONE WHO NEEDS CHANGE), followed by a sea of shocked faces as his body hit the tracks.

It was funny what he thought of in the few seconds that passed as he lay there. His right arm. Would his right arm be okay? As the sound of the train grew louder, he wondered whether his mother would find out why he'd been in the Times Square transit station after school instead of behind a cash register at Mr. Robinson's paint store.

Reflexes kicked in. More than reflex: a deep desire to live. Without any conscious thought, he pressed himself flat between the tracks. More screaming.

He closed his eyes, hoping he wouldn't feel the impact.

And then he felt something he hadn't expected: his body being lifted from the ground. He opened his eyes but saw only white. Was this heaven?

The plane of white moved, making way for the scene of the subway platform again. People staring. Screaming. Asking if he was okay.

He looked toward the blurred, fading plane of white. It was her sweater, topped by the strawberry-blond ponytail, still tightly in place. The forearms were pumping as she took the stairs two at a time, no pause in sight.

She held her recovered iPhone in her hand.

And Nicky?

Nicky was going to live.

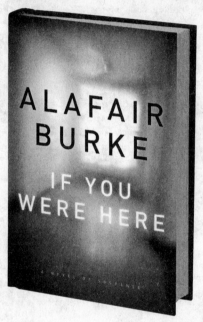

ALSO BY ALAFAIR BURKE

NEVER TELL
A Novel of Suspense

ISBN 978-0-06-199917-8 (paperback)

Alafair Burke delivers another addictive thriller, returning to
heroine Ellie Hatcher in a case centering on the death of a
young girl with connections to both New York's wealthiest
elite and downtown's most dispossessed.

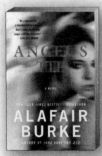

LONG GONE
A Novel of Suspense

ISBN 978-0-06-212015-1
(paperback)

Not long after Alice Humphrey lands her dream job as the
manager of a Manhattan art gallery, she arrives at work to
find that the place has been vacated overnight—and the man
who hired her is lying in a pool of blood on the floor.

212
A Novel

ISBN 978-0-06-156132-0 (paperback)

After the vicious murder of a New York University student
who found menacing, personal threats posted to a campus
website, NYPD Detective Ellie Hatcher must track down
the killer before another young woman dies.

ANGEL'S TIP
A Novel of Suspense

ISBN 978-0-06-211423-5 (paperback)

When a college student is found dead after spending the
last few hours of her spring break at an elite Manhattan
nightclub, NYPD Detective Ellie Hatcher begins an
obsessive hunt for the co-ed's killer—placing her directly in
the sights of a psychopath.